S0-BFA-040

The Killing Storm

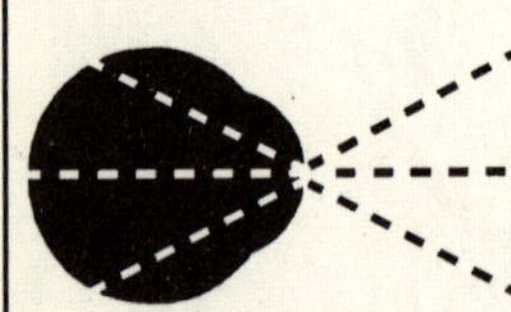

The Killing Storm

Kathryn Casey

THORNDIKE PRESS
A part of Gale, Cengage Learning

Detroit • New York • San Francisco • New Haven, Conn • Waterville, Maine • London

A Sarah Armstrong Novel.
Thorndike Press, a part of Gale, Cengage Learning.

Thorndike Press® Large Print Thriller.
The text of this Large Print edition is unabridged.
Other aspects of the book may vary from the original edition.
Set in 16 pt. Plantin.

LIBRARY OF CONGRESS CATALOGING-IN-PUBLICATION DATA

Casey, Kathryn.
The killing storm / by Kathryn Casey.
p. cm. — (Thorndike Press large print thriller)
"A Sarah Armstrong novel."
ISBN-13: 978-1-4104-3563-7 (hardcover)
ISBN-10: 1-4104-3563-6 (hardcover)
1. Texas Rangers—Fiction. 2. Armstrong, Sarah (Fictitious character)—Fiction. 3. Criminal profilers—Fiction. 4. Kidnapping—Investigation—Fiction. 5. Murder—Investigation—Fiction. 6. Texas—Fiction. 7. Large type books. I. Title.
PS3603.A8635K55 2011
813'.6—dc22 2010049213

Published in 2011 by arrangement with St. Martin's Press, LLC.

Printed in the United States of America
1 2 3 4 5 6 7 15 14 13 12 11

For my children, with love

One

"Have you seen my puppy?" the man asked. They were in the park, a span of thick green with black-trunked oaks and soaring, spindly pines nestled among sprawling subdivisions northwest of Houston.

Caught up in an imaginary world, a sandbox desert of hand-shaped hills and roundabout roads, the boy pressed down hard on a bright yellow-and-red plastic dump truck, pushing it up a make-believe ramp, then pulling it down again. All the while, his soft pink lips vibrated, *brrrrrrrrr,* mimicking an engine.

"Did you see my puppy?" the man asked again, louder. The boy glanced up, startled, but then smiled at the man. When he saw the frown on the man's face, the boy thought that the man looked troubled.

"No," the boy said, shaking his head, his clear blue eyes wide with worry. "Is your puppy lost?"

The man's brow furrowed and his lips pinched, as if he were ready to cry. *The puppy must be lost,* the boy thought, and then the man confirmed it. "He ran away," he said. "My little puppy ran away. Will you help me find him?"

A worried look on his face, the boy swiveled toward his right and saw his momma sitting on a picnic bench, talking on her cell phone and staring off into the pond, where the ducks with the green heads and the snow-white geese milled about, plucking at the water. It was a school day, and the park was deserted except for the boy and his mother and the man who'd lost his puppy. The boy thought about the puppy and wondered where it might be. *I should tell Momma that I'm helping the man,* he decided. *She's upset about the big storm, the one they keep talking about on television.* "Just a minute," he said, turning to run to his mother.

Before the boy could leave, the man reached out and gently touched the child's shoulder. "Don't go!" he pleaded. "You've heard about the hurricane. I need to find my dog before the bad weather comes. Please help me. He's not far away. It won't take long."

As the boy dropped his gaze to the sand,

deep in thought, the man glanced at the woman and smiled. The boy's mother remained on her cell phone, and it appeared she hadn't even looked their way. "Your mommy is busy," the man said, wearing his best you-can-trust-me expression. "I know her, and I know she likes it when you help people. She'd want you to help me."

Concentrating on the face of the man who towered over him, the boy wondered if the man looked familiar. Maybe. His momma knew a lot of people. The man had a nice smile, the kind adults have when they're worried but they want to be nice anyway, to not look upset. The boy's momma did that, tried to look like everything was okay when the boy knew it wasn't, like the day his poppa moved out. That afternoon, the little boy heard loud arguing, his momma screaming at his poppa, telling him that he'd be sorry if he left them.

After his father slammed the apartment door, the boy rushed to his mother, frightened. "It's okay," she said. The boy looked up as his mother reassured him with a tightly drawn smile. "We'll be fine."

Again, the boy glanced at his mother and saw she still talked on the telephone and gazed out at the water. Every day his momma brought the boy to the park to play, unless it rained. On those days, they stayed inside their small apartment, and she watched television while he played with his toys on the stained tan carpet. Once in a while, when she was in a happy mood, they played games, Candy Land and Chutes and Ladders.

"I need you to help me find my puppy," the man insisted, reclaiming the child's attention. "It'll only take a minute. I bet my puppy will come if you call him."

The possibility that the puppy would listen to him caught the boy's interest. "Your puppy will come for me?" he asked, excited by the prospect. "If I call him?"

"I bet he will," the man said, his hands palms up as if weighing the likelihood. "He's a good puppy, but sometimes we play this game. Like playing hide-and-seek. He hides, and I have to find him. I like games. Do you like games?"

The boy thought again about Candy Land, Chutes and Ladders, and this time hide-and-seek. "I like games," he said. "I like games a lot!"

"You look like the kind of boy who would," the man said, with not only a smile, but a soft chuckle. "I play games a lot. All kinds of games."

"With your puppy?" the boy asked.

"Yes, with my puppy, and sometimes with little boys and girls," the man said. "It's my favorite thing to do."

The boy looked at his momma a third time. She was still talking on the phone. She looked serious. Maybe it was about the storm. Or maybe she was talking to his poppa. The boy wondered sometimes where his poppa lived now that he didn't live with the boy and his momma. Considering what he should do, the boy gazed up at the man again, stared at the leash in his hand, and then asked, "What's his name?"

"His name?" the man replied.

"Your puppy's name," the boy said.

"Buddy," the man said. "My puppy's name is Buddy."

The boy laughed. "That's a silly name."

"Why is that silly?"

The boy thought about it and wasn't sure. "I don't know," he said. "It just is."

The chains squeaked wearily as the humid, hot breeze picked up, and the eight swings with their thick brown leather seats swayed lazily back and forth, back and forth. How strange that the sky was so blue and the day so tranquil when a violent storm circled in the Gulf. Sometimes the boy liked to swing. His momma pushed him so high that he thought he should be able to stretch out his legs and punch his feet through a cloud.

"And your name is Joey," the man said.

"I'm Joey!" the boy said, then felt confused. "How did you know my name?"

"I told you, I know your mommy," the man said with an indifferent shrug.

Joey Warner thought about that. The man knew his name, and he didn't seem like a stranger. He was a nice man with a nice smile. And the man was right, Joey thought. His momma liked it when Joey helped, like picking up his toys or cleaning his room. And he was supposed to be respectful of adults. His momma said that, too.

"Okay," Joey said, nodding. Then he cried out, "Buddy! . . . Buddy!"

Above the boy, tree branches rustled and the still green leaves shimmered, showing off their silver underneath. Joey looked over at his momma and thought again that she had to be talking to his poppa, because that's the way they talked now, angry with loud voices. Although he couldn't hear her, he knew his momma was upset.

"I saw my puppy over there," the man said, pointing near a stand of trees bordering the parking lot. "That's where Buddy ran off."

"Oh," Joey said. *Then that's where the*

puppy must be, he thought. With the man following, Joey ran fast toward the parking lot, shouting, "Buddy! . . . Buddy! Come, Buddy!"

The man glanced back toward the picnic table, wondering if the boy's mother would finally look in their direction. But even with the boy shouting, she never turned around, instead staring out at the shimmering water. "That's right, Joey. Let's play the game," the man murmured. "Call the puppy. Come with me. It's all part of the game. Someone hides, and someone seeks."

Two

Hands on my hips, I pondered the body that lay before me. Eighteen years as a cop, ten profiling murder scenes, I'd seen stranger killings, but this one was up there near the top of the bizarre list. Overhead, I heard a crackling, drawing my attention to the strong, gnarled branches of an oak tree, draped with long, flowing, feathery tendrils of pale green Spanish moss. Midway up perched a dark, hooded figure, watching, beady eyes staring down at me, waiting.

"I hate vultures," I said with more intensity than I'd intended. I grabbed a tissue out of the back pocket of my black Wranglers to mop up a bead of sweat tracing its way down the back of my neck. When that didn't help, I gathered my shoulder-length, straw-colored mane in one hand and hoisted it up, hoping for a breeze to cool the exposed skin. No luck. "Damn buzzards are the ugliest birds."

"Gotta say I agree, Lieutenant," Sergeant George "Buckshot" Fields growled back. In a similar pose standing beside me, Buckshot had a look of pure disdain on his broad, mustached mug. A big, sinewy man, he took up more than his share of space. I'm not a small woman, a little over average height and a good weight, not heavy but not too thin, a little broad through the hips, yet my fellow Texas Ranger towered over me. When I said nothing, he went on, contending, "Those damn birds are even uglier than my ex-wife, and that's saying a mouthful."

I looked over, and the sergeant sneered, exposing saliva-coated teeth, yellowish brown from the plug of tobacco he gnawed religiously. He had a roguish sparkle in his intense dark eyes, seated under the ridge of a prominent brow. "That gal, she could stop a train with her face," Buckshot said about the woman he'd once loved. "And don't get me started on her figure. Not sure she had one."

"You forget, I know Peggy," I said with a blank stare. "Beautiful woman, at least on the outside."

Buckshot shrugged. We both knew that he hadn't forgotten, just felt like grousing out a bit of frustration.

"Yeah, Sarah, that's true enough. Most

likely why she left me," he said with a sheepish grin, ruffling up his wavy salt-and-pepper hair, wet with perspiration. He mopped off his forehead with the back of his hand, thoughtful. "Can't blame a man for complaining, way she hightailed it out of here."

I nodded, figuring he had a point. A year earlier, Peggy had taken up with one of Buckshot's best friends, a guy he'd known for decades who'd won somewhere around four million in the state lottery. After the divorce, they moved to Southern California, where Buckshot said the happy couple lived in a house with a maid and a kidney-shaped swimming pool. "Lieutenant Armstrong, you want me to kill that damn bird?" the sergeant asked, cocking a pistol fashioned out of his right index finger and thumb and pointing at the vulture hovering above us. To make sure I understood, Buckshot followed it up by suggestively placing his hand on the 9 mm in his holster.

He looked pleased at the idea, and I momentarily considered the possibility, sizing up the repulsive thing and figuring the world wouldn't miss one homely scavenger. But then, maybe it would. After all, the vulture wasn't doing anything it wasn't designed to do. And it was waiting politely, not in a hurry for dinner. I couldn't think of a justification for killing it simply for being what nature intended. "Nah," I said. "Leave him. When we're done here, it'll call in its friends, have a party, and help clean up this mess."

It was then that the sergeant voiced what so many on the Gulf Coast felt, the uneasiness that comes from impending danger. It makes your senses keener, but it comes along with a sense of dread. "Guess you're right. Damn ugly, but those birds don't usually bother me. It's this blasted, never-ending heat. It's long past time for summer to pack it in for the year. Don't know if I believe in all that global warming mumbo jumbo, but this is the hottest October I remember. And I don't much like having that damn storm out in the Gulf. Never cared much for vultures, but I like hurricanes even less."

"Yeah," I said. "You'll get no argument from me."

The hurricane had a name, Juanita, and it had been trekking toward land for the better part of a week. An impressive category four with 145-mile-per-hour winds, it measured more than four hundred miles in diameter, and it was deadly. On satellite photos, Juanita filled much of the Gulf of

Mexico. Two days earlier, the storm had flooded and ravaged northern Cuba, leaving it in shambles and putting thirty-five men, women, and children in their graves.

Stalled over the unseasonably warm Gulf waters, Juanita grew stronger with each passing day. It was a nervous time, too early to know where Juanita would come ashore, despite the best efforts of the predictors. "So far it looks like it's heading farther south. They're not saying it'll hit us," I pointed out. "Still, with hurricanes you never know."

Buckshot nodded, and I expressed the dilemma of living in hurricane country: "Sure don't want it here, but I'd hate to wish a killer storm like that on anyone else."

"I know what you mean," Buckshot said with a sickened frown. "I can't think of any good place for a hurricane but spinning to its death out at sea."

At that, Josh Braun sauntered over. While we discussed vultures, the unseasonable heat, and hurricanes, Braun had been on his cell phone, checking in with his insurance people. He had a claim to file, no doubt about that. "Well, Sarah, my agent's going to give you a call. He'll need a copy of the police report. But the big question is, what the hell happened here?"

Thick-necked and stubble-faced, Braun had graduated a few years ahead of me from high school, which I figured placed him in his early forties. Folks in my hometown, Tomball, worship local football players with the intensity much of the world reserves for movie stars. Braun had been the star quarterback and a notorious ladies' man, deflowering, legend had it, most of the high school cheerleading squad. Middle-aged, overweight, and balding, he still had a certain cachet as the head of a family that owned twenty-six hundred prime wooded acres grazed by the largest herd of cattle in the hills north of Houston.

In the past decade, the city had gobbled up ever-larger pieces of Tomball, a once sleepy burg half an hour north of Houston. Six months earlier, my mom had been approached about selling the Rocking Horse, our place, where she boards horses. Rumors said developers were clamoring to buy the Braun family's cattle ranch, the last major spread close to the city that remained undeveloped. Mom turned down the offer for the Rocking Horse. But folks had bets on how long the Brauns would hold out and how high they'd drive up the price. I wondered if what we were looking at was in any way related.

"Anyone have a reason to be mad at you, Josh?" I asked. "Could this be someone's way of persuading you to sell your land?"

The rancher mulled that over for a few moments, as if considering the likelihood. Then he shook his head and waved his right hand, pushing the thought aside. "Don't think so. I really don't. We're talking to a few folks interested in buying the place, sure, but nothing all that serious, and there's been no hard feelings. At least, not yet."

I thought about that, then asked, "Okay, what about anyone else who has a reason to be teed off at you? Somebody you fired or had a run-in with, or someone you've wrestled with in the past?"

This time, Braun grimaced, furrowing his heavy brow. Time passed, and no one talked, until he again shook his head. "Well, Sarah, I guess there's nearly always someone mad at me," he admitted with the certainty of a man who'd been in more than his share of sticky situations, including, if the other rumors were true, with the angry husbands of a good number of lovers. "But for the life of me, I haven't got a clue who'd be bastard enough to do something like this. You know how much that damn animal was worth?"

All three of us stared down at the bulky

beige-and-tan body splayed out on the ground. Someone had drawn a circle around it in the coarse, red-brown earth. Habanero, Braun's prize-winning Texas longhorn bull, lay in the center, dead long enough in the incubator-like heat that the pasture smelled of decomposition and flies buzzed the beast's face.

I sensed the sergeant wanted to put Braun on notice. "I believe you already told Lieutenant Armstrong and me how much you figure that animal was worth," Buckshot said, never one to belabor a point. He stopped to spit a cheek full of tobacco juice onto a pile of red sumac leaves. "Actually, Josh, I think you've told us a few times how much that bull of yours was worth."

The rancher grimaced. "I don't mean to repeat myself, Sergeant Fields, but I want you both to understand that I've suffered a sizable loss here. This animal was valuable," Braun said, his voice impatient. "Now that I really think about it, I had Habanero underinsured at a hundred grand. The past couple of years, we shipped straws of that bull's semen across the world. Last week we even got an order from Australia. That animal was a gold mine, and we had a lot more years to cash in on him."

When we'd been summoned by a frantic

call, I'd been reviewing cases for other agencies. As the Texas Rangers' only criminal profiler, I assess evidence and work on investigations with law enforcement agencies across the Lone Star State. In all the other cases, the victims were human. Responding to a scene where the deceased was a nine-year-old longhorn? Well, I had to admit this was the first time I'd had that pleasure.

Shaking his head, Braun folded his arms across his chest, steadfast. "I shoulda been more careful, kept Habanero closer to the rest of the stock, instead of letting my prime sire wander so far out," he said, sounding like a man plagued by regret. "Least I should have done was made sure he was fully insured. I'm going to have to rethink what I've got in insurance on my stock, if this sort of thing is going to go on."

Then he said what we were all wondering: "Who the hell would murder a bull just to paint some blasted symbol on him? How's that make sense?"

Not sure, I didn't answer, which appeared only to irritate the cattleman more. "Is this some kind of gang ritual or something? Some city kids from Houston come up and do this?" Braun asked, looking perplexed. "Sarah, I could use some answers here."

Not eager to commit until I had a shot at being at least close to right, I kept my mouth shut and considered the possibilities. At first, the men followed my lead and no one spoke. Finally Buckshot spit again and then, it appeared, felt compelled to defend my honor. "Lieutenant Armstrong here's real good at figuring these types of things out. This here's a strange one for sure, but you give her a chance and she'll decipher it. That I guaran-damn-tee you."

What was apparent was that both men were angry, and not surprisingly so. To the rest of the world longhorns might seem like just livestock, but in Texas the animals, descendants of Spanish cattle introduced to the New World by Christopher Columbus, verge on sacred. This isn't like India. We eat longhorn meat all right. I haven't met a lot of Texans who don't enjoy a well-marbled rib eye. But the breed is part of our heritage, our image, and we take the animals seriously.

Wanting a closer look, I crouched down, covering my mouth and nose with a tissue, as much for the smell as to keep away the flies. The symbol was drawn on the dead bull's hide in thick black ink, painted with broad downward sweeps to accommodate the beast's short, soft hair. Sizing it up, I noted that the diagram was made up of a large triangle divided into four parts, each holding a cross, the tips of the intersecting lines ending in circles. At the top of the main triangle were three lines, double-arched and resembling birds in flight. Pointing at the corners of the triangle's base were figures that resembled arrowheads.

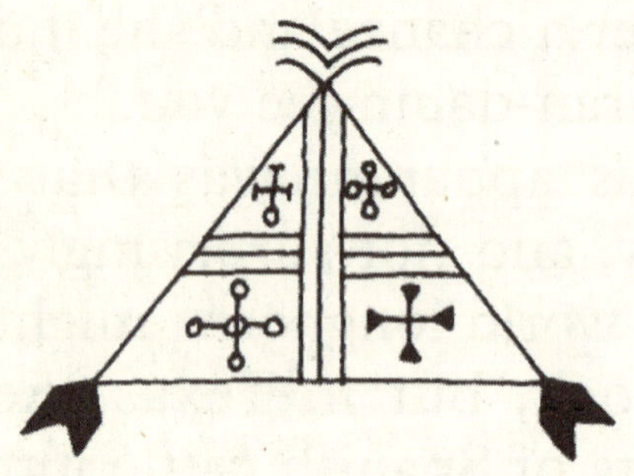

Was it some kind of Native American reference? Or a gang symbol, as Braun suggested?

"Sergeant, I need paper," I ordered, and Buckshot complied, handing me his lined spiral-bound report notebook and a pen. We'd already photographed the bull's corpse, including multiple close-ups of the drawing, but in college I was a psychology and art major, and sometimes sketching helps me analyze what I'm seeing. Abandoning the tissue, which wasn't helping anyway, I swatted away flies as I drew the symbol, outlining it and then filling in the solid parts with the black ink. While I worked, I thought about the animal's coloring, buff with scattered caramel-colored spots. The interesting thing was that the area where the symbol was drawn, smack on its side, midway from head to tail, was completely pale. That was obviously the part of the animal the killer cared to preserve, since the bull's head had been nearly blown away. Most of the skull had been cratered and emptied out, blood and brain matter splattered across the dirt and the side of a nearby oak tree, the one the vulture was using as a perch.

"I know this beast isn't a human, but I need you to take the case seriously," Braun said, looking even more disgusted. "I raised Habanero, and he's worth more to me than money."

A stand of pines bordering the pasture filtered the searing rays of the sun. I leaned over the bull, on closer inspection, and noticed bits of lead pellets and wadding, the ingredients of a shotgun shell, mixed in with the brain matter fanned out behind the bull's head. Braun described Habanero as an even-tempered animal, not afraid of humans. I figured the killer walked right up to him, raised the shotgun, and pulled the trigger. Habanero's head exploded, and the animal maybe staggered some or simply dropped where he stood. The killer painted the symbol, whatever it was, on the carcass with some kind of thick black marker and then dragged a stick or something through the dirt, to draw the circle around the bull. It seemed a vile thing to do to any animal, to sacrifice it for no apparent reason, not food or even sport.

"Habanero's value makes this a serious offense. We'll have to consult the district attorney's office, but to my mind, this person robbed you of valuable property, and we'll view this as a high-level felony," I said, noticing Braun relax as he nodded in agreement. "We'll do our best to investigate."

"That's all I'm asking, Sarah," said the aging jock. "Just that you look carefully at this case, don't shelve it because it's about a dead animal and money."

"The sergeant and I will do our best," I reassured him, pushing up and again standing between the men. "There's a professor at A and M, one who works with bugs. She's the best in the state, and she may be able to analyze the larvae on the carcass to give us a rough estimate of time of death. And I have a crime scene unit on the way. It may be tough to pull up a print since the bull's hide is covered with hair, but we can try. I doubt it, but they may decide to take the bull in for autopsy."

"That wouldn't make that old guy happy," Buckshot offered, nodding up at the vulture. "I think he had big expectations."

All three of us looked up at the buzzard in the tree and frowned. "Damn birds," Braun said. "Guess I shouldn't begrudge him. That's how we knew something had happened. We saw them circling. We shooed the others off. That particular vulture refused to go."

Looking around the setting, a remote location far from the ranch house, I could see the wheels turning when Buckshot asked, "You figure the guy did it way out here to hide the thing?"

It had never occurred to me that the killer wanted to conceal his handiwork. It seemed obvious that he wanted folks to notice. Why else choose a prize-winning bull to slay? If he'd just wanted the thrill of shooting a cow, there were plenty out in the fields. Folks would miss them, sure, maybe report the killing to the local police, but they didn't belong to bigwig ranchers who'd call the governor and request that the Texas Rangers investigate.

"No. I don't think so," I said to Buckshot. "Where's the fun in leaving behind an obscure message on a dead animal's hide if you don't want anyone to find it? My guess, it was just the opposite, that this lowlife figured the bull was expensive enough that someone would go looking for him."

"Guess you're right," Braun said. "But it sure is a puzzle."

"I can understand rustlers, stealing animals and selling them to pocket the cash. This I don't get," the sergeant said. "The bull was just a way to send some kind of message?"

"Yeah. The way it looks, this is all about that drawing," I said, pointing at the symbol.

"Sheesh." Braun looked disgusted, furious at the culprit. "When you find the bastard, tell him to send an e-mail or a letter next time. Leave my livestock alone."

"We'll do our best, Josh," I said. With that, I started walking back to where we'd left our vehicles, fifty feet away in the cattle pasture. Careful where I put my boots down, I explained what would happen next, that Buckshot would stay at the scene to oversee the CSI unit and work with the entomology professor. We were still discussing plans when my phone rang.

"Sarah," David Garrity said.

I was glad to hear his voice, and I reacted with a slight quickening of my pulse, then silently scolded myself for my response. David is an FBI agent, a fellow profiler. We'd been officially dating for about six months, and I'd grown to enjoy hearing him say my name. At first, it had all seemed relatively simple. We enjoyed each other's company, maybe more than we were ready to admit. At least, I suspected that was true from my perspective. But then, a month earlier, a wrinkle had developed, an unforeseen complication we had yet to navigate our way through.

"Yeah, hi, David," I said, glancing at my watch. Half past six. I'd told him I'd be ready for dinner at seven. I had to get home, get the cow dung off my boots, and change into something at least flirting with feminine. It was part of the new me. David hadn't complained about the old me, but I was taking a stab at trying at least vaguely to dress like a girl, especially under the current circumstances. I thought about my hair, frizzy. I'd need a shampoo.

But then, maybe not.

"I can't make it. At least not at seven," he said. "We've got a kidnapping, a little boy, four years old, from a park in Houston. The Amber Alert is out, and I'm on my way to the scene."

"Where?" I asked, feeling my body tense.

I've never liked missing kid cases, anything involving a child, really. And there'd been a rash of them lately, all little ones. The others had turned out badly.

"Northwest side," David said.

"Maybe the kid just wandered off into the park?" I ventured, getting a sick feeling that betrayed the optimism in my question. "Are you sure it's a kidnapping?"

"We're not," he admitted. "Might not be that at all. They're doing a preliminary search of the park, but so far no little boy. The sheriff's department responded to the 911 call and requested FBI assistance. The deputies on the scene tell me the mom's a bit odd. She waited a full hour before she called it in. Her husband was at the scene, and he says she wanted to search the park on their own, before bringing in the police. We're looking at her pretty hard."

"You've got a mom, though," I said. "This isn't like the others?"

"Yeah," he said. "We've got a mom and dad, an ID on the kid. It's not like the other two, the unknowns."

"That's good," I said, thinking about the two partial skeletons of children found over the past year and a half. This case was different, but I wasn't ready to give up on the possibility that David's missing child case could be related. "This kid is about the right age to be connected to the others, though."

"I thought about that," David said. "But nothing else matches. This isn't a case of unidentified remains. Our boy's been reported missing. And like I said, we've got parents and an ID."

I thought about that and decided I was undoubtedly grasping at straws, hoping for any possible clues to the deaths of the unidentified little ones, unsolved cases that had been haunting me for months. "You're right, of course. You need any help? Should I meet you there?"

"No. We're okay. The sheriff's department is flooding it with talent. Half of major crimes is investigating. I'll call you later." He paused and then added, "Sarah, I still hope this'll be quick, that we'll find the kid and have time to get together, but it might be pretty late."

"No problem. Hate to think of the little guy lost or worse. I'll head home and get ready, in case it works out, and wait to hear from you. Let's see what happens."

"Great. I'm sorry. I was looking forward to tonight," David said, sounding genuinely disappointed.

"Me too," I admitted. Maybe I had more reason than he did to regret calling off our date. "I hoped we could have that talk you've been postponing."

"Ah," he said, his voice soft, regretful. "Yeah. I know. The truth is that I'm not sure I'm ready. I haven't really figured it all out. But I understand why you're impatient."

Silence on the telephone, then David said, "I'll call as soon as I know what's up."

"Okay," I said. "Now go find that kid."

"Fingers crossed," he said.

When I clicked off the cell phone, Buckshot grinned at me. "You and that FBI agent going to make it legal?"

That's one of the things about working with strong, opinionated, protective men: as soon as a woman's dating, they figure she needs to be looked out for and that she needs a wedding ring on her left hand to make it respectable. "Hasn't been discussed," I said.

"I didn't know you were single, Sarah," Josh said. He stood up straighter and smiled, one of those smarmy, suddenly-I'm-so-interested grins. The legendary philanderer had the audacity to straighten his shirt collar and move closer to me. "You know, I had kind of a thing about you in high school. When I heard you married that Texas Ranger, I figured I was out of luck, since the guy would be a deadeye shot.

When was the divorce?"

"No divorce. Bill's dead," I said, narrowing my eyes and giving him a cold, calculated look intended to cut off the conversation. Braun took two steps back. People react that way a lot to finding out I'm a widow, unsure what to say. "My daughter and I are living at the ranch with Mom. Bill was a great guy, wonderful father. He died two and a half years ago, and I miss him every day."

"Sorry," Braun said. Yet he took only a minute to regroup and then moved closer. He seemed confused when I shook my head.

"Josh, I'm not a high school cheerleader, and you're not the star quarterback," I said. Out of the corner of my eye, I saw Buckshot chuckle, enjoying the exchange. "It's my job to figure out who killed your bull. That's it. I'm busy, so I'd like to avoid distractions and tie this up."

I shot the cattleman a smile and then waited. He frowned at first, then shrugged, undoubtedly realizing that solving Habanero's killing was worth more to him than a flirtation with me. A commotion overhead, and I realized the potential diners had multiplied. Four vultures batted their long black wings, riding the air currents and gliding above us, while two on the ground picked greedily at the carcass.

"Now, about the dead longhorn, chase those buzzards away and get more photos before we lose the light, Sergeant," I said. "Then guard the scene until the forensic unit gets here."

"Those birds are going to be more than disappointed," Buckshot said with a wink. He seemed delighted at the prospect of sending the birds packing with empty stomachs.

"Yeah, well, when it comes to disappointment, there's some of that going around," I said, thinking about David's phone call. "All that 'best laid plans of mice and men,' I guess."

The sergeant and Braun looked at me as if confused, but I didn't bother to recite the verse or credit Robert Burns. Instead I simply said to the sergeant, "Keep me posted."

THREE

"Sarah, help me haul the bottled water into the house," Mom shouted when I pulled up in my state-issued burgundy Chevy Tahoe and parked next to her old blue Ford pickup, the paint bleached and pockmarked by Texas's harsh summer sun. Her cap of loose white curls was flopping, and she was wearing jeans and a denim work shirt. Mom had a five-month-old silver F-150 in the garage but refused to use it, afraid she'd scratch the black vinyl bed liner. She also had a red silk shawl I gave her a decade ago, in its original box, in her dresser drawer, waiting for a special occasion that apparently had to be of the magnitude of a presidential inauguration.

"Are you ever going to start driving the new pickup?" I asked as I bent down and grabbed two cardboard cartons of plastic water bottles. With dusk minutes away, the sun rested on the horizon, and the sky shone orange with gold streaks through the pines, as vibrant as strokes from a wide brush thick with coats of oil paint.

"Sarah, I do. I drive it, sometimes. But this old girl's got a lot of life left in her," Mom said, gesturing proudly at a truck that had been around for a chunk of my adult life. "I'm going to see what I can get out of her before I pasture her."

The water was heavier than I'd expected, so I put one case down and then carted the remaining one toward the back door. When I was halfway up the porch, my twelve-year-old, Maggie, less formally known as Magpie, swung open the screen door and held it for us. I trudged in with Mom, carrying two brown paper grocery bags, behind me.

"Looks like you're stocking up," I said, stating the obvious. "We expecting company?"

"No, a hurricane," Mom said, her well-lined face weary from what appeared to have been a hectic day. "I've got bottled water and fresh batteries. I found a battery-operated radio at Target. That old one we have picks up a lot of static, and I figured we might be out of power for a while, like last time."

Last time was five years earlier. The thing about hurricanes is that the hurt comes in waves. First there's the storm itself, fierce winds and torrential rains, like the worst possible thunderstorms, multiplied exponentially, sometimes enduring for twelve hours or more, spawning floods and spinning off tornadoes. Later there's the aftermath: destroyed homes and businesses, fallen trees, and cleaning up the damage. One of the biggest problems is waiting for the crews to repair downed power lines. Last hurricane, we went without electricity for two weeks.

"What about bigger flashlights?" Maggie asked, wide-eyed, with kind of a nervous smile, one that showed off her new braces with the purple rubber bands. Her mop of thick dark hair framed hazel eyes. The kid had been excited about the storm for days, ever since it popped up on the weather reports. Seven when the last one hit, Maggie didn't remember the danger and apparently saw the prospect only as a potential adventure.

Still, since the Rocking Horse was eighty-five miles from the Galveston coastline, more than thirty miles northwest of downtown Houston, we wouldn't catch the brunt of it, not the storm surge or the flooding. Yet even so far from the Gulf, the possible damage from a category three or four wasn't to be underestimated. We'd been lucky last time, just a minor leak in the stable roof and one shutter blown off a second-floor window. But if Hurricane Juanita turned in our direction, there were no guarantees we would fare as well this time.

"Sorry, dear," Mom said to Maggie. "The flashlights were all sold out. We'll use the four we have, but that's okay. Bobby called, and he found a generator for us. So even if the electric's out, we should have lights, a couple of ceiling fans, and the refrigerator and freezer working. The bad news is that I could only fill two gas cans. They're rationing at all the stations. We've only got a couple of days' worth of fuel."

At that point, I looked up and realized Mom and Frieda, our ranch hand, had already duct-taped Xs across all the house windows, to keep them from shattering into the house if they broke from flying debris. Something bothered me. "While I believe in being prepared, I'm confused. Is the storm headed here? Do we know that?"

"Not for sure, but the weatherman said on the news this afternoon that it looks more like the storm will change direction. He thinks it could hit us!" Maggie said, her voice edged with exhilaration. "And Mom, the longer the hurricane stays out over the water, the stronger it will be when it hits land."

"Perfect," I said, sarcasm dripping.

"We just need to keep our fingers crossed that it'll miss us, but make sure we have everything we need in case it doesn't," my level-headed mother advised.

We were back at the truck, and I hoisted the second case of bottled water while Mom grabbed two more grocery bags. "They're looking at the storm making landfall in a few days, probably sometime late Saturday," Mom continued, looking perplexed by the entire situation. "Who'd have thought we'd be talking about a hurricane in late October? Why, Saturday is trick-or-treat, Halloween. It's too late in the season. Guess it's just that we've had such hot weather." Stating the obvious, since we'd been breaking records all fall, she added, "Doesn't really feel much like summer has ended."

Just then Bobby Barker, Mom's suitor, pulled up. We walked outside again, in time to see the white-haired oil exec with the thick laugh lines around his brown-green eyes brace a piece of plywood like a ramp on his pickup, then slide a red generator off the truck bed. The thing had thick black wheels, so he gripped it by the handles, like a wheelbarrow, and rolled it toward the garage. "Look what I've got," he said, nodding back toward his pickup and a lineup of six fifteen-gallon gas containers. "All full."

"Well, aren't you the hero," Mom said with a half smile. Then to Maggie and me as we walked in the house, low enough so her frequent companion couldn't hear: "Sometimes there's a comfort to having a man on the spread."

An hour later, I'd showered, put on makeup, and dressed in a pair of black slacks, strappy black heels, and a white T-shirt with lace trim that dipped low at the neckline. I was even wearing jewelry, a pair of silver earrings and a chain necklace. I looked at myself in the mirror, long and hard. Up until the last few weeks, life had felt pretty good. Now I had the feeling I was waiting in the wings for someone else to decide my future. The situation with David made me uneasy. *It's not fair,* I thought. Life was simpler when I was young. When Bill and I met, we fell in love and married, started a family. Now, with David, both of us came toting heavy baggage.

In the kitchen, stew simmered lazily on the stove, filling the house with a rich aroma. Mom held a long wooden spoon and was giving the thick brew a stir. Eyeing my getup, she asked, "Are you going out with

David?"

"I'm not sure, still waiting to hear from him," I replied. She didn't say anything, just pursed her lips. We'd had the discussion before, and I knew what she was thinking. Mom has a way of getting her point across without a lot of words, and she'd made it clear that my current situation with David wasn't to her liking. "Check the horses, will you, Sarah?"

Moments later, the outdoor lights clicked on, powering the strands of small white bulbs that line the corral elm tree's branches and the top of the surrounding fence. The lights were Maggie's idea, her way of feeling as if her dead father watched over us. They illuminated my path up the hill to the stable, where a dozen horses, four of ours and eight boarders, munched on oats and hay. I stopped at Emma Lou's stall to say good night, but Maggie's black-and-white pinto sized me up, suspicious. I wondered if the scent of bad weather had the mare jumpy. In the next stall, Emma Lou's colt, Warrior, must not have developed his bad-weather sensors. Six months old, all black and growing quickly, he playfully nuzzled my chest with his long, velvety soft nose.

"Hey there," I said, pushing him away and laughing. Although I wasn't sure it would prove true, I added, "I've already got a date."

After closing the stable doors, I walked back toward the garage and climbed the stairs to my combined office and workroom, drawn to what waited high on a shelf. Before long, I'd taken down two boxes. Carefully, one after the other, I removed two small skulls on pedestals. Each wore a mask sculpted from clay, work I'd done six months earlier, attempting to replicate the lost faces of the two unidentified children.

A chemical plant shift worker had found the skeletons while four-wheeling through a field far south of Houston. A macabre scene, the two sets of small remains lay side by side, arms crossed over their chests as if positioned in a coffin. No clothing, nothing to help identify them, had been recovered. After lining up the skulls on my workbench, I stared at my handiwork, memorizing, not for the first time, the faces of two young children. We had so little to go on. Just to determine their sexes, the M.E. had to bake samples of the bones and then add liquid nitrogen to pulverize the chunks. From the powder, he'd pulled the DNA of a boy and a girl.

"Who are you?" I whispered. "Who?"

We had two more bits of information from

the M.E.: both children were Caucasian and, based on the development of their joints, between three and five years old. As I'd worked on them, I'd fashioned finely cut features in clay with the lightest of tints. But skin tone, along with nearly everything else, was at best a guess.

"Where are your parents?" I asked, looking into the blue-and-white unseeing plastic globes that were now their only eyes. "Why isn't anyone looking for you?"

I wondered again if David's missing boy could be connected. That he was four, about the estimated ages of the dead children who'd found what appeared to be a permanent home in my workroom, troubled me. Then I reconsidered the circumstances and had to conclude that David was right. With the two children in the boxes, no parents had come forward. We'd searched long and hard but found no reports of missing children that even remotely matched their descriptions. We'd run pictures in newspapers across the state and reported them to all the national Web sites, looking for someone to identify them, hoping it would spur memories and bring us names. But nothing. Not a single phone call.

At that moment, my phone rang, and David's number flashed on the screen.

"Change of plans," he said when I answered.

"Tell me you found the boy, or that there's something I can do to help," I said as I reached out for the first skull, the nameless little girl's, to put it back in the box. For the time being, I needed to concentrate on cases where I had clues, ones I had a hope of solving. I needed to think about children I might be able to save.

"You must be reading my mind," David answered.

FOUR

"So this is where the kid was the last time his mother saw him," David explained, motioning toward the sandbox. His eyes lingered on my date clothes, settling on my T-shirt's lacy neckline. "You look great, by the way."

"Thanks," I said with a shrug. I'd been excited about getting dressed to spend the evening with him, but now I felt vaguely awkward. Maybe Mom was right, and I needed to raise my guard and not try so hard. After so many years married, the whole man-woman thing sometimes struck me as too complex to tackle. "But to be honest, if this is where I'd foreseen spending the evening, I would have dressed down a bit."

David shook his head, and his mouth curved into a lopsided frown. "Nobody wants to be here. Just wish we could find the kid."

The park crawled with law enforcement. The county sheriff's department had been the first on the scene, calling in the FBI when they realized they might have a kidnapping. Deputies ringed the park, protecting the perimeter, while the crime scene unit searched for clues and detectives in plain clothes bunched together, comparing notes. Letting the others do their work, David explained what he knew. "The last time the mother says she saw the boy he was playing here, in this sandbox, rolling a plastic truck with his name written on it around in the sand."

Glancing down at the sandbox, which had yet to be processed, I saw the grooves in the sand from what were most likely the toy truck's wheels. "Didn't find the kid's truck, I take it?" I asked.

"No truck. But the boy's Batman tennis shoe was found near that stand of trees, on the edge of the grass near the parking lot, like it fell off in a struggle when someone grabbed him," David continued, motioning toward the area. He then turned in the opposite direction and pointed toward a large pond that backed up to the woods. "The mom says she was over there, sitting at that first picnic table, watching the ducks, while she talked with her estranged husband on her cell phone. She had her back turned to the kid for approximately twenty minutes. She says she thought they were alone."

Sometimes I can't help say what I'm thinking. Mom calls it a character flaw. "The boy's mother should have turned around and watched the kid. The ducks can take care of themselves."

David sighed. "Sarah, stay on point here."

"I know," I said. "Just makes me mad. People are so careless."

"Understood," he said. "But look around, ask anything you want. The mom's name is Crystal Warner. She's twenty-two, unemployed, separated from her husband. We have her at the sheriff's department, in an interview room in major crimes, waiting. They've brought in the husband for questioning, too. The mom says she's willing to give a formal statement, and I'd like you to be there. She's high-strung, rather difficult, acts like she's got a chip on her shoulder. I figure we have a better shot at getting her to open up with a woman."

David's a muscular man with strong features, graying brown hair that curls around his collar, sturdy hands, and a calm manner. When we're together, I often have the sense that he finds me more than a little exasperating. Still, it can't be too bad. He keeps coming back for more. I gave him a quick once-over and said, "You know, you call off our date for a bank robbery or a burglary, I might argue with you about not feeding me."

"Not this case?" he asked.

"Not a chance. Not when a child's missing," I said. "Tell me about the kid."

"Joey Warner," David said, handing me a snapshot of a young boy sitting on a rocking chair. In the photo, Joey had long, shaggy light brown hair and bright blue eyes. He had a shy smile, a quiet child, I guessed, one of those you forget are in the room. This is the part I always hate, seeing the faces of children I know are either dead or in danger. Mom says some things tug at your heart, children at the top of the list. From the first look, like those two unidentified kids waiting in my workroom, Joey Warner had a hold on mine. I wasn't hungry any longer. It had been a long day, but I wasn't tired.

From that moment on, I was furious.

I looked around the crime scene at everyone gathered. A horde of reporters clutched together on the rim of the crime scene tape, with spotlights from TV cameras throwing shafts of light into the park. The black-and-whites parked along the perimeter shone their lights on the sandbox and the edge of the parking lot, where the kid's shoe had been found, making light for the CSI unit. Throughout the park, boxed-off sections of light interrupted the darkness, courts and fields all lit, although no one played tennis or soccer. Despite the patches under the lights, most of the park's three hundred acres remained clothed by night, including a hiking trail that wound through the bordering woods.

"You're certain that Joey didn't just wander off?" I asked, searching the shadows. "Pretty dark. He could even be scared and hiding in the woods."

"We had the dogs out, and they lost his scent at the edge of the parking lot, near where the mom says she found the tennis shoe," David said. He looked upset, and I knew he had to be thinking about the four-year-old, dead or frightened, if not lost and alone, assuredly with someone who meant him great harm. The next twenty-four hours would be crucial. Most missing children are found with a family member or are freed by their abductors during the first day. For those who aren't, the statistics aren't hopeful. "When we got here, it was light enough to see, and we searched and didn't find him. I hope he's hiding in the park, waiting for morning, safe. Maybe we'll be lucky and he'll just walk out of the woods at dawn. But it doesn't look that way."

"Okay," I said. "And this mom, tell me more about her."

David appeared to consider how to portray Crystal Warner and then opted not to. "I'd like you to make up your own mind. Let's just finish up here and we'll head out."

"I've told y'all that a thousand times. Just stop asking me all this stupid stuff and go find Joey," the boy's mom snapped in response to my first question: What was her son doing when she last saw him? "You're wasting time."

A full Amber Alert was out on the boy, notifying every law enforcement agency in the state and the nation, along with the media. Detectives working the case were following leads as they were being phoned in. In Harris County, somewhere around thirty cops were searching for Joey, so the boy's mom didn't have a real gripe, but we'd already explained that to her, and that information hadn't appeared to make an impression. While the others followed leads, our hope was to generate some from those closest to the boy, his parents. Plus, there was that doubt that had to be satisfied.

Stranger abductions are exceedingly rare. In any case involving a missing child, statistically the most likely suspects are the parents.

We were at Lockwood, an aging, nondescript building ringed by a chain-link fence on Houston's southeast side, home of the Harris County Sheriff Office's major crimes division. The interview room had four off-white walls, a door with a window, a second mirrored window that led to an observation room, a table, chairs, and nothing else. Nothing to distract from the business at hand. I tried to decide what one word I'd use to describe Crystal Warner, if I had only one to use. Bristling, I guessed. She was a slender young woman, with long dark hair that hung loose around her shoulders. A pair of blue jean short shorts with rhinestones on the back pockets and a white T-shirt wrapped her body so tightly that neither had the opportunity to wrinkle or sag. Even though her son had vanished only hours earlier, Crystal didn't appear frightened. Fuming at whoever took Joey? Sure, but even more so at David and at me, as we talked, a videocamera recording our every word, hoping to glean any information that could help us find the boy.

When all else fails, my best philosophy is to smile. I did just that, sitting back in the uncomfortable metal chair with its too-straight back. Crystal didn't blink, just stared at me unwaveringly, as if girded for my next move. She didn't trust me. Of course, she had no reason to, especially since she undoubtedly sensed that I didn't trust her.

"Mrs. Warner, please, we're not the enemy," David suggested. "Let's keep focused on why we're talking with you. Law enforcement personnel are out looking for your son, and at my request Lieutenant Armstrong has agreed to help us. She's asking questions . . . we're asking questions for only one reason: to find out if you know anything that might help us find Joey."

The woman didn't buy it; that was obvious. She shook her head in disgust. "I know I look young, but I've been around, and I'm not stupid," she said. Before we could argue either point, she went on. "I've seen those movies on TV, the ones where the kid disappears and the cops don't even look for him, because they're so busy pinning it on the mom and dad. You need to leave me alone and go figure out where Joey is."

Frowning, I gave the woman another skeptical stare. "You know, funny thing," I said. "When a kid goes missing, it *is* almost always the parents." I waited to see what she'd say, but she simply swiveled her gaze from David's face to mine with no less anger. Since she kept mum, I decided not to. "That said, no one here is trying to pin anything on you. We don't know what happened in this case, and our intention is simply to find out. How cooperative you are, how eager you are to help us, that will help us decide what we believe about your possible involvement in your son's disappearance. If we can eliminate you, we move on. If not?"

I left the latter thought hanging, hoping she'd jump in. She didn't, so again, I continued, "Mrs. Warner, the truth is that Special Agent Garrity and I are doing two things here. Besides looking for clues to your son's disappearance, we're gauging your cooperation."

I saw David resolutely examine the young woman's expression as I bent closer and lowered my voice. "What do you want us to think about you, Crystal? Do you want us to believe you have something to hide? Do you?"

Jerking her head to the side to avoid me, she clamped her jaw down hard, yet I didn't see it tremble. Based on appearances, her clenching wasn't a result of being afraid that she'd cry, but rather a futile attempt at containing her anger. David and I said nothing, waiting to see what she'd do next. The boy's mom took a deep breath and turned to me, this time with a strange smile, broad yet unnatural, as if she were determined to hide her true feelings. "Okay, ask away. But one more time, a few more questions, and I'm done. I'm out of here. If you're not going to look for my kid, there's no reason for me to help you."

"I assure you, as I explained earlier, that there are detectives and deputies all over Houston looking for Joey," David said.

"Yeah," Crystal answered. "That's what you said."

"Okay, tell us this — if you were us, where would you look for your son?" I challenged. If the woman had any theories, we needed to hear them. "Where would you start?"

At that, she pinched her lips together and frowned, as if she hadn't considered the possibilities. "I'm not sure," she said, pausing a moment before shaking her head. "I can't think of anyplace except the park."

"Any guesses on the identity of the person who took Joey?" David asked, sizing up the young mother with a quizzical gaze. "That's not a hard question, and it's one you want to answer, right? I know you want to help us. Don't you?"

This time a long silence, then she closed her eyes as if concentrating. "I can't think of anyone," she said. "Nobody in particular pops into my head."

Surprised that she didn't have a single direction to send us in, even a guess at someone we could investigate, I gave her a puzzled look. "Okay. Let's take this from step one. Let's see if we can piece together a few clues, so we've got a whisper of hope of searching the right places. Did you see anyone in the park, at any time today?"

"No, we were there alone. Or at least I thought we were," she snapped, pointing at David. "Just like I told him."

"Have you gone to that park in the past?" I asked.

"Yeah. All the time, if the weather's good. Joey likes the park, and it gets us out of the dump of an apartment we live in, since his dad left us," she answered. She held on to the chair arms as though she thought they might keep her stable. Maybe she thought that if she let go, the storm out in the Gulf would sweep her away. "Most of the time, since school started, we're pretty much the only ones there."

"Okay, so think back, anytime in the past," I said. "Did you see anyone who appeared to pay any attention to you or to Joey? Did he talk with anyone? Did you?"

"This is important, Mrs. Warner," David stressed. "Think hard."

The room grew silent, and Crystal lowered her head and again closed her eyes. At such moments, there's electricity in the air, not knowing if what the source says next will break open the case. This time around, we weren't so lucky. "No," she said. "Like I said, since school started, we're usually about the only ones there. That's what I like about the park. It's quiet."

"What about a car?" David asked. "Did you see any cars there today?"

"No," she said, shaking her head. "The other cops asked me that, too."

"Okay," David said. "What about earlier this week, or any other time? Anything you remember for any reason?"

Again, Crystal took her pose, head bowed, thoughtful. This time, she looked up, appearing hopeful, as if something had just occurred to her. "Sometimes, but I never saw anyone get out of it," she said. "Sometimes lately, now that the park's so deserted, this car shows up, kind of an old white sedan, you know, four doors. I don't know what kind."

"How old?" I asked.

"I don't know, just old, not new," she said.

"Did you see anyone inside?" David prodded. "Anything unusual about the car?"

"Yeah. I think it was a guy. The car's always parked too far away to see what he looked like. But like I said, he never got out," she said, shaking her head. "I just always thought that was odd, that he came to the park, then sat in the car with his windows all up."

"How often was he there?" I asked.

"Maybe three or four times," she said, tying her mouth into a bow. "Over the past month or so."

"Think back to be sure. Did you see the car today?" I asked.

"No," she said, again shaking her head, irritated at the question. "Like I said, I didn't see any cars today. But I wasn't looking, either. I was talking to Evan, Joey's dad, on the phone, listening to him tell me I was spending too much money. That I couldn't have the three hundred I needed. I was kind of distracted."

Leaning forward, David appeared to consider what she'd said. "Okay. But think back to those other times, when you saw the white sedan. What else did you notice about the person inside, or about the car?"

Again a pause, then she said, "Nothing. Just that there was this kind of older-looking car with a guy inside, and that he didn't get out of the car or roll down the windows to get fresh air. Why go to the park just to sit in a car?"

"Maybe to enjoy the view," David suggested.

"Well," she said, hesitating. "I guess."

In case it could be tied to Joey's disappearance, David wrote down the description of the car. Yet there must have been a hundred thousand white sedans in Houston, so with nothing to differentiate the car, Crystal's lead didn't promise much help. "Are there family members or friends, anyone who'd take Joey? Anyone who was upset with you or your husband?" I asked. "Maybe someone said they didn't think you were taking good care of the boy?"

"What's that supposed to mean?" she railed, sitting up pin straight and eyeing me. "I take good care of Joey. I'm a good mother!"

Ignoring her irritation, I went on, "Focus here, Crystal. Agent Garrity asked this earlier, but think hard about it. Do you know anyone who wanted but couldn't have a child? Anyone who might be desperate enough for a child to take your son?"

Still miffed, Crystal quickly shook her head. "No one I can think of. My parents see Joey lots, probably more than they want, 'cause they babysit. And Evan's parents could care less. Evan and me, we had a good life together, and we were pretty happy, but his mom and dad trashed us when we got married. They just saw the marriage as a stupid mistake. Which I guess it was, since he left me for that Barbie doll."

On the way to the interview, David had filled me in on what Crystal had to say about her not-yet-ex-husband, none of which qualified as flattering. The guy sounded like a lowlife, uninvolved in his son's life, unfaithful. Yet from the melancholy look on her face, I had the feeling Crystal wasn't finished with Evan Warner yet, that she still wanted him back. And after meeting the young mother, I figured there were definitely two sides to this particular story. The boy's dad waited in another room, but we had business to finish with the mom. First off, I had something I wanted cleared up.

"Crystal, Agent Garrity showed me the photo of Joey you gave the deputies, the one released to the media. It's the one that went out with the Amber Alert," I said, broaching something that had been bothering me ever since I'd looked at the photo. "Maybe I'm wrong, but Joey looks younger than four to me. When was it taken?"

With that, the young mom shrugged, as if I were bothering her with something irritatingly inconsequential. "About six or seven months ago, I guess," she said with a smug frown. "It could be as long as a year, but I don't think so. When he was three."

David flinched. His voice rose, although he kept it tight and in control. "You told the officers the photo was recent."

A rueful huff, and Crystal said, "I told that cop that it was the most recent photo I had. I didn't have anything newer on me, and I didn't want to go home to get one. That would have been a waste of time. Why? What's the problem? A photo's a photo."

I took a deep breath, too angry to answer.

"The problem is that you've got the police, the public, everyone, looking for a kid who probably doesn't look like that photo anymore. Children change quickly. Joey is older, bigger, his face has matured," David said, glancing over at me. "We need a new photo. A current one."

At first Crystal simply stared at us, then her eyes searched David's face. She said nothing, but I had the sense that she understood we were serious about the magnitude of her blunder. "I have some at home," she said, for the first time with an attitude that bordered on demure. "When I leave here, I'll get them."

"That's good. That's very good. But there's something else," David said, leaning forward, intentionally invading Crystal's space. Uncomfortable, she sat back, trying to lengthen the distance between them. "Before anything else, you have a job to do. You need to convince the lieutenant and me that you're not involved in your son's disappearance."

"I knew you thought it was me," she said, and shook her head as if we were all she expected, two dumb cops without a clue, Barney Fifes reincarnated. "Sure, like, how am I supposed to do that? Swear on a Bible or something? You'll believe me if I do? Get real."

"Take a polygraph," David said, sitting back and watching. "We give it to you, now. You pass it, we believe you, and we look elsewhere."

The young mother folded her arms across her chest. "No," she said, resolute. "Not a chance."

"Now that's not smart, assuming you're not involved," I suggested. "It's all ready. The examiner is waiting in the next room. You pass the polygraph, and we're on your side. We believe you."

Slouching in her chair, Crystal seemed to give that some thought. "I've heard those things don't really work," she remarked with a nonchalant shrug. "What if it says I'm lying, and I'm not? That can happen, can't it?"

"The tests aren't foolproof, but they're a pretty good indicator," David said. "And the examiner who'll conduct your test is good. He's been at this a long time. If you're telling the truth, passing a polygraph is the quickest way to convince us."

Crystal shook her head and stared down at her hands. If that was supposed to mean no, we weren't jumping on it. She was going to have to spell it out. We waited, and she looked up. "Okay," she said. "I'll do it."

Five

The truth was that we hadn't expected Crystal to agree, but David did have Ralph Goodson and the polygraph machine ready in an interview room two doors down. We escorted Crystal and made the introductions, then waited while the stooped man with the bow tie and high-water pants hooked her up. Crystal fidgeted in the chair, uncomfortable for obvious reasons. It wasn't exactly like settling in to watch television on a favorite recliner at home. After Goodson secured sensors around Crystal's chest, one on her finger, and a blood pressure cuff on her arm, David and I left and walked one door down, into an adjoining observation room to watch and listen through a one-way window and an intercom.

"I don't think these machines really work," Crystal complained with a disgruntled frown. "I'm willing to try it, but you make sure you don't ask any trick questions."

Goodson, a former private investigator, nodded as if in agreement. He looked like a high school chemistry teacher, and Crystal seemed to take his gesture as reassurance. "Young lady," he said, peering over the top of his wire-frame glasses, "you just relax and tell the truth. No problem, right?"

"Okay," she mumbled. "No problem."

From where we stood, David and I watched the machine trace graphs measuring Crystal's blood pressure, breathing, heart rate, and perspiration. Goodson asked the control questions, her age, her name, where she grew up, Joey's name, and his birth date. To my surprise, the resulting graphs appeared odd. If Crystal was telling the truth, the lines should form an even pattern. They weren't.

"Was your son at the park with you this afternoon?" Goodson asked.

"Yes," Crystal answered, her heart rate increasing.

"Do you know where he is now?"

"No," she said, clipping off the word. On the graph, her blood pressure rose, making an elongated arc.

"Do you know who has him?"

"No," Crystal said, again causing another jagged blip.

"Are you a truthful person?" he asked, his

voice even.

"Yes," she said, fidgeting in the chair, and the stylus careened upward.

As the test went on, Crystal's results began to look like a piece of paper she'd had Joey scribble on. Afterward, we stood with Goodson in the hallway while Crystal waited in the original interview room. "I'm not sure," the polygrapher said. "I wish I could be more helpful, but it's a strange result."

"How strange?" David asked.

"It appears she was deceptive even on the control questions," he said. "Usually when I see that, it means the subject is attempting to beat the test by confusing the result. That they've prepared, either taking some kind of drug or psyching themselves into it, by muddying up their minds or using physical tricks like muscle tightening. But that young woman had no idea she was taking the polygraph until she was already here. Right?"

"That's right," David said. "We just told her minutes before we walked her in."

"That doesn't make sense," Goodson said, shaking his head. "When did she prepare? How did she know what to do to try to confuse the test?"

"Unless she suspected she might have a

reason to be given a polygraph and she did some legwork beforehand," I speculated, glancing at David. "Maybe she knew it was a normal investigator's tool, and that we would ask the parent of a missing child to take one."

"But then she had to know her son would go missing," David said, connecting the dots. "Otherwise, why prepare?"

"Yes, she would have to have known the boy would be missing," I said.

"I guess that's possible," David said, running his hand over his chin while he mulled over the possibility. "We know she didn't prepare for the polygraph after the abduction. Until she came here, she never left the park."

"Maybe we're off here. Is there some other possibility?" I asked, gesturing at Goodson. "Bottom-line this for us."

"The report is going to read that she shows signs of deception," the polygrapher said, frowning. "My take is she intentionally manipulated the test to prevent us from getting a good reading. I can't tell you if she knows where the boy is and who has him or not. I can tell you that she's not cooperating with the investigation."

Minutes later, Crystal stood at the front desk, announcing she was leaving. She never asked if she'd passed the polygraph, which seemed odd, so David told her anyway. "The polygrapher says your test showed signs of deception." He let that sink in, then added, in case she needed an interpretation, "We continue to have the impression that you aren't being honest with us."

"It's all witchcraft," she said, her eyes narrowing. "I've told you everything I know. If that's not enough, I can't help you. I don't know where Joey is, but I think you should all be looking for him, not harassing me."

I leaned closer. "Young lady, you have some things to think about. The first one is, do you want us to spend our time investigating you or looking for your son? Because if you're intentionally screwing us over, all you're accomplishing is putting the focus on you and taking it off finding Joey."

"I've told you the truth," she said, defiant. She had a deputy beside her, one who had been assigned to take her to her apartment to find a more recent photo of Joey. As she turned and they walked away, Crystal ordered: "Now find my son."

"So what's she covering up?" I asked a few minutes later.

Before we introduced ourselves to Joey's dad, David and I detoured to the break room for a cup of coffee. David's face was flushed, and I knew why. I was angry, too, and disgusted. First she'd given us an old photograph of the kid, and now it appeared Crystal was trying to beat the lie detector.

"It has to be something that ties her to the kid's disappearance. Otherwise, why lie?" David answered. "Funny thing is, why'd she talk to us without a lawyer? Why'd she agree to take the lie detector? If she's screwing us around, why's she acting at all as if she's cooperating?"

"Probably figures she's smarter than we are, that she can fool us. The old photo," I asked, "you think it's on purpose?"

"Could be," he said. "I don't know."

"How much damage did releasing it to the press do?" I asked, figuring I knew the answer but wanting to hear his thoughts.

David frowned. "Substantial. The television stations have already shown it. We'll try, but it's most likely too late to stop the newspaper from running it in the morning. We'll put the new one out, but we'll never erase the old one from memories. It's like Crystal Warner is trying to throw up roadblocks, keep us from finding the kid. What do you think?"

"I don't know," I admitted. "It could be that she consciously misled us, or it could be that she's young and ignorant, and too angry to understand that what she's doing could get her son killed. Let's go talk to the ex-husband."

"In a moment," David said.

I turned and looked back at him, wondering. He had a glimmer in his eye, one I'd come to recognize. He pushed the break room door shut. The heavy aroma of a popcorn bag inflating in the microwave and the sound of snapping kernels enveloped us, while under the fluorescent lights, David pulled me close, slipping one arm around my waist. His right hand migrated around my neck and he urged me forward, until his open lips were full on mine, and my breathing became quicker. Then he whispered in my ear: "You look so beautiful. I can't tell you how much I regret not being alone with you tonight."

Rather than answer, I kissed him back and then whispered in his ear, "Now let's go find Joey Warner."

SIX

"So that's what I know. We were on the phone. Crystal wanted money, again, and we were arguing, again. I got sick of it, and hung up on her. Maybe five minutes later, she calls back and says Joey is missing. I didn't believe her, because Crystal lies. She'd lie about the time of day. I figured she just wanted me to go to the park so she could get me to talk to her in person, to ask for the cash."

Evan Warner sat in the same interview room where we'd talked with his wife. A gangly young man, he had a thick crop of curly dark blond hair and the same round, bright blue eyes he'd passed down to his son. In the chair, Evan sat at attention, his left leg propped on his right knee, holding on to his left shin with both hands, as if to keep it from sliding off. His son was missing, but, like his wife, Evan didn't look worried, only irritated.

"Crystal will say anything for attention," he told us. "Anything. Like I said, she lies when there's no reason. I wouldn't put it past her to stage a fake kidnapping to make everyone feel sorry for her. She'll probably want a ransom for Joey, then pocket the money."

David and I both looked at the guy and wondered, but David was the one who formed our thoughts into a question. "You really think your wife would do that to her own child? You're comfortable saying that's what happened?"

I figured the boy's dad would recant, but he nodded. "Yes, I am. She told me I'd be sorry for leaving her. Crystal is a pathological liar. She's capable of absolutely anything. She tricked me into marrying her, got pregnant so I didn't have a choice. I know Crystal. If she thought stashing Joey somewhere and claiming he'd been kidnapped would drop a bunch of cash in her lap, she'd do it in a heartbeat." With his final sentence, Evan pointed at both of us, as if emphasizing his certainty.

Even before we sat down with Joey's dad, David had confirmed that Evan Warner was working at the bank when his son disappeared. Of course, it was still possible that he'd hired someone to scoop up the boy.

The father had a financial motive, in two words: child support. If that turned out to be the incentive, it could be bad news. A father willing to take such drastic measures wouldn't be worried about keeping Joey alive. The boy's death would be a financial boon, since judges don't force parents to pay cash to support dead children.

"What happened when you got to the park?" I asked.

"It took me half an hour to show up. I wasn't sure I'd go at first," he said with a self-righteous shrug, as if still unsure he should have responded when his wife called him. "I get out of the car and the first thing out of Crystal's mouth is that she wants to look around the park before calling the police. So that's what we did."

"What was Crystal like when you arrived, how was she acting?" David asked.

This time, Evan threw back his head and looked at the white-tiled ceiling for a few moments before continuing, as if pulling together his thoughts or, perhaps, deciding what he wanted us to know. When he lowered his eyes, he looked directly at David, attempting a man-to-man connection I apparently wasn't part of. Lowering his voice, he said, "Crystal was upset, but that's not unusual. She's got this whole routine that she's used on me before, lots of tears, makes her look like a real victim. It took me a couple of years after we got together to figure out that it wasn't real."

"Mr. Warner, when is the last time you saw your son?" I asked, reinserting myself into the mix.

"Last Sunday, when I took him out for pizza," he answered. His grip tightened on his shin, and he frowned, his fury at his wife mounting. "When I picked him up, Crystal was mad. Her parents hadn't been willing to babysit the night before. She couldn't stop talking about how they ruined her Saturday night. She had some big plans, and Joey got in the way."

"Did she say what the plans were?" I asked.

"No," he said. "But they probably involved a bar and some guy she met there. That's Crystal's speed."

"How often do you see Joey?" David asked. "On the average."

"Once a week, sometimes less," he admitted, his eyes downcast, as if ashamed. "I'd take him more, but that'd mean I'd have to see Crystal more, and even seeing Joey isn't worth having to spend any time with his mother. I'm done with her. As much as I love Joey, I wouldn't live with Crystal again for anyone. Not even him."

Evan Warner had been more than forthcoming about what he wanted us to think had happened to his son. Now we only needed to figure out if we could believe him. If we could, maybe there was a way to use the information to find Joey. "If your wife is involved in this, is there someone she'd ask to help her?" David asked. "Who is she closest to?"

For a few moments, the boy's father appeared to consider the possibilities, and then he shook his head. "Crystal's kind of antisocial. People don't like her. It takes a while, but eventually they figure her out and don't want anything to do with her. She says she's got some new friends, but I don't know them. Like I said, my guess is she met most of them in a bar," he said. "Her parents are the only ones she's got any kind of real relationship with. They're not my favorite people, mainly because they believe everything Crystal tells them like it's gospel, when most of it's lies. But they love Joey. They'd never hurt him. As much as I dislike Ginny and Danny, I don't think they'd be involved."

That question answered, I wanted him to consider other possibilities. "Mr. Warner, suppose for a moment that your wife isn't involved. Is there anyone who'd be angry enough with you or with her to do something like this?" I asked.

Again, he didn't appear even to consider the possibility. Instead, he looked me in the eyes, annoyed. "The only one who'd be angry enough is Crystal," he said without hesitation. "And ask anyone. The way she talks about Joey, no one who knows us would be surprised if she's behind this. Crystal complained that the kid was ruining her life. I figure she found a way to turn him into an asset and cash in on him."

I looked at the guy and wondered, Was he telling the truth? What if the boy's mother hadn't taken him? "You know, Mr. Warner, you want to hear what I'm thinking?"

"Sure," he said with a frown. "Why not?"

"I'm thinking you don't seem very worried about your little boy," I said with what I was sure was outright doubt printed across my face. "Not very worried at all. If that were my child, I'd be frantic, doing whatever I could to help, including searching for the kid myself. You don't look like you care."

Warner smiled back at me and at David, a scornful smile that came with a slight shake of the head. "You're right, I'm not worried about Joey. That's absolutely true. Why?

Because I don't believe anyone really took him."

"How can you be so sure?" David asked.

"I saw Crystal at the park, kind of half-hearted looking around, spending most of the time talking to me about coming back to her. The usual Crystal stuff," he said. "I'm telling you the truth. Crystal is behind this, and at some point Joey will turn up, safe and sound. Only, if her scheme works, Crystal will have a pile of money to spend."

"Mr. Warner," David started, "maybe, but —"

"What you two cops need to do is pin this kidnapping thing on her," Warner cut in. "Crystal needs to go to jail. I want her out of my life, and then I'll be free to take care of my son, while she rots behind bars."

Watching the boy's father carefully, David asked, "Crystal tells us that you have a girlfriend, a teller at work, a pretty blonde. Is that true?"

I had to give Warner credit, because he didn't back down. "Yeah, I have a girlfriend," he said without any sign of guilt or remorse. "So what? I'd be happy to introduce you sometime. But that has nothing to do with Joey's disappearance. I love my son, and I'd never do anything to hurt him."

"Okay, I'm sure Agent Garrity or one of

the detectives on the case will take you up on that," I said. "But first we've got a request. We have a polygraph machine down the hall with an expert to run it. Crystal agreed. She cooperated and took the test, answered questions for us with the lie detector hooked up. We'd like you to do the same."

"I bet she didn't pass, did she," he said with an air of certainty.

"That's not the issue on the table," David said. "What we want to see is that you're cooperating as fully as your wife."

"I don't know," Evan said, giving a slight shake of the head that appeared noncommittal. "I've never done anything like that before. I mean, do those things really work? What if I didn't like what I was being asked? Would I have to answer? I mean, you could ask anything, right?"

"What wouldn't you want to answer?" David said, deflecting a question with a question. "Wouldn't you be willing to answer anything that would bring Joey home?"

"Well, I guess it would be all right," Evan said. "I'm telling the truth, so —"

A sharp knock on the door, and Evan was interrupted. David, with his tendency to forget to hang up his suit at night, was an oddity among investigators. Most of them looked like the detective who stuck his head in, a precisely cut flattop, spit-and-polish neat, maybe to the point of appearing square. “Agent Garrity,” the detective said, “there’s someone out at the front desk demanding to see you.”

“Not now,” David said. “Tell them to wait.”

“They’re causing a commotion. I think you’d better talk to these people,” the detective answered. “Right away.”

SEVEN

"We insist that you stop interrogating our son," demanded the woman, with all the conviction of someone who routinely got what she asked for. There were three of them in the reception area, the woman and two men. It was after eleven, and major crimes was quiet, with just a few detectives in the office, most of those on duty out on the street working the Warner case, following up on tips generated by Joey's photo on the ten o'clock news.

My empty stomach rumbled. Of course, now that I'd seen Joey staring up at me from the photo, I'd long since forgotten dinner. Unfortunately, my body wasn't in agreement. Still, something nagged at me. David's kiss in the break room reminded me that we had unfinished business. As worried as I was about the kid, I couldn't help consider that at some point I really needed to figure out where my personal life was heading and whether or not David Garrity was going to be a part of it.

"Hello. You must be Special Agent Garrity and Lieutenant Armstrong," said an affable-looking man in a navy blue jogging suit with wide white stripes down the sleeves and pant legs. "I'm Randy Rogers, Mr. and Mrs. Warner's attorney. A deputy called this evening asking questions, and we understand that you have their son, Evan, here. Excuse my appearance, but we rushed over, and I was at the gym when Alice and Jackson called. Is Evan under arrest?"

"No," David said, shaking the man's hand. "Evan's son, Joey, disappeared late this afternoon from a park, where he was with his mother. We're looking for the little boy and just asking questions."

"That woman probably did something to that child," said Alicia Warner, a tall, straight woman with rowdy brown highlighted hair that she'd undoubtedly struggled with most of her life. Her face was weathered with thick creases etched down from the corners of her lips, not up — from frowning, not smiling, was my guess. She wore big silver jewelry and a loose black dress. Her husband, Jackson Warner, looked her male mirror image, as resolutely erect as she, with thick, unruly gray hair and restless, faded blue eyes.

"That child isn't a concern of ours. He's his mother's problem," said Jackson, his expression cold. "But our son is. We'll take him with us and leave."

"We have questions for your son, Mr. Warner," David said. "It's important that we find your grandson quickly, and we need Evan's cooperation and yours to help make that happen."

"We don't consider that child our grandson. In fact, we've never been at all sure that he is," Mrs. Warner snapped. "Tell Evan we're here, please."

"Why won't you help?" I asked, peeved. I felt my blood pressure rising along with my anger. "Has this four-year-old insulted you somehow, enough that you would let him disappear, perhaps die? A child's life is in danger, and you're too busy to be bothered. Is that what you're telling us?"

"Lieutenant," the lawyer chastised, wearing a cautionary frown, "I must ask you to refrain from talking to Mr. and Mrs. Warner that way. You have no right to expect them to become involved in this situation. Now please tell Evan that we're here."

"Seems to me that common decency requires their involvement," I said, half expecting David to jump in to stop me. He didn't, and I figured I was saying pretty much what he was thinking. "Any moral code, even a halfhearted imitation of one, requires assistance when an innocent young child may be in danger."

"Your code, not ours," the grandmother said, to my astonishment. "Our code says that the boy doesn't exist, and he's not our problem."

At that point, Evan trailed out from the interview room. We'd asked him to wait, but he'd apparently inherited his parents' uncooperative genes. "What are you two doing here?" he asked, shooting them both a brooding glance. "I can take care of this. I don't need you or your lawyer."

"Your parents are here to take you home, son," the attorney said. "Get your things, if you brought anything with you. We're leaving."

"I just told them I'd take a lie detector test," Evan said, as if it were no big deal. "I think it'll take a while. I'll come home when I'm done."

"No!" his mother shouted, visibly alarmed. "Grab whatever you have here, if you have anything, we're leaving."

Evan paused for a moment, then shrugged and moved toward his mother, indicating he'd decided to follow orders and would soon be out the door. If we had any hope of convincing him otherwise, we had to talk fast.

"Even if your clients don't, Mr. Rogers, you know this isn't smart," David told the attorney, pushing ever harder. "Let Evan take the polygraph. Why not? Do you *want* us to think he's involved, that his parents are tangled up in this somehow? Why else would they be so uncooperative with the life of their own grandchild hanging in the balance?"

"You're not listening to us. We're not involved with that child. We've never even seen him," Alicia Warner fumed. "Our son was tricked into marrying that awful girl. She's the one you should be questioning."

I grabbed a flyer with the outdated photo of Joey off a nearby desk and thrust it in the face of his less-than-devoted grandmother. "This is your grandson. He's a little older now, four, and he has light brown hair, round blue eyes like your husband's and your son's. His name is Joey, and he likes to play with trucks in the park sandbox," I said, holding it up so both Evan's parents had no option other than to look into their missing grandchild's sweet face. "This is *your* grandson. You need to talk to us and help us save his life."

For the wink of a moment, I thought it might work. Both Alicia and Jackson looked at the photo, stunned. But I was wrong. "Evan, we're leaving, and you're going with us," Alicia ordered, turning away resolutely. "Now!"

Casting an angry glare in my direction, Jackson grabbed his son by the arm and coaxed him toward the door as the attorney in the jogging suit led the way. "Don't you care about your own son, Evan?" I called out. "He's a child, a little boy. Your parents may not know him, but you do. You're his father. And if you don't help us, he may die. Don't you care?"

His head spun around as his parents urged him out the battered metal door to the corridor that led to the stairs to the lobby. In minutes, Evan would be gone, and we had no way to stop him. "If I thought Joey was really in trouble, I'd help you. But he's not in danger. Go after Crystal," Evan shouted on his way out the door. "That bitch has our son stashed somewhere. She's doing it for the money. You check it out. Crystal knows where Joey is, who has him, and everything she does is for money."

EIGHT

After a quick good-bye from David, I was on my way home. He had work to do. I wanted to stay, but Joey's disappearance wasn't my case. From the beginning, it was clear that I'd been asked only for a consult, to help with the interviews, which hadn't gone particularly well. But David would be working the kidnapping throughout the night, starting at Crystal Warner's apartment. He had a search warrant to execute, which the kid's mom probably wasn't going to like. She'd be even more upset if she realized the green van parked in the apartment complex's lot housed high-tech listening devices, including everything needed to tap her phone. With a signed court order to back him, one he'd talked a judge into by showing him the polygraph results, David also planned to bug the apartment. Maybe it would work. Maybe Crystal would say something that would lead to Joey. Or maybe the kidnapper would call.

As I drove through the darkness, I couldn't get the little guy's picture out of my mind, half wishing David hadn't shown it to me. My subconscious was already cluttered with victims' faces, including those of the two children whose skulls waited patiently for names in my workroom. Frowning, I thought that the last thing I needed was the face of yet another four-year-old to carry around with me for the rest of my days.

Halfway home, I suspected sleep was probably not going to happen, so I detoured one exit past the ranch and into the countryside to the field where hours earlier I'd inspected the carcass of a cold, dead longhorn named Habanero. As I assumed I would, I saw lights in the distance after I drove past the barbed-wire gate and out to the far pasture. The moon hung high and bright, the stars shone in the velvet black sky, and cattle lowed in the distance as I walked up to a light glowing under a weathered tan canvas canopy, erected over the corpse of the dead bull. Kneeling beside it was a woman with long white hair pulled tight into a severely twisted bun anchored by a tortoiseshell pick. She'd seen me coming, I knew. There was no way she could have missed the truck's headlights or the wide beam from my flashlight. But she never looked up. Instead, she concentrated on carefully removing fly larvae, small, squirming off-white maggots, from inside the dead bull's gaping head wound, not an easy task since the animal had a full seven feet of horns that had wrenched his head lopsided when he fell.

"That you, Sarah?" Gabby Barlow asked when I loomed above her. Some folks might have spooked, seeing someone approach in a dark cow pasture so late at night, but Gabby wasn't the kind who let much of anything distress her.

"Yup," I said. "It's me all right. Where's everyone else?"

"Crime scene has come and gone. So has the vet. The sergeant is off in the trees, taking care of some business," she said, a slight chuckle in her voice. "I'm sure he'll be back soon."

As promised, moments later Buckshot emerged from the darkness, readjusting the zipper on his tan Wranglers. I pretended not to notice.

"We're almost done here, Lieutenant," he said. "Doc Larson didn't see any reason to autopsy the bull, since it's blatantly obvious that the shotgun shell through the brain killed it. But after forensics finished dusting the body and the horns for prints, they skinned off the section of hide with that picture drawn on it and took it with them, figuring it'll dry out and you can keep it for evidence."

I scanned the carcass and saw the patch of missing cowhide, exposing thick bands of muscle shriveling from loss of blood. The symbol must have been important, otherwise why take time to leave it? Something odd was going on here; I just had to figure out what.

With that, Gabby Barlow stood, unfolding until she made me feel small. At five-six, I'm not petite, but Gabby towered a full six feet. At nearly seventy years old, she took longer moving around, but she still seemed to have a full complement of working brain cells and more energy than a lot of middle-agers. "I've got pretty much what I need, more than enough samples to give you a ballpark on time of death. I'll have results sometime tomorrow," she said, the deep creases around her eyes drawing narrow. "Damnedest thing I've ever seen. Who the hell would kill a longhorn to use its side to draw on? Have you figured this out? Got some ideas?"

"Only guesses," I said. "I'm thinking maybe kids, like a gang ritual. But there's no real evidence of that. I'm open to suggestions."

"I haven't got a one," she said. "I do, however, have a colleague at the university who may be able to help you with that drawing. That's his specialty, deciphering symbols."

"That would be appreciated," I said. I'd been planning to do a little investigation of its meaning on my own, but if Gabby knew someone who could help, all the better.

"Tell you what, e-mail me a photo of the drawing, and I'll run it past him in the morning," she offered. "One way or the other, if he can help or not, I'll get back with you."

"Buckshot, you'll do that for Gabby, when you get home tonight?" I asked.

"Yeah," he said with a grunt. "I'll e-mail it. As soon as I clean a day's worth of cow pasture off these boots."

At that point, we closed up shop. Gabby had her samples, Buckshot, appearing understandably exhausted from the day in the field, headed home, and as I walked to the truck, I heard the beating of thick, long wings against the calm night air. "Dinnertime," I said, assuming the vultures had been waiting at a distance and now realized we were leaving. Once we were gone, the place would flood with scavengers fighting over the remains. The vultures were already present. Maybe a bobcat would wander by. Even a bald eagle wasn't above fighting over scraps of meat. When the larger diners finished, the crows would show up, and through it all the flies and ants feasted. I hoped they savored the meat. That bull was an expensive dinner.

Even the fast-food restaurants were closed, so I arrived home and helped myself to a bowl of Mom's stew out of the fridge, warmed in the microwave. Bobby had left hours earlier, and Mom and Maggie slept. I sat on the porch, looked up at the stars, and spooned down the rich stew with its salty broth, wondering about little Joey Warner. I'd hated to leave, but David had insisted that between the FBI and the homicide detectives, they had the investigation well in hand. I knew they did, but that didn't make me any less sad about not working to find the kid.

Half an hour later, I peeked in on Warrior in the barn, found him sleeping soundly. On my way back to the house, I thought again about how odd it was that the world seemed so peaceful, the sky above so clear, with a monster storm collecting energy, brewing in the Gulf. In four days, when nature's horror made landfall, people could die and homes and businesses wash away, ending some lives and changing others forever.

"I hope wherever you are, we have you home safe and sound by then, little Joey," I whispered to no one except, perhaps, the Almighty. Minutes later, I checked Maggie and found her peacefully asleep, then made my way to my room. I heard Mom's soft snoring behind her closed bedroom door and thought about safety and family and love.

Nine

The boy's head hurt, bad, and he wondered how long he'd been in the dark. Where was he? Joey thought back, trying to remember, but he couldn't, and he started to cry. He wanted his momma and his poppa. He wanted his oma and his opa. He'd left his favorite truck in the sandbox at the park. His momma would be mad. She scolded him when he lost his toys. "Money doesn't grow on trees, Joey," she said. Once, when he didn't pick up his toys, she had threatened to throw them all away.

It was black dark, and Joey saw the thinnest light, just a line along the floor, coming in from behind what felt like a door. He put his head down and tried to look through the opening, his tears puddling on the floor beneath his cheek, but he saw only a strip of worn wooden floor. Then, in the distance, someone whistled. Scrunching down even closer to the floor, Joey tried to peer through the sliver of light into the room outside the door, but he saw no one. He listened, wondering if he'd imagined it, but then, again, the boy heard a long, thin whistle.

Someone was outside, in the light. Someone who could help. "I'm in here," Joey said. No one answered. Then louder, "I'm in here!"

At first nothing, then footsteps and a creaking floorboard. Tensing, Joey waited, sensing someone standing silent, motionless, just outside the door. Why didn't the person say something and open the door? Suddenly, Joey couldn't stand another moment of uncertainty. A cry caught in his throat, one that turned into racking sobs.

"Let me out!" Joey screamed, standing up and pounding on the door. "I want to get out!"

In the darkness, a key turned in a lock and then a doorknob twisted. The door swung open and Joey fell forward as the closet he'd been locked in flooded with light. But after hours in darkness, it hurt his eyes. Covering his face with his hands, Joey rubbed his closed eyelids until the confusion cleared. When he finally looked up, he saw someone looming above him, a man with a familiar face.

"Did you find Buddy?" Joey asked with a

hopeful smile.

"Buddy?" *The boy's so small,* the man thought, staring down at the figure before him. *Small and trusting. They're all that way, the children. So easily fooled.*

"Your puppy," Joey said, happy to see the man he'd tried to help, thinking now there was someone able to contact his momma. "Did you find him?"

"I don't own a puppy," the man said, enjoying the boy's confused look. "I don't even like dogs."

Joey cocked his head to the side and thought about the man, about what he'd said, and about the park. He remembered being excited about helping the man find the dog, remembered running toward the trees, where the man said his puppy was hiding. Then, something tight wrapped his mouth and nose, a hand covered by a cloth. Joey struggled, but someone held tight. A sickening smell, and Joey's lungs burned as his legs bent and his body slumped. Then nothing, until he woke up in the closet's darkness.

None of it made sense.

"But what about Buddy?" Joey asked, appearing puzzled. "He's your puppy. Didn't you find him?"

The man laughed, a coarse, rueful laugh.

"There is no Buddy. I made him up," he gloated, his excitement building. He enjoyed the child's inability to grasp what was happening. The man liked them that way. Their innocence made them helpless, more easily controlled. "I told you, I don't even like dogs. All they do is eat and shit."

For a moment, Joey appeared too bewildered to respond. Then he looked up at the man, and tears again filled his eyes. "My head hurts," he cried, putting his hands on his forehead. "It hurts bad."

"The drug does that at first. It'll go away," the man said with a disinterested shrug. It seemed such a pitiful complaint, such a banal whimper from the child, when so much had already happened to him. Of course, the past was nothing when compared with the boy's future. Taking Joey had been thrilling, as it always was. The man enjoyed the quest of convincing a child to ignore everything he'd been taught about strangers, about the danger of the unknown. But what waited, that was what gave the man a reason to live. Just thinking about it made him ache with anticipation.

"Where's my momma?" Joey asked, his voice hoarse, a sick feeling in his stomach as he thought about what the man had said, about not even having a dog. As hard as he tried, Joey couldn't understand why the man was looking for a puppy. Especially when the man said Buddy didn't exist. Not sure what was happening, the boy collected his courage. Wrapping his hands across his chest as if defiant, he looked up once more at the man, demanding, "I want my momma and poppa."

"Or you'll do what?" the man mocked, relishing the power he had over the child. "I'm the only one here, Joey. I'm the one in charge."

The boy's face formed a tight, fearful mask, and he gulped so hard the man saw the soft muscles in the child's neck contract. "From now on, Joey, you do what I tell you. Anything I tell you," the man said, glaring down at the child. "From now on, as long as I want you, you belong to me."

Tears running down his cheeks as he stared up at the man, Joey thought about what his oma had told him, about never talking to strangers. The boy wondered if the man even knew his momma. The man lied about the dog, maybe he'd lied about knowing Joey's momma, too. Again, the boy swallowed hard, and he felt his belly roil, empty. Acid etched its way up his throat, and Joey wondered if he'd throw up. If he did, maybe the man would get mad. Maybe he would hit him. Reining in panic, Joey again looked up at the man's face, set as impenetrably as a cold marble statue. "Please. I can go home?" Joey begged. "I can go home, now?"

"No," the man said, his voice level and calm. "You cannot go home."

Ten

"The hurricane's turning north!" Maggie screamed up the stairs the next morning as I hobbled toward the bathroom, stiff-jointed after a restless night of half sleep. "There's an even *bigger* chance it'll hit Galveston. Thirty percent instead of only twenty, Mom. Did you hear me? The storm is turning, and it's bigger and stronger!"

"On my way, Magpie," I shouted in response. "I'll be right there."

In the kitchen, Mom's pancakes bubbled on the griddle. If there'd been any doubt that she was worried about the storm, the mixing bowls, eggs, sugar, and milk put it to rest. On the side, Mom, whose name is Nora Potts, runs a little company called Mother Adams Cheesecakes, baking desserts for caterers and fancy restaurants. Since she went pro, we have to have a crisis for her to pull out the cake tins for us. Otherwise, she pretty much sees it as work.

The storm, it appeared, had done the trick, and Mom's anxiety had birthed a baking binge, evidenced by enough home-baked breads and desserts cooling on the counters to keep us on a weeks-long sugar high.

I gestured at the stacks of ingredients, and she smiled a bit awkwardly, then laughed. "Well, dear, look at the bright side. At least you'll have chocolate cheesecake tonight," she said.

"Mom, really, the storm is still three days away, and we don't even know it's coming this way," I protested.

"I know. I really do," she said. "But it looks more and more like it might. And I wanted to use up some of the milk and eggs, in case the generator isn't enough to keep the refrigerator running, or we can't get enough gas for it. I would hate to see it all spoil."

"You sure?" I asked, doubtful. It seemed the older Mom got, the more cautious she was about things. The more she worried.

"Well, the truth is, yes, I'm nervous. There, I said it. I keep thinking about all those people who died when the hurricane hit Cuba. Terrible," she said, shaking her head as if in disbelief. "This is my way of handling it. And that's good, right?"

"Of course," I said. "Handling it is good."

A nod of the head and a grimace that turned to a smile, and Mom went back to kneading a loaf of jalapeño bread, working out her anxiety on the dough as she threw it against the floured counter and massaged it with her palms. Meanwhile, I turned my attention to a stack of blueberry pancakes and watched the morning news. It was predicted to be another hot day, with temperatures in the nineties and humid. The aerial views of Juanita were breathtaking, and I understood Mom's concern. The storm was growing, collecting around a clearly visible opening, the eye of the hurricane. Stalled, it continued to absorb power from the unusually warm waters. When it hit land, forecasters were predicting a twenty-foot surge and damage that could be catastrophic.

"Gram, don't forget to pick up extra horse feed, to stock up before the storm," Maggie said on her way out the door to catch the school bus. The kid worried almost as much about being prepared as Mom, which was saying something.

"Yes, Maggie," Mom answered, smiling at me. After the screen door slammed, she laughed. "You know, that girl of yours reminds me of you at her age. I remember the time you stayed up all night waiting for a hurricane. Missed us completely, and I was pretty sure you were disappointed."

"Ah, I don't remember that," I protested. Actually I did, kind of, but it was one of the things from my childhood that I'd been hoping for a long time Mom would forget. "You sure?"

"Sure as I am about that storm coming somewhere close. I can feel it in my bones," she said.

Just then, footage of the park the night before flashed onto the television screen. David and I could be seen in the squad car headlights. Mom, it appeared, didn't notice, and I didn't point myself out. The night shots cut to morning, and a reporter, voice lowered and somber, as if in a funeral home, described how the city was responding to reports of a missing child. Where we'd stood the night before, where Joey's Batman tennis shoe had been found, was a growing memorial of flowers, teddy bears, and notes, many written by children who lived in the neighborhoods surrounding the park. One said: "Joey, come home!" Another: "To the bad man who took Joey Warner: Bring him back!" A third simply: "Don't hurt Joey!"

At the end of the segment on Joey's disappearance, the reporter held up the flyer with the boy's photo, to my deep dismay the same one I'd seen the night before. Somehow, even the following morning, word hadn't gotten out to the television station that the picture they were showing of the child was an old one.

"Damn," I muttered, shaking my head.

"What's wrong?" Mom asked.

"Nothing," I said. Then, "Everything. I have to go. I need to get to the office."

I stood to leave, but the anchorwoman announced that the station was cutting away to a news conference where the mother of the missing child would make a statement. Then there she was, Crystal Warner, with an odd expression on her face, as if caught somewhere between terror and jubilation, including just the slightest tug of a smile. Standing in the street outside an office building, beside a man and woman who looked much like her, only older, I assumed her parents, she read from a sheet of legal paper clutched in her hands.

"I'm appealing to everyone to help us find my son," she said. "Joey is four years old, and he's been missing for sixteen hours. My parents and me are worried that someone took him. We don't believe he wandered off or that he's lost in the park."

In the kitchen, Mom moved up and stood beside me as the television coverage continued. "Joey is a good kid, and we love him and want him back. Please help in the search. Watch for my son." With that, Crystal held up a new photo of Joey, a more recent one. Maybe, I was thinking, the mom was on the level. Maybe she loved the little guy and she wasn't involved. But then something else happened, something that reminded me of what Evan Warner had predicted the night before, that his soon-to-be ex-wife was involved and had a motive.

"Crystal Warner says she's doing all she can to help police find her little boy," said the reporter, a bright-faced young woman with a shrill voice. "And to help defray costs associated with the search and her inability to work until her son is found, the family has set up an account at a local bank where people can donate, either via the Internet or by stopping in at a branch office."

"Money," I muttered. "Maybe it is all about money. But where's the kid? Did she pay someone to stash him?"

"Did you say something, Sarah?" Mom asked.

I was still thinking and didn't answer.

"You know," Mom went on, "in my opinion, that girl's statement seemed a little strange. I mean, she didn't seem quite right. Is that the way a mother with a missing child would act? I could be wrong, but to me, she actually looked happy."

Just then the telephone rang, and within minutes I was on my way.

Eleven

"The fax came in a few hours ago," the captain said, staring down as I was at the papers spread out on my desk. I had all four images fanned out, showing the drawing from different angles. Like the first one, this new symbol had been found painted on the side of a dead longhorn, another expensive, prize-winning bull, shotgunned through the head and with a circle drawn around his carcass in the dirt. Instead of in the forested hills north of Houston, this grisly discovery had been made by a rancher on a flat, treeless pasture south of the city. Like the first, this longhorn was caramel-colored and light tan with a pale midsection big enough to frame the drawing. Instead of a dissected triangle, however, the new symbol resembled a claw perched on a thick black stem, crossed by four heavy black lines.

"You have any theories about all this?" Captain Don Williams asked. A tall, dark-

skinned man with a rounding belly who'd played basketball in college, the captain had just turned fifty-six. To mark the event, his secretary, Sheila, had brought in his favorite German chocolate cake and we'd all patted him on the back. Afterward, he'd told me that fifty-six wasn't bad, except that it was only four years away from sixty. I figured for his age the captain looked pretty good, and I told him so, but he appeared unconvinced. "Seems to me that these symbols mean something. Haven't you got any ideas yet?"

When I didn't answer, he shook his head, as if the whole thing were totally nonsensical. The captain's like that, a big, blustery man without a lot of patience. He glowered at me, as if trying to decide how to stress the importance of the two dead bulls. Buckshot had already warned me, saying that news about the killings was spreading through ranching circles faster than fear of mad cow disease, and the governor's office had been inundated with phone calls from worried cattlemen. "You know, these crimes are adding up. That's a small fortune in livestock this criminal, whoever he is, has shotgunned and left to rot."

"I understand that, Captain," I said, shuffling the photos around on my desk. "I get that the bulls are expensive."

Staring at the images, I thought about the scene the day before, Habanero's decomposing body used as a bizarre medium for a yet-to-be-deciphered message. There had to be something this bull killer wanted to tell someone. Maybe that was the place to start, to figure out what audience he wanted to communicate with. Texas ranchers? Maybe it was some kind of antimeat campaign. But that didn't wash. It was hard to picture a vegan executing bulls even to make a point. And what was he or she trying to say? Wouldn't someone who wanted to get a point across leave a message we could interpret? Maybe not. Maybe knowing that we were baffled was a big part of the thrill. Maybe that was the enjoyment, that he had a bunch of cops bamboozled.

"So what are you going to do?" the captain demanded. "How do you figure out what those symbols mean? How do you catch this guy?"

I thought about that for a moment. I kind

of wished he hadn't asked, but he had, so I needed an answer. "I'm going to e-mail these photos to Gabby Barlow at A and M," I said. "She has a fellow professor, one who specializes in symbols. He may be able to help. And I'm going to search past records, see if we've had anything like this anywhere in the state. Maybe this has happened before. Maybe there's a link to an old case we can use to pull the clues together. If not in our files, maybe a computer search will turn up something, anything, to help us get a bead on this."

The truth was that I'd never seen anything like these symbols before, so I kind of doubted we had anything in the data banks that could help, but it didn't hurt to try. Compared with my efforts, I figured Gabby's colleague offered the most hope.

"Once we make an arrest, what kind of charges are we looking at, Captain?" I asked. "Have you run this past the D.A.'s office?"

A glum frown on his face, the captain eyeballed me. "Yeah, after the first bull's demise. Due to the value of the animals, we're talking first-degree felonies, a few, animal cruelty, criminal mischief, and theft. We're still refining. But don't you worry about the prosecutor's angle. Concentrate on figuring out what's going on and catching this guy. Put him out of business before we've got more dead longhorns."

Just then my cell phone rang, and I saw David's phone number before I flipped it open. I gave the captain a sorry-I'd-better-take-this look and answered.

"Sarah," David said, "we're running on fumes here, and this missing kid case is heating up. The national press is all over it. We just heard through the grapevine that Crystal and her parents are scheduled to be on the *Today* show tomorrow morning, and a group is putting together a candlelight vigil for Joey tonight in the park. We've got to solve this thing and get this kid back quick, especially with that storm maybe coming and shutting us down."

"Sounds like a nightmare," I said, thinking yet again about the photo of little Joey, the boy's sweet face. "What can I do to help?"

"I'd like to request your services from the captain, just for a few hours. Any objections?" he said. Before I had time to answer, he added, "I need someone to do an important interview. None of us have slept. We're all bone-tired."

I'd been waiting for this. I wanted to help find the boy, but I hesitated. Inserting myself into the center of what was fast becoming a big national news story, the biggest thing on the Gulf Coast next to the storm, gave me pause. The last couple of years, I'd been on the front pages more than I cared to be. Neither time had it been anything close to fun. Glad my fifteen minutes was over, I wasn't in the market for another brush with fame. "I can work in the background," I said, not needing to explain my concern to David, who'd been with me through the turmoil of two cases that had my face front page. "No one mentions me to the press?"

"Sure, but you have to understand how big this is blowing up," David said, agreeing yet at the same time sounding as if he were cautioning me that it might not be possible. "Before you decide, turn on the TV."

"Why?" I asked.

"Just do it."

As instructed, I clicked on a small television I keep in a corner bookshelf and switched it to Houston's ABC affiliate. While the reporter did a voice-over, I saw David on the screen, in the same park where we'd been the night before, this time in the distance, talking on his telephone but surrounded by searchers, men and women, volunteers, preparing to walk the park, others on horseback getting ready to look for the boy or his body.

"Okay, so it's a madhouse, I get it," I said.

"Headquarters won't let me leave here," David said, his voice low. "It's a public relations catastrophe if we're not on-site and they find the boy's body. Now that it's daylight, we've got more forensics to do. I don't know these detectives well, and I want someone I trust on this interview. Will you help?"

"Absolutely. Captain Williams is right here. I'll put him on."

With that, I handed the telephone to the captain. "David Garrity would like to talk to you," I said.

Twelve

On the way out the door I handed Sheila, the captain's secretary, the photos of the symbol painted on the second dead longhorn and Gabby Barlow's e-mail address. My own investigation into the matter would have to wait. When I arrived at the park, I flashed my badge, and an officer logging in law enforcement personnel motioned me through to a parking space near a row of picnic tables covered by an awning, which appeared to be a makeshift command center. Despite blocking the unrelenting sunshine, the canvas shade did little to abate the ruthless heat. Still early in the morning, it had to be in the high eighties and climbing, a damp, sweaty heat that would build throughout the day. I'd left my jacket in the Tahoe, but my white cotton shirt, crisp in the morning, hung on me, wrinkled and damp. David was nowhere to be seen. I stopped an officer in a uniform and asked for the FBI special agent in charge, and he pointed toward the body of water at the back of the park.

When I walked over, I realized there were two small boats with divers in the center of what was perhaps a twenty-acre pond, a dammed-up section of creek surrounded by trees with a gritty dirt bank. Spying David, I walked up behind him, then tapped him on the shoulder. He looked terrible. The kid had been missing for going on eighteen hours, and I didn't doubt that David had suffered every minute of it.

"Sarah," he said, and despite his fatigue, he managed a smile. "Thanks. More than I can say, this is appreciated."

"No problem," I said. "What's going on? Dive team searching?"

"Yeah, but they're running into problems," he said. "The bottom's muddy and the water's murky, nearly opaque. We're talking about dredging, bringing in the hooks."

That made sense, of course. If the kid was in the pond, he wasn't alive. "I hope you don't find him, not here, not dead," I said, feeling a rush of incredible sadness. "I hope this isn't the way it ends."

"Yeah," David said. "Me too."

"What else?"

"The equine folks are searching the creek

banks, and we've got volunteers walking the park," he said. "But I don't think the kid's here. I think he was taken, gone. I hate this. I want to leave, to follow the leads, but until we're sure Joey isn't here, I've got orders. I can't."

"So what do we know?" I asked. "Anything more than last night?"

"You saw the news conference?" David asked. When I nodded, indicating I had, he added, "What did you think?"

"Obviously, it made me wonder if the boy's dad is right and the mom is behind Joey's disappearance. Crystal Warner does appear to be planning to cash in, doesn't she," I said.

"Yeah," he replied, wiping the back of his left hand across his forehead, blotting a thin layer of sweat. "Plus, the detectives have talked to a couple of the mom's friends, mainly women she went bar-hopping with. I'm hearing that Crystal hated being a mom, made her miserable."

"How miserable are we talking? Miserable enough to kill her own kid?"

"That's what you're going to find out," he said. "We've got a list of leads. The one I want you to take is a sit-down with a guy Crystal hooked up with in a bar sometime last weekend. He left a message at my office. Says Crystal was complaining all night long about the kid cramping her style. Says she made some incriminating statements."

"Okay. Sounds good." Looking at David, I realized yet again how exhausted he had to be. "But promise me something?"

"What?" he said. The bags under his weary eyes drooped into sad creases, hanging like draped funeral banners. Still, he managed another small smile. "That when this is over I'll cook you that dinner you missed? You've got it. Just promise me that you'll wear that T-shirt you had on last night. When I close my eyes, I can still picture you in it."

As tired as he was, David shut his eyelids tight and flashed a wicked grin, mischievous. Unable to help myself, I chuckled. "While that all sounds promising, it's not what I had in mind. Promise me that you'll get somebody else to take over for you, and that you'll go home and sleep, at least for a couple of hours. Take a shower and get a little rest."

That he seemed less certain of. "We'll see," he said. "It's only been one night. I can manage. It's my case, and I don't know that, well, even if I went home, I don't think I could sleep knowing the kid's out there somewhere. The clock is ticking, that damn storm is coming, maybe here, and we need to find him."

"You also don't know when you'll get the chance to catch a nap again. Could be another long night," I said. We both knew that cases like this one can drag on for a very long time. "Come on. Promise me."

David smiled, and I knew. "You're not going to, are you," I said.

"No," he said with a shrug. "But I do love having you worry about me."

I smiled and then thought, again, that I had to pull back from David, for my own protection. I had to disconnect some, at least until I understood where we were going and if we were going anywhere together.

THIRTEEN

For a scumbag, Jimmy Fernandez wasn't bad looking: twenty-eight, curly black hair, big almond-shaped eyes the black-brown of Greek olives, a bit of a swagger in his walk, and a smirk that never quite disappeared, even when he asked if I thought Joey was dead.

"We don't know, but we haven't found a body, so we're hoping he's still alive," I said. "What can you tell me about Crystal?"

Our sit-down was at a Starbucks not far from Fernandez's apartment. It seemed he didn't want me dropping in. I wondered why, until I noticed his wedding ring. From that point on, his reluctance to talk about Crystal Warner in his living room made sense. "My wife will kill me if she finds out about this," he said, the smirk growing longer, revealing a glimmer of pride at the thought of a woman killing over him. Odd, I thought, since he was predicting he'd be the victim. "I could tell that Crystal hag was trouble. She's been calling my cell all morning. I had to turn the damn phone on vibrate, so my wife didn't catch on. If she finds out, like I said, I'm dead meat."

"I'm sure you exaggerate, Mr. Fernandez," I said, thinking that his wife probably understood he wasn't worth killing. But then, you never know. After all, I'm often amazed at the insignificant motives folks have for murder. "Of course, the simple solution is not to mess around. Then you don't have to worry about strange women interrupting family time with your wife and . . . I suppose you have children?"

"Two," he said. "A boy and a girl, six and two and a half."

He flipped open his wallet, and I looked down at the faces of children who bore a striking resemblance to the man seated across from me, same dark eyes and hair. Maybe I was simply jumping to conclusions, but it struck me that the youngest, the son, already wore his father's less-than-endearing grin. "They're darling," I said with a smile. "How sad it will be if you and your wife split up over your inability to keep your pants zipped."

Fernandez frowned for the first time during our meeting but didn't seem to take offense. Perhaps he'd thought about the same thing over the years but never put enough stock in it to change his behavior. As he described it, the previous Saturday night, about ten thirty, he was cuddled up to the bar in his favorite country-western joint on Houston's north side, a place called Spurs, hobnobbing with the bartender, a guy he'd once worked a security job with, and watching the women come and go, when Crystal approached him and asked for a light for her cigarette. The only catch was she held up two fingers as if she were holding one, but they were empty. No cigarette. When he asked where it was, Crystal put her hand down, laughed, and said, "I don't smoke. But I do lots of other naughty things."

The girl was obviously a card. Such a soft, subtle sense of humor. "What happened after that?" I asked.

"Pretty much we talked," he said with a shrug. "About an hour. She's pretty. Nice figure. A little ways into it, I started doing a little exploring, just some touching. She was primed all right. Ready for some action. Problem was, we had no place to go."

"No place to go?"

"She said her parents couldn't babysit like they usually do. She was really teed off about it. So instead of at her parents' house, the kid was at home. I had a wife in my bed," he explained, eyebrows lifted in an expression of what I interpreted as resignation. "No money for a room. I've been unemployed for about six months. Lost my job over some missing tools, a bullshit charge since I wasn't involved."

"Of course you weren't," I said, shutting down the topic. "But for now, let's focus on Saturday night and Crystal. What happened next?"

"She said she was tight for cash, too. Her ex was holding the money hostage. She figured he had a bunch, just wasn't giving it to her. His parents are loaded, or at least that's what she said. They hate her. She figured once he dumped her and moved back home with them, they'd open up their wallets, happy he got rid of her. Really teed her off, big-time."

"Cars don't work anymore?" I asked. When he appeared confused, I added, "For sex."

"Not comfortable," he said. "I threw my back out doing that once. Crystal is hot, but I didn't want her that much."

"Ah, I see," I said as a picture I tried to erase flashed in my mind. "This is all fascinating, but what I need to know is what Crystal Warner said about her son. Did she mention Joey?"

"Mention him? He was all she talked about," he said, taking a sip of his latte and leaving behind foam in the corner of his mouth. I pointed at the corresponding spot on my face, and he wiped off his upper lip with one of those earth-friendly, recycled paper napkins. "But she didn't talk about the kid in a motherly kind of way, if you know what I mean."

"No, actually I don't, Mr. Fernandez." I couldn't believe this guy. He needed to move it along. "Please recount the conversation as accurately as you can. What did Crystal tell you about Joey?"

"I told her I had kids, and she said she had one, too. But she said she was sick of taking care of him. She never got to go out partying. She was always stuck at home with the kid, and she said she was tired of it," he said with what I interpreted as empathy for Crystal's predicament. "She talked for a long time about the kid. I could tell she was getting ticked just thinking about it. At one point, she said she wished her son would just disappear, so she could live her life and not have to worry about taking care of him. I didn't believe it at first, but then she said it again."

"She said that?" I asked, openly skeptical.

I wondered if this guy was to be believed. After all, what were the odds a mother would say that on Saturday and her kid would be missing on Wednesday? Unless she had a plan to make that happen. "This is important, Mr. Fernandez. I need you to be as precise as possible. Tell me *exactly* what Crystal Warner said to you."

"She said it twice, and I already did," Fernandez insisted, looking hurt by my doubt. "Crystal said exactly what I just told you, that she'd be better off if the kid disappeared, because then she'd be free to do whatever she wanted."

Considering what I'd just heard, I tallied up the evidence. From all indications, Crystal had both prepared for a polygraph and, five days before Joey went missing, mused about him disappearing. The odds had to be infinitesimal that both those facts were true and she wasn't somehow connected to the boy's disappearance. The more I heard about this mom, the worse it looked for her. "What else did she say?"

"That was pretty much it. A lot of the time, we weren't talking. We were making out some, and she was trying to talk me into getting a hotel room. She was kind of busy being persuasive."

"How?"

"Nothing too wild. Just kissing and stuff," he said, chuckling. He moved forward, this time whispering, "Maybe a little touching."

"Ah," I remarked.

Sitting back in his seat, he took a swig of the latte and then gave his mouth another swipe with the napkin. "She seemed pretty needy, like she was looking for someone. I had the impression she was shopping for a replacement."

"In your case, someone else's husband?"

"I don't wear my wedding ring on Saturday nights," he said with a vague nod. "We talked about my kids, but my wife never came up."

Fourteen

Although I was on loan for only one interview, I wasn't eager to go back to investigating dead longhorns. Joey's case gnawed at me. I couldn't stop thinking about the kid, wondering where he was, who had him, and if we'd find him before he ended up like those kids on my workroom shelf. It was nearly noon when I detoured back to the park to relay what I'd learned from Fernandez. I saw David the moment I exited the car and walked toward the pond. There seemed to be a lot of commotion; the others were standing back some, and one of the divers had a shovel and was stabbing at the ground. When I walked up, I saw what had all the others mesmerized, a two-foot-long coral snake — headless, thanks to the diver with the shovel. David started to bend down to pick up the head.

"Don't do that," I shouted. He looked up at me, unsure.

It was painfully obvious that David, a Yankee who'd grown up in Connecticut, needed a lesson on poisonous snakes. "The thing's dead," he said.

"The snake is, but its nerves and muscles aren't yet," I said. I grabbed the shovel from the diver and touched the snake head. As if it were still alive, the venomous reptile opened its mouth, clamping mindlessly onto the shovel. "They keep moving for a while."

The diver, wearing a slick black wet suit, undoubtedly planned to give the northerner a fright.

"You know better," I said, eyeing him unhappily.

"Sorry, Lieutenant," he said with a shrug. "Didn't figure we'd let it hurt him, just get close enough and then we'd stop him. Show him how the thing could jerk a little and give him a scare. Just having a little fun."

The diver took the shovel, scooped up the head, and then grabbed the long, thin body. It reacted immediately, twisting in his grasp. We watched the dead snake writhing as he walked it toward a garbage can near the parking lot.

David and I sauntered off a bit, and once we were alone, he shook his head. "Just what I need. As if I'm not punchy enough. We've been at this for twenty-one hours now. We didn't find Joey's body, which is good because it may mean he's still alive, but we don't have a single solid lead. No one saw anyone around the park yesterday afternoon, but we've got lists of calls from moms who say they've seen suspicious cars and people hanging around in the past. The problem is that the descriptions are all over the place. It's interesting, though, that no one has mentioned a white sedan, as Crystal described. I'm beginning to think it doesn't exist."

"You're exhausted, David," I said, at the risk of sounding like a nag. "You need to go home, at least for a couple of hours. Catch a nap."

"I can't, not with that kid missing, in danger," he said, wiping his hands over his eyes. "Tell me you found a lead, any lead?"

After I relayed the conversation with Jimmy Fernandez, David shook his head and closed his eyes, as if in deep thought. "Sounds more and more like the mother's involved all the time. Let's go sit down at the picnic table," he said. "Let's go over this piece by piece and see what we know."

"Sure. I don't think the captain will miss me yet," I said. "And I'd like to help you find the boy."

On a pad of paper on a clipboard, David

had already constructed a timeline of the events, as he knew them, leading up to Joey's disappearance. Above the first entry, David wrote the information on the Saturday before: Crystal pairs up with Jimmy Fernandez at the bar and says she wishes Joey would disappear.

"You don't think this guy's making this up?" David asked. "Maybe he just wants to get in on the publicity bandwagon."

"No. I don't think so. Fernandez is no great guy, but he insists he doesn't want anyone to hear about this. He's got a jealous wife and two kids," I said. "But you could send someone to interview the bartender, to find out if he overheard anything. Fernandez says the guy was standing nearby."

"Of course," David said. "We'll send somebody over."

The next entry on David's list was the day before Joey went missing, when a store manager reported that Crystal's credit card was rejected. At that point, she had Joey with her. Later that night, a neighbor in the apartment complex where they lived saw Crystal and Joey arrive home, late. He said Crystal looked upset.

"Over the credit card rejection?" I asked.

"I don't know," David said. "But it sounds

like our kid's mom has money troubles."

"She told us that," I reminded him. "She said she and the ex were arguing about money on the phone when the boy disappeared."

"Yeah," he said. "I forgot. Maybe you're right. Maybe I'm tired."

"Tell you what," I said. "You can leave here now. You're not far from the ranch. Drive out, take a nap, just a couple of hours."

"Nah," he said. "Not yet. We need to find that kid."

David's cell rang and he picked up. As if in chorus, only moments later, my phone rang, too. In my case, Gabby Barlow had news about Habanero, the first dead longhorn.

"Sarah, there's quite a bit of insect activity on the carcass, mainly larvae. You know, bugs aren't that precise, it's hard to be certain, but based on what I'm seeing in the lab and the condition of the corpse, my best guess is that the bull was dead twenty-four hours or so when I got there to take the samples," she said. "I'm thinking that the bull was shot sometime the prior evening, sometime before midnight."

"Huh, I guessed it was a pretty fresh kill, just from the state of decomp, although the heat was a factor and my experience is more with people than livestock. Anything else?" I asked.

"Yeah, that colleague of mine, he says your symbols are African."

"African?" I repeated. "Like Africa African?"

"Yes, African," she explained. "It's not my colleague's expertise, but for the past month, he's been working with another professor, a Dr. Alex Benoit, who relocated here from New Orleans. Dr. Benoit is a former Tulane prof in the process of cataloging artifacts found on the grounds of the old sugarcane plantations south of Houston. From what I hear, he's one of the foremost experts on African symbolism in the country."

"That's a stroke of luck," I said.

"Sure is," Gabby said. "In fact, Benoit just happened to call my colleague today on another matter."

"Did you ask him if he'd be willing to help?"

"Dr. Benoit agreed to talk to you. I've got his phone number, if you're interested."

Fifteen

Hour after hour Joey lay quiet, unmoving, waiting in the dark closet, for what, he wasn't sure. The house remained stone silent, and he felt certain he was alone, but his fear kept him motionless. The man had left him a thin blanket, a pillow so flat that it barely cushioned his head against the hard wood of the closet floor, a bottle of water, and a funny-shaped plastic thing with a handle to pee in.

Sometime, maybe late in the morning, the four-year-old simply couldn't stand it any longer. The darkness had worn on him until his nerves pricked his body, as if he lay on a bed of nails. He had to do something, find a way out of the closet and home.

His first push against the door was tentative, soft. No movement. Gathering his strength, he pushed harder and then harder again. After taking two steps back, all he had room for in the closet, he rushed forward, hitting the door the way he'd seen the police do on TV, with his shoulder. Like a rag doll, he tumbled backward, hit the back wall with a thump, and then dropped to the floor. The door hadn't budged.

"I want to go home!" he screamed. "I want to go home!"

In the closet, Joey sobbed, while from the house he heard only quiet.

Long minutes passed. An hour or more later, he'd collected himself, calmed his crying. He thought about the closet and wondered. The night before, when the man let him out, Joey decided he should have taken a look, to see if there was anything inside that could help him. He hadn't felt anything, but maybe he could find something to pry the door open. On his knees, the boy desperately felt about the floor, his hands spreading over the rough, uneven boards, searching but feeling nothing but the old wood planks that made up the floor. Then he stood and ran his hands over the walls, from the floor to as high as he could reach on his tiptoes, hoping for a light switch, something, anything that could help. All his soft, small hands encountered were cracks in aging plaster.

Finally, he reached up, thinking maybe something hung, like in his closet at home, clothes on hangers maybe high over his head. If he found one, maybe he could use the hanger to get out. But all Joey's outstretched arms encountered was the sticky hot closet air, stagnant and smelling of his own urine. That was until he stretched high on his toes, waving his arms, jumping up and up, reaching. Finally, he touched something soft, cloth. On instinct, he pulled back, afraid. He waited and thought. Then, in the darkness, Joey jumped again, grabbing at whatever the cloth thing was and pulling it toward him, hoping to bring along a hanger with his prize. Three more tries and a supple round object fell into his arms, furry and familiar.

For the rest of the day, Joey sat, knees crossed, in the center of the closet, clutching what felt like the stuffed animals he had lined up on his bed at home. He buried his face in it and cried. Holding it brought modest comfort as he waited for something, anything, to happen. At times, he talked reassuringly to his only friend. "My momma and poppa are looking for us," Joey whispered. "They'll come and beat up that bad man. Then we can go home."

Gradually, he fell asleep.

When the door jerked open and light poured in, Joey felt confused. Curled in a ball on the closet floor, holding his hard-won trophy against him, he looked up at the man.

"Have a nice morning?" he said, an amused smile on his face. Joey stood up and stumbled out of the closet. It was then that the man focused on the toy, in the light a worn, dark brown teddy bear with black shoe-button eyes. "How did you get that?"

Joey didn't know why, but he felt the way he did when his momma caught him coloring on his bedroom walls. "It was in the closet. Up above," Joey said, flinching at the anger in the man's eyes.

Seething, the man put out his hand and waited. At first Joey held the toy tighter, afraid but not wanting to give it up. Moments passed, until he reluctantly put the bear in the man's hand.

"Is that your bear?" Joey asked, looking beseechingly at the man, then at the object that had given him brief solace in his closet prison.

"It belonged to a little boy," the man said matter-of-factly.

"Where is he?" Joey asked. "Is he your little boy?"

"In a way, he was mine. In fact, he'll always be mine," the man said. Joey couldn't decide what the man meant, but then he smiled down at him and explained in a cool, uncaring voice, "The boy who owned this bear is dead."

"Did he get sick?" Joey asked.

"You could say he got very sick, all of a sudden," the man said. For a moment, he was quiet, staring down at Joey, inspecting him as if he were somehow subhuman. "What's important here is that this is my bear. Not yours."

As Joey watched, the man returned to the closet, and Joey looked up at a shelf he hadn't been able to see in the dark, one the bear's long, skinny legs must have been dangling from. To get a better look, Joey took two steps into the room, and what he saw frightened him even more. On the shelf, the man sat the teddy bear beside a battered baby doll, dirty, with one eye missing. Then, next to the doll, Joey saw something familiar, something red and yellow, with his name written in black marker on the side.

"That's my truck!" he demanded, reaching up toward it, although the shelf towered over him, out of reach. "I want it. Give me my truck!"

"It used to be yours, but now it's mine," the man said, gazing down at him. "I like to call these my souvenirs."

Sixteen

My left arm had been aching all day, the one that has a metal rod and screws holding it together, the result of a six-month-old gunshot wound. The standoff the day I got shot could have ended a lot worse, so I didn't like to complain, but I'd noticed that the arm throbbed when bad weather brewed. Maybe that was what Mom meant when she said she felt the storm's approach in her bones. Funny how body parts and animals sense bad weather before humans feel it in the wind and see it in the sky.

After talking to Gabby and checking in with the captain, I reluctantly left David at the park. I wanted to stay and work on the investigation into Joey Warner's disappearance, but David insisted that wasn't necessary. That didn't relieve my conscience, but it did convince me that I had no other choice. It wasn't my case, and I had an investigation of my own to work. During the drive to meet Professor Benoit, my cell phone rang again. I'd already heard that no fingerprints were found on either of the longhorn carcasses. This time, our ballistics guy had the results on the shotgun shell fragments and pellets recovered from the bulls' remains.

"Not surprising that it cratered their skulls," he said. "The weapon was a twelve-gauge shotgun loaded with triple-aught buckshot."

"Triple-aught?" I repeated. "The shooter wasn't taking any chances."

"I've never actually tried to kill one, but I figure that's enough firepower to bring down a water buffalo," he estimated. "On the good side, if you catch a break, it'll make it easier to make a match when you find the weapon, as long as it's loaded with the same ammo. People don't use triple-aught much. Too big for birds and most game. We've got enough wadding and fragments to make a firm ID."

"Any chance you can recognize the brand from the samples you have on file, or through the computer data banks?" I asked. "If they're rare enough, maybe we can track down who sold them and even, if we're really lucky, who bought them."

"I tried that," he said, ending the conversation. "Didn't work. Nothing we have is a match."

"Ah, well. It was a shot," I said. "Anything else occurs to you, keep me informed."

I'd arranged to meet Professor Alex Benoit at the Westover spread, an early-nineteenth-century sugarcane plantation in Brazoria County, less than an hour south of Houston. Settling in for the drive, I clicked on the car radio, only to wish I hadn't when I heard that the storm had turned even more to the north. Still two and a half days out, Hurricane Juanita was sowing panic. The reporter said fights were breaking out among folks scouring Houston stores looking for staples, bottled water, batteries, and ice, the things Mom had stocked up on a day earlier. I'd chided her for it, but it appeared her senses had kicked in even before my bionic arm took notice that the storm was heading our way.

"Yes, Sarah, we're fine," Mom said when I called the ranch. "Frieda and I were outside working on the stable, nailing some loose boards down. We've got a month's worth of horse feed. Maggie's still in school, but when she gets home, we're going to put her to work helping to get the horses ready for the storm."

"Do we have everything we need?" I

asked. "Because from what I'm hearing, the odds are increasing that —"

"I know what you're hearing, that the storm's looking more and more likely to come ashore somewhere around Galveston," Mom cut in, impatient. "Sarah, we're as ready as we can be. Once the bad weather blows in, we'll hunker down and ride it out."

I thought again about little Joey Warner, wondering if he was in a safe place to survive the coming storm. My heart felt as if it skipped a beat or two when my mind strayed from where the kidnapper had him to what he might do to the boy.

"Sarah, are you still there?" Mom asked.

"Yeah. Okay. But if there's something I can pick up on my way home tonight, let me know," I said. "And I may be a little late."

"Meeting up with David?" Mom asked, suddenly sounding concerned. "Have you two had that talk yet? I think the world of David Garrity. You know that. But he owes you honesty, and you deserve to understand what his intentions are."

She was right, of course. But that didn't make it easy. Nothing seemed simple when I stepped back and looked at the situation. David had been divorced for years. When we'd begun dating, his past life was in his past. Then his ex-wife called him. She'd left her second husband, and she wanted David back, to try again to make their marriage work. To sort through the situation, David went to Denver for a visit but came back as confused as when he'd left. "If it weren't for you, for us, what we have, I'd put in for a transfer," he'd said to me over a candlelit dinner after he'd arrived home. "But now I'm not sure what to do."

If I were honest, I'd have to admit that I wanted him to say it wasn't a tough decision, that as soon as she'd asked, he'd told her he wouldn't go. But in addition to an ex-wife, David had someone else who wanted him in Denver, his teenage son, Jack, a kid David rarely got to see. Stuck in limbo while David made up his mind, I thought about asking him to stay in Houston but felt selfish, not so much that I was willing to tell David to leave, but enough not to ask him to stay. Still, part of me wondered, *If he's considering the move, what does that say about us?*

"You two need to get away to talk, without a lot of distractions," Mom rattled on. "I don't like the way he's doing this. The longer it drags on —"

"I know, Mom. I know." I didn't disagree, but I didn't want to hear it. "This just isn't the time. David's knee-deep in that missing kid case, and I'm heading south to Brazoria County, to talk to an anthropologist about two very expensive, very dead longhorns."

Mom paused and then said, "Okay. I understand. No more motherly advice." I could picture the look on her face as she nearly bit her tongue to keep quiet. "We'll table this for now, Sarah. Until things settle."

"Agreed," I said, wondering if she'd be able to live up to the bargain.

Settling in for the rest of the drive, trekking southwest, I traveled ever closer to the storm churning in the Gulf, yet the graceful trees that lined the highway barely rippled in the stifling hot breeze. I switched channels, and a preacher with all the fire and brimstone of a Pentecostal railed about Hurricane Juanita, calling it the hand of God, a storm akin to the one in the Old Testament that Noah and his herd rode out in the Ark. "The Father Almighty will raise His great hand and strike down the sinners, using the storm to punish the evil," he hissed, his fervor building. "Bodies will float in the bayous, many carried out to sea. Will the innocent die? Yes, as casualties of God's war against the wicked. Those who are taken will perish only because their deaths are needed for God to strike vengeance. But for the innocent, their suffering will be brief, as they're welcomed into the heavens, to the strains of harps and the joyous music of salvation!"

How did he know the innocents were only casualties of the war against evil, not those intended to perish? I don't pretend to understand how it is in heaven, but in my world, the victims were too often like Joey Warner, who'd hurt no one, those who deserved the opportunity to grow old. I liked the preacher's view of the world, that if folks died in the storm, they'd mostly be those who deserved such a tragic end. I liked it way better than my own worldview, one that held that more often the innocent suffer.

I pushed another button on the radio and Brad Paisley crooned, as I imagined what it must have been like before the days of TV weathermen with Doppler, before planes flew above to catch aerial views of approaching typhoons. Hurricanes must have hit like earthquakes, unexpected and therefore even more deadly. When you know a storm's coming, you can flee or take cover. I wondered how much notice my ancestors had of approaching storms, if any, and where they went to escape. I'd heard of my mother's great-great-aunt Constance, who drowned as a young girl in the devastating hurricane of 1900. The way the story goes, my ancestor, who lived in Galveston, was a bit touched and ran to the beach that morning to swim in the storm surge. Maybe Great-Great-Aunt Constance didn't understand how deadly the undertow could be.

SEVENTEEN

The Westover Plantation lay on the north bank of the Brazos River, a twisting ribbon that takes shape north of Abilene and meanders and bends through Texas, eventually emptying into the Gulf of Mexico. Since its discovery, the river's been the stuff of legends, and the early Spanish settlers who inhabited this part of Texas called it Río de los Brazos de Dios, in English the River of the Arms of God. That name has always puzzled me. Floating down a river named after "the arms of God," I imagine a crystal-clear stream. South of Houston, the Brazos is as brown as its muddy shores.

Listening to the radio, I drove across the flat coastal plain, lined by open fields and short, scrubby stands of trees, exposing a nearly uninterrupted dome of brilliant blue sky. A white wooden cattle fence lined the road as I approached the plantation, and a sign at the entrance warned: PROPERTY OF

THE STATE OF TEXAS — NO PUBLIC ACCESS.

As Benoit had instructed, I removed the chain loop that anchored the gate, and I entered the gravel road leading to the main house. The road ran between two-hundred-year-old oaks, their branches a canopy so dense that it admitted only narrow shafts of light. As I drove, the shadows and light pulsed through the interior of the Tahoe, as in a theater during an old black-and-white movie. A few minutes later, whitewashed sheds became visible off in the distance, then a straight, austere house with six thick, square pillars. Built in the 1820s, decades before the Civil War, the house was brick painted white, and the double front door must have been fifteen feet high. I walked inside, onto bare pine plank floors that creaked beneath each step, into a parlor. Directly across from the main doors stood another set of double doors leading to the back porch. I'd seen homes built this way before, old structures that dotted the countryside. For more than a century, until air-conditioning, the residents left both sets of doors and rows of tall windows open for cross-ventilation, to soften Texas's unrelenting summer heat.

"Dr. Benoit," I shouted. "It's Lieutenant

Armstrong."

No answer.

The mansion was in a state of disrepair, with plaster separating from the interior walls, showing their core, like the outside of the house brick and mortar. The rooms were empty, upstairs and down, except for lawn chairs with frayed woven green and white straps and a dirty white plastic table, a cooler filled with bottled water. I heard no one, no one answered my calls, and before long, I walked out the back doors along a covered brick walkway, to a shedlike structure. As was common in those days, trying to keep the heat out of the house and fearing fire that could consume the entire mansion, the original residents built a freestanding kitchen. A pot hung in a fireplace below a stone chimney, and the place smelled of mold. The room felt heavy with gloom, the only windows skinned with decades of grime.

Outside again, on a path cut through the underbrush, I noticed stables in the distance. The soft breeze smelled of deep pink roses blooming on a fence line, undoubtedly planted generations earlier by someone long dead. At the stable door, I peered up at the loft and again called out, again waited, but heard no reply. Dr. Benoit had said I would see him working around the place. I felt certain he heard or saw me. Why wasn't he answering my calls?

On a slight hill, a monument stood in the distance, an obelisk. Up close, its stone was pocked by nearly two hundred years of wear and etched into it were the fading words *gone but not forgotten.* Running my hand over the once deeply carved letters on the obelisk's base, worn shallow by wind and rain, I read the name Westover. Surrounding it were gravestones marked with the names and dates of the Westover family, the plantation's original owners, members of the colony that settled this part of Texas, led by the man considered the Father of Texas, Stephen F. Austin. Piecing together the clues on the markers, I learned that Colonel James Westover was born in 1794 and in 1832 fought in the Texas Revolution. He lived a long life, burying three wives and more than half of his thirteen children. On one grave, it read, "Little Nell, left this earth at three years and three days, succumbing to the fever."

As I stooped over the child's lonesome headstone, I sensed someone standing behind me. I hadn't heard anyone approach, and out of instinct, my hand went directly to the Colt .45 holstered on the rig under my jacket. Quickly I stood and turned, and found myself face-to-face with an angular man I judged to be in his early fifties. His features were finely cut, aristocratic, his hair a tree-bark brown only touched by streaks of gray, combed back in waves, framing deep-set grass-green eyes. His skin was well tanned, as if he worked long hours in the sun; he stood well over six feet and wore a wide-brimmed canvas hat, a white linen shirt, and khakis with boots.

"Lieutenant Armstrong?" he asked, eyes narrowed, questioning.

"Yes. And I assume that you're Dr. Benoit?"

"Of course," he said, his manner one of absolute calm. "Who else would be foolish enough to be out here on the plantation with that hurricane in the Gulf?"

"I didn't see a car when I drove up," I said, slowly removing my hand from the grip of my Colt .45. He watched, as if amused. I was anything but pleased. "I called out and looked for you, but you didn't respond. I was beginning to worry that perhaps you weren't here."

"My truck is in one of the outbuildings. I like to protect it from the sun." His expression was blank; it was as if he stared through me. "Unseasonable heat, and now a hurricane. I should be at home, barricading my house, instead of attempting to salvage what may be unsalvageable. Or interrupting my afternoon's work to talk with you."

"I do appreciate your assistance. We were grateful for your offer," I said, and Benoit shrugged, not acknowledging that he was the one who'd offered to see me. I wondered what he was referring to, what might be unsalvageable. "Are you talking about the mansion? It's been here for a long time, through other hurricanes. Why the concern now?"

"No. Not the house. Follow me," he said.

As we walked, he talked in a strange, detached monotone, detailing a brief history of the plantation. Before the Civil War, the sugarcane fields were tended to by as many as sixty slaves who harvested more than four thousand acres, first burning away dry brown leaves and killing the venomous snakes drawn to its rich cover. Pointing at round, cast-iron bowls, eight feet in diameter and three feet deep, discarded in a field, Benoit explained, "After the slaves harvested the cane by hand, they used a mule-powered press to crush it, then boiled the juice down in those pots, transforming it into a thick, brown sweet syrup, used for cooking."

As we walked on, he explained that Colonel Westover's only surviving son left the plantation to his children, who sold it after the Civil War, when a scarcity of cheap labor made sugarcane farming in Texas unprofitable. After a string of owners, a wealthy oilman purchased the spread in the 1950s, later bequeathing it to the state to be preserved as a historic site.

"Since then, the place has pretty much been left to rot, with only a few coats of paint and a new roof twenty years ago on the main house," said Benoit as we approached a long, narrow wooden building with doors every ten feet across the front. Benoit stopped in front of the first door, looked at the place for a moment with a glimmer of pride, then motioned for me to go inside. I entered and found myself in a ten-by-ten room, dark, with the only light penetrating through slats in two boarded-up, glassless windows. The floor was compacted dirt, and the walls were the bare frames of the outside siding.

"What is this?" I asked.

"Slaves quarters. An entire family once lived in this room," he explained with a solemn frown. "Each door is an entrance to another room just like this one. Each room housed another family of slaves."

"Hard to believe," I said.

"Believe it," he said, his face expressionless.

"Is this the building you mentioned, the one that's in danger of being destroyed?" I asked.

"Yes. This structure was scheduled to be moved next week," he explained. "It's slated to become part of Sam Houston Park. I've been preparing the area where it will be relocated. Do you know the park?"

"Yes, very well," I answered. "It's one of my daughter's favorite places. We've spent many an afternoon there, enjoying the setting and the city's skyline behind it. It's high on our list of favorite places for an afternoon picnic."

"Ah, well, then you understand the allure," he said.

On green rolling acreage at the edge of downtown, Sam Houston Park is sandwiched between I-45 and Houston's mountain range of skyscrapers. In the beginning the city's first official park, over the decades the property became home to various historic buildings relocated by the city's Heritage Society, most of them dating back to the early 1800s. After being restored, each was meticulously furnished with period pieces, to give visitors the ability to see how their lost ancestors lived. On long, leisurely summer afternoons, Maggie, Mom, and I had eaten lunch on benches under the park's impressive oaks, then toured the homes of those long dead, a wealthy financier, a freed slave turned preacher, and the quaint old, white-sided St. John Church. Always in favor of big, flashy, and new, Houston is a place that routinely demolishes rather than preserves, and the park is an unusual escape from the frenetic onslaught of modern life, recalling a forgotten time when swings hung from front porches and pies cooled on windowsills.

"The site is perfect, picturesque, on a slope near the pond," he said, staring at me oddly, his eyes a cold mask, his look contained, as if he were holding himself back from saying more. "We've built the piers because in any tropical storm or hurricane, that part of the park, the section closest to the pond, floods."

My heart beat faster, but I wasn't sure why, other than that the way he looked at me made my skin crawl. "I guess it's good you're not moving it yet, then, with the hurricane perhaps heading our way."

"Yes, very true," he said, his voice emotionless. "But once it's on the piers, it should be safe."

I waited for him to continue, but he remained silent, his eyes focused resolutely on mine until I felt exceedingly uncomfortable. "That sounds exciting," I said, wondering about the man with the odd, coldly distant manner. "Moving the building to the park, I mean. It must be exciting watching your plans take shape."

"Yes, very," he said, again keeping his eyes on me, as if waiting to see what I would do next. I sensed a curiosity in his expression, as if I were as much a specimen as an old building needing restoration. "If the slaves quarters survive this Hurricane Juanita, we'll begin the work."

"Fascinating," I said, as curious about the man as he was about me. "How did you get into this?"

"I grew up in Louisiana," he explained, as if he'd been asked the same question often. "In the seventeen and early eighteen hundreds, my ancestors bought and sold slaves."

"So this is personal."

"Not really," he said with a shrug. "It's the restoration and the history that interest me, not the injustices of slavery."

That surprised me, but I hesitated to comment, instead saying, "How ironic it would be if now, after surviving so long, this building were destroyed before you could save it."

"Irony is a good word, just as it's ironic that you would come to me with your symbols," he said with the first show of emotion since I'd set eyes on him, a self-satisfied grin.

"Why is that ironic?" I asked, puzzled, feeling with each passing moment more ill at ease being close to Benoit.

"Perhaps 'surprising' would be a better word choice, that our paths had crossed through our professor friends precisely at the time you had the symbols to interpret. Surprising that events fell in place that led you to me," he said, that same thin half smile etched across his face. Then the subject changed. "Before we begin, let me show you what else we found."

I followed Benoit again, this time toward a door at the far end of the same building. Just outside the threshold stood the leafless skeleton of a six-foot tree, its trunk impaled in the ground. From the branches hung bits of metal and glass, animal and bird bones, branches encased in old soda bottles that had been slipped over the ends. In the sunlight, the glass shimmered clear, green, and some brown, looking ancient and weathered.

"What's this?" I asked.

"I constructed it myself, out of pieces I found scattered around the place. The slaves made bottle trees like this, believing they protected the household, kept away evil spirits," he said, fingering a piece of round green glass hanging from a crimped wire. In response to his touch, the tree shook slightly, filling the air with the clatter of clinking glass. "These trees trace their beginnings to the decorating of graves in Africa. Once the slaves landed in the New World, they used bits of glass, bones, and utensils they found on the plantations to build them. As early as the late seventeen hundreds, decorated trees were placed near doorways. Some believed that the bottles covering the tips of the branches kept the limbs from ending, as a way of ensuring that life doesn't truly end in death."

"Fascinating," I said, but he frowned and shook his head.

"Not really," he said, his expression leaving no room for argument. "Only fools believe a bit of sparkle and the sound of glass and metal in the breeze can keep away evil. You don't believe that, do you, Lieutenant?"

My body tensed, I didn't know why. All I said was, "No, Professor. I'm sure bits of glass and metal have no power over evil."

With that, he again gestured, and we walked through the door into yet another room, this one lined with shelves holding rusted tools and bits of china and glass. "This is why I'm here, to pack these things up and move it all to higher ground. These are artifacts found on the property," Benoit explained, fingering one, a long, curved hook with a hinge. Opening the hook, he moved closer to me, as if to make sure I saw it, and I felt his breath against my face, hot even in the stagnant air of the steamy afternoon. "This, for instance, looks like an early Christian symbol of a fish, but it's not. People read false impressions into simple objects. This has no religious value. It's simply a hook, one the slaves used to hang pots over a fire."

"Again, fascinating," I said. Not sure why, but uncomfortable with being around Benoit, especially alone on the plantation, confined so close to him in the tight quarters of the room, I said with a forced smile, "As grateful as I am for the history lesson, I'm here for something very specific. Perhaps I can show you these symbols we've found."

"Of course," he said, offering a polite nod.

Despite its monotone, his voice betrayed flecks of a New Orleans drawl. "I'm happy to look at them and see if they are in my area of expertise."

I removed the photos from a small black canvas folder I carried and handed them to Benoit. He took his time, looking at each, turning it in different directions, then clearing a shelf so he could line them up one next to the other, to look at them all at once. For what seemed like a very long time, he said nothing. Eventually he chose two, one of each symbol, and placed them side by side, slipping the discards back into the envelope.

"The professor at A and M who referred me to you believes they're African," I said, trying to spur on the conversation. "She seemed to think that perhaps you'd be able to tell me what they mean."

My attempt failed, as Benoit silently assessed the symbols, a taut smile on his lips. He appeared enthralled with them, soaking them in. I had a sense that to him, they were of significant beauty.

"Professor Benoit," I said, "please, my time isn't unlimited. If you know something, I'd appreciate your help."

He turned and looked at me and said, "Of course, you have an investigation to continue, don't you."

"Yes, I do," I said. "And a long drive back to Houston."

"Please forgive me for my thoughtlessness."

"Do you recognize them?" I asked.

"Yes. Your professor friend is right. They're African."

"Tell me what they mean. Everything you can about them."

Benoit nodded, then began, "To put it in context, when the Africans were enslaved and transported to the New World to work the plantations, they brought with them customs and symbols from their native homelands. Some of the Africans arrived directly in North America. Others first made stops on islands on the way here, including Cuba. That symbol, your triangular figure, it's Afro-Cuban."

"Afro-Cuban?"

"Yes, from the black Cubans, both those who as slaves worked in Cuba and remained there and those who were transported first to Cuba and then, later, to the States to work when the harvesting of sugarcane came to Louisiana and Texas."

"And what does it mean?"

"The symbol is called *Abakuá,* the war and blood sign," he said. "It's thought to have originated in Nigeria, may have begun as part of a secret society, and it dates back to the Spanish occupation of this part of Texas."

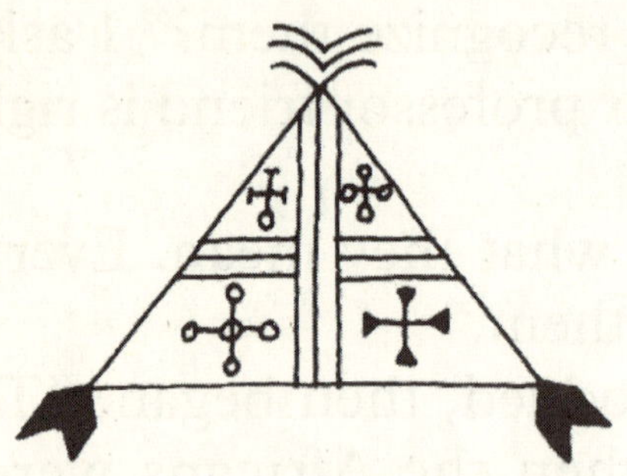

Pointing at the crosslike figures, he explained that they had no Christian connotation, but rather the circles on the ends of each line stood for drums of honor and symbols of danger. The dark blocks that looked to me like arrowheads, he described as signifying war.

"Why would someone paint this symbol on the hide of a dead bull?"

With that Benoit frowned, as if disappointed in my question. "I thought you understood," he said, devoid of all inflection. "I can only interpret the symbols. When it comes to solving these crimes, you'll have to do your own work."

"But it's a warning?" I echoed.

"Yes," he said, sizing me up with resolutely

cool eyes. "At least, that's the way *Abakuá* is normally used."

I thought about that, wondering why someone would execute a longhorn to send out a warning and to whom it was intended. "The other symbol," I said. "Is that a war sign, too?"

"Well, that's interesting as well. It's an *Adinkra,* a symbol used by the tribes of West Africa," he said, pausing for a moment, as if considering, before going on. "Which symbol did you say was left first?"

"The triangle. The one you're saying is a symbol of war."

"Ah, well, that makes sense," he said. "This person obviously understands the symbols well."

"Professor, please. You need to spell this out for me," I urged. I had the impression that he was dragging it out, enjoying my impatience.

"See the shape?"

"Yes, of course. Is it some kind of claw or club?"

"No, it's called *Ako-ben,* and it's a war horn," he said. "This symbol is meant to show a readiness to join the battle."

"That's why the order makes sense, because the first is a symbol of war and the second is a kind of call to arms."

"That's exactly right, Lieutenant," he said, giving me the feeling that I had momentarily, at least, redeemed myself.

"So, tell me who would use these symbols. Have they been claimed by any type of street gang? Maybe a militant group of some kind?"

Benoit appeared to think about that for a moment, as if considering the possibility. "Not that I know of. I've never heard of that."

"Who would know about them?"

"Lots of people, including academics, but really anyone who has studied African and African-American art and culture," he explained. "And, of course, with today's technology, a few hours on the Internet are enough to stumble upon these symbols. Scholars have studied and continue to study such drawings and publish their work."

"I see," I said.

"You know, when the slaves built the plantations, they often carved symbols into the walls, at the cornerstones. Sometimes they left animal bones between the bricks, in the mortar," he said. "Some were thought to ensure health and bring good luck. The culture was heavily into symbolism, much of it dating back for centuries."

"Is there anything else you can tell me about these two symbols?" I asked. "Anything that will help with the investigation?"

This time, his answer was even slower coming. A wry smile, and then he shook his head slightly, again giving me the impression that he found my quandary amusing. "Nothing else, Lieutenant," he said. "When it comes to figuring out who's behind this, you're on your own."

Eighteen

The meeting with Benoit left me uneasy, and on the drive back to Houston, I called Sam Houston Park to speak to the curator, asking the woman if she knew a Professor Alex Benoit.

"Of course," she said. "He's been working with us for the past two years, helping us pull together our restoration of slaves quarters to be moved to the park. Why do you ask?"

"Can you describe him to me?" I said, wondering if there could be any possibility of a mistake.

"He's tall, rather good-looking, with brownish hair and I'm not sure what color eyes," she said. "He has just a little Louisiana drawl. Have you met him? Is this because he can seem a little odd?"

"Actually, yes," I said. "Tell me what you mean by odd, just to make sure we're on the same page."

"Rather a flat affect, I guess," she said, uncertain. "It put us off at first, but as we've gotten to know him, it's just the way Alex is."

"And you've checked him out?"

"No need to, we knew of him before he knocked on our door," she said. "Benoit is famous when it comes to African cultural studies. He hasn't published much in the past twenty years or so, but his work in the field is highly respected."

"Why did he stop publishing?" I said.

"We were curious, too. We asked why, and his answer was that he's reached a point in his life when instead of writing about the culture, he's trying to preserve it."

"That all makes sense," I said, yet still feeling vaguely uneasy about the encounter.

"We're grateful for his help," she insisted. "It's unusual for someone of his stature to volunteer his services. The slaves quarters project is very exciting, and none of this would be happening without his involvement. I know he's a little strange, but, Lieutenant, you'll get used to him."

After thanking the woman, I hung up, deciding the hurricane's threat had to be getting to me as well. Benoit had said nothing overtly odd, nothing even close to threatening.

That issue settled, I called Buckshot and went over what I'd learned from Benoit, explaining the symbols. "Well, ain't that a kick in the pants," the sergeant mused. "You mean to tell me that somebody's out there shooting bulls through the head to write African symbols threatening some kind of war?"

"It appears that way," I agreed, struck by Buckshot's bare-bones interpretation and how bizarre it made the entire case sound. "At least, as far as I can tell, that's the most likely explanation."

"Damn," he hissed. "So, who the hell is this asshole declaring war against, and why? I gotta tell you, Sarah, this sounds downright peculiar to me." Others may search for deeper meaning, but the sergeant routinely called them the way he saw them, in this case twisted.

"I agree, but the symbols mean something significant to the guy we're looking for, so maybe they can give us a clue to help us figure out who he is," I said. "But at least at this point, I can't answer your questions. I don't know who's behind this or why he's doing it."

"Geez," he said. "This world gets stranger all the time."

I laughed and then explained, "Buckshot,

I'm heading home, and I'll be there about five. I'm planning to work on my computer, see if I can dig anything up in old cases with similar MO, including maybe these or other African symbols, plus e-mail a few of the other agencies in the area, ask if they've seen anything like this case. We'll talk in the morning."

"You got it, Lieutenant," he said. "Glad you found that Benoit guy to help us out. At least we've got a direction to take this thing."

"You bet," I said, momentarily thinking back to those awkward moments with the professor and feeling silly for reacting as I had. At that, my call waiting buzzed. "Gotta go. See you in the morning." I clicked the phone off and on, heard David's voice, and in an instant changed my plans.

Nineteen

Driving up to the park, I noticed that many of the squad cars were gone, but a bees' nest of SUVs and sedans buzzed about the lot, searching for parking spaces. I watched as women unloaded children, pulled out strollers for babies, and guided their toddlers by the hands. When I spotted David leaning against a pine tree far from the crowd, I pulled over and parked.

"Okay, I'm here," I said. "I'm ready."

His eyes red from fatigue, he frowned, and I wondered if I sounded miffed. I wasn't. In fact, I'd been eager to put aside the longhorn case and relieved to get David's call, since I'd thought of little other than Joey Warner for most of the day. The plain truth was that I was itching to help find the missing kid. As David had instructed, I'd stopped at the ranch and changed into jeans and a T-shirt and swapped my boots for a pair of tennis shoes. My hair cinched in a ponytail, I had on a Nike baseball cap, and I figured I looked like a suburban soccer mom. Around my neck I wore a small digital camera I keep in the Tahoe. Now I had a question David needed to answer: "Explain what I'm doing here."

Although it was after seven, the sun had yet to set and the temperature still hovered in the mid-eighties, as it had all day. Off in the distance, the demonstrators congregated near the makeshift altar of flowers, notes, and stuffed animals. It was there, before it, that the candlelight vigil was to be held, where they'd bow their heads and pray for Joey's safe return. I knew the crowd was an intrusion for David and the others working the case, yet another wrinkle to contend with, but I didn't blame the moms for wanting to help. I, too, was worried. The boy had now passed the all-important twenty-four-hour mark, and if we didn't find him soon, it might be too late. With the clock ticking and the hurricane approaching, odds were quickly mounting against finding Joey Warner alive.

"I want you to act like part of that crowd," David said, motioning toward the demonstrators. "Blend in. We have videocameras set up around the perimeter and we're photographing cars and license plates, but from the inside, you'll have a better perspective. I'd like you to take pictures of anyone acting oddly, in any way. Anyone who doesn't fit in."

"Guess you're figuring the kidnapper might show up, like an arsonist who returns to the scene to experience the excitement of watching the firemen try to put out his handiwork."

"We're hoping," David said, an air of resignation to his voice that gave the impression the possibility didn't register high on his perceived scale of what was likely to happen. "So far, we've got nothing. No notes. No phone calls. No evidence. All we have are two uncooperative families, a mother who wished the kid gone and tried to beat the polygraph, one Batman tennis shoe, and dead-end leads phoned in by well-meaning people who think they might know something but, as far as we can tell, don't know anything that can actually help."

"Okay," I said. We stood concealed behind a stand of trees on the far side of the parking lot, hidden from the crowd. I thought about trying to be accepted as just one of the moms. That wouldn't be possible if anyone pegged me as law enforcement. Worried someone would notice us talking, I scanned the crowd, saw no one looking our way, but decided it wasn't a good situation. "If that's the plan, I need to take off and join the crowd. Here on out, I'm just here to attend the vigil."

He nodded and stayed put while I quickly splintered off. In the parking lot, I got in the Tahoe and left. After circling the block a few times, I drove back into the parking lot, this time parking in the middle of the mass of cars and detouring to where the demonstrators congregated. On the edge of the crowd, I turned to talk to a mom with a toddler balanced on her hip. "I'm here for the candlelight vigil for that cute little boy who's missing. Do I need to sign in or something?"

"No," she said with a worried expression. "Isn't it horrible that a child could just disappear like that? Poof, he's gone." I nodded in agreement, and she continued, "Just go over to that woman with the shopping bag and grab a candle."

She pointed at a matronly woman who looked happy to see me when I explained I'd come to help. "We're hoping to get two hundred people here tonight. We have a minister coming to lead a prayer service, and some of the churches are bringing members," she said when I asked what the plan was. "We're going to light candles and sing hymns. We'll kick in right at nine o'clock for the FOX news broadcast, then we'll keep it going through the ten o'clock news programs."

"You sound like you've got this figured out," I remarked, taking from her bag a small, off-white taper candle, its base surrounded by a disk of cardboard covered in aluminum foil to catch the drippings.

"I hope so. We do this all the time," she said. "A bunch of us are kind of regulars, whenever anyone goes missing."

"Ah, that's great," I said, meaning it. "What a wonderful thing to do."

Walking away, I slipped — inconspicuously, I hoped — into the crowd, which continued to grow, a tense hum in the air as many talked about Joey and wondered what could have happened to him. At around eight thirty, the parking lot overflowed and the crowd looked to number somewhere around the anticipated two-hundred mark, when reporters arrived. Holding spiral-bound steno notebooks, they mined the crowd, asking questions, looking for the passionate to interview. "If that were my little boy, I don't know what I'd do!" a plump woman with a short brown hair and a smattering of freckles said on-camera. "My best guess is that I'd be out with a gun looking for the criminal who took my kid."

"The police obviously aren't doing enough or they would have found the little boy," said a balding, middle-aged man with a fringe of long dark hair pulled into a ponytail at the nape of his neck. "I'm sure there's some way to find that kid if they stopped eating doughnuts and just focused."

Perhaps I should have anticipated that Crystal would attend, but no one had mentioned her coming, and I was surprised when at nine, just before the nightly newscasts, an SUV pulled up, and Joey's mom and the middle-aged couple from the morning newscast, the ones I suspected were her parents, clambered out. The woman was stout, with reddish brown hair cropped short, wearing khakis and a flowered blouse, while the man beside her, in beige shorts and a black shirt, had a splay of silver-gray hair. Beside them, in an ill-fitted, wrinkled suit, stood a heavyset man whom I pegged as the newly hired family lawyer. I doubted that Crystal had the cash to pay him, but a healthy percentage of attorneys took headline-making cases pro bono, banking on the star power of a front-page photo and an appearance on the local news to lure lucrative paying clients. Worried Crystal would recognize me, I pulled down my baseball cap to veil my eyes and kept circulating. When I noticed her looking my way, I hid behind my camera, snapped a few pictures, and then moved even farther back in the crowd.

"Form a circle," the woman with the candle-filled grocery bag ordered shortly after nine, and those gathered did as instructed. There were so many that we ended up with eight rows, stacked outward. I claimed a slot at the very back, watching, scanning the crowd as David had suggested, looking for anyone out of place. If someone else was observing the gathering, I had no doubt she'd take a picture of me. I had to be the oddest one in the group, my hat pulled down, skittishly making my way through the throng. I looked for someone, anyone, who didn't belong. No one stood out. Most appeared to be simply concerned parents, predominantly women with children. The candles were lit, and a minister, a thickly built woman with a booming voice, recited the Lord's Prayer. Others joined in: "Our Father, Who art in heaven, hallowed be Thy name."

As they murmured, I watched. Most folks had their eyes closed, concentrating on the words to the prayer. Some gazed about sadly, perhaps thinking of the lost four-year-old and wondering, as I was, if he was still alive. "Deliver us from evil," the crowd prayed, and I hoped God heard and that He'd help Joey escape whatever evil had taken over his young life.

"Amen," the minister called out, and the crowd cried out a resounding, "Amen."

With that, the man in the suit introduced himself to the television cameras. "I'm Erick Barnett, and I'm here on behalf of Joey's mother, Crystal Warner, and her parents, Danny and Ginny Farris," he said, gesturing toward the couple who stood anxiously beside their daughter. "I'd like to begin by thanking you for coming tonight, to support this family through this very difficult time."

He paused, looking about the crowd, a sober expression on his face. "You all have work to do. You need to make your voices heard. Police aren't looking for Joey. Instead they're harassing this fine family," he said, sweeping his arm back toward the Farrises and their daughter. Crystal smiled, nodding at the crowd and, unless I was paranoid, casting her eyes twice in my direction. "We need to insist that instead of focusing on the innocent, law enforcement concentrate on finding the guilty. We need to hold the police accountable for bringing Joey home."

In the crowd a murmur of support, and

someone yelled out, "Bring Joey home!"

"Crystal and her parents aren't wealthy people, but they're good people. This mother," Barnett said, pointing at Crystal, who stood primly, hands behind her back, smiling shyly at the crowd, "this young woman loves her son, and she's answered all their questions. She's given them all the help they've requested. So have her parents. But instead of acknowledging that a stranger has little Joey, that police need to go out into the world and find the monster who has taken him, those investigating this case continue to focus on Joey's family. Instead of looking for the man or woman behind this heinous crime, investigators have grilled this poor young mother, and detectives showed up at the grandparents' home and leveled unfounded accusations, focusing on their daughter's relationship with her beloved son."

A buzz went through the audience, an angry rumble. Some in the crowd cried out, "Stop that. Stop that."

"Tell the cops to look for the kid!" shouted an unseen man in the crowd.

"We need your help. Call the county sheriff's office and tell them that you demand law enforcement leave this fine, God-fearing family alone and start looking for the boy and the fiend who abducted him," the lawyer demanded. "Don't leave any room for misinterpretation. Make sure you tell the sheriff that you'll remember this case when he's up for reelection next fall, and let him know that you're paying attention to how this matter is handled."

Watching the crowd, I saw a woman walking along the outside of the circle. I wondered where she was going, and I backed up and stood off to the side to watch, thinking perhaps this was someone of importance, finally someone worthy of a photo. As I moved back, so did the object of my interest, disappearing behind other demonstrators. I couldn't see her face, just dark reddish brown hair. I thought about that, where I'd seen that hair before, when the woman cleared the crowd.

"My daughter says that you're a Texas Ranger, a Lieutenant Armstrong or something," Ginny Farris shouted, shaking her finger at me and closing in. "What are you doing here? Why aren't you out looking for Joey?"

Exposed, with eyes in the crowd locking on me, I turned, head bowed to avoid the cameras, and began walking toward the parking lot. Ginny followed. "I asked you a question, Lieutenant. Why are you here watching these nice people who are trying to help us, when you should be looking for my grandson?"

As quickly as I moved, she kept up with me, shouting so loudly that soon the crowd stood quiet, focused only on me. As she sidled up beside me, I tried to calm her, keeping my voice low. "Mrs. Farris, I'm here to help find your grandson, but this isn't the time or the place to explain. I'm happy to discuss this with you, but not now. I'm sure once we've talked, you'll understand that I'm here to help the investigation, to help bring your grandson home, but, please, we need to talk about this privately."

Her flushed face contorted into sheer anger as the cameras shifted from the lawyer and followed Joey Warner's grandmother, recording her angry confrontation with a woman in a Nike baseball cap walking away from the crowd. "That woman is a Texas Ranger, Lieutenant Armstrong!" Ginny Farris screamed, pointing at me, the interloper, fingering me as if I were a pedophile at the elementary school gates. "Instead of searching for my grandson, our little Joey, she's here, at this vigil, watching us! Investigating us! This proves that the police are wasting their time and not looking for Joey."

With the television cameras on me, I had

few options. Not authorized to make a statement, not even officially on the case, I did the only thing I could: I walked faster toward the Tahoe. I wished I could have turned and defended myself, explained why we were there. But that wasn't in the best interest of the case. Although I kept silent, behind me reporters shouted: "Lieutenant Armstrong, is it true that you aren't looking for Joey Warner?"

Steadfast, I hurried off.

After fleeing the park, I called David on his cell. "Sorry about that," I said. "Guess I didn't quite blend in well enough, even hiding behind the camera and baseball cap. It obviously could have gone better."

"It's okay," he said, his voice weary. "It was my fault. I should have known the family might show up, that you could be recognized."

"So what now?"

"As disappointing as this has been, now I call it a night," he said, his voice thick with regret. "There are three detectives working leads who'll call me if anything heats up. Meet me at my house in half an hour, and you can cash in your rain check from dinner last night. Bring a bottle of wine."

"I can do that," I said, still thinking about the little lost boy, but knowing for tonight, without a solid lead to follow, there was nothing we could do to help him.

When David opened the door on his bungalow in the Heights, with the downtown skyline in the distance, he looked me over and frowned. I hadn't gone home, so I still wore my soccer mom duds, except for the bill cap, which I'd left in the Tahoe. Since I always assume red when wine is mentioned, I held a bottle of Cabernet. "You were hoping for a Pinot Noir?" I asked.

"I was fantasizing about the low-cut T-shirt you had on last night," he said with a playful shrug.

"For sexy I need more notice," I said, shaking my head. "Spur of the moment, you get me as I am."

As David laughed along with me, his disappointment quickly melted. The moment we were behind closed doors, he held me close. I nuzzled against his chest, breathed him in, familiar and strong, and thought about us, in a holding pattern, waiting to find Joey Warner and waiting to figure out if we were to have more than a brief romance. As tired as we both were, I wondered if now was the time, if I should ask if he'd decided what lay ahead for us. Would he be staying in Houston or leaving for

Denver? But then I felt him relax in my arms, the weariness of the past few days fade, and I couldn't ruin the rare moment of peace.

"I'm exhausted and hungry, but this is what I really wanted," he whispered.

"Me too," I said softly, running my hands lightly across his face and into his hair. "Maybe a woman's not supposed to admit that?"

"If there's a rule against it, it's a stupid one," he said.

Under the circumstances, maybe I should have, but I didn't hesitate when he guided me to his bedroom. I wanted him as much as he wanted me. On his cool white cotton sheets, for a very long time, we simply held each other and kissed. When I noticed a tear on his cheek, I wiped it away, lightly running my lips over the damp skin and then holding him close.

"I hate cases like this," he said. He didn't have to say any more.

"I know," I said. "Me too." I unbuttoned his shirt and ran my hands over his taut body. That night, unable to forget the disappointment of the previous day and the uncertainty of the future, we made love slowly, not in the heat of passion, but as two injured human beings, each reaching out for the comfort the other could offer. I'd been hungry for this, the closeness, yet the free abandon of our usual lovemaking wasn't present. My body responded, and I moaned as he moved on top of me, holding myself tight against him, feeling the rhythm of each muscle, the jumble of joy and agony as he rocked against me. My heart drummed in my chest as he fell upon me in a painful release. Afterward, he lay at my side, never relaxing the hold of his arms wrapped gently around my waist.

For more than an hour, I cradled his head in my arms, stroking his forehead and his face as he drifted off to sleep. I watched him, and I thought about how much I would miss him if he disappeared from my life.

Silently, I slipped back into my clothes and tennis shoes. On the drive home, I wiped away a tear of my own, wondering about David, where my life was going, and the little boy with the golden-brown hair and the round blue eyes.

TWENTY

Joey spent the rest of the day locked in the dark closet, thinking about the toys on the shelf, wishing he could hold the teddy bear or play with his truck, missing his momma and poppa, wondering what it all meant. Based on the silence, the boy thought the man was again gone. When he returned and let Joey out, it felt very late, and the man's clothes were soiled and his shoes were caked with mud.

After handing Joey a peanut-butter-and-jelly sandwich on a thin white paper plate and a green plastic glass of cold milk, the man began to undress. While he greedily assaulted his first meal of the day, Joey stood outside the closet in a long narrow bathroom. Another door, a few feet away, opened to a bigger room, a bedroom. As Joey watched, he realized the man looked tired and that he was getting ready for bed.

Once the sandwich was gone and the glass

was empty, Joey put the plate and glass on the floor, then stood off to the side. In the closet, he'd decided on a plan. His back against the wall, the boy squeezed his eyes shut and concentrated on disappearing. Like the cartoon characters he watched on television, the ones who hid behind magic spells and amulets, Joey was convinced that if he remained absolutely quiet and willed himself invisible, the bad man wouldn't be able to see him. Then all Joey had to do was wait, like Jack did for the giant to fall asleep.

The main problem, Joey figured, was that he didn't know where he was. The bathroom connected to the man's bedroom, but the bedroom door was locked, blocking him from the rest of the house. Shutters covered the windows, nailed in place. What waited for him outside the bedroom and the house was unknown. But in his plan, once the man drifted off, Joey would find the key, unlock the bedroom door, and run.

Once he escaped, the boy had his actions all mapped out. His oma and opa always said that if he needed help, Joey should watch for a police officer. But the boy wasn't sure that would work. He didn't know if there would be a policeman or even a fireman close enough to help. Instead, Joey planned to run as fast as he could to another house. If someone was home, the people would answer the door, hide him, and call the police. Once the man was arrested, Joey could go home to his momma. *She must be worried,* Joey thought. He remembered how they played games together and sang along with the radio in the car. *She must miss me.*

Reviewing his plan to run fast, Joey looked down at his bare feet and wished he had his Batman tennis shoes. He wondered where they were and thought about asking the man, but then he remembered that he had to keep quiet, keep his eyes shut, or he wouldn't become invisible.

Then, suddenly, as he stood there outside the closet, Joey heard his name coming from the adjacent bedroom. Curious, he opened his eyes and walked in, only to see that on the TV, a woman was talking about how he was missing. His oma and opa were on the screen with his momma, but Joey didn't see his poppa. He wondered why he wasn't there, too, looking for him.

"This Texas Ranger, Lieutenant Sarah Armstrong, has been harassing us," his oma said. "That's why she was here tonight, instead of looking for our grandson."

"I want my son back," his momma said, and Joey started to cry. "Bring our little boy home to us. We love him."

Behind him, a voice, startling the boy.

"There you are," the man growled. "It's time for bed."

"I'm not tired," Joey said, disappointed that he'd forgotten to keep his eyes closed and get invisible so he could trick the man. "I want to watch TV."

"It's time for bed. Go to the bathroom first," the man said, walking over and turning off the television. The boy didn't move, and the man warned, "Now."

"I don't have to go," Joey protested, his hands in tight fists at his sides.

"Go, now," the man said again, this time raising his right hand as if he might strike the boy. Seeing the threat, wondering if the man would hit him, Joey walked slowly to the bathroom. Standing at the door, the man stared at him as Joey pulled down his khaki shorts, releasing a cloud of urine and sweat.

"Give me those," the man demanded. "You reek."

"No," Joey said, his voice a determined whisper.

Again, the man raised his hand, and Joey did as ordered, peeling off his shorts and his Spider-Man underwear and throwing them at the man, who let them fall to the white-and-black tile floor.

"Your shirt," he said. "Take off your shirt."

Joey began to cry, "No, no."

"Your shirt, too!" the man said.

Again, the boy did as ordered, pulling the shirt up over his narrow chest. It caught on his left ear, and he tugged it harder until it slid over his head, and then he dropped it on the pile with the shorts and underpants. The man stood there for moments, looking at the naked child.

"Wait here," the man ordered. Joey watched as the man walked into the bedroom and opened a drawer in a battered wooden dresser, retrieving something from inside.

"I want my clothes," Joey said, wrapping his arms around his chest.

When he turned toward the boy, the man ordered, "Come here."

Joey didn't move. He looked at the man, focusing on the short thick black object he held.

"Come here, *now,*" the man said, this time with a deep, angry voice.

Joey hesitated, then reluctantly moved forward. As soon as the boy was within reach, the man grabbed the boy's right hand, isolated his small middle fingertip. He then flipped open a knife, exposing its long thin silver blade. At the sight of it, Joey shook uncontrollably. He tried to pull away, twisting his hand, crying, "Don't, don't."

Going in, the knife slid effortlessly through Joey's pale skin, then came out quickly, leaving a wound that pumped out a stream of dark red blood.

"That hurts!" Joey screamed, pulling to wrench his hand away, the cut stinging, the finger throbbing. "I told you, don't hurt me!"

Ignoring the boy's pleas, the man held the bleeding finger tight while he bent down and claimed the boy's soiled underwear off the pile. Then he stared without emotion into Joey's eyes as he smeared the rich blood flowing from the wound onto the front of Joey's underpants, covering Spider-Man's face.

"Stop that!" Joey said, tears running down his cheeks. "Stop that! That hurts!"

The man looked at the boy and said nothing, but he dropped the boy's bloody hand, and the boy rushed the finger into his mouth. "You made me hurt," Joey cried. "Why did you hurt me?"

The man smiled, a small, self-satisfied smile. "For some things in life, Joey, there are no good answers." For a moment, the man looked as if he might say more, but instead he pointed at the closet. Crying, the naked child turned and walked inside. The door shut, the man locked it, and Joey was again surrounded by darkness. Overflowing tears slipped silently down the boy's soft cheeks, and he sucked on his injured finger, tasting the salt of his own blood.

"My momma and the police are looking for me. I saw it on the television," the boy called out. "And when they find me, you'll be sorry."

A curt laugh, and then the man said, "You don't realize how lucky you are. You're very special, little Joey. You will be my masterpiece."

Twenty-One

A night of little sleep, and I knew what I had to do. The captain would be furious, but I had no choice. I couldn't continue looking for some creep dispatching expensive bulls while the boy remained missing. At the break of light that Friday morning, I was dressed and drinking black coffee on the back porch, deciding how best to handle the situation. The rising sun crept up from behind the trees and cast a rosy glow, and I retreated to the kitchen for a second cup and one of Mom's cranberry muffins.

As I slathered on a thin layer of butter, I turned on the television. The hurricane remained stalled over the warm Gulf waters, two days from land, and the storm's projected path had veered even farther north. Chances were yet again multiplying that Juanita would come ashore near Galveston. I watched the prediction of the storm's path, and I could think of only one thing: in two days, all of Houston would close down. We were running out of time. We had to find Joey, and we had to find him soon.

"Our best guess is that Hurricane Juanita will make land somewhere between Freeport and Galveston either late Saturday or very early Sunday morning," explained the TV weatherman. "We're anticipating a mandatory evacuation of all coastal and low-lying areas to begin early this afternoon."

Looking out the window as I sipped my coffee, I saw Frieda carrying the horses' morning oats into the stable. Upstairs, Maggie could be heard walking to the bathroom, and the creaking of the old boards on the steps announced Mom before she entered the room. Her white curls stood at attention, flat on one side, as they did most mornings before she brushed them, and her bathrobe gaped open, showing off her favorite cotton nightgown scattered with small yellow daisies.

"Good morning, dear. Nice of you to make the coffee. That's unusual," she observed with a concerned glance. Mom's like that — she seems to be able to home in quickly when something is bothering me, even at my age. "Why up so early?"

"Couldn't sleep," I said. Then, to change

the subject, I gestured toward the television. "Looks like this could be bad."

"The hurricane?"

"The hurricane. They're going to start evacuations this afternoon," I said. I thought about how prepared Mom was already, how she'd started so early, before the storm was projected to hit Houston. That was unusual for her. Mom was conscientious, true, but not that conscientious. "How did you know the hurricane would turn and head in our direction?"

"I've seen my share of hurricanes, and it just looked like it would to me. I suspected that we were in for it," she said, the creases between her eyes deepening as she frowned. "Some of it is, I've just had this feeling lately, kind of a premonition, that all wasn't well, that something bad might happen. Then when that darn hurricane popped up in the Gulf, I started to think maybe that was it."

"So you've become clairvoyant?" I teased.

She thought about that and appeared to enjoy the prospect. "Could be. Maybe I'll open a booth at the church festival next month: Nora the fortune-teller. For a dollar, I'll predict the future." She laughed softly, then her mood changed again, and she was suddenly quieter. At first she said nothing; then: "Sarah, I'm scared. I don't know why, but I am. The storm bothers me more than it should."

"I am, too," I admitted. "A hurricane this size, we'd be fools not to be concerned. But we've both lived through storms before, Mom. We've been careful, done our best, and we've been okay. My guess is that we'll survive this one, too."

That didn't seem to settle her doubts. "Logically, I know you're right. We're far enough from the Gulf to escape the worst," Mom said, looking as uncertain as when our conversation began. "But that part of me where the premonition's in charge, that part's still worried."

"I know," I said. Just then I heard Joey Warner's name, and I turned back to the TV, a finger across my mouth. "Shush. I need to hear this."

On the television, the hurricane coverage ended and footage played from the candle-light vigil the night before, including images of Ginny Farris chasing me to the parking lot. "This Texas Ranger, Lieutenant Sarah Armstrong," Ginny said to the cameras, "has been harassing us. That's why she was here tonight, instead of looking for our grandson."

I groaned.

"That's not good," Mom remarked.

"No," I said, thinking about how the captain was going to react to my face and name on the news. Rangers have as one of our edicts that we work in the background, avoid the press. For the past couple of years, that was one part of the job where I'd failed. "That's not good."

Meanwhile, the local anchor pitched an upcoming segment: "This morning from Houston, Crystal Warner, the missing boy's mother, and her parents are on the *Today* show. Stay tuned to find out why they say local law enforcement and the FBI are botching the investigation into the boy's disappearance."

"That's not true," I said to Mom, waiting impatiently for the commercial break to end.

"I told you that mother seems odd to me, Sarah," Mom offered, watching the television, distracted momentarily from her hurricane worries. "There's something not right with that young woman."

Minutes later, Crystal and her parents appeared on the screen, with a graphic of the Houston skyline behind them. "The police made their minds up that I was involved right away, and I'm the only one they're investigating," said Crystal, perched with her parents on stools at the Houston NBC affiliate, talking through a hookup to the *Today* show's reporter, a dark-haired, middle-aged man with a slight overbite. "I talked to that FBI guy and that Texas Ranger. I even took a lie detector test. I did everything they asked, but I don't think they're following clue one."

"So, Mrs. Warner, you're saying that this is a rush to judgment?" the reporter asked.

"Yes, it is," her father answered. "Lieutenant Sarah Armstrong, the Texas Ranger on the case, even showed up at the candlelight vigil last night, watching the people who came to support my family instead of going out looking for our grandson."

The *Today* show reporter looked skeptical. "But shouldn't law enforcement investigate all possibilities, especially the parents?" he asked. "Doesn't that make sense, since statistically most children know their abductors and the vast majority are family members?"

"That's fine, but Crystal cooperated and told that ranger everything she knows. Danny and I have talked to detectives, too," Ginny Farris said, clacking her tongue in irritation. "They don't have any evidence we're involved, so they need to leave us alone. Instead of wasting time on us, they should find out who took Joey and bring him home."

"One last thing, Mrs. Warner. You took a lie detector test, as you mentioned. Did you pass it? We're hearing you didn't," the reporter said.

I was surprised that someone had leaked the information but at the same time grateful Crystal wasn't getting away with acting like the persecuted victim. She hesitated, looked at her parents, and then flushed, angry.

"I, well, it's all junk science," she blurted out. "They won't even let lie detector results in a courtroom."

With that, the *Today* show broke away for a commercial, and I was left thinking about Crystal Warner. She wouldn't like what I had in mind.

Twenty-Two

Photos of a third dead bull painted with a symbol and surrounded by a circle waited on my desk when I reached the office at eight that morning. This one, like the others, had unusual coloring, nearly all buff, very little caramel brown, with a particularly pale area on its side. An eleven-year-old rodeo champion, it weighed close to twenty-two hundred pounds, and its graceful horns extended an impressive six feet. Its name was Simon's Reassurance, not at all reassuring, however, since where its head used to be was a bloody crater. The symbol on its side was different from the others yet similar, drawn with a thick black marker: a post with two pear-shaped loops at the base, the staff branching out like ribs off a backbone.

I e-mailed Alex Benoit a photo on his Heritage Society account and then called him.

"Nicely drawn," he said, as if assessing graffiti on a wall rather than a slaughtered bull. "This longhorn killer of yours is an artist. I'm impressed."

"Forgive me if I have less enthusiasm," I said. "What I need, like before, is a translation."

Uncharacteristically, based on our previous encounter, he released a short laugh. "You must learn patience, Lieutenant," he advised coolly. "Our minds work best when we don't crowd them with irritation and anxiety."

"Point well taken," I agreed, as much as anything to move the conversation along. "Now, the meaning, please."

"If you must. This symbol is *Aya.* On the surface, it's literally the figure of a fern."

"Tell me more."

"Like *Ako-ben,* the call to arms, *Aya* is *Adinkra,* from West Africa," he said. "This is actually a more common symbol, often used on textiles."

"Okay," I said. "What does it mean?"

At first a pause, then Benoit said, "I am not afraid of you." With that, the connection between us became a long, empty silence.

"I didn't intend for you to be," I said, wondering why the conversation had taken such an odd turn. Despite the Heritage Society director's assurance that I'd get used to Benoit, the more I interacted with him, the more he troubled me. "Did I say something to indicate that you should be afraid of me?"

"No," he said, his voice mocking. "Lieutenant, you're not paying attention. You asked me what *Aya* means, and I told you: I am not afraid of you."

"Ahhh," I said. "Sorry. I've got it." Putting my irritation with Benoit to the side, I thought about the new symbol's meaning: "I am not afraid of you." The killer was taunting us, flaunting that he was in charge. This person, whoever he was, saw himself as superior, and he liked playing games. "Well, thank you, Professor Benoit," I said, eager to hang up. "This is helpful."

But then Benoit challenged, "Is it, Lieutenant?"

It took me by surprise. I wasn't sure how to respond. Why would he doubt that?

"Yes," I said, wondering if perhaps he was looking for more gratitude on my part. But that wasn't the inflection in his voice. What I heard was contempt. Not knowing what to say, I offered, "I appreciate your assistance. You're kind to help us."

For the second time I was ready to say good-bye, but Benoit again stopped me cold, this time by saying, "You know, there's more going on here than *you* realize."

If I'd been ready to hang up, that had changed. Suddenly, the conversation had become interesting. "What do you mean?"

"I've considered your situation," he said. "What if this man is trying to warn you, perhaps not you as an individual, but the police? Based on the meanings of the symbols, that could certainly be his intention."

"Warn me of what?" I was used to folks playing cop, giving me advice on cases, but something about the way Benoit approached it struck me as downright strange. Every instinct I had was on high alert.

"Maybe he wants you to stop him, to stop the killing."

What was going on? Of course, Benoit did have a point. On one level, letters and symbols from criminals were sometimes intended not just to taunt police, but to aid in the search: the hunted's conscious or subconscious way of helping the hunter. There are those criminals who crave the added excitement of knowing police are just one step behind them, of knowing the cops are hot on their trails. They're thrill junkies, and the danger heightens their excitement.

Yet why was Benoit saying these things? And how serious was it, really?

The insurance companies had to pay out a great deal of money. That was true. And the bad guy deserved to get caught and punished. When we found Joey, I'd tackle the longhorn case head-on, find the creep, and put him out of business. But at that moment, I had the missing boy to think of. More than ranchers losing livestock, there was a human life, that of a small child, hanging in the balance.

"Thanks for your input," I said, tired of whatever game Benoit played. "But I need to go."

Distracted, I glanced at my watch. Eight thirty. The captain and Buckshot were both in the office, which was good luck. If I corraled them, I could fill them in on the third dead bull and then turn the case over to Buckshot. If everything fell into place, I could be gone by nine, on my way to the sheriff's department. The night before, David had said they had a strategy meeting on the Warner case planned for nine thirty. I might miss the beginning but would be there for the last half. Earlier, I'd called the captain in charge of the case at the sheriff's department to offer my services, contrary to regulations, which specified that the local agency was supposed to request my assistance. Fifteen minutes later, David called back, sounding grateful to have the help. If they didn't want me intruding, they covered well.

I had what I needed from Benoit and was only half listening, again ready to hang up, when the conversation took yet another strange turn. "Lieutenant, you shouldn't write this guy off as a mere nuisance," he said. "Doesn't it make you wonder?"

"About what?" I asked, no longer trying to mask the irritation creeping into my voice. "If you have something to tell me, Professor Benoit, you need to spit it out."

"Wonder about someone who enjoys killing so much, if he is truly only targeting cattle."

With that, Benoit went silent. He said nothing, but he didn't hang up. When the silence endured long enough to become uncomfortable, he said, "It would seem to me that eventually this victim choice would be less than satisfying."

I'd been told the man was a respected scholar and teacher, but nothing about him rang true to me. Something was wrong.

"Would you elaborate on that, Professor?" I asked.

Again, a long, drawn-out silence. He was toying with me.

"I'm only trying to help, Lieutenant," he said, his voice level, without emotion. "It seems to me that a person who enjoys killing so much, who is so attuned to the beauty of death, which this person must be to feel compelled to decorate what he's slain, I only wonder if such a person wouldn't be drawn to continue to kill. And if he'd want more of a thrill than slaying longhorns."

"Are we talking about someone who'd graduate to killing human beings?"

A long pause, and then Benoit demurred, "I don't know. I'm an anthropologist, a student of history, but not a psychiatrist. What do you think?"

Over the years, I'd learned to listen to my intuitions, and they were on full alert with Alex Benoit. "I'm asking for your opinion, Professor," I suggested. "You've made some fascinating points here. Those who murder human beings sometimes begin by torturing or murdering animals. I have a great deal of respect for your viewpoint, and I sense that you've given this a considerable amount of thought."

"You flatter me," he said, sounding decidedly insincere. But then: "Are you *really* curious about my theories?"

"Yes, I am."

Another short laugh. "Well, it makes sense to me that this person, man or woman, takes pleasure in killing," he said matter-of-factly. "And I believe he's enjoying playing with all of you in law enforcement as well, showing you how much smarter he is, while leading you down a path."

The conversation got more alien the longer Benoit talked, yet on another plane, he made sense. That was precisely what the longhorn killer was doing. "Very true. Very perceptive of you," I said. "Anything more you'd like to share?"

"It seems to me that this man has something planned," Benoit said, his silky smooth voice intense. "Something more serious than dead bulls."

For a moment, I said nothing, considering where the conversation was leading. "Again, Professor, are you saying this person is or will be targeting human beings?" I asked.

For the third time, Benoit laughed. "I told you when we met, Lieutenant, that all I can do is interpret the symbols. I have no other expertise in these matters," he said dismissively. "I do hope I helped you, but I have to go. I'm working at the plantation again today, cataloging the last of the artifacts. I'll be there all day, tidying up loose ends. Everything has to be done before the hurricane hits, of course."

After he hung up, I held my cell phone and looked down at it, rethinking the conversation. Was it possible that Benoit was simply trying to be helpful? Maybe he'd become caught up in the case and it had his imagination working overtime.

Twenty minutes later, I'd gone over the new developments with the captain and Buckshot, and I'd filled them in on my tête-à-tête with Alex Benoit. "So what does all that mean?" the captain asked, appearing as confused as I by the discussion. "It sounds ominous, but it's not unusual for folks to play cop. Maybe that's all this professor of yours is doing, having fun knocking around possibilities with the police. Some people get off on that."

"I don't know, Captain," Buckshot said, tugging at his mustache in deep thought. "Reminds me of the time when I was still a trooper, and I pulled over a guy driving a fancy silver Porsche for speeding. While I write the ticket, he starts telling me how easy it would be to steal an expensive car, about how all he'd do is pretend to be a valet and hold his hand out for the keys. I ran a check and the license plates weren't reported stolen, but it smelled fishy enough to make me decide to call for backup and talk to him long enough for them to get there. By then I had a bump on my radio. Turned out the Porsche had disappeared from some high-priced restaurant parking lot before the owner sipped his first cocktail of the night. He'd walked outside, asked the real valet for his car, and found out it'd been stolen."

"I'm with Buckshot on this, Captain," I said. "Professor Alex Benoit makes my skin crawl. I want to know more about him."

Captain Williams shrugged, as if he'd been outvoted. "Okay," he said. "You both agree, so, Lieutenant, I suggest you do a little scouting around and figure out who this Benoit character is. See if there's any more there than a healthy curiosity and a little game playing."

"Well, that's the thing, Captain," I said somewhat sheepishly. "I'm not going to be available to do it."

"Why not?" Buckshot asked, instantly appearing concerned. "Are you okay, Sarah?

Maggie and your mom all right? Is something wrong?"

"We're all fine," I reassured them both. "But you can handle this, Buckshot, just make some phone calls around Houston, maybe check with New Orleans PD. Check up on this Benoit guy. The thing is, Captain, that I've got another case to work."

"Not that missing boy case," the captain wailed. I'd been wondering if he knew about my appearance in the morning news but thought maybe not — until he said, "I saw you on the news this morning, Lieutenant, and I'm sure headquarters will hear about it. I was willing to overlook it, not push the point, since I was sure you thought you were doing the right thing. But you're getting yourself into a world of hurt if you overstep your bounds on this case. The plain truth is that you're not authorized to be involved in the Warner case."

As I recounted my morning's conversation with David, the captain's anger at my behavior became even more evident. "Sarah, you know that this isn't the way it works," he said after he'd followed me back to my office, where I grabbed a few things before heading out the door. "Other law enforcement agencies ask the rangers for help. They request us. Unless they ask for us or the governor orders us to take a look, we don't move into a case. Plus, they've got the FBI, with all their resources, looking for that little boy. What makes you think you can do any better than they can?"

I hated it when he asked questions like that. Sincerely hated it, because he was right, and I had no good answers. So I smiled at the captain and shrugged. "I don't know," I said. "I'll check in with Buckshot later this morning. I'll keep tabs on the longhorn killings and help as much as possible. But I need to help find that little boy. I can't look back and live with it if Joey Warner's murdered or never found and I didn't at least try to save him."

Minutes earlier, frowning and shaking his head at me, the captain had looked angry enough to order me to forget such nonsense and go back to work. Now, although he was still scowling, he appeared resigned. I guess we'd been through enough together for him to know that issuing a command probably wasn't going to change the final outcome. "Okay," he said. "But make sure that you keep in touch with Buckshot, shoot him ideas. Half the cattle ranchers in southeast Texas are up in arms about these killings. We don't need them calling the governor, saying we're not doing our best."

I slipped my Colt .45 into the holster on my rig, a tooled black leather double belt.

"And stay out of the goddamn newspapers and off the TV," he said, so frustrated that he practically sputtered. "I don't want to see your face anywhere associated with this case! You've made enough headlines in the past couple of years."

"Yes, Captain." I threw my navy jacket over the shoulder of my white cotton button-down shirt, grabbed my weathered saddlebag purse, and headed for the door. "I'll stay in the background. You can count on it," I said, and I was gone.

Twenty-Three

"Hey, television star," one of the detectives shouted out just after nine forty-five that morning when I arrived at Lockwood, the floor with DETECTIVE BUREAU stenciled across the door.

"Hold your applause," I suggested with a half smile that was my best shot at looking less than annoyed. "I don't deserve all this. I just arrived and I haven't done anything yet."

"The way that mom tells it, none of us are doing anything," jeered a white-haired detective in a baby blue polyester-blend sport coat. "You just got to be front and center, the public face of the incompetents."

"Lucky me," I said, brushing past on my way to the strategy meeting already under way on the Warner case. But when I arrived, the conference room was empty, except for David, who appeared to be organizing a stash of black vinyl three-ring binders.

"Hey, Sarah, looks like you got here just in time to see the case come together," David said, looking better than I'd seen him since the kid disappeared. "We're writing an arrest warrant."

"Whose name is on it?" I asked.

"Crystal Farris Warner," he said.

Since there wasn't any celebrating in the room and the mood was far from joyous, I had a bad feeling, but I asked anyway. "My guess is that this doesn't mean you found Joey."

"I wish," David said. "More than I can say, I wish we had. But no, we haven't found him, and I don't know that we will."

"What have you got?" I asked.

"This is a conversation that took place last night, one the surveillance team picked up on the bug we left in the apartment during the search," David said. With that, he hit a button on a CD player. At first there was static. A television or radio played in the background, at times so loud that the words and the sounds of those in the room became indecipherable.

"I'm telling you, Joey isn't coming back," Crystal could be heard saying over swelling music in the background, sounding like a movie score. "You two have to accept that. Joey's gone, and he's not coming home."

"How can you say that?" Ginny screamed, her voice laced with panic. Whatever they were watching went to a break, and a Jack in the Box commercial could be heard in the background. "How can you know Joey isn't coming home? Did you do something to him, Crystal? Did you?"

"New, at Jack in the Box," the commercial blared even louder as Danny Farris cried out something I couldn't understand, a reference to the police, but what came through loud and clear was one word: "body."

"Why are you asking me that?" Crystal shrieked, so loud that even the television couldn't disguise it. "I'm not telling you two anything. You two talked to those detectives after I told you the cops are trying to trap me."

At that, Ginny wailed with pain and screamed, "Crystal, how could you? How could our own daughter —"

His wife never finished her accusation, but Danny threatened, "If you've done anything to that boy, you'll answer to me!"

An announcer shouted, "For a limited time!" and the tape cut out.

"After that, there's a lot of crying and muffled screaming we can't understand. We think they were bunched together someplace the bug didn't pick up well," David explained. "But talking of a body and saying Joey would never be coming home, it sure sounds like this mom knows way more than she's admitted to us."

I thought about what we'd just heard. David was right, it did sound incriminating. But what did we really know? It seemed reasonable for Crystal to be fearful that Joey would never be found. And we couldn't really make out what her father shouted. The word *body* was unsettling, that was true, but we didn't know the context. This family was in crisis, so it didn't seem odd that the Farrises circled the wagons in public while badgering Crystal with questions behind closed doors.

"I don't know, David," I said, picking my words carefully. "If this is all you've got, I'm not sure there's enough here —"

"It's not all we have," he interrupted. "Look at this."

With that, he flung open one of the black binders on the table. On the cover it read: "Crystal Warner, computer records." Halfway through was a list of recently visited Web sites. Two-thirds of the way down the second page, the subject read: "How to beat a lie detector test."

"The date on that entry is two weeks ago,

before she had any reason to believe Joey would be abducted and that she might have to take a polygraph," David said. He sat down at a nearby computer and pulled up the site. On it were instructions on how to do exactly what Ralph Goodson, the polygrapher who'd administered her test, thought Crystal might have done, manipulate her body by tightening muscles to raise blood pressure and invalidate the results.

"So you've got her preparing ahead of time," I said. "And you've got her talking as if Joey is gone forever, perhaps even dead."

"Yeah," David said. "And one more thing."

I looked at him expectantly and waited. I could tell this wasn't something he wanted to say, but he took his time and spit it out. "We think that maybe she sold the kid," he said, as if it were too awful to even suggest. "We ran a check and found a savings account in her name. A deposit was made, a wire transfer, the morning after the boy disappeared. Thirty grand."

Stunned, I sat down, wondering if David's reasoning could be possible but seeing no other alternatives. All the pieces of the case were lining up. "Crystal Warner sold Joey, her own kid," I repeated. "For thirty grand, she gave him away."

"Yeah. Stinks, doesn't it?" David said, his voice low. "But, yeah, we think so."

The horror of Joey Warner's young life assaulted me, and I sat quietly, unwilling to speak. He was a little boy, a handsome child with hair the color of ripened wheat and big, sky-blue eyes, and it appeared possible that his own mother had handed him over to someone for a fistful of cash.

"You okay, Sarah?" David asked. He looked as injured as I felt. Sometimes cases tear away the illusion of living in a civilized society, where husbands and wives love each other, where parents cherish and care for their children, and where a mother would never give away a child for anything, especially not money.

I thought about what we knew, about what we suspected. "So did this person show up at the park, and Crystal just handed Joey over? Or was it kind of the way she described? Did she take Joey to the park, make a phone call, and turn her back?" I asked, visualizing the scene as it might have played out two days earlier. "When it was over, maybe she called the boy's name a couple of times, in case someone was watching. Then she called the boy's father and said Joey was missing. She ate up time waiting for the dad and then another hour looking around the park, although she knew the kid wasn't there. That gave whoever had Joey time to get away. Finally, she called the police, and then she sat back and let us spin our wheels. She confused the issue by not helping, making unfounded charges against those looking for Joey, even gave us an old photo, one that didn't look like him, to make sure he wouldn't be found. It was that easy?"

"Yeah," David said, his face mirroring my disgust. "I think so. I think it was that easy."

Still, even as the depression settled over me, somewhere a thought needled at my subconscious. David had sounded so resigned to it being the worst of endings, yet I wondered, "You can't be sure Joey is dead."

"No. I didn't mean to imply that. There is the possibility that he's still alive," David said with a shrug. "But we're figuring that by now the abductor has either killed the kid or taken him away, somewhere we'll never find him. We're going to keep looking, but it's been nearly two days, and now it appears that the scumbag who took Joey had his mother's cooperation and plenty of time to plan and escape. We figure that this isn't looking good."

I thought about that. "What about tracking the money back to the source? You've done that, of course."

"We tried," he said, sounding resigned. "We hit dead ends. It originated somewhere overseas. So far, no luck. We'll keep trying, but at this point, it's not promising. Our computer experts figure we'll ultimately be led to some dummy account in a fake name. This guy planned well, figured out how not to lead us back to him."

"I gather our only shot at finding the boy is getting Crystal to open up," I speculated. All the tips investigators had chased led nowhere, disappointments one and all. "There's no one else who could point us in a direction."

"That's all we've got going for us, that maybe the mom will talk," he said. Yet he shook his head, as if it were inevitable that we'd come away disappointed. "From past experience with Crystal Warner, I'm doubting that that's going to happen."

Just then, one of the detectives came by, gave David a tap on the shoulder, and said, "We've got the warrant. We're rolling."

After slipping his suit coat on over his holster, David walked with me out the door. "Saw you on television this morning," he said. "You looked good, but you should have lost the bill cap."

"Thanks. The captain enjoyed it even

more than you did. I've been ordered not to do an encore."

Twenty-Four

Crystal lived at the Regency Arms apartments in a second-floor corner unit, minutes from the park where Joey disappeared. Despite its impressive name, the aging complex had seen better days. Curls of paint peeled from window frames and trim, and the siding buckled with dents and tears in the green vinyl. On the landing, at the threshold of unit 209, sat a battered Big Wheel and two pairs of flip-flops, one small enough for a four-year-old.

When we arrived just before ten thirty that morning, David, flanked by two detectives, pointed to the side walkway. I nodded and, as we'd planned, made my way around, taking a position on the balcony that ran along the side of Crystal's apartment. I had my Colt .45 drawn and ready, just in case. Once I was in position, David pounded on the door and shouted, "Mrs. Warner, open up. It's Special Agent Garrity, with the FBI."

There was scuffling inside, and then someone cracked open the apartment door. In a single breath, it slammed shut. "We have a warrant for your daughter's arrest," David shouted. "Open up and stand back, Mr. Farris. Open up and stand back. Now!"

A pause, and again the door eased open. I heard David talking and caught a glimpse of him walking with the detectives inside, then I heard a window inching open. Planting my feet, I waited, my gun aimed at the source of the scraping sound. Cocking my head to the right for a better view, I saw four smallish hands straining to push the window farther up. Once it reached the top, a trim bare ankle slipped through, the body of the person it belonged to still hidden behind a dingy beige curtain.

"Now, go to Aunt Helen's and wait for us there," a woman's voice whispered. "Don't forget or get any other ideas in your head."

"Shut up, Mom," Crystal said, seething. "You never believe it, but I know what I'm doing."

Slowly an arm and a leg appeared, then a face, her neck craning to the left, checking to see if the proverbial coast was clear, until she turned right and stared directly at me. Eyeing my gun barrel, Crystal let out a yelp and then lurched back into the apartment.

After that, all was nervously quiet.

"Come on out, Mrs. Warner," I ordered. "This time, all the way!"

A moment passed, then her arm and leg appeared again, followed by her upper body. Appearing uncertain, she cocked her head to the side and glared at me. I felt as if I could hear her thinking, considering possibilities, not realizing she didn't have any.

"Agent Garrity is inside, so there's no way out. You might as well climb out here, onto the balcony, Mrs. Warner," I ordered again, this time motioning with my gun to stress the direction I wanted her to exit and the wisdom of complying. At first, I thought the standoff was over. Then somehow the threat my message carried appeared to escape her. Suddenly, Crystal slid all but her left leg back inside.

"Stop!" I ordered, moving forward until I could see her inside the apartment. Looking directly at her, I ordered again, "Out here, now!"

By then, I heard David shouting from somewhere inside, "Do as the lieutenant ordered, Mrs. Warner. All the way out of the window onto the balcony. Move it. Now!"

This time, Crystal did as instructed, slipping the rest of the way out until she stood firmly on the concrete balcony, nervous, waiting.

"Hands up, and turn and face the brick wall," I ordered, and slowly, reluctantly, she complied. One of the two detectives moved in quickly, grabbing Crystal's trembling hands and pulling them together, anchoring them in place behind her back with handcuffs, then giving her a quick search.

When we had her safely secured, I shouted at David, "Everything okay in there?"

"Yeah," he said. "Bring her to the front door."

By the time the three of us arrived, Crystal leading the pack, David waited. He had the second detective inside the apartment, watching over Crystal's parents. "Well, Mrs. Warner," David said, "thank you for giving us another charge to level against you. Fleeing arrest is always a quality addition."

"My lawyer warned me not to talk to you," she said.

"That's okay," David said. "This is one of the times when I don't mind doing all the talking." With that, he began reading her *Miranda.* "You have the right . . ."

When he finished, he ordered one of the deputies, "Take her downstairs to the squad. Transport her to Lockwood and hold her in lockup. We'll get the CSI unit going on the new search warrant and meet you there."

The deputy grabbed Crystal by the crook of the arm and did as instructed while we walked inside the apartment, where bent blinds and stained curtains hung heavy, filtering the light. Danny and Ginny sat on a careworn, tan corduroy couch, his arm around her and her hands over her eyes, crying.

"What are you doing here? Haven't you done enough to us?" she screamed. "Get out of here! Leave us alone!"

Ignoring the woman's pleas, David moved forward and ordered her to stand up. "Your daughter is under arrest, and you're lucky we're not taking you in for trying to help her escape," he said. "And we have a search warrant for the premises. One of our officers will escort you downtown. We'd like to ask you both more questions."

Crystal's parents appeared bewildered, as if neither had envisioned the possibility of such a turn of events. "We don't have anyplace to go," Danny said. "We were staying here with Crystal, through the hurricane."

"What about your house?" David asked.

"It's a mobile, double-wide," Danny said. "The management at the RV park suggested we all get out."

While David talked to the Farrises, telling them again they'd have to vacate until after the apartment was searched and released, I wanted a good look around before CSI moved in. I circulated slowly, finding traces of Joey visible in every room. In a corner of the living room sat a plastic laundry basket filled with toys: Lego's *Star Wars,* Thomas the Tank Engine, Diego, and SpongeBob. Next to the basket waited a riderless rocking horse, painted black and white like Emma Lou, Maggie's pinto. I nudged David. "The toys are still out," I whispered. He looked at me, puzzled at first, but then glanced around and shot me a wary look.

"Why are you doing this?" Ginny asked, cheeks flushed and tears streaming. Danny shook his head, still in disbelief. That his daughter might be arrested was incomprehensible. While her husband remained speechless, she turned to me and charged, "Are you here because we embarrassed you on TV? Are you getting even?"

Although tempted to confront her, I ignored the question, turned my back, and walked farther into the apartment. Next to the couch, more toys were stowed in a bright blue vinyl box, and in the kitchen, a small plastic picnic table with child-size benches was topped by a single dinosaur place mat, as if waiting for Joey to eat his lunch.

The bathroom was cramped and cluttered, but a pile of plastic containers nested beside the tub, ready for warm soapy water to be poured from one to the other, and a bottle of SpongeBob bubble bath waited on the sink. In the first bedroom, I found a queen-size mattress with bright yellow sheets and suitcases on the floor, leading me to believe that the Farrises were bunking there. The sheets were disheveled, thrown off to the side, the bed unmade. The second bedroom had one twin bed, also consisting of simply a mattress on the floor. Yet it was immaculately made, the sheets and blanket pulled up over the pillows, and a knobby-jointed Woody from the *Toy Story* movies had been lovingly placed on the pillow. To the right lay a pile of blankets and a pillow, where it appeared Crystal, who'd given up her bed to her parents, was spending the nights. *Is she feeling too guilty to sleep in the kid's bed?* I wondered. *Or is she keeping it pristine for his return?* Joey's clothes hung in the closet, toddler three and four shorts and jeans and small T-shirts with comic book characters on the front. I fingered a pair of cotton pajamas covered with trucks that hung from a hook inside the closet door and thought about the little boy who might never again wear them.

In the living room, David escorted the Farrises outside, explaining again that they had to leave the apartment so forensics could work and that they could follow the squad cars to Lockwood, where he wanted to take statements from both of them.

"There won't be any statements. This is harassment," Danny warned, his face glowing so red-hot that I had no doubt his heart was beating double time. "We're calling our lawyer."

"Tell him to meet us at the sheriff's department, major crimes," David suggested. "There's room enough for all of you there."

Twenty-Five

"You don't have evidence to hold her, much less charge her," said Erick Barnett, the same attorney who'd addressed the crowd at the candlelight vigil, giving us a too-casual wave of the hand. "A few snippets of conversation that you can barely make out over the sound of the television. You can't even tell what they're talking about. This is ridiculous. Come on, Sylvia. Get real here. This isn't an arrest warrant. It's fiction."

"Putting all the pieces together, the evidence forms a damning picture. You're not looking at this as a jury will." Chief prosecutor in one of the county's felony courts, Sylvia Vogel shook her head, as if Barnett weren't to be believed. Assigned to the case by the luck of the draw, manning intake when the warrant was drawn up, Vogel was stick-figure thin, an image not eased by her habit of having one eyebrow poised higher than the other. "Agent Garrity and the detectives presented their evidence, and what you have to be worried about, Erick, is that the judge disagreed with you. In fact, he didn't ask a single question before signing the arrest warrant. There's a lot of smoke here, so I'm not anticipating that it'll be hard to convince a jury that your client set the fire."

With that, Vogel lowered both eyebrows, squinting at the defense attorney. "So it's you who needs to get real."

"There's just not enough here, Sylvia," Barnett scoffed, sizing her up through cloudy blue-gray eyes. A stocky man in a too-small pinstripe suit, one I doubted he could button across his round belly, he pulled forward in his chair and then leaned toward her, as if physical closeness could sway her. "Take an objective look at this case. All you've got is a gut full of suspicion."

A pen stuck above her ear, protruding from a thick mass of premature gray, Vogel surveyed Barnett with open skepticism. "You know, Erick," she said, her voice noticeably perturbed, "you've personally said that to me on multiple cases in the past, and every one of those clients you were so sure we had no evidence against, well, correct me if I'm wrong, but I believe that they're all now spending long stretches in Texas prisons."

Miffed, Barnett sat back and shifted uncomfortably in his chair, while Crystal, who'd spent most of the time staring down at her hands, shot her attorney a questioning glance. Standing off to the side, David and I confined our involvement to listening and letting the attorneys hammer out the situation.

"I'm telling you that Mrs. Warner is not involved in her son's disappearance, and no matter what you think you've got on that audiotape, it's not her saying she knows the boy is dead or that she knows where the kid is," the attorney said. At the word *dead,* he pounded his fist on the table for emphasis. I figured he was pretty good in a trial, slapping legal pads and tapping pencils to make sure the jury paid attention to him and not the opposition. A lot of attorneys had their methods. I once saw a defense attorney in a murder trial go so far as to attempt to stand pencils on their erasers, luring the jurors' eyes away from the prosecutor questioning the state's star witness.

"Okay, Erick. Let's not get hung up on the audio. Don't forget that we've got the guy she cuddled up with on Saturday night saying she wanted the kid to disappear," Vogel pointed out, counting off bits of evidence on fingers. "And there's that computer search two weeks before Joey disappeared, the one on how to beat a polygraph."

"So what? The lie detector test isn't admissible in a courtroom," Barnett charged, his voice rising. "You know you'll never get that in."

"About that, you're right. The jury won't hear that she failed the lie detector," Vogel said with a shrug. "But we *will* get in that Mrs. Warner searched the Internet for information on how to get away with lying to investigators, two weeks before her son disappeared."

Barnett squirmed in his seat. "Yeah, well —"

Vogel didn't wait for him to finish, instead clicking off another point on yet another extended finger: "And there's that other little matter, the thirty grand little loving mom here had deposited into her savings account the morning after her kid was kidnapped. What are the odds of that not being related?"

At that, Crystal sat straight up and immediately went into attack mode. "You didn't tell me about thirty grand," she said, glaring at Barnett. "You didn't say a thing about money. Where'd I get thirty grand?"

"Mrs. Warner, shut up," her attorney ordered, lowering his voice and covering her hand on the table with his. "You shouldn't say anything. They're baiting you."

Adjusting in the chair to sit core straight, she brushed off his instructions. It seemed apparent that she wasn't any better at being a client than she was at being a mom. "I don't care. This is some kind of a frame, or there's some kind of a mistake. That's not my money. I don't have any thirty grand. They're lying," she said, eyes wide, looking frantically about the room. "I haven't got a clue what you're talking about. What thirty grand?"

"Come on, Mrs. Warner. You know what money. The thirty grand in your savings account, the money somebody paid you the morning after you arranged to hand over Joey," Vogel said.

"I love my son. I didn't sell Joey," Crystal insisted, emphasizing each word. She'd been fish-eyed unemotional throughout the meeting, but now she began to weep, wiping away tears that tracked slowly down her cheeks. "If someone put money in my account, they're trying to frame me!"

Barnett held up his hand to shush his client, but Crystal continued to sob, hands over her face. I had to admit that she appeared convincing. If it was a performance, Crystal Warner wasn't a bad actress. "Listen, you've got the wrong account, screwed up the numbers or something," she said, shaking her head emphatically and looking directly at David and me. "I've got two hundred in my account, maybe. Money I was keeping for an emergency, like a doctor bill if Joey got sick. That's it. No kidding."

With that, Vogel motioned for David, who handed over an envelope. Vogel took her time squeezing the prongs together, lifting the flap, and pulling out a copy of Crystal's savings account statement, building the suspense. The entire time, the prosecutor stared down Crystal with as much contempt as if she were sizing up a two-inch roach scurrying across her kitchen counter. Once the prosecutor unsheathed it, she handed the information from the bank to Barnett and his client. I'd already reviewed the paperwork and knew that it read that Crystal's savings account balance jumped from $192 the morning of Joey's disappearance to $30,192 the next morning. For a few moments, neither Crystal nor her attorney said anything; then Barnett whispered in Crystal's ear.

"No, it's not mine!" she shrieked, appearing furious. "You think I'd beg that deadbeat husband of mine for three hundred bucks on the day Evan was kidnapped if I had thirty grand coming in?"

Shooting Crystal a glance that ordered her to shut up, Barnett said, "I'd like to talk to my client alone."

"That actually sounds like a good idea. We'll be outside. Pound on the door when you're ready for us to come in," Vogel said. She rose and then bent over the table to be at just the right level to glower head-on at Crystal. "Think it over, Mrs. Warner. Right now, you've got leverage to cut a deal. We haven't found the kid yet, so if you can help us recover Joey, you've got something we want. Once we fill in all the blanks on our own, we won't need your help. Then, no deals. You're out of options." Vogel frowned at Crystal, a long, contemptuous accusation. "A jury would love to come down hard on a mother who sold her kid, and I promise you that I'll go for blood."

We walked out the door, closing it behind us, and then slipped around the corner into the adjoining room, to watch through a one-way mirror. We didn't turn on the sound. Crystal and her attorney were entitled to talk without us eavesdropping; that's the law. The conversation was protected. But there was no statute that said we couldn't watch. At first, Barnett listened and Crystal talked, throwing her arms up in the air as if exasperated. She kept picking up the bank statement and staring at it as if it weren't to be trusted. Then she threw it down on the table as Barnett moved closer to her, putting his hand on her shoulder, attempting to convince her of something, perhaps that the evidence against her was too much to fight, that she was better off thinking about other alternatives, like authorizing him to negotiate a deal.

"You know, I'm not sure about this," I said to Vogel and David as we watched the drama unfolding in the interview room. "That apartment didn't look to me like she sold the boy. It didn't look like she'd given up on him coming home."

"We don't have the forensics in yet," Vogel said, watching as in the next room Crystal grew angrier with each passing moment. "What're you talking about? How can you tell there isn't something there until they process the place?"

"Sarah's talking about Joey's toys," David said, shooting me a knowing glance. "I noticed them, too."

The prosecutor continued to watch through the window, but I saw her lift her left eyebrow even higher than usual, peeved.

"Crystal didn't dispose of anything. She didn't put anything away," I explained, going through the laundry list of what I'd seen, from the SpongeBob bubble bath to the picnic table with the dinosaur place mat. "If Crystal sold Joey, she wouldn't expect him to return. On some level, she would most likely feel guilt, and seeing all of his things in the apartment, being forced to look at his toys in the living room and his clothing in the closet day in and day out, would be too much for her. If she's a true sociopath and has no guilt, she still would have either gotten rid of the stuff or put it away. Then it would have been an unemotional, logical decision, as in why keep Joey's things cluttering up the apartment if the boy's not coming back."

Vogel thought about that for a few minutes. "You agree?" she asked David.

"I'm not sure," he said, eyeing me. "But on one level, yeah, it makes sense. It's certainly an indication that we need to bear in mind that we could be wrong about Crystal Warner."

"Lord, save me from the profilers," the prosecutor said with a perturbed frown, undoubtedly annoyed that we had brought the case to her when we now had doubts. "What do you want me to do? What are we hoping for here?"

David took a deep breath and said, "This arrest could be wrong, but we could be right, too. We don't know for sure yet what happened to Joey. What we do know is that there's more than ample reason to be suspicious that this woman is involved, because she isn't cooperating."

"None of us will argue with you about that," the prosecutor said. "But what's your point?"

"A couple of days in the county jail could do wonders for Crystal Warner's attitude, maybe convince her to help the investigation instead of hindering it," David pointed out. "I don't know if Sarah agrees, but my take on how to proceed is that we go ahead and run Crystal through the system. Try to keep her behind bars for the time being. We keep pushing her and see if she'll talk."

Vogel looked at me, questioning. "We decide to do this, we all need to agree, and we need to keep our mouths shut. No one hears that we're not sure we're arresting the right person. That information doesn't leave the room."

"I'm okay with that," David said, looking at me.

I'd never been much for using an arrest warrant as a strategy in a case unless I figured the person behind bars was the right one. But in law enforcement, as in life, there are always exceptions. "Yeah, David's right. We need that woman to talk to us. A few days in jail could help. After all, what's important here is finding the boy." I looked at the young woman in the next room, crying and protesting. "Everything else is negotiable."

"Then we're on," Vogel said, watching Barnett get up and knock on the door. "Let's get back in that room."

Twenty-Six

Once we were all clustered again in the interview room, Crystal's tears were gone. Instead she sat calmly behind the table, with that same strange smile she'd had on her face when I'd first met her. But I noticed she didn't react at all, no look of concern, regret, or even of interest as Barnett said there'd be no deal. In fact, her demeanor had melted from outrage and anguish to the appearance of utter serenity.

"Well then, we're going to proceed with booking," Sylvia informed Barnett while staring at Crystal, eyes on eyes, intent.

"You go for it," Crystal said, grinning back up at her. "You know, lady, that you haven't got anything on me."

"Crystal, shut up," Barnett said, putting his hand on her shoulder. She glanced up at him and snickered, as if her attorney were nothing more than a fool.

"Just try proving that wasn't some kind of

a frame job, putting that money in that account," she jeered. "Find something, anything, that says I had any part in that money hitting my bank account. You can't because I didn't. Nothing. I had no idea until you told me that it was even there."

I watched her and wondered. Of the small group in the room, with the exception, perhaps, of her attorney, I was the only one who thought that maybe, just maybe, she was telling the truth. Still, I disliked the woman enough to not be sure if I cared. Part of me just wanted her punished. "Aren't you at all worried about your son?" I said, incredulous and furious at the same time. "Is that all you care about? Your own hide?"

Crystal smirked, then her lips parted and she released a short laugh. "You know, I don't know where that money came from, but it's really nice to have. For all I know, someone heard that we needed money from the announcement on the news about the fund at the bank. Maybe some anonymous person decided to help me out because she felt sorry for me, with Joey kidnapped and all. When you look at it that way, that money is mine, and I don't see how anyone can prove that it's not. And it sure doesn't mean I'm involved in Joey's kidnapping."

"Shut up!" Barnett said yet again. This time, Crystal's eyes shot up to his and she paused, taking in his frustration. Before his client could charge ahead, Barnett turned to Sylvia and tied up the interview. "This is over. Lock her up if you have to until we get bail figured out. She can sit out the hurricane here, and we'll get her out in a few days."

"A few days?" Crystal screeched, her jeering instantly replaced by fury. "You've got to be kidding."

"No, he's not kidding," Sylvia said, still targeted on Crystal, but now with a self-satisfied grin. "You weren't counting on that, I'm sure. But with the hurricane coming, your attorney doesn't have any other options. The courts closed down about fifteen minutes ago, as of noon today, to make sure those who need to evacuate can. No judges on duty, no one to decide how much you have to put up to get out of jail. It's ironic. Even if you wanted to tap into that nice bundle you say some kind soul dropped in your lap, to use the cash to buy your way out of jail, it won't help. Not until the storm passes over and the courts are up and running."

I couldn't deny a feeling of satisfaction when two deputies handcuffed and escorted

Crystal to a cell. "This'll be a piece of cake," she said as they led her away. "Once you have to drop the charges, I'll sue all of you and the county."

Moments later, she disappeared behind the heavy steel doors that led to the holding cells, and David, Vogel, and I left, driving separately to Vogel's office.

With the hurricane threatening, downtown Houston was nearly deserted, more of a ghost town than I'd ever seen. On my car radio, newscasters said the freeways were bottling up on roads with people fleeing the storm. Outside the city limits, the interstates had all been reassigned to outbound traffic only, doubling the number of lanes leading out of the city. With the storm's arrival estimated at thirty-five hours away and counting and more than a million folks who'd been ordered to evacuate, there was little time to spare.

"Everything okay there?" I asked when I called Mom at the ranch.

"Fine, dear," she said. "They released the kids from school early, and Maggie is here helping. We're marking the horses." Marking meant that Mom, Frieda, and Maggie were putting breakaway halters onto the horses, marked with Mom's name and phone number, and braiding luggage tags with the same information into their manes. The horses were all microchipped, but Mom still liked to do it the old-fashioned way. If the stable blew down or something else happened like a wall collapsing and they scattered, it was our best chance at getting them back.

"The highways are backed up, Sarah," Mom said. "We're hearing on the television that it's taking folks hours to get out of the city. When are you heading home?"

"As soon as I can, Mom, but I'll take side roads," I said, wondering if that would actually help. "Is Maggie okay?"

"We're all fine. She's still acting like the hurricane is a great adventure," she said. "Don't worry, but call and let us know when to expect you?"

"I will," I said.

Soon David and I sat in Vogel's office, on the fifth floor of Harris County's criminal courthouse, in downtown Houston. The windows were floor to ceiling, and outside, the mirrored-and-granite skyscrapers danced in reflected sunlight. Mementos were scattered throughout the office, including a Styrofoam wig stand with bullet entrance and exit wounds drawn on it, an aid from an old trial showing the trajectory of two bullets a husband shot at a wife. Half the woman's face was ripped off, blinding her. It was one of Vogel's favorite cases. The victim lived, but Sylvia got a seventy-five-year sentence for the shooter by employing the old eye-for-an-eye closing argument and convincing jurors that the husband effectively imprisoned the woman for life, leaving her blind and disfigured, and they needed to do the same to him.

"What if this really is some kind of frame?" I asked, playing devil's advocate. "You came down hard on Crystal Warner, Sylvia, saying you'd go for blood. If Crystal knew something, don't you think she would have wanted a deal?"

"We don't know that," David insisted, appearing weary and discouraged. "It's just as reasonable to assume that Crystal is guilty as hell, involved in all of this somehow."

"Maybe. Maybe," I said. This was something new. David and I had never been on opposite sides of an investigation before. "But like I said, Sylvia, you were pretty scary in there. I think we have to look at this from all sides, David, including if we're wrong."

"Yeah," David said. "You've got a point. But we need a lead, something to go with. That kid's still out there somewhere, and we've got nothing. The storm's coming tomorrow night, and once it hits, all bets are off."

David's agreeing with me didn't sit well with the prosecutor. "Agent Garrity, I don't like being in this situation," Sylvia said with a penetrating glare. "This could put us in a bad light if it turns out your assessment of the evidence is wrong. If we've arrested that mom and she's not involved, with all the publicity, it won't be pretty."

"I understand, but we're at a loss here. We don't have any other leads," he said. "You have to —"

"No, maybe *you* have to, but I don't," Sylvia broke in. "I thought we all agreed on this, but the unmistakable problem here is that if we don't have the evidence to go against the mom, this arrest is going to look like harassment." She looked unhappy, not a good situation. I'd once seen her lay into a detective who'd misrepresented evidence with so much venom that the man literally limped out of her office. "The mom's already screaming that we're incompetents on national TV, that we're messing with her instead of looking for the boy. Think about the publicity she'll get if it looks like she's right. That happens, I'm going to let the two of you explain to my boss why we arrested the mom of a kidnapped kid without enough evidence to make the charges stick."

David rubbed his forehead with his left palm, as if to quell a migraine. "Listen, how about this?" he said. "We've got Crystal's computer on premises, still in the process of being examined. We haven't looked through all the e-mail accounts yet. It appears she has a dozen or more."

"Your point?" Vogel asked.

"Maybe this guy communicated with her via e-mail. Why don't we let her cool her heels in the holding cell for a couple of hours while Sarah and I see if we can find anything else on the computer that ties her to the abduction?" he said. "Then we figure out what to do, where to go with this investigation and the charges against her."

The prosecutor considered David's proposal and then said, "Okay. Just remember that it's your heads on the block along with mine. You don't find anything, you think about this and figure we're skating on thin ice, you call me, and I'll make a phone call and spring the mom from jail before the hurricane. All right?"

"Yeah," David said. "All right."

Two hours later, after sitting in the tech room at the sheriff's department with a tattooed computer geek named Salvatore, David looked at me and shrugged. We'd run searches on all Crystal Warner's e-mail accounts, looking for two dozen keywords including payoff, $30,000, the name of the park, polygraph, lie detector, Wednesday (the day Joey disappeared), Crystal's bank account number, and police. We'd come up with a few matches on "park" and "Wednesday," but nothing connected with the case.

"We have nothing," David said. "Do I call Sylvia, tell her to release Crystal?"

I thought about that and hesitated. While I wasn't sure she was guilty, the toys around the apartment, her convincing confusion when we first told her about the thirty grand, all made me second-guess my instincts, which still cautioned me that she had to be involved. "I know I'm the one who rained on the parade," I admitted, wishing I had a clearer take on what to say. "Still, I'd like to keep Crystal in jail. We know she's not telling us the truth. We know she's hiding something. Right?"

"Right," he said.

"So I vote we keep her locked up, and keep trying to track down where that money came from, find out what her involvement is," I said.

"I agree," he said. "But we've got to think about possible repercussions."

I knew he and Sylvia had a point. I could picture Crystal and her parents back on the *Today* show, telling the reporter, who'd be übersympathetic, how we kept her in jail during a hurricane without the evidence to back it up. But was it that out of line, based on what we did have: an uncooperative mom, the thirty grand, her own words that she wanted the kid to disappear, and the tape-recorded conversation?

"When you take a good look at all this, I think Sylvia's overreacting," I said to David, voicing my thoughts as they were forming, as if testing them on him. "Crystal may not turn out to be involved, but we legitimately still had enough to book her. The judge signing the warrant verifies that. And that means we have enough to keep her in jail while we investigate."

David frowned, ruffling his brow, and then closed his eyes. "You're right. The judge thought we had enough when we got the warrant or he wouldn't have signed it, and nothing has really changed. That evidence all still stands," he said. "The problem is, as vocal as this woman and her parents are, whether or not it's justified, the arrest could be a public relations disaster."

I thought about that. It was hard not to agree. "Yeah, I know you're right."

"I wish that we could figure out where the kid is, and get out of this quagmire," he said. "What're you thinking?"

"I'm thinking I feel better with Crystal Warner in jail for the time being," I said. "I'm thinking we leave her there. I know it's risky, but I'm willing to take the heat if you are."

He barely considered the alternative before shooting me a warm smile. "Okay," he said. "We're in this together. Only one problem."

"Yeah, I know," I said. Before I went any further, he said what we both painfully knew to be true.

"We haven't got a freaking clue what to do to find the kid," he said. "Not a damn idea here. Or am I missing something? Have you figured this out and come up with a plan?"

I was about to admit that I had no idea what to do next, that I couldn't suggest a single alternative. The truth was that I didn't have even a plausible theory on what we could do to find the boy. Looking back later, I'd believe that either we were simply due for a break, or God, or fate, or flat-out luck interceded — for just then one of the detectives on the case motioned at us.

"Caller on the line for Agent Garrity," he

said. “Joey Warner’s dad.”

“Evan Warner?” I asked, surprised.

“One and the same,” the detective said. “Sounds like maybe he wants to talk.”

Twenty-Seven

Getting out of downtown and past I-45 took a full twenty minutes, even with the siren wailing on my Tahoe. I wasn't trying to get on the freeway, just take an underpass to cross it. With the storm coming, folks were rattled, and since little was moving, they had nowhere to go to get out of our way. Once David and I cleared the freeway, we made a beeline for the Warner home in West U, a trendy, well-heeled section of Houston near Rice University and the priciest shopping, trendiest restaurants, and most expensive art galleries. We pulled up to a redbrick colonial with a rose garden and a well-tended lawn.

"Evan was the one who made the decision to call you. Our attorney has evacuated, and we couldn't get in touch with him," Jackson Warner said when David and I arrived. "But we understand our son's attachment to the child, and now, with what happened this morning, we believe it may be time to become more helpful."

David and I shook the man's hand, murmured something about being grateful for their cooperation, and we were motioned toward the living room, where Evan sat holding a large envelope. "Lieutenant Armstrong and Agent Garrity," the young man greeted us, his face a blank, as if he were only half-aware of what was going on around him. "Thanks for coming. I apologize for the other day. I didn't really understand. I thought it was just Crystal being Crystal. I never thought —"

"No problem," David said when Evan choked up and couldn't finish. "What's happened? Why did you call us?"

"This," he said, holding up the envelope. The envelope was padded, white with green markings, a common type sold in office supply stores. Nothing was written across the front.

"When did this come?" I asked.

"It was outside this morning, on the front porch, when we opened the door to get our newspaper," said Alicia Warner, seated in a chair near a window looking out toward the front yard. Her eyes were red, as if she'd been crying. The mood in the room was somber, filled with what I suspected could be a rather bitter dose of regret. Subdued, Evan's parents weren't issuing orders, as they had been at the sheriff's department two nights earlier, just hours after Joey disappeared.

As I watched, David claimed a latex glove out of his back pocket and slipped it on. He then splayed open the envelope far enough to reach inside and pull out something that looked like a ball of fabric. As it fell open, I saw that what he held was a small pair of boy's jockey shorts.

"I recognize them. They're Joey's," Evan said, his hands tucked under his arms, holding back anger and fear. "Look at the front. It looks like there's blood on them."

With two fingers, David held up the garment and examined it. The little boy's underpants were dirty, stained with urine and, on the front, over Spider-Man's face, a smear of what appeared to be dark, dried blood.

"I'll get evidence bags," I said, and I turned and rushed out. I didn't want anyone, especially Evan and his parents, to see how upset I was. On the street, I hit the unlock on my key twice and opened the Tahoe's rear door, pulled out a box that had evidence bags tucked inside, grabbed a few, then took a moment to wipe my eyes before

I walked back toward the house, thinking about the contents of the envelope.

Inside, Alicia Warner cried openly while her husband attempted to comfort her. Evan sat alone, barely holding on to his self-control. His left fist opened and closed, pumping with anger. On the edge of the chair, he appeared poised to jump up, to do something, anything, but apparently he didn't know where to go or what to do. "I keep thinking about how small Joey is," Evan said, his words stumbling over one another, tears running down his cheeks. "He's always been a little runt of a kid, you know. A funny little guy. Always following me around. Poppa this. Poppa that. He's so small, his hands barely fill my palms."

Holding up his right hand as if he wanted us to see, he lowered his head and wept. His parents scurried closer to comfort him, and his mother handed her son a tissue she'd already dampened with her own tears.

"What changed besides this envelope?" I asked Evan's parents. "Why are you cooperating now?"

Jackson looked at me and shook his head, as if unable to speak.

"When you showed us Joey's photo, we recognized him," Alicia said, holding her son's shoulders as he cried. "We now believe he is our grandson. He looks just like Evan did at his age."

In that instant, perhaps it wasn't fair to deliver a blow while they were already reeling. But I didn't think about that. I had to know. "So, if that little boy wasn't related to you, you wouldn't lift a finger to help him? Even to save his life?"

"Sarah," David chastised, his voice barely above a whisper, although I knew he had to be thinking the same thing. "Not now."

"There's something else in there," Evan said, bringing our attention back to the envelope. "A note, I think. Once I saw Joey's jockey shorts, I didn't want to touch anything else, so I didn't open it, but there's a piece of paper."

First things first. I opened an evidence bag, and David dropped the Spider-Man underwear inside. He then reached back inside the white envelope and pulled out a folded sheet of paper. Using his gloved hand, he flipped it open. The paper was unlined, from appearances standard printer paper. He slipped it in an evidence bag, and my heart quickened when I saw what was on it: a symbol drawn with a thick black marker, an eight-point star with an empty circle in the center.

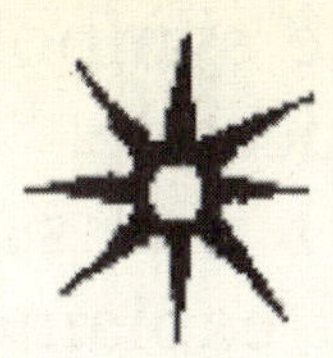

Images of the lifeless cattle, their heads reduced to gaping, angry wounds, filled my mind, and the first thing I thought of was what Alex Benoit had said to me only hours earlier: *It seems to me that this man has something planned. Something more serious than dead bulls.*

"What does that mean? Is it some kind of code? Is he asking for money? What does he want?" Alicia Warner asked, frantic. "Anything. We'll give him anything he asks for, if we can get the boy back."

Sometimes knowledge hits with all the force of a physical blow. *Oh, my God, no,* I thought. What I said was directed at Evan's father, Jackson Warner. "May I use a computer, one hooked up to the Web?"

"Sure," he said, searching my face for answers. "There's a laptop in the study."

While I walked to the study with David, I thought over what had just happened. The blood on the underwear was the kidnapper's way of upping the stakes, flaunting that he had the boy and that Joey was in grave danger. The symbol? That I needed more answers to decode.

Minutes later, I was searching Google. Since Benoit had explained the origins of the three symbols left on the longhorns, I keyed in *Adinkra* and then "star." A list of links filled the screen. The one I clicked on read, "*Adinkra* Symbolism," and the page that came up was from a university Web site, and it bore depictions of the symbols in the left column along with explanations on the right. I didn't find *Abakuá,* the war and blood sign, but I didn't expect to. Benoit had said that particular sign was Afro-Cuban, not *Adinkra.* I did, however, quickly focus in on both *Ako-ben,* the call to arms, and *Aya,* the fern that depicts defiance, meaning "I am not afraid of you."

Near the bottom, I discovered the third symbol I was looking for, an eight-pointed star with an open circle in the center, similar to the star on the piece of paper in the envelope. This particular symbol's name was listed as *Nosoroma,* and its meaning was "a child of the Supreme Being."

I looked at David. "We need to find Buckshot," I said. "Now."

TWENTY-EIGHT

I called Buckshot from the Tahoe, but he didn't answer. On the way to my office, I filled David in on the longhorns, the symbols painted on their sides, and Benoit, repeating the menacing conversation I'd had with him early that morning. When the captain got on the line, he said Buckshot was out working the case and checking up, as I'd requested, on Benoit. When I still couldn't reach my fellow ranger, I called Benoit myself, twice, but he didn't answer.

"So we think this professor was intuitive enough to figure out there was more going on than someone killing livestock? Or that he's the one killing the bulls and that maybe he has Joey?" David said, piecing together the puzzling picture I'd drawn.

"Yeah, maybe. I'm not sure," I admitted, fighting back a growing sense of anxiety. "The conversation struck me as peculiar at the time, enough to ask Buckshot to look into the guy. But yeah, thinking about all this, Benoit's either qualified for a second career as a forensic psychologist or he knew what the kidnapper had planned because he was the one who took Joey."

Just then my cell rang, and Buckshot said, "You trying to reach me, Sarah?"

Relieved to hear his voice, I asked, "Where are you?"

"On my way to hook up with Benoit, maybe fifteen minutes away from the Westover Plantation," he said. "That's where he told you he'd be, and I've been calling the SOB, but he's not answering his cell phone. We've got to powwow. I've got some questions to ask, and I want to do it in person, make sure I get the right answers."

Without taking time to consider what I should do, I turned the Tahoe around. I'd been driving to the office, but instead I made a left at the next corner and took a side street, heading south, toward Brazoria County and the plantation. The back roads would mean a longer ride distancewise, but the freeways were nearly at a standstill with hurricane evacuees.

"What did you find out?"

"Not who he is, but who he isn't," Buckshot explained. "Turns out that there sure enough is a Professor Alex Benoit who taught at Tulane University, and he moved to Houston a few years ago. All that's true."

"Then why do you think this man isn't him?"

"The real Benoit isn't at all like you described him. The real professor Benoit is eighty-two years old, and he's living in a west Houston nursing home," Buckshot said. "This fellow you've been dealing with, well, the guy's an impostor. Must have come here and just said he was Benoit, and no one checked up on him. Why should they? He was doing all these nice things for the folks in that history society, donating his time."

I thought back to the morning's conversation, when the man I then believed was Professor Alex Benoit warned me that human lives could be at stake. Now I knew that man to be a fake. I no longer had any doubt. "I think this impostor has Joey Warner, the kid we're looking for, Buckshot. An envelope with a drawing of a symbol like the ones left on the longhorns was dropped off at the boy's father's house this morning. This one symbolizes a child."

"Why, that sick son of a bitch," he snarled. "I get my hands on that twisted pile of —"

"Yeah," I interrupted. "You won't get an argument from me or from David. We want to talk to this guy, too. In fact, we'd like to be there with you. When you get to the plantation, hold up and call us, and we'll let you know when to expect us. This guy may be dangerous. Don't go in until we get there. We're on our way."

"I'll try, Sarah," Buckshot said. "But if you think he's got that kid, and I see evidence he's on the premises, I may not wait for y'all to get there. The traffic's a disaster, and no telling how long it'll take."

I didn't like the idea of Buckshot going in alone, but he had a point. The longer Benoit, or whoever he was, had Joey, the more danger the boy was in. "Okay, understood, but this guy's a strange one. Be careful. And don't go in alone. If you can't wait for us, call the locals for backup," I said, trying to steer around cars piled up at an intersection. Apparently as frustrated as I was, the driver of the car in front of us threw a U-turn and drove two wheels over the curb onto a sidewalk to try to get out of our way. "Listen, Buckshot, like I said, be careful. Don't underestimate this guy."

"You've got it, Sarah," he said. "I guarandamn-tee you that I'll keep my eyes on him."

I closed my cell phone, lowered the window, smacked my portable siren onto the roof, and turned it on, and the car that had just made the U-turn pulled over immediately, the driver no doubt figuring he was in line for a ticket. But I just kept going, maneuvered around the traffic, through the intersection. For a short distance it looked more promising, but two blocks down the road, David and I sat at a dead stop, trapped at yet another intersection, cars piled up and idling at a green light. Even the side streets were blocked.

"This isn't going to work," David said, stating the obvious.

Without further conversation, I made a U-turn of my own and headed toward the office, tossing my phone at David. "Call the captain," I said. "Tell him that we need a chopper at headquarters, ASAP."

Twenty-Nine

When we drove into the office parking lot, the captain greeted us with the chopper, engine running, waiting in a section of cleared-out parking lot. "We're ready for you," he said. "The pilot has the coordinates for the plantation. Says it shouldn't take more than twenty minutes once you're in the air."

"Have you heard from Buckshot?" I asked as he ran alongside us.

"No, and we've been trying to reach him," the captain said, appearing worried. "I can't understand why he's not answering."

"David's been calling, too," I said. "Same result: the phone just rings, then goes to voice mail."

"I called the locals," the captain explained. "Buckshot requested backup half an hour ago, but they couldn't spare any. Those towns are in a mandatory evacuation area, and all their personnel are on the street, directing hurricane traffic."

"Damn," I said as the captain backed up to get out of the way. He waved at the pilot, who pushed down the throttle, and we were off. The chopper hovered briefly over U.S. 290 and Houston's 610 Loop, both clogged with traffic streaming from every direction, cars filled with folks desperate to flee the hurricane. Then we took a sharp turn, heading south to Brazoria County and the Westover Plantation. As far as we could see below, on all the streets and freeways, traffic crawled.

"Looks like we did the right thing calling for the chopper," David observed. "None of this traffic is going anywhere."

"Let's just hope we're in time," I said, although I wasn't sure for what. All I knew was that the man I'd been introduced to as Professor Alex Benoit was an impostor and that he could be involved in Joey Warner's kidnapping. That Buckshot wasn't answering his phone worried me. By now, he must have realized we were anxious to reach him. Why didn't he call?

Beneath us, the city was a tangled web of freeways as we flew south, toward the plantation. The minutes dragged, and Houston's trees and neighborhoods gave way to green fields scarred by country roads. Then, in the distance, we saw something odd. The pilot pointed at a plume of thick black smoke rising and drifting off in the clear blue sky, like the exhaust from a colossal chimney. "That should be right about where we're going," the pilot said. "What's going on?"

"Don't know," David said, glancing over at me. "But let's make a loop above it, see if we can find out."

We flew on, approaching the fire, and the pilot maneuvered around the smoke, skirting close enough to the source to see but not so close that we'd feel the heat or get sucked into the currents of hot air. As we passed the source, we looked down and saw bright yellow-and-orange flames coming through the roof and licking the sides of a great house. "It's the mansion," I confirmed. "The Westover Plantation."

As we cleared the smoke, I noticed a black vehicle parked behind the burning building, under an aged oak tree. "Buckshot's Suburban," I said with a sense of dread. "Over there."

We landed in an open field, and David and I barely waited for touchdown before we jumped out and sprinted toward the burning mansion and Buckshot's truck, guns drawn. The greedy flames crackled and tore away at the nearly two-hundred-year-old structure, destroying what had survived freezes and hurricanes, droughts and floods. "You go to the right," David shouted as he ran to the left. I circled, gun drawn, my face flushed from the heat radiated by the blaze. Heart pounding, I peered inside, hoping to make out a figure emerging, someone alive. But I saw only fire and the mansion's toppled brick walls. The house was engulfed in flames, and anyone inside had to have perished. We saw no one on the grounds. I looked for Buckshot to run to us, but he didn't appear, and the only vehicle was his Suburban, with his silver-belly Stetson, 9 mm pistol, and cell phone abandoned in the front passenger seat.

"Damn it, where's Buckshot?" I asked David, who stood surveying the property, watching. By then, sirens whined in the distance. The pilot had called in the fire, and firefighters in yellow-and-red ladder trucks arrived, unloading hoses and quickly going to work. So little remained of the house, so much of it had already been destroyed, that it took little more than an hour to reduce it to a smoldering mass of charred black soggy ruins that belched from smoldering pockets. The captain still hadn't heard from Buckshot, neither had we, and as the minutes passed, my last remaining grasp on hope gave way. An ambulance sat nearby, the EMTs waiting as we were, but for what? Anyone caught in that fire surely died.

Yet as the firefighters walked the sodden and charred ruins, no one called out to announce discovering a body. Was it hidden beneath the debris, under a fallen ceiling or a collapsed brick wall? The lead firefighter, his face blackened by soot, walked toward me. "We didn't find anyone. Your ranger could be in there, but we'll have to bring in the cadaver dogs when it cools to look. Can't right now, though. We're spread thin with the hurricane, and we've got to leave," he said. "We've got another call."

"Where?" I asked.

"Down the road a piece," he said. "Somebody called 911. There's a body on fire."

"Come on," I said to David. "We're going."

We hopped onto one of the fire trucks, the siren wailing, and we held on as it sped down the long gravel driveway and then swung left onto the road. The ambulance followed, and we continued down deserted streets. This was shallow coastal plain, prone to flooding, and the folks who lived nearby were mostly already on the road, heading north or west, away from the Gulf and the storm. Two more turns, and minutes later we stopped abruptly at the intersection of two country roads surrounded by trees and fields. Out in the Gulf the hurricane churned, but the only wind was a stifling hot breeze, and the sky was picture-postcard blue. The putrid smell of burning flesh coated my nostrils and burned my throat.

In the center of the intersection, something flamed.

On closer inspection, I saw the outline of a body on its left side, its arms and legs raised as if ready to fight. I'd seen this stance before with fire victims. The medical folks call it a pugilist's pose, caused when muscles contract from intense heat. Whoever it was, we'd arrived too late. The burning remains were completely still, the only motion the black smoke drifting upward. A firefighter rushed forward with an extinguisher, and David and I fell into line behind him. The man unleashed a funnel of cloudy discharge, quickly snuffing out the still burning flames. What remained was the stench of burned flesh and a disfigured, charred corpse. The hands, eyes, and most of the face, including the nose, looked like ash and crumbled off like bits of spent charcoal.

"Buckshot?" David whispered.

"Oh, God, no," I said, covering my mouth with my hand. I could barely stand to look at the blackened corpse. It sickened me to think he could be my fellow ranger and my friend. Still, I had to know. Drawn to its side, I knelt beside the still body. Although the limbs and face were burned beyond recognition, nearly all the clothes reduced to ash, the trunk of the body, especially the area flush with the ground, on its left side, appeared unburned.

"He must have already been dead when the fire was lit," David said. When I looked up at him, questioning, he said, "From appearances he was dumped here and didn't try to run away."

"Do you have a pen?" I asked. Staring at the body as if stunned, he didn't respond, and I asked again. "David, a pen."

I took the black ballpoint offered and pushed away fragments of a charred sport coat. The one Buckshot had worn that morning, when I last saw him, was lightweight and a camel color, one more befitting summer but practical for our fall heat wave. There was no telling what color this coat had been before the fire. As the fabric bits fell away, I saw peeking out from underneath the dead man's torso the burned remains of a tooled leather belt, an empty holster, and a half-melted silver badge, like mine, a lone star surrounded by a wagon wheel. My heart drilling against my rib cage, I stared at the body, trying to think of a way I could be wrong.

"It's Buckshot," I whispered. "It has to be." Once I'd formed the words, I couldn't move. I simply felt incapable of it.

"Come on, Sarah," David said, gently urging me back to my feet. "I'll call the captain. You need to go sit down on the fire truck and wait."

Slowly, I made my way back up onto my feet, but I couldn't take my eyes off the body. Buckshot was my friend. We'd worked cases, eaten meals, and laughed together. When my husband, Bill, died, he and the captain went with Mom and me to the mortuary to plan the funeral; we sat on a bench together, and I cried inconsolably on his shoulder. I was the one who got drunk with him when Peggy, his wife, took off with his good friend. Buckshot and I once spent a full forty-eight hours together on a stakeout, taking turns sleeping in my Tahoe, and afterward joked that we should get married because we never argued.

David guided me to the fire truck, and for just a moment, I thought about asking why anyone would do that to my friend. Then I remembered something I'd realized long ago: there are people in this world who don't need a reason.

THIRTY

David called it in, and not long after, another helicopter arrived, this one carrying the captain, an assistant medical examiner he'd brought from Houston, and a small, two-man forensic team. David did all the talking, leaving me to stare at Buckshot's body in the road, covered by a white sheet. The assistant M.E. pulled away the sheet and began processing the body, removing Buckshot's burned clothing, picking up the fragments to be sealed inside airtight paint-type containers. Looking at it as if it were just another crime scene, I understood they wanted to preserve the evidence, to check the fabric for accelerants like gasoline. On another level, it wasn't just another crime scene, and it was one I'd never forget. After the forensic team finished, Buckshot's corpse was wrapped in the sheet, zipped into a white body bag, and loaded onto the helicopter.

In the morgue, the M.E.s would compare dental records, but I had little doubt that what they'd determine was that the burned corpse was all that remained of my dear friend.

"Sarah, we need to talk," the captain said, standing over me. His face sagged, and he looked a decade older than he had that same morning, when I'd dropped the longhorn case in Buckshot's lap and taken off to try to help find Joey Warner. Now Buckshot was dead, murdered. Perhaps it was my fault. After all, I'd deserted him. And the boy? We suspected Benoit had him, but we were no closer to finding him.

"We don't have anything on this guy who's been calling himself Alex Benoit, no photos, nothing to identify him," the captain said. "And he's smart. We dispatched a couple of squads to a house the folks at the Heritage Society were letting him camp out in while he was working at the plantation, an old Victorian about half an hour west of here, but by the time our guys got there, there'd been an explosion. The place, like the mansion, was burned to the ground. We don't have a single fingerprint."

I nodded, numb. "You didn't find bodies? Joey wasn't there?"

"No bodies, at least not yet, nothing to

indicate anyone was in the house when it blew up," he said. "But we need to find this guy and the boy. The only driver's license photo we have is from Louisiana, and it's of the real Benoit, an old man. We didn't find any auto registration in the entire state of Texas to get us a description of a vehicle or a license plate number. We need to know what this guy drives, what he looks like."

"What do you want me to do?" I asked.

David had been standing next to the captain, but now he sat beside me and held my hand. "Draw his face for us, Sarah," he said. "Show us who we're looking for."

I nodded again. It wasn't such an odd request. Over the years, I'd often drawn composites when there wasn't time to wait for a forensic artist and I needed to get out a description. This time, however, it would be different. This time I wouldn't be pulling a face out of someone else's head. Benoit's features would be reconstructed purely from of my own memory.

"I need paper and a pencil," I said.

One of the crime scene guys came up with a pencil and a notebook, unlined, that he used to sketch crime scenes, and I sat on the fire truck drawing while the others worked the scene. I closed my eyes and thought back to the only time I'd talked in person with the man who'd called himself Alex Benoit, not quite twenty-four hours earlier, when I'd shown him the longhorn symbols at the plantation. I opened my eyes and began sketching, but my hands trembled so that I couldn't. Fighting for control, I put down the pencil and clenched my hands into tight fists as I sucked in one, two, three, four deep breaths, holding each, counting down the seconds, desperate to clear my mind and quell the anger and grief that had invaded every cell of my body.

On the fifth breath, I turned the notebook to a clean page and reclaimed the pencil.

I began by drawing the line of a cheek, a high forehead, a face that was not young but not old, thready wrinkles around the eyes, hair combed back in waves, and handsome, patrician features. I don't know that I'd ever appreciated how difficult recalling a face could be, remembering the small nuances, the minute features. Did the man I'd met really have a mole on the left, above his upper lip? Or was I manufacturing that bit of information, false memory? If I could have, I would have turned back the clock and taken a closer look, but I'd missed my opportunity. The last time I saw Benoit he wasn't a suspect, merely a source. When and if I saw him again, there would be no time for taking stock of his physical features, not until I had him handcuffed and in custody.

I finished the drawing, shading the areas under his cheekbones and smudging his hair to give it the look of thickness. "Best I can do," I told the captain. "He had a little southern drawl, but only a slight one, maybe an affectation, since we know now he isn't Benoit. We don't know if he's really spent any time in Louisiana."

"Thanks, Sarah," he said. "Looks like this is all we've got. They're searching the scene at the house, looking for prints, but there's so much damage, we don't think we'll be lucky."

I thought for a minute, recalling the afternoon before with Benoit at the plantation. "Is the tree still there?" I asked. "Back at the Westover place. Are the slaves quarters and the tree still there?"

"I don't know. What tree?" David asked.

"The bottle tree," I said.

Including a forensic guy with supplies, we hitched a ride on a fire truck back to the plantation. The captain's chopper had taken off with the body, heading to the Texas medical center, where it would land on a helipad atop one of the skyscraper hospitals. Buckshot's body would then be transferred to a stretcher and taken to an ambulance, to be transported to the medical examiner's building, which housed the morgue. The captain had already called ahead and made sure the autopsy was scheduled for that same night, before the morgue, like everything else, closed down for the hurricane.

"Someone needs to call Buckshot's family. I know they're divorced, but Peggy will want to know," I said. "Their daughter is at the University of Texas, in Austin. I think he said she's living in Jester Hall."

"We'll take care of it," the captain said as we turned back down the long gravel driveway onto the plantation. "That's not yours to do."

He leaned closer to me, whispering, "Buckshot's death isn't your fault, Sarah."

My response caught in my throat, the words refusing to leave. *How do you know?* I'd wanted to ask. *How can we ever know?*

The chopper that had transported David and me to the scene still sat parked in the field behind the smoldering ruins of the mansion, and I instructed the fire truck driver to take a side road past the stables. When the road ended, we got out and walked a short distance to the slaves quarters, or rather, where they used to be. As with the mansion, only fire-scarred ruins remained.

"So much for his love of preserving history," I muttered. David looked at me quizzically. "Never mind," I said.

"Where's this bottle tree?" the captain asked.

"It's gone," I said. Where it had been, the end of a thin, burned tree trunk protruded a few inches out of the scorched earth. Yet it seemed that it shouldn't all have disappeared. Scanning the ground, I pushed with the toe of my gray lizard-skin boot at something green, the edge of a long thin jagged piece of glass protruding from the soil, and the broken neck of a soda bottle popped out. "Here," I said. "Here's something."

"Over here," the captain shouted at one of the forensic officers. Soon we were all searching, uncovering broken glass, scattered on the blackened earth, evidence that was slipped into bags, to be transported to the lab in hopes of finding a fingerprint.

"Will you be able to get any prints off these?" I asked the CSI officer. "Would the heat destroy them?"

"It could, if they got hot enough. And, of course, if he left prints in the first place."

I thought about that. "Yeah, sure, of course. All I can tell you is that Benoit said he made the bottle tree himself, so my guess is that he touched all that glass," I said. Yet I felt less than hopeful, less than certain any of it would matter. "It's all I've got for you, all I can think of to help figure out who he really is."

As we prepared to leave, I looked around the plantation, and I thought about my first visit there, recalling how I'd knelt at the graves from a forgotten era, reading the inscriptions. On that afternoon, I'd been listening for Benoit, but he still surprised me, crept up on me so silently, I didn't know he was there until I sensed him standing over me. I wondered if he'd done the same thing to Buckshot, if Benoit had eased up directly behind my friend, holding a gun to his head before Buckshot even realized he was in danger. I found myself praying it happened that way, that my fellow ranger died before he confronted his fate.

"Let's get out of here, Sarah," the captain said gently. "It's time to go."

As we walked slowly to the helicopter, David slipped his arm over my shoulder. "Where will he take him?" I asked.

Looking at me as if I should have known that, he explained patiently, "Buckshot's remains are on their way to the morgue, Sarah."

I closed my eyes for just a moment,

overcome with sadness. As much as I wanted to give in and grieve, I couldn't. Somewhere the man responsible was still out there, free, and if we were right, he held an innocent child hostage. "No," I said. I didn't have another name for him, so I continued to use the only one I knew. "Where will Benoit take Joey? This man, whoever he is, doesn't have a home anymore, a safe place to hide the boy. Where will they go?"

David drew in his lips, appearing weary and almost resigned that all might be lost. I couldn't accept that. The possibility that Benoit had escaped with the boy and that he'd never be brought to justice for murdering Buckshot was more than I could bear. "There are other questions here," David said. When I looked at him, questioning, he said, "Is the mother involved? What's Benoit planning to do with the boy? If we can answer those questions, maybe we can figure out where he'll take him."

The first question, I couldn't shed any light on. Crystal Warner's involvement, if there was any, was still a mystery. So far, she wasn't talking. When it came to what Benoit had planned, no one wanted to speculate, but I couldn't help thinking about what he'd said on the telephone, that the killer wouldn't be satisfied slaying longhorns.

"If we only had a clue where to look, anything that pointed to a location. There has to be something we can do," the captain said. He grew quiet, as if searching for options. Then, resigned, he said, "We'll circulate your sketch, get it on television, but with the hurricane coming, people are distracted. The timing is bad, really bad."

Like the captain, I needed something, anything, to hang on to, any shred of hope we would find this monster. I thought about Benoit walking out into the cow pastures, shotgun in hand. Three mornings. Three dead longhorns. When Gabby Barlow looked at the insect evidence, she said the first bull died the night before it was discovered. "When is sunset?" I asked, and then realized that it was late, that the sun was already low in the sky.

"Less than an hour," David said. "Why?"

"He kills the longhorns at night, one every night for the past three nights," I said. "The first one north of Houston. The second south. The third west."

"You think he'll kill another one tonight?" the captain asked.

"Could be. I don't know," I admitted. "But it's all I've got that I can think of right now that might help."

"So the next one is east," David said.

"That's my guess," I said. "I don't know why, but he appears to be keeping to some kind of a pattern."

"But there have to be a hundred cattle ranches east of Houston, small ones hidden in the countryside. How do we find the right one?" the captain asked. "How do we figure out which one?"

"Well, there's this thing about the longhorns," I said. "There's something I've noticed about the bulls."

Thirty-One

On the way back to the office in the helicopter, we watched cars fleeing the hurricane, snaking out of the dark city below us, visible only through long strings of slowly moving red and white tail- and headlights. I called Gabby Barlow, asking for more information on Habanero, the first bull. The best Gabby could figure, based on the stages of the bug population in the corpse, was that the bull died sometime the night before it was discovered, most likely before midnight. But bugs aren't that precise, and the estimate was as much guess as science.

"That's assuming blowfly patterns are the same on longhorn cattle as on human corpses. I believe they're probably close, but there's no research on bulls that I've been able to find," she said. "I can't give you a guarantee, Sarah. This is maybe not even a ballpark. And you can't lock me into any of this in a courtroom."

"That's not why I'm calling," I explained. "This isn't for testimony. It's to help us figure out how to catch the guy."

"Ah," she said. "Not calling it a day, even with the hurricane coming tomorrow night?"

"We think this guy who's killing the bulls is the same one who kidnapped the missing little boy, Joey Warner." I took a deep breath and added, "And it looks like this same guy murdered Buckshot."

"Oh, my God," Gabby said. I heard a painful catch in her voice. "No."

"Yeah. And we haven't got much to work with, but we really need to find him now, rescue the kid, and bring this piece of human debris in before the hurricane hits and chaos takes over."

Gabby was quiet for a moment and then said, "I wish I had more for you, Sarah. All I can say is that my best guess is that Habanero died sometime before midnight."

It was going on eight o'clock when we landed, and it had been dark for an hour. That meant, if Gabby was right, we had at most a few hours to prepare and get in place. "How are we going to find the right ranch?" David asked.

The only one of the three who'd seen the cattle firsthand, I'd been considering that problem in the chopper. "This guy had to find the cattle somehow, figure out which ones worked for what he wanted. As I mentioned in the chopper, all three of the bulls had similar coloring, a pale area on their sides for him to draw on, so the symbol would stand out and be easily seen," I explained. "We need to find a bull with the right coloring east of Houston. Since the three ranches where killings have already taken place are around fifty miles from downtown, that's my best estimate on distance."

David gave me one of those looks, the kind that suggests *You've got to be kidding.* Yet that thought he kept to himself. Instead, he asked, "How do we do that?"

"It's not impossible," I assured him, hoping I wasn't lying. "When I was thinking about this the other day, I figured the guy was finding the cattle on the Web. These are all prize-winning bulls, and their semen is sold and shipped all over the world. It's been so crazy, I never had time to check, but my theory is that the bulls are advertised on the Internet."

"With a photo," David said, nodding that he understood.

"With a photo," I echoed.

Word had already spread about Buckshot,

and our offices at the Texas Department of Public Safety building on the West Loop swarmed with uniformed state troopers, my fellow rangers, and civilian personnel, secretaries and clerks, who'd come in well after hours to grieve together. That morning, we'd had eight rangers working out of Houston's Company A. With Buckshot dead, we now had seven. The others watched us, angry and apprehensive, as we walked toward my office. Some of the secretaries cried. I didn't realize I was until David handed me a tissue. I said nothing to anyone. If I had, I might not have been able to keep putting one foot in front of the other, much less accomplish what we had to.

Minutes later, David and I had a map covering the area in question. We then Googled "prize-winning longhorn bull Texas." When the list of Web sites came up, we searched for zip codes that matched our map and pulled up ranchers' Web sites with pictures of their top bulls. One by one we scanned the possibilities. In the end, three longhorns at three different ranches matched the physical description we were interested in, bulls with buff-colored midsections large enough to draw a symbol on.

"We need help," I told the captain when I

showed him the map and printouts of the results.

"That's not a problem," he said. "You've got an office full of angry rangers and state troopers who'd like nothing better than to catch the guy who murdered Buckshot."

Explaining what we'd discovered on the Internet, David and I laid it out for the captain, showing him where the ranches were located.

"Let's call ahead and get the ranchers on board. Then we'll station three people at each site, one of us with a ranger and a trooper," David suggested.

"That works," the captain said. "We've got one helicopter outside and two more on standby. Let's move out."

I grabbed the information on the first bull, handed number two to David, and gave the third to the captain. "We'll keep in touch," I said. "There's not much time. We're going to need to get really lucky to make this work."

THIRTY-TWO

The pilot set the helicopter down behind the ranch house, a low-slung, one-story structure of cream-colored brick with brown shutters. I'd called ahead and discussed the plan with the owner, and he had horses waiting, including one for himself, to guide me, my fellow ranger, and the trooper who'd accompanied us to the remote pasture where the family's prime sire, a twelve-year-old longhorn named Curley Moe, would be roaming. In the darkness, the cattleman led the way. Plump with a sagging belly that hid his leather belt, the rancher took his time as we ventured ever farther down a narrow trail that twisted between the trees. Above us, a nearly full moon illuminated the sky, casting a soft glow. The air, cooled by evening, smelled of rich dark earth and the heavy pine-scented oxygen of forest. I looked at my watch; it was ten thirty. I'd been on the first helicopter out, which meant that David and the captain were still en route. "We're running out of time," I whispered to no one in particular.

The bay filly I rode wound sure-footed on the narrow path, but before long, our short caravan stopped. We'd already been told that we'd have to finish the trip on foot. We got off our horses and tied them to trees, and then the rancher whispered, "This way."

We started down another slim path, on what the rancher estimated was a ten-minute walk, when suddenly, from somewhere ahead, we heard a loud crack echoing through the forest. It rushed past us into the night, then all was silent.

"What's that?" the rancher asked. The man's eyes narrowed, and I saw sweat collecting on his forehead and upper lip. I couldn't blame him for being scared.

"A gunshot," I said, peering ahead. We still had a substantial distance ahead of us. But if that was Benoit, he didn't know we were coming, and he wasn't done. Curley Moe might be dead, but Benoit had a symbol to paint on the bull's hide, another clue to leave behind. If we hurried, cornering our prey wasn't impossible.

"Let's go," I ordered. "We need to get there, quick."

As we ran, edging closer, I turned off my flashlight and the others followed suit. Now we had only the light of the moon to guide us, shafts of which made its way down between the trees. The rancher's eyes widened as my fellow rangers and I pulled our guns, but the man didn't back off. Instead, he motioned down the path and led us forward. We followed close behind, hurrying toward the pasture and the source of the gunshot. In the near darkness, I tripped on a gnarled root and fell against a tree trunk, scratching my shoulder against the rough bark. That delay put me in the rear as the others rushed past.

"Just ahead!" the rancher yelled out as we neared a clearing.

"Quiet," I ordered, reining in my voice from a shout.

We had to surprise Benoit. We had to catch him unawares, or he'd run and in the forest, in the darkness, disappear. Mindful of the danger, we rushed down the last of the path, watching, and soon the trees gave way and the moon shone overhead, its light allowing us to scan the pasture. At first nothing, then the trooper pointed to the far end of the clearing and hissed, "Over there!"

A man's silhouette was visible, hunched over something on the ground. Benoit. And someone else, in the shadows, a small figure. Joey!

"Be careful. He has the boy," I whispered, but just then the man looked up, saw us emerging from the forest, and turned and ran into the woods, dragging the child, who attempted to wrestle from his grasp.

"Joey, get away, run!" I screamed.

"Come on," I urged the others, my pulse quickening. "Watch out for the boy. Try to take Benoit alive, but if you get a good shot, take it!"

Sprinting as fast as our legs could carry us, we rushed across the open pasture, toward the trees where Benoit and the boy had disappeared. The night air burned my lungs, but I ran as if driven, determined, only one image on my mind, the face of the boy in the photo, the innocent child who could still be saved. One four-year-old boy waited for us to free him. Here, this night, in this place, we had the chance to save Joey Warner from the evil that had already claimed my friend's life.

By the time we reached the tree line on the opposite side of the pasture, we backed off, paused, and waited. Listened. At our feet lay Curley Moe, his head blown away, a bull so massive that his body bulged cumbersome upon the earth, still warm from the searing hot day. Benoit had fled in such a hurry, he'd had time to draw only half a circle around the bull's remains. I thought about the forest, the darkness, how if we spread out within it, we'd become easy targets. Benoit could hide anywhere, behind any tree, watch and wait, taking his time before he opened fire. In the night, going into the woods was suicide. Every cell in my body wanted to catch Benoit and free Joey, but this wasn't smart.

"What's back there?" I asked the rancher, who had followed us, either out of instinct or fear of being left alone.

"Through those trees?" he asked, short of breath, sucking in air in a whooping sound.

"Yes. Back there, behind the woods."

"The highway. That's the way to the main road."

"Back to the chopper. Now!" I screamed, and again we were running.

I'd ordered the pilot to be ready to take off, but it took longer than I'd hoped to reach the chopper, climb on board, and lift off. Soon, we hovered just above the trees, then the pilot nosed the chopper over and we aimed in the direction of the main road. Once there, we followed it along, on a route to return to Houston, my best guess at Benoit's destination. At nearly midnight, in the rural darkness, we saw no traffic, nothing on the road, not until we'd traveled two miles from the ranch. Then, ahead, red taillights.

At first, I thought it was a van or a small bus, but as we approached from behind, I realized the vehicle was a truck, a bright red pickup with an extended cab. "The only driver on the road. That has to be him. We've got to stop him. Pull above it," I ordered the pilot. "Then turn on the lights."

As instructed, the pilot maneuvered overhead and then slowed to a hover just above the truck, tracking it along the road, with all the searchlights pointed down. I commandeered the chopper's PA system and bellowed, "Pull over. Police. Pull over, now!"

Below us, the pickup's driver laid on the gas, cranking up the speed, and the vehicle careened dangerously around a corner as we flew directly overhead, with the spotlights focused on the truck along with flashing red and blue warning lights.

"What now?" I asked the pilot. "We've got to stop him."

"Watch," he said, a grin on his face. "This is where we have fun."

Increasing the airspeed, the pilot maneuvered the chopper past the pickup, then whipped it around and again hovered, bringing the craft down until it nearly blocked the road. "This almost always works," he said as he nosed down at the road. I peered at the slowing pickup, wishing I could see through the windows, but they were coated with a thick black sun film. The truck stopped, and the pilot's grin locked in place as he lowered the chopper, getting ready to land in the center turn lane, directly in the middle of the road. That's when the pickup's driver threw the truck into reverse. It lurched backward, and it was off, backing down the road, weaving erratically between lanes while we flew forward just feet above it, trailing it down the road.

We rounded the first curve, then the next, and the driver in the pickup wound back and forth, ignoring lanes and swaying at times onto the shoulder. At the third curve in the road, the driver attempted to swing the truck into a tight U-turn, apparently to drive forward. In the process, the pickup spun out of control, nearly flipping. It landed instead with its back end hanging over a steep ditch on the side of the road. The truck's wheels spun, but it went nowhere.

The chopper put down a short distance from the red pickup, and we jumped out just in time to see someone pop a door and run, a man but no child. I ran forward and screamed, "Stop! Police!" The man sped up, sprinting full speed, heading toward the trees. Determined to stop Benoit, my anger building, I screamed, "This is over!" as I pulled the trigger, the sound waves bouncing off the road, the chopper, and the trees.

Benoit didn't fall. I'd missed. I sucked in my breath and lined up a second shot, taking my time to make sure this one brought him down, when he suddenly put up his arms and stopped running.

The others rushed forward to corner Benoit while I ran toward the pickup truck to find Joey. The passenger-side door was locked, so I rushed to the driver's door, which was gaping open. There was no one in the front seat. I looked in the back: empty. Where was the boy? Had Benoit thrown Joey out of the speeding pickup during the chase or left him in the forest?

"Lieutenant," one of the other rangers shouted, "come take a look."

"Where is he?" I screamed as I ran toward where the driver was handcuffed and on the ground. "Where's Joey Warner? What have you done with him?"

But when I looked down at the man on the road's black asphalt surface, splayed out on his back over the center line, a teenager stared back up at me, not more than fourteen, a pimply-faced kid so frightened that he'd urinated all over the front of his pants. Looking at all of us gathered around him pointing guns, thinking of nearly running the kid down with the chopper, shooting at him as he ran, I didn't blame him.

Taking a deep breath, I asked, "Who are you?"

"One of the Thompson boys," he said, his voice cracking. "Rick."

Shaking my head, I asked, "Why didn't you pull over? Why didn't you stop running? I nearly shot you."

The teenager's mouth contorted, as if to stifle a sob. "My dad doesn't know I have the truck," he said. "I didn't get permission."

The chopper pilot called the main office, asked them to get in touch with the boy's parents, and we left him there while we headed back to the pasture, where Curley Moe waited. Minutes later, we put down not far from the carcass. We weren't worried any longer about Benoit hiding and waiting or clueing him in to our presence. He knew we were there, and he was undoubtedly long gone. We'd missed our chance. We'd come close, but he'd escaped.

What we did know, because we'd seen him, was that he had Joey Warner and the boy was still alive.

"Let's take a look," I said to the others, fighting crushing disappointment. On the ground lay the bull, like the others covered in caramel-colored patches except for his side, where yet another symbol waited, etched in thick black marker.

"Benoit was here, but we lost him," I said when I got on the phone with the captain. "Tell David that we've got another symbol. I'll meet you both back at the office."

THIRTY-THREE

Sally Mae Harper had been working third shift at the twenty-four-hour Full Pantry convenience store on Telephone Road, southeast of downtown Houston, for ten years, the last five buzzing about the place on her motorized wheelchair, a necessity brought on by the advance of the diabetes she'd been fighting since middle age. At sixty-eight, she was a fully rounded woman with a pleasant smile; she could walk, but not well, and she feared falling. Her hair didn't look as realistic dyed black as it once had, but she appreciated the way it brought out her playful dark brown eyes, and she had an eyebrow pencil to make everything match. The store's owners liked Harper. She was reliable and cheerful, and the customers chatted happily with her when they stopped in. The owners were so fond of her, in fact, that when Sally took to the wheelchair, they hired a handyman to lower a section of the checkout counter eighteen inches so she could ring up orders sitting down.

One added benefit to the arrangement, in Harper's opinion, was that the lower counter put her at kid level. She loved children, always had. Would have had ten of her own if her body had held up. The way it was, she'd given birth to six, four boys and two girls. The problem was when they became teenagers. Up until then, she got along with them fine. Once they grew up, the relationships cooled. As adults, none of the six talked much to her anymore. All of them had families and jobs and not enough time for Sally, but she didn't hold that against them. To her great disappointment, Sally saw her grandchildren rarely. But none of it changed the way she felt about the little ones. If she could have, she would have given up on the adults and spent all her time with the young ones. "You should have been a kindergarten teacher," she told herself often, and never doubted that it was true.

"What're you looking for?" Harper asked the man, a tall, good-looking guy, who stood at the counter holding a little boy's hand. He was a beautiful child, light brown hair and round blue eyes. She smiled at the boy and asked, "What's your name?"

"Jo— ," the boy started.

"Please, don't talk to my son," the man said, flashing the boy an angry frown. "That's not what we're here for."

"Sorry," Harper said, thinking the man was kind of a snooty type, the kind who must have thought he was better than everyone else. Why folks had to treat other folks that way was something Harper never understood. Wasn't everyone in this mess called life together? She thought about that and wondered how hard it would be for people to just show a little common courtesy. Glancing at the boy, Harper smiled again, but this time she didn't talk. She noticed that the boy didn't have any shoes on, and his bare feet were dirty. The man's shoes were filthy, too. A glance at the floor, and she realized they were tracking clumps of mud and dirt through the store.

"Would you point us to your restroom?" the man said. "My son would like to use it."

The man *looked* like a snooty type of person, too, Harper thought. He had the face for it, those small features, a well-bred-looking nose, one he'd spent his life looking down at folks, she figured. Now he was going to walk through the store with his grubby shoes and get the floor all dirty, then probably wouldn't even buy anything. She thought about saying that to the guy, then looked at the little boy again. He looked tired and frightened, and she didn't have the heart to make his night any worse. "Back at the corner there, next to the milk and margarine," she said, pointing. She frowned at the man, irritated, then remembered he was the customer and she needed him to come back and buy groceries, or she'd be out of a job. Despite her irritation, she smiled, showing off the gap between her two upper front teeth.

"Thank you," he said, more polite this time. "Do we need a key?"

"No," she said. "It's open."

The boy and the man shuffled off toward the back of the store, and Harper thought nothing of it. She had cigarettes to stock. With folks nervous about the hurricane, water, ice, soda, chips, canned goods, beer, wine, and cigarettes were selling well, especially the alcohol and cigarettes. The store was already out of bottled water and ice and running low on everything else, although now it appeared that maybe the rush was over. Most folks were apparently done stocking up and settling in for the next day, less than twenty-four hours before the hurricane was scheduled to hit.

Thinking about how she had her own supplies well in hand at home, Harper turned her back on the cash register and stood up briefly to slip a few packs of generic menthols into the display's top rack, when she noticed something in the round mirror, shaped like a hubcap, over her head, the one that reflected the right back end of the store, near the restrooms. The man was talking to the little boy, and the kid was crying.

"Nice father," Harper jeered under her breath. "Not any nicer to his son than he is to other folks."

But there was something about the way the man was talking, cool and collected, even though the kid looked terrified. It was then that Harper saw it, when the man opened his jacket to show it to the kid, tucked in his belt, something that looked like a gun.

It's a robbery, she thought. *That psycho brought his kid with him to rob the store!*

Harper remembered reading about something like that once or seeing it on television. A dad in New Mexico brought his ten-year-old daughter to a store when he robbed it and then told the clerk he needed the cash register money to feed the girl, as if that made a hill of beans difference. Harper thought if the boy needed food, she'd be happy to give him some. She didn't want the kid to starve. But when somebody pulls a gun, there's no explanation that makes it right.

Harper turned and sat back down in her chair, then hit the release and opened the cash register. She wasn't taking any chances. She pulled out two torn dollar bills stapled together from the far left compartment in the cash drawer. Instantly, the store filled with the blare of the alarm. She watched as the man rushed toward her, carrying the boy. By then, Harper had grabbed a twelve-gauge shotgun from under the counter and cocked it.

"What's that?" the man asked. "What did you do?"

"I called for help, because you've got a gun!" she said, staring at him down the barrel of the shotgun. "You better listen up. I know how to shoot this thing, and the police are on their way. They'll be here any minute. You just stay put and don't you even think about giving this old lady any trouble."

"You stupid bitch," the man said as he backed toward the door.

"Get back here, you piece of white trash," Harper said, fuming. "You're waiting for the cops."

The man kept moving gingerly back, holding the boy in front of him as a shield, watching her, calm but focused on Harper and her shotgun. "You're not going to shoot a little kid, are you, lady? You wouldn't do that."

The boy looked petrified, his eyes big and his flesh pale. Harper gulped, thinking about what to do. She could shoot the guy and try to miss the kid, maybe wound the man enough so that he couldn't leave, but what if she missed? Here she was, nearly seven decades old, and despite what she'd told the man, Harper had never pulled the trigger of a gun, wasn't sure she could, and certainly wasn't confident that she knew how to aim the shotgun well enough to hit the right target. Feeling helpless to do anything else, she held the shotgun and watched as the man backed through the door. Before it swung shut behind them, the boy shouted at her.

"Joey!" he screamed. "My name is Joey Warner!"

At that, the man's free arm swung out from around the boy, and too late Harper realized he held the gun. "Lord help me, don't shoot!" she screamed, but by then the man had aimed at Sally Mae Harper's chest and fired.

THIRTY-FOUR

A few strokes of the keyboard in my office, and the captain, David, and I assessed the meaning of the fifth symbol, the one drawn on the hide of the fourth dead bull. In the photographs, it resembled a heart with curlicues reminding me of a silver necklace Bill gave me one Valentine's Day, not long after we married. This *Adinkra* was called *Sank ofa,* and the Web sites I found said it represented the wisdom that comes from knowing the past when planning for the future.

"So what does this mean?" the captain asked. "What's he trying to tell us?"

Not sure, I clicked the back key and returned to the list of Web sites, then clicked on another link.

"Look at that," David said, pointing farther down the computer screen. There on the new page I'd pulled up was a mention that up until recently, clothing made from fabric stamped with the symbol was reserved for funerals, and something else, a translation of the word *Adinkra:* "saying good-bye to the dead."

"This looks worse all the time." David shook his head, and there was silence. There had to be dozens of interpretations, but every one that popped into my mind threatened the life of the boy while offering no clues on how to find him. I felt my shoulders sagging, and I had a pain in my forehead, kind of a dull throb. I thought about Maggie, wondering if she'd heard about Buckshot's death on the news. By now, she and Mom were both asleep, but I made a mental note to call first thing in the morning. I needed to warn Mom, to tell her to keep the television off until I got home to tell Maggie about Buckshot myself. It all felt lost and hopeless.

"Maybe if we think about the purpose of the symbols," David said, his voice reminding me that we hadn't given up hope.

"Sarah, Benoit suggested the killer was trying to guide you, didn't he?"

"Yeah, he did," I said, wondering if any of the things the man had told me were true. Obviously he'd lied about even the essentials, including his name. "Although, as I told him, I wasn't impressed with the level of help." Thinking about what David had just said, I realized Benoit had been truthful when interpreting the symbols. I took out a piece of paper and listed all five: *Abakuá* = war; *Akoben* = a call to arms; *Aya* = I am not afraid of you; *Nosoroma* = a child of the Supreme Being; *Sank ofa* = the wisdom of learning from the past.

We stared at them, exhausted, feeling defeated, and wondering how to interpret any of the clues Benoit had left us to help us find him. "Looks like the first three were threats, declaring war, and a statement of defiance," David said. "The fourth tied him to the child, another indication of his defiance, his belief that he is superior to us, like rubbing our faces in it, saying, 'You dumb cops, look here, I'm the one who took the boy.' "

"That fits," said the captain.

"So that leaves us with *Sank ofa,* the fifth symbol, the only one that points toward an answer, suggesting we look to the past," I said, rubbing my temples, hoping to relieve some of the tension that had my forehead tied up in knots. "The question is how do we do that?"

No one spoke while we all considered what to do next. Out of ideas, exhausted by death and waste, I wanted to go home to sleep and to wake up the next morning without a hurricane bearing down on us, with Buckshot still alive and well, and with little Joey Warner safe and loved. As much as I wanted the other two, especially that Buckshot could be resurrected, of the three, there was only one goal I had a hope of accomplishing. I couldn't blow away the hurricane or breathe life into Buckshot's burned corpse, but maybe, with a little luck, I could help find the missing four-year-old.

"On the telephone, Buckshot said that the real Alex Benoit lives in a nursing home west of the city," I said, grasping the only idea that stirred my weary mind. "Perhaps he's the link to this guy's past, the one the symbol is supposed to direct us to. Maybe he ties all of this together. I know it's the middle of the night, but maybe David and I should drop in for a visit."

The two men looked at each other and shrugged. "I don't think we've got any better ideas," the captain said. "Go wake that old man up. See what you can find out. I'll be here in the office. Let me know what happens."

"This is a mandatory evacuation. Hurricane Juanita is projected to land somewhere just south of Galveston. It's the most dangerous storm to hit the Gulf Coast in decades, a category four, with current wind speeds of one hundred and forty-six miles per hour. Water surge in Galveston is expected to be twenty feet. This is a potentially catastrophic storm, a deadly hurricane, and it will flood low-lying areas not only on Galveston Island, but inland," Houston's mayor explained in a prerecorded announcement David and I listened to in the car on the way to the nursing home.

Despite the impending natural disaster, the city appeared quiet. Traffic had let up enough so the roads were navigable. Many of those who'd been ordered to leave their homes, it appeared, were already well on their way, far from the city, north and west, of the projected path of the storm. "Once Hurricane Juanita comes ashore, currently projected to be between ten and midnight Saturday night, everyone in the area is advised to take shelter. Throughout the duration of the storm, there will be no emergency services. Please, don't call 911. It will not be safe for rescue and emergency personnel to travel during the hurricane, so they have been ordered not to respond. Only after the hurricane passes through our area will emergency services restart."

I looked at the clock in the Tahoe: 2:36. That was A.M. Once the storm hit in approximately nineteen hours, David and I, like everyone else, would have to put our lives and our work on hold to stay safe and ride out the hurricane. As it trekked in from the Gulf of Mexico, the full force of the storm would hit Galveston and the southern reaches of the city first. There it would be at its most deadly. Once on land, Juanita would slowly weaken but still be a formidable storm, with more than hundred-mile-per-hour winds, torrential rains, flooding, and the threat of spawning lines of deadly tornadoes. Thinking about the days ahead, I decided it was time to ask David something I'd been considering. "Mom has Bobby staying at the ranch through the storm," I said. "The land is high, and we don't flood. And the hurricane will lose some steam before it hits us. If you'd like to, you're welcome to ride it out on a cot in the living room."

David eyed me.

"Plus, my guess is that you've been too busy to prepare, buy supplies, and we have," I said. "Mom and Maggie have stocked up. We've got water, food, everything we'll need."

"Is that it?" David asked with a questioning smile. "Those are your only reasons? Just my personal safety?"

"Yeah," I said, finally admitting, "Pretty much, I guess, under the circumstances, not really knowing where we stand, those are my motives."

David appeared not to know what to say. "I'm sorry, Sarah. I know this is tough. It is for me, too," he said, his voice hoarse and tired. "But you're right. Things are kind of uncertain. Maybe I'd better just plan on staying at my place during the storm. Until this is all straightened out between us, I'm not sure it would feel right to act like part of the family."

"Sure, but that wasn't what I was suggesting, that you're part of the family," I said, sorry I'd brought up the subject. "I was just offering a safer place during the storm."

"I know. I really do. And I know we need to talk, and I need to decide what I'm doing. Until we do, maybe we shouldn't subject Maggie to this."

"That's true," I said, disappointed but seeing his logic. "You're right. Now's probably not a good time for you to camp out at the ranch."

Taking my hand, he asked, "Just give me until all this quiets down, to think things through?"

"Okay," I said. Maybe I should have stopped there, but I didn't. "But part of me wonders, if we were really right for each other, would this be a hard decision?"

David looked at me, his eyes sad, and just shook his head. "I don't know. What I am sure of is that I do care about you. But right now, I can't think about us. There's too much going on. Sarah, I need time."

"Yeah," I said, feeling much the same way despite my need to know. "That I can understand."

The rest of the short trip was made in silence, until we neared the nursing home. Then David turned to me and said, "Sarah, it wasn't your fault, you know."

"My fault?" I said.

"Buckshot," he answered. "What happened wasn't your fault."

The captain had said the same thing, but I'd been thinking about that, about all the things I could have, perhaps should have, done differently. No matter what, I never should have walked out on Buckshot, leaving him to investigate the case alone. Yet in a sense, it seemed like a perfect storm, the hurricane making it impossible for him to get backup, the missing boy, the ranchers demanding action on the dead longhorns, so many events that had all conspired to transport Buckshot to the plantation. But I was the one who'd dumped the case in his lap as I ran out the door to help David find the four-year-old. Would it have changed things if I had been with Buckshot?

"I know Buckshot's murder wasn't my fault," I said to David, my voice tight, betraying an overwhelming sadness. "But I'm not sure I'll ever stop feeling guilty about walking out on him, handing him the case."

"You can't be sure that being there would have changed anything," David reasoned. "And if you hadn't been at the Warner house to see the symbol left on the doorstep and connect the dots, we might never have linked the two cases and figured out who had the kid."

"All true," I said, my heart heavy with regret. "But I still walked out on my friend, and now he's dead. And we'll never know if my being there could have saved him."

We pulled up in front of Weldon Manor Nursing Home, a gray stucco structure with white trim, and parked under the porte cochere. At the entrance, David reached out to open the door, but it was locked. "The middle of the night, that's smart," he said, reaching over to ring a bell.

Moments passed, and then from somewhere inside, a voice said, "Yes. May I help you?"

Thirty-Five

"It's highly unusual for someone to visit this time of the night," said the reed-thin woman with dark chocolate skin as she escorted us into the nursing home. "I'm sure the nursing home's director won't be happy about this. I mean, couldn't it have waited until morning?"

"No," David and I said in unison.

The woman frowned, drawing harder on the right, giving her face an uneven look. "Oh," she said. "Okay. But you're going to have to wait until I wake Professor Benoit and help him out of bed."

We did as instructed, in the beige hallway with framed prints of forest scenes on the walls. Exhausted, I leaned on the railing, the one residents undoubtedly used during the day to prop themselves up when walking or to pull themselves along in their wheelchairs. The place smelled of antiseptic, and it looked clean, if not homey. A short time later, the nurse returned and motioned us inside.

"Please don't stay too long," she requested. "It's late, and he needs his sleep. He's a rather frail old man."

"I heard that, Isabelle," shouted a gravelly voice from inside the room.

"Well, it's true, Professor," she answered.

"Yes, but is truth always a defense?" the voice prodded. "I like to think of myself as merely age-disadvantaged."

"Frail and ornery," the nurse said as she turned to leave. Facing back toward the professor's open door, she added, "And I hope you heard that, too!"

Inside the small room sat an elderly man with trim white hair. Nestled in a corner chair, a recliner, with his feet propped up, he chuckled softly, as if the enjoyment of the exchange with his night nurse lingered. The room was dark except for a long fluorescent light-bulb glowing over the bed, turned on with a pull cord. The light illuminated the right side of Professor Benoit's craggy face but left the rest in shadow.

"Come in," he said, his voice strong, even if his body was withered with age. "Come in, please, closer where I can see you. The nurse says you're police officers?"

"Yes," I said, leaning down to shake his hand. "Professor Benoit, I'm a Texas Ranger, Lieutenant Sarah Armstrong, and this is FBI Special Agent David Garrity."

"Well, isn't that impressive," he said, taking my hand, then David's, and grasping them warmly. "I'd say happy to meet you, but it is the middle of the night and there's a hurricane coming, so I'd rather ask, why are you here?"

"You are Alex Benoit, who was a professor at Tulane University?" I asked. "You're an expert in African symbolism?"

"Yes." He may have once been a tall man, but he was so bent over with age, crumpled, it was impossible to tell. "I am Dr. Benoit from Tulane. And again, because it's very late, and I'm very tired, why are you here?"

"We have a sketch we'd like you to look at," David said, pulling my drawing of the man who'd called himself Alex Benoit from an envelope. "Please, does this person look familiar to you?"

The old man took the sketch in a twisted, disfigured arthritic hand, the joints swollen and painfully askew. "My glasses, please," he said, motioning toward the nightstand. David grabbed the round wire frames and began to hand them to the man, then thought better of it and opened them up and helped him slip them on. The elderly man appeared not to notice, as if at peace with such concessions for his age. In the dim light, he looked at the drawing, and soon he closed his eyes and lowered his head, enveloped in a deep sadness. The hand that held the paper sank to his lap.

"What has he done?"

"You know this man?" I asked.

"Unless there's some other explanation, this drawing resembles my son, Peter," he said. "He's why I moved to Houston, to be closer to him, so he could watch over me in my old age. That was a mistake. I knew he was troubled, but I didn't really understand what he was capable of. If I had, I would have stayed far away. In all honesty, I believe the boy is mad."

"Why would you say that?" David asked. "What did he do?"

"I was only living with him for a little more than a month, when he tried to kill me," the old man said with a slight shudder, bringing his trembling right hand up to his forehead and pressing his palm above his eyes. "I would be dead now if it weren't for the doctor who discovered I was being poisoned."

"Why?" I asked.

"Why?" he repeated, his faded, aged eyes

glancing up at me, questioning. "What are you asking?"

"Why did your son try to kill you? For money? Out of anger?"

The old man shook his head gently, and I saw confusion. "Who knows? I don't know. I have no money. I live here on a long-term-care insurance policy, or I wouldn't be able to afford such a nice place. My university pension is small, and it ends when I die. I have little else."

"Don't you have some idea?" David asked. "Why would he try to kill his own father? Something must have happened?"

The old man appeared at a loss for words, then simply shook his head and said, "In a place like this, you have a lot of time to consider the past. I've done that, and I've only come up with one answer to your question. I think my son wanted to kill me so he could watch me die."

We learned that Alex Benoit had taught his son African symbolism, but in many ways, Peter's studies were a disappointment. He'd barely finished high school. Although exceptionally bright, he was unable to focus on his studies and had gotten in trouble even as a boy, fights and angry outbursts. Most frightening, he'd once tied up a neighborhood girl for half a day and kept her hidden in a garage, while his parents and the girl's mother scoured the neighborhood, searching for her.

"We did realize after that incident that Peter was disturbed. My wife and I thought we'd addressed his problems. For years, we sent Peter to therapy. The psychiatrist told us Peter had changed, that he was no longer dangerous. The therapist described what had happened with the girl simply as Peter acting out a natural curiosity, kind of a coming-of-age, where a boy searches for control and power. He said Peter had learned that his actions were inappropriate. We had no further such incidents," Benoit said, again dropping his head and closing his eyes in deep sadness. "Peter grew up and moved on, and my wife and I traveled often. We spent a lot of time in Africa for my work. The result was that we saw less and less of our son. We heard he worked in restaurants in New Orleans for a long while. I don't know that he forged any real relationships. I don't believe he ever married or had a child, although I'm not certain. We saw him rarely. Four years ago, my wife died, on her deathbed lamenting that our only child hadn't found his place in the world."

"How did you end up in Houston?" I

asked. "Why would you come to be near him, if you so rarely even saw him?"

"After his mother's death, Peter called and reconnected with me. We rebuilt our relationship, or at least I thought we did," the professor said, his aging face taut with worry and his eyes wet. "I lived alone in our old home, and I began falling and needed help, and Peter sounded so kind. It was such a relief to have him in my life, especially when he offered to take me in and watch over me. I moved to Houston and into his apartment with him. He was working then, lunches and at night, waiting tables in a little restaurant, and we had my pension and Social Security check. At first, all was well, but before long, I grew ill. One day, when Peter wasn't home, I asked a neighbor to take me to a physician with a nearby office. I'd been asking Peter to, but he never had time. The poison showed up on my bloodwork, and as soon as the doctor called, I knew immediately that Peter hadn't changed. If anything, he was worse."

The old man hadn't seen his son in more than two years, not since the murder attempt. He didn't know where he'd been living and couldn't help us with ideas about where his son could be found. "There's only one thing I can do for you. I have a photograph of Peter on file at the front desk, along with instructions warning that security is to be called if he comes to visit me. Take the photograph. Perhaps it will help," the old man said, reaching out and taking my hand. He held it and looked into my eyes. "Can you imagine being terrified of your own son?"

Thirty-Six

We stopped at the desk and picked up Peter Benoit's photograph from the night nurse, then commandeered the nursing home fax machine to send it to my office. "We'll have this out ASAP, and we'll start running records on Peter Benoit. Now that we have the right name, maybe we'll be lucky and get a car description and license number. Anything that could help us spot him on the road, recognize him with the boy, could help," the captain said when we followed up with a phone call. "Good news from the lab, by the way. They found a couple of latent fingerprints on pieces of the glass from the plantation."

"That is good news," I said. Although we'd identified the man and had his real name, in a courtroom, when Benoit was tried for Buckshot's murder — a day I looked forward to — the fingerprints would be evidence. "Anything else for us?"

"Yeah. I know you're both tired, but we have a lead down in the medical center, a convenience store clerk. She was shot, and the woman says the guy who did it had a little boy with him. They fit the description, and the boy said his name was Joey Warner."

Hooked up to a web of machines, Sally Mae Harper lay beneath the hospital emergency room's bright lights, their harshness leaching the color from her skin and calling attention to her dyed black hair. Nurses circulated in and out, and Harper's blood pressure was being tracked, along with her oxygen and pulse, a heart monitor recording every beat. "It's amazing that she survived. If that bullet had been a quarter of an inch to the right, it would have sliced through her aorta. She'd pulled the alarm, and police were on their way. Otherwise, she would have bled to death," the young ER doc told us when we arrived. "I'm telling you all of this because I need both of you to understand that my patient is very weak. Based on her medical condition, I was against her talking to you, but she insisted. She wants to help you find the boy."

As soon as we introduced ourselves, Sally Mae started right in, breathlessly detailing her encounter with the man and the boy that led up to her shooting. She described both Benoit and Joey to a tee, but I'd taken the precaution of pulling together a photo spread on my laptop, including the photo of his son that Alex Benoit had just given us. On my computer screen, I showed the woman six different middle-aged white men.

"Do any of these men look familiar?" David asked.

"That's the guy," Harper said, hacking and wheezing, holding her hands against her chest, as if to quell the pain. She pointed at Benoit's photo. "He's the creep who shot me."

I then pulled up a snapshot of Joey on the screen. "And that's the kid," she said. "Really sweet-looking boy. He looked so scared. That poor baby. Made my heart hurt to look at him like that, so upset."

"Anything else you remember that could help us?" I said. "Did you see a car? Anything?"

"The man was really stuck-up, not nice. The boy was barefoot," she said. "And the man . . . well, he had shoes, but both of them, the boy and the man, too, tracked mud into the place. I was pretty ticked off, figuring I was going to have to clean it up. The man must have had a car, but I didn't see it."

Turning to me, David said, "I'm going to duck out and call the captain. Maybe that dirt's from the pasture where the fourth bull was killed earlier tonight. Let's get forensics to take samples at the store."

"Good idea," I said.

David left, and I stayed with Harper, listening as she recounted the events in full, flinching when she talked about the crack of the gunfire and the burst of pain as the bullet entered her chest.

"Does the convenience store have surveillance cameras?"

"Yeah," Harper said, getting excited. One of her monitors beeped urgently, I couldn't tell which. "You should get the video. That'll help! That's a great idea. I should have told you about that first thing."

"Mrs. Harper, calm down. We will get it," I assured her as a nurse ran into the room to investigate. "Believe me, we will."

A second phone call to the detective handling the case, and we learned that he had already confiscated a video from inside the store, from a camera pointed at the counter and cash register. But there was a hitch: A second camera, one that scanned the parking lot, was out of order. It had been for months. Since the place had never been robbed, the store owner had procrastinated about spending the money to get it fixed.

"Let's hope Benoit parked close enough to the building for the inside camera to nail the car," I said as David and I drove to the major crimes division on Lockwood, where the Houston PD detective in charge of the shooting case had taken the video, at our request. At nearly six A.M., it remained dark, but a glimmer of light shone east of the city. In another hour it would be daylight, and out in the Gulf, the hurricane trudged ever closer. We passed through downtown, usually bustling early in the morning, even on a weekend, but on this Saturday it remained quiet, with few lights shining inside the skyscrapers that loomed overhead. Everywhere we drove, the streets were nearly empty. "It's so deserted, we could land a chopper on these streets," I said, and David nodded. What neither of us said was something we both understood: we were running out of time.

In Houston, the weather remained unseasonably hot and muggy, with a slight breeze barely ruffling the trees, but a radio announcer described Galveston as experiencing the first signs of the approaching storm. "The waters are rising along the Seawall," she cautioned. "In four more hours, everyone needs to be off the island, as authorities predict flooding will make the causeway impassable."

In the robbery division, the HPD detective cued up the video from the store and pushed play. On the screen, a man and a boy walked into the store, while Harper, behind the counter, sat in her wheelchair. They approached her, and the three of them talked momentarily, Harper gesturing toward the back of the store, as she'd told us she had, indicating the location of the bathroom. The man nodded, his head down, as if trying to shield it from the cameras he must have assumed would be pointed at him. But while Benoit ducked the cameras, Joey, bless his heart, looked straight up at them. He stared sadly at Harper and therefore directly into the camera above her, as if willing her to recognize him.

"You can't see a car in the parking lot," David pointed out, running his fingers over the window area visible on the screen. "Benoit kept it far enough back to make sure you couldn't."

"Yeah," I said. "If the parking lot camera had been working, it would have picked up the car. Our luck, the parking lot camera is broken and this video doesn't help."

On the screen, Harper filled the cigarettes

and then turned, suddenly alarmed. She opened the cash register and pulled out the bills that triggered the alarm. Instantly, Benoit rushed forward, using the boy as a shield. Meanwhile, Harper wielded the shotgun. "It would have been poetic justice if she'd fired that thing at his head," I said.

"She did the right thing, Sarah," David cautioned. "She could have hit the boy."

"Sure," I said. "Of course, you're right."

In the video, it appeared Benoit intended only to flee, until Joey said his name, then Benoit's hand swung out with the gun, fired, and he turned and ran, while Sally Mae Harper collapsed in her wheelchair, her body slack. She held up a hand to her chest, and when she pulled it away, it was covered in blood.

"We catch him, this'll work in court on the shooting," David said. "But how's it going to help us find him?"

"It's not," I said, dismissing it as another lost lead.

Moments later, the captain called. Buckshot's autopsy was completed, and as we'd expected, he was dead when Benoit set him on fire. "No soot in his trachea," the captain explained. "And they found a gunshot wound in the back of the skull."

"Have you notified his family yet?" I asked.

"Yeah," he said. "The daughter took it hard. We had a couple of counselors from the university go over to tell her. She's coming in after the storm to make arrangements. Once the hurricane passes, the ex-wife is planning to fly in from California for the funeral."

I thought about the conversation I'd had with Buckshot standing over the first longhorn, about Peggy and his disappointment that she'd left him. He'd be happy that she was coming home to bury him. I had the impression he'd never stopped loving her. Maybe, despite everything, including the new millionaire husband, she still had some love in her heart for Buckshot.

"Great," I said sadly. "The least we can do is give Buckshot a good send-off."

"By then, we better have the crazy bastard who murdered him behind bars," the captain added.

"Let's hope," I said. "On that end, anything to help us?"

"Not really," the captain admitted. The captain had found no car registration records or driver's license in Texas for a Pete or Peter Benoit, so we still didn't have a license number or a description of a car to go out with the alert asking officers to be on the lookout for Benoit. "We're checking Louisiana," Captain Williams said. "But being a weekend, it may take a while. We've got other folks on this now. While you're waiting, you two should get some rest. It's been a long night without sleep."

It wasn't what David and I wanted to do, but there seemed little choice. The sun was up, the storm lurked offshore, and neither of us had slept in more than twenty-four hours. I called the ranch. "We're just finishing up, Mom," I said. "What's going on there?"

"Frieda, Maggie, and I are done with breakfast," she said. "We're going to keep battening down the hatches. This morning, we're nailing the shutters on the stable shut."

"Anything you need?" I asked. "Anything I can do?"

"No, Sarah," she said. "We're okay. We really are."

"I think David and I will stay downtown for a while, then grab some breakfast and see if any new leads come in," I said. "I'll drive out to the ranch late this afternoon, in plenty of time to beat the storm."

"That's fine, but just don't wait too long," Mom cautioned. With that she lowered her voice, confiding, "Maggie's been asking for you. We saw about Sergeant Buckshot on the news this morning, and she got pretty upset. That poor man. It's awful, so awful."

"I know," I said, wishing I'd remembered to call and warn Mom before Buckshot's murder hit the news. "It is."

"The sergeant's death and that darn hurricane, I'm thinking maybe Maggie's getting a little scared. The weather reports look pretty bad, and she's been watching nonstop. I finally made her turn off the television. But most of all, I think, she's worried about you. She keeps asking where you are and when you'll be home. Sarah, it wouldn't be good if you were stuck somewhere and not here when the bad weather hits."

"I'll be there," I said, again thinking about Maggie. Under the best of circumstances, cops' kids worry. They grow up knowing instinctively that a job that requires their mom or dad to strap on a gun every day isn't, by definition, safe. Thinking about Maggie at the ranch, anxious about the storm and perhaps even more about what danger I might be in, especially now that a ranger she grew up knowing was dead, his body on a slab at the county morgue, I had a hard time not feeling guilty. I wondered, not for the first time, if my job was at all fair to my daughter.

Worn out, David and I went to his house in the Heights, where he made bacon, eggs, and English muffins while we reviewed everything we'd done, everything we knew about the case, looking for some way to figure out where Benoit would take Joey. Shelters were set up north and west of the city, and David wondered if he'd take the boy there, where they could blend in and hide in the masses of evacuees forced from their homes. There they'd be just faces in the crowd.

"I don't think so," I said. "Benoit has something planned. Something he's working toward. Otherwise why all the symbols, all the prep work to get here?"

"But maybe the hurricane's changed his mind. Made him postpone," David offered. "Maybe he's had to come up with a new plan?"

Before I could, David answered his own question. "No," he said. "Joey was abducted on Wednesday afternoon. By then the hurricane was already in the Gulf and there was a good chance it would hit here. Some of the experts were already predicting that conditions were right and Galveston was a likely target. This is a guy who pays attention, who works things out. He knew the hurricane could be coming, if not here, close. Somehow, he didn't think it would affect his plans."

A few moments of silence, and then I threw out another possibility. "Maybe it's part of his plan."

"What is?" David asked.

"The hurricane."

Again, we considered. Instead of brainstorming ideas, we kept quiet, each of us trying to understand the distorted mind of a dangerous killer. I thought back to our meeting with Peter Benoit's father and the mention he'd made of the day his son held a child hostage. The elder Benoit had made the event sound relatively unimportant. The girl hadn't been molested or abused. David and I had endured a long, hard, emotional day, and perhaps we weren't thinking as clearly as usual. I began second-guessing, wondering if we should have asked more questions. I picked up my cell phone and called the nursing home, asking the nurse on duty to patch me through to Dr. Benoit's room.

I waited what felt like an eternity before Benoit's voice was on the telephone, then turned on the speaker so David could listen. "Yes, Lieutenant. And how may I help you?"

"Dr. Benoit, I want you to tell Agent Garrity and me more about that little girl, the one your son tied up and kept hidden," I said. "I believe you said he kept her in a garage?"

"Yes, he did," the old man said. "But is this really necessary? How can it help you?"

"I don't know," I admitted. "But we have nothing else to work with."

We could hear the old man sigh. "What do you want to know?"

"Anything you can tell us," I suggested. "Whatever comes to mind about that day."

The old man was silent. These were painful memories of an event he had no desire to relive, but slowly he began talking, his voice ragged with emotion. That morning, the professor had classes, and he returned home early. "It was spring," he explained. "I thought I'd get my wife and son, take them for a ride in the countryside. Abigail, my wife, always loved that. She said a change of scenery made her feel like she'd had a little vacation, time away to reawaken her senses."

"What happened when you got home?" David asked.

"Well, I couldn't find anyone. The house was empty," the professor said, sounding as tentative as he must have felt that day. "I called out for Abigail and Peter, but no one answered. Peter was about twelve at that time, and he'd been in a little trouble, but nothing important, nothing serious. I never thought . . . I never thought anything truly bad could happen, that he was capable of hurting anyone."

"Go on," I urged. "Tell me what you saw."

"I was home only a few minutes when a neighbor woman rang the doorbell. She asked if my wife was home yet, explaining that Abby had gone to drive the neighborhood in our old Ford station wagon, looking for the woman's daughter, that the girl was missing. She was a pretty little thing, four or five, all blue eyes and dark blond, or maybe kind of light brown hair."

I thought of Joey, a boy who fit that same description.

"Anyway, I told the woman I hadn't seen my wife, that she wasn't home when I arrived," the professor continued. "We walked out onto the front porch to wait. While we stood there, the neighbor woman explained that her daughter had been missing for much of the day. The woman started crying. I tried to calm her, but she was inconsolable. Very afraid. Very worried, not knowing where the girl could have gone or what could have happened to her."

"Keep going. What occurred next?" I asked.

"Abby drove down the street in our car, then pulled up in front of our house and parked," Benoit explained. "As the woman said, my wife had been riding through the neighborhood, helping to search. She hadn't seen the child, and she looked upset as well. Looking back, maybe I had a hunch, a sense that somehow our son was involved. I asked Abby where Peter was, and she said that he'd told her earlier in the day that he'd be playing baseball at the park. I remember being pleasantly surprised, since he had so few friends. The boy was something of a loner, even back then."

"You said he was how old?" David asked.

"Twelve," the professor said. "Peter was about twelve, a handsome child but quiet, and always very much to himself."

"Did you help the women search?" I wanted to know.

"Yes, I did," the professor said. "Actually, before long, we had nearly every parent on the block looking for the girl. They were circulating through the streets, talking to other children, but no luck. We thought maybe she'd wandered off. We called the police, and a couple of officers were sent in a squad car to the neighbor woman's house.

They took a picture of the girl out of a frame to use to identify her, and that's when the woman became hysterical. 'You think she's dead,' she screamed. 'You think my daughter is dead.' It was horrible."

At that, the professor grew silent, lost in his memories. "How did you find Peter and the girl?" David asked.

"I didn't. My wife did," he explained. "It had been a wet spring in New Orleans, more so than usual, and the bayous were high. It had rained the day before, torrential rains, and the pumps hadn't been able to keep up. The water was rising. The Corps of Engineers had said they were going to fix it, but while we lived there it was a constant problem. I don't know if they ever did. The bayou backed up often, but especially so that spring. My wife and I had spent a lot of time worrying about the rising water, talking back and forth, wondering if the bayou would overflow and the water would make its way toward the house, perhaps flood our home." He drifted off, as if having a difficult time focusing, continuing with his story.

"Go on, Professor," I prodded. "Please."

"Yes. Of course," he said. "So that afternoon, after we'd spent hours looking for the girl, we gave up. Abby and I were both upset, worried about the child, and I went in the house to change from the clothes I'd worn to the university that day. Meanwhile, my wife said she wanted to check on the bayou. She walked back through the trees, to see how high the water was, how much it had risen with the latest rain. Abby was gone a few minutes, and I had thrown on some clothes. The bedroom window was open, and I heard her scream."

The old man stopped. The longer he talked, the more ragged his voice became, the more agonizing it must have been to relive those moments. "Please, Professor," I urged. "I need you to tell me everything. Please continue."

For a moment, only silence. "Why?" the old man finally asked. "Why does this matter now? I'm sorry about your friend, that my son might be responsible for murdering that ranger, but how can this help?"

At the nursing home, David and I had told the old man only that his son was a suspect in the murder of a Texas Ranger. We didn't tell him that he was also a suspect in a kidnapping. I'm not sure why, other than that the professor was already so upset and appeared so fragile that we took pity on him, thinking there'd be time enough in the future for him to hear the whole story. But now, I had no choice. "We believe your son has abducted a young boy," I said.

Again, a horrible silence. "Another child. He's taken another child?"

"Yes, so I need to know what happened to the little girl," I said softly. "And I need to know now."

"Oh," he said, more a grunt than a word. "Well, I understand. I do. Another child. A boy."

"Yes, a little boy named Joey Warner, about the same age as the girl you've been telling me about, four, with light brown hair and large blue eyes," I said. I gave him a moment to understand fully, then urged him, "So pick up your story. Tell me what happened."

I heard a long, deep breath, then: "I ran, following my wife's screams to the bayou. The earth was wet from the recent rain, and it was slippery. I had on an old pair of shoes with smooth soles, and I lost my footing, tumbling down the slope behind the house, as I reached the woods. When I got to the bayou, I was covered in mud. It was then that I saw the girl. I didn't understand at first why she was in the water, why she was so still. Then I saw the ropes. She was tied up, wrists and ankles, to tree branches extended along the bank. She had her head up, trying to keep above the water, to breathe."

Again a brief pause, then he went on. "Peter stood just above the waterline, with my wife screaming something I couldn't understand. I realized she was trying to get to the girl, but our son was pushing his mother back. It may seem odd, but at first I didn't comprehend what was happening. Then I realized that he'd been sitting on the bank, watching the water rise, waiting for the child to drown. He had a strange look in his eyes, an emptiness."

"What happened next?" David asked.

"I ran toward the water, grabbed Peter's arms, pulling him off of my wife. Once she was free, my wife rushed into the bayou and untied the child, rescuing her from the water. The girl kept gasping for air, and my wife wailed and screamed at our son, 'What did you do? Why? Why? Why?' The poor little girl, the beautiful child, cried as if the world were ending. I carried her to our home. She felt wet and heavy in my arms, and she sobbed, her face pressed up against my muddy shirt."

Such horrible memories from agonizing days long past.

"Why drowning?" David asked.

"Pardon me?" the professor asked, sounding confused.

"Agent Garrity wonders why your son would try to drown the girl," I explained. "Did something happen, anything at all, that in any way helps this make sense?"

Benoit again seemed reluctant to continue, but then he began talking, his words a slow, aching progression. "When Peter was a toddler, about three, I believe, my wife once went to answer the phone while she was bathing him. She was gone only minutes, but somehow he slipped, and when she walked back into the room, our son was unconscious, facedown under the water," he said. "Abigail was a registered nurse. She began CPR and resuscitated him, but for a short time Peter wasn't breathing. We talked of it often, and he grew up fascinated with that story, how for a few brief moments he didn't have a heartbeat."

I wished again that we'd asked more questions sooner, but at least now we understood. "I thought that you said the girl was kept in the garage and that she wasn't hurt," I pointed out.

"Well, what I'd said was that she hadn't been molested, and what I'd meant by unhurt was that she'd suffered no permanent scars. Reconsidering, I admit that it was an unfortunate word choice. Perhaps I should have said no physical scars," he said. "But, as I told you, Peter had kept the girl in the garage. Our son told us that was what he'd done up until shortly before we found him at the bayou, and we later found evidence that suggested that was true, including the remainder of the rope he used to tie her."

"Was this reported to the police?" David asked.

"No, which was now, perhaps, in hindsight, a mistake," he said. "At the time, we thought it would never happen again. We moved away, which is what the girl's mother wanted to keep what happened quiet. She didn't want her child's name sullied, people speculating what Peter had done to the girl, so she was amenable to keeping the event a secret between our two families."

"So you left and never spoke of it again?" I asked.

"Not exactly. As I told you, we did take Peter to counseling, years of therapy," he said. "And it seemed to be the correct decision, when nothing else terrible happened. Nothing, at least, as far as we ever knew. Not until my son attempted to murder me."

"Did you report that to the police? When your son tried to murder you, what did you do?"

Again a pause. "No. I didn't tell anyone," he said, his voice a hoarse whisper. "I just wanted to get away. I moved to this nursing home and gave instructions not to admit him. And I tried to forget."

"So what do we take away from that?" David asked after we thanked the professor and hung up. "Is Peter Benoit going to drown Joey? And if so, is the hurricane part of his plan?"

"I don't know, David," I said, pacing his dining room. "I just don't know. Some of this doesn't make sense to me."

"Maybe the hurricane is simply playing into his hands. He'd already made up the plan, fashioned the symbols he'd leave as clues, and when the hurricane changed course and headed toward Galveston and Houston, he decided to take advantage of it."

"Maybe," I said. "But why now? If he's had this fantasy, why did he wait until now? Why aren't there other victims?"

"I don't know. Maybe there are, and we just haven't tied him to the cases yet," David said. "Maybe Joey's the first. Maybe we'll never know."

"What about those unidentified kids, the ones I did the facial reconstructions on? We don't know cause of death, but they're the right age and race." I'd thought about them often since the Warner case began, wondering if they could be connected.

"They're so different, skeletons found in fields, none of this staging with the bulls and the symbols. Age and race are the only factors connecting them," David said. "I don't know. Could be, I guess, but I don't know."

I thought about that for a few minutes, digested it. "Maybe it doesn't matter right now. Maybe this isn't the time to think about it," I said. "All that's important is that for whatever reason, Peter Benoit has Joey, and he's playing some kind of hideous game."

I thought about what we'd learned and wondered what it all meant, if it told us anything useful, especially about where Benoit had the boy.

"So what we do know is that this guy is into drama, right?" David offered. "The symbols, all this ritual, including the sacrificing of the bulls. It's all a grand play. Some kind of theater he's constructing by mixing what he knows from his father's work in African culture with his own fantasy of murder, drowning, and death."

"I guess," I said. Then, after more thought,

"Yes, of course, that's true."

"So where would you go? What would you do to heighten the drama?" he asked. "In the middle of a hurricane, if you wanted the setting to give the biggest thrill, where would you take the boy to drown him?"

Thirty-Seven

"Galveston PD has a dozen officers available to help us, part of a squad who stayed behind to ride out the hurricane, to prevent looting," the captain said when David and I returned to my office. The reports on the radio still pegged Juanita as a category four, with winds nearing 150 miles per hour. It was nearly noon, and the hurricane stalked the island and Houston, ten hours from shore.

"This is crazy," I argued. "Even if David is right about Benoit taking the boy to Galveston, what are the odds that you'll find him? You don't know where to look. He could be anywhere. The West End, the Strand, on the Seawall. You don't even know what kind of car he's driving."

"We'll figure it out on the way or when we get there," David insisted. "We've only got another hour or two to get over the causeway. The winds are picking up and it's already growing dangerous. Once the water rises, we'll be out of luck."

The idea of driving into Galveston, where the storm would come ashore, felt crazy. Juanita would be at full bore, loaded for destruction. "We don't know. We don't know that Benoit has Joey there. This is all conjecture, a guess. But if you're both going, then I should go, too," I said. "We'll take separate cars, spread out. My coming gives you another set of eyes."

"No," the captain said. "Absolutely not."

"Yes," I countered. I thought about Maggie, wondered how she'd fare without me through the storm. But there was a little boy's life at stake, an innocent child I had no doubt Peter Benoit intended to murder. Maggie had Mom, Bobby, and Frieda to comfort her through the storm. Joey Warner was in the hands of a madman. "I'll go. I insist. I won't take no for an answer."

The captain's glare didn't bode well. "You will take no for an answer, because this time, Sarah, it's not a suggestion, it's an outright order," he bellowed, glowering down at me from the advantage of his extra foot in height. "And this is one order you won't ignore, Lieutenant. I won't have it. You're not going."

"Captain, let's talk about this. I should be there."

With that, David moved forward and took my hands. "Listen, Sarah," he said, softer. "This isn't negotiable. The captain is right. First, we don't need you. Second, Maggie does. She's already upset about Buckshot. You can't do that to the kid, not on a hunch, not when we have no real evidence Benoit has taken the boy to the island, that we'll even be able to find them if they are in Galveston."

"But this is all we've got, our only lead. Nothing solid, just suspicion, I know, but it's something," I argued. "And if we don't find Joey, he'll die. We've got to stop Benoit. We have to bring him back to pay for Buckshot's murder. Why else would Benoit take the boy except to drown him the way he intended to murder the little girl? To watch Joey die the way he wanted to watch his father die? Why else?"

"Okay, it's a bad situation. The captain and I get that," David said, appearing increasingly angry about my insistence. "But this time, this one time, you're going to sit this one out. You need to trust us that we're going to do our best to save Joey Warner. You're needed at home. This one time you're going to ignore the fact that you're a Texas Ranger and remember that you're a mom. There's a hurricane coming, and you need to put Maggie first."

"That's not fair," I said. I knew what they were doing, playing the woman card, expecting me to go home. There were times I kind of played it myself, I had to admit, when being one of the only two women rangers in the entire state got me what I wanted. But this time, that wasn't what I had in mind. Sure I was scared. No one wants to drive into the eye of the storm. And I was worried about Maggie. I wanted nothing more than to be with her, to help her through Buckshot's death and assure her that I was safe, to watch over her. But there was a missing boy, a little kid in danger. "I have as much right to continue on in this investigation as you do. And I have never expected either of you to cover for me, ever."

"We know," the captain said. "That's not what's going on here."

"But the truth is that you don't have standing in this case. You were never invited in. You asked to work the case," David said, his eyes intent on mine. "This is my case, and, Lieutenant Armstrong, I don't need you."

The captain glanced uncomfortably down at his desk, then back up at me and shook his head, impatient. "We're wasting time. With the storm coming, we can't fly in. We need to get out of here now and get across the causeway before it closes. We're leaving, and you're staying behind, Lieutenant. And this conversation is over."

With that, the captain turned to leave, and I gave it one more try. "You need me there," I shouted. "Captain, you need me there."

"No, Lieutenant." About to rush through the door, he turned back to confront me. "We need you at home with your daughter until the hurricane blows over. God knows we shouldn't be driving into that monster storm, either, but someone has to. If there were another way, none of us would go, but there isn't, and we are, and you, Lieutenant? You're going home. That's an order."

With nothing left to argue, I grabbed David as he rushed out. "Call me. Let me know," I insisted.

"As soon as there's anything to tell," he said. "As long as the phones are working."

"And stay safe, both of you," I shouted. But by then, they were gone.

Thirty-Eight

I considered heading straight home, and I got on the freeway heading north. There seemed to be a new wave of stragglers bunching up, trying to get on and off the expressways, maybe those who'd procrastinated and then, at the last minute, based on the size of the storm on their television screens, nervously decided to leave. I went one slow mile before reevaluating and instead turning on my siren and heading back downtown. Sitting in traffic, I'd decided on one last stop, a detour to the county jail, where Crystal had been taken to ride out the storm until her bail could be set.

On the way, I called the ranch, hoping to reach Maggie. But Mom answered and told me she was out in the barn. "How's my daughter?" I asked.

"Still asking for you," Mom said. "But okay. Hanging in there."

"I'll be home soon," I assured her. "Within a couple of hours."

After that, I called Evan Warner and asked him to meet me at the jail. I waited half an hour or so before he walked in with his parents. The Warners all looked as fatigued and anxious as I felt. The jail's lobby was nearly empty, just a skeleton crew on, guards and personnel who were preparing the building for the hurricane and making plans to keep the facility secure throughout the storm. After Evan and his parents placed their belongings in lockers and I checked my Colt .45 at security, we walked through the scanners and then toward a rear elevator we took upstairs to the women's floor. When we arrived, I asked to use an empty lunchroom. Surrounded by vending machines, a gurgling coffeepot, and the aroma of an unidentifiable brown liquid that had thickened on a day when few had taken the time for a cup, I explained to the Warners why I'd asked Evan to come to the jail. I wanted him to talk with Crystal, to urge her to admit her involvement in Joey's abduction and tell us everything she knew about the man who'd taken him, especially anything about Benoit's car or where he might be.

In contrast with our first meeting, this

time Evan's parents said little. They appeared apprehensive but resigned to the prospect that their son was the only one who might be able to help save the life of the little boy they now acknowledged was their grandchild.

"Why do you think Crystal will talk to me?" Evan asked, his expression doubtful. "I left her for someone else, and we've done nothing but fight."

"I noticed when she talks about you, she's angry, but she still sounds as if she's sorry the marriage ended, that she wants you back. And I know something else," I said, nodding at Evan's parents. "She thinks the two of you, Mr. and Mrs. Warner, are rich, and she regrets not ever being able to tap into any of your money."

Evan's parents exchanged a knowing glance, as if signaling that they had both understood that from the beginning.

"So you want me to do what?" Evan asked, unsure.

I sighed. This was delicate. "Listen, Evan, I can't make false promises to Crystal. But you can."

"Why would she listen to me?" Evan asked again, combing through his hair with his fingers and looking both frightened and frustrated. "Why would Crystal do anything to help me?"

"She won't. But she'd do anything to get what she wants. And what she wants is you and a foothold into your parents' checkbook," I said, laying it out. "I can't tell you what to say to her, Evan. I can't tell you to lie to her. All I can say is that we need to get her talking, and you're the only one who can make that happen."

"You?" Crystal mouthed, shooting her husband a questioning glance as a white-shirted guard unlocked the handcuffs on her wrists. He sat her down in one of the stiff, high-backed metal chairs, then stepped back, far enough to assure her that he couldn't hear. With the hurricane bearing down on Houston, Crystal and Evan were the only ones in the jail's cavernous visitors room, separated by thick Plexiglas. Each picked up a black headset mounted on the divider and put it to an ear.

"Why did you come?" she asked, peeved. We had the audio feed plugged into a phone I sat listening to in a nearby office, peering through a one-way mirror at them while a recording device ran on the line. We weren't breaking any laws. Inmates were told when booked that anything they say over the jail phones could be monitored, recorded, and used against them. "Did you come to rub it in? To see how I look locked up?"

"I miss you," Evan said, I thought rather convincingly, looking a bit doe-eyed at her. "I've broken up with Sami, that woman I was seeing from work. I know now that I'm not in love with her, and I've been thinking a lot. With Joey gone, I've been thinking about what we were like as a family, missing him and missing you."

Crystal appeared more than dubious. "Sure," she scoffed. "You bet. Suddenly you're the great husband and dad."

"I understand why you don't believe me, but you have to understand. Something's happened," Evan said. He fidgeted just a bit in the chair and leaned forward as if reaching out to her. "This whole thing with Joey got me thinking, how he's our son and we're his parents, how we need to take care of him. And there's this other thing. I've been thinking a lot about it, and I figure most of our fights were over money, Crystal. Weren't they? Don't you think that was our real problem?"

She turned her head slightly, held the phone away from her ear, then replaced it and said, her voice thick with doubt, "Yeah. I guess."

"Well, I love you, and I love Joey," Evan

said, giving her a warm smile. "It wasn't ever that I didn't love you. It was that I couldn't take care of us. I wanted to finish college, to get a degree and be able to support both of you, but without my parents' help, I couldn't do it. That made me feel bad, and we had a lot of fights."

"Yeah," she said, eyeing him as if he were a stranger, a man she wasn't sure she could trust. "So what changed?"

"Everything," Evan said. "That woman ranger showed my parents Joey's picture. My mom, well, she never thought he was mine. My dad didn't believe it, either. But once they saw Joey, they realized he had to be mine. They said he looks just like me at that age. They believe now that he's my kid."

"Yeah," Crystal said with a sullen sneer. "So now, with Joey gone and me in here, now they believe he's yours?"

"I know the timing sucks," he said, putting his hand on the window as if wanting to touch her. "I understand. But they're offering to help us out. They want their grandson to live a good life, with both of his parents. If we get Joey back, my mom and dad offered to buy us a house and pay our expenses, including my tuition, until I graduate from college. Then I can get a really good job and support us. I'll be able to pay the bills, and we can be a family again, but without the money problems."

From her expression, Crystal wasn't convinced, and she didn't raise her hand to meet his on the window. "You think they mean it?" she asked. "Really?"

"I know they do," Evan said, his eyes intent on hers, as if willing her to believe him. "I love you, Crystal, and I want to be with you and Joey."

With that, Crystal sat back as far as she could in the chair, as far as the telephone cord would stretch, thinking. "But Joey's gone," she said. "What if we can't find him?"

"We have to find him," Evan said.

"But Evan, what if we can't? Maybe we'll never find him." When her husband didn't answer, Crystal leaned forward, narrowing the distance between them. "We could still be a family, have more kids, couldn't we? Wouldn't your parents be happy with that?"

For perhaps the first time in days, I smiled. Evan was leading her down a path, and he just had to nudge a little harder to close the deal.

"No. I love you, Crystal, but my parents want Joey. There's no other way. We have to get him back. Plus, I don't think we'd make it in our marriage if we didn't find him. It would just be too painful to lose him like this," Evan said, beginning to cry. That part I figured wasn't acting. "And my parents, part of this is that they want to get to know their grandson. If we don't find Joey, they won't help us. Things will be like they were. No house. No tuition money. And if that happens, we can't make it. Crystal, we already tried that and it didn't work. I want to take care of you, but I can't, not without a good job, and right now, I can't get one. We need my parents' help, and to get it, we need Joey."

Since he'd first put it on the glass, Evan's hand waited. Now Crystal raised hers and put it parallel to his, as if touching, the window separating them. "Really, Evan?" she asked. "You really do love me? Are you sure?"

"Yeah," he said. "I'm sorry for everything I did, for making you sad."

"I love you, too, Evan," she said, a smile inching its way into a grin. She looked happy, content, as if all her problems were over. Then, as if she'd just remembered: "But what are we supposed to do about Joey? How do your parents expect us to find him?"

"I don't know," Evan said, shaking his head. "I really don't. I wish there was something, anything you could do to help that Texas Ranger find him. If you did help, I know that my parents would be grateful to you, that you'd be a hero. They'd be even happier to accept you and help us build our new life together."

At that, Crystal's hand slunk down off the glass onto the ledge in front of her. She looked at it, then up at Evan's face, as if considering what to do.

"I'm sorry you don't know anything to help," Evan said, his voice shaking. "I wish you did, so we could get our family together again, only living in a nice house, without any money problems, without all the trouble we had before."

Crystal bit her lower lip, as if in pain. Moments passed, and she said nothing. Then: "Maybe I know something," she said tentatively, her mouth sloping into a downward comma. "Maybe I do. But, Evan, if I tell the cops, we'll never be together. I'll be in jail. My lawyer said not to talk to them."

"But if you don't, we won't get Joey back," Evan said, wiping away a tear. "And if we don't get Evan back, Crystal, it's over. All of it, us, the new house, our new life. It'll all be gone."

Again, Crystal cinched in her lip and held it in place with her teeth, biting down hard. "That lawyer I have, he's not very good. He didn't know how to negotiate a good deal," she said. "But maybe, if you brought that ranger and the prosecutor back, we could work something out."

Evan wiped away another tear. "Do you think so? Will you be able to tell them everything, so they can find Joey, Crystal? Do you know enough to help?"

"Yeah," Crystal said. "Just tell them that I'm ready to talk."

THIRTY-NINE

Hoping Crystal's soon-to-be ex would pull it off, I had Sylvia on standby, and we were seated in an interview room fifteen minutes later. Evan and his parents waited anxiously in the lobby while Sylvia asked Crystal if she wanted to wait to consult her attorney.

"No," Crystal said. "I figure we can make a good deal without him. I have information you want, and what I want is to not spend any time in jail."

"What have you got to tell us?" Sylvia asked. "We need to know what you have to bargain with. Do you know where Joey is? Do you know where this person has taken him?"

Brokering a deal is a lot like poker, and Sylvia and I were doing our best to hide what we had in our hand. Meanwhile, Crystal grinned as if she figured she held a straight flush. "I can describe the guy. We met in the park. I know a lot about him, including his name."

"But can you tell us where to *find* him?" I asked, eyes flat on Crystal's face, watching every nuance. Despite her apparent confidence, she squirmed in the chair, displaying an ounce of discomfort. Unconvinced that Crystal could help us, I repeated what Sylvia had already warned: "Before we agree to any deal, we need to know what you have to bargain with. Listen, Crystal, the bottom line here is that if you want a good deal, your information needs to be useful to us. If it's not, we have no reason to offer you anything."

"Yeah. I get it. I know the guy's name, where he lives, everything about him," Crystal jeered. It didn't take much to get this woman riled up, and I could see her blood pressure mounting. "I can tell you a lot."

Sylvia and I exchanged a brief glance, and I nodded. No matter what, I needed to know what Crystal could tell us. We might be giving up some options when it came to prosecuting her, but we'd think about that later. Right now, all I cared about was finding that little boy alive. We'd come so close in the pasture, only to lose him.

Once she had my agreement, Sylvia pulled out the first form, the one that stipulated

Crystal was voluntarily waiving her right to an attorney. "You have to sign this if we're going to negotiate with you without Mr. Barnett," she explained. "If you decide at any time you want your attorney present, the interview will stop. Do you understand?"

"Yeah," Crystal said, signing her name in a loopy, childlike handwriting. "I understand."

"Okay," Sylvia said, all business. She then pulled out a second sheet of paper. "This is part two, our offer. It's a ten-year probated sentence. That means ten years' probation, no jail time, for the charge of offering a child for sale, the Texas statute that includes selling a minor."

"Let's do five," Crystal said, smiling at us. "Bring it down to five, and I'll sign it." She sat back in the chair, arms folded. It had been only one night, but black circles ringed her eyes, and she began rubbing her wrists, as if sore from the handcuffs she'd arrived in.

"Not much sleep in here, huh?" I asked.

"They leave the lights on," she said. "And people talk and scream and stuff all night long. Plus, I'm pretty sure those mattresses have bedbugs. There's something, bites all over my stomach."

"Poor you," I said, decidedly unsympathetic. "Imagine what it's like in a Texas prison. No air-conditioning in the hot summers. No telephone privileges."

Sylvia sized up the young woman, frowning. The prosecutor had been around a long time, long enough to understand how to ignite fear. When she smiled, it was cold and hard. "Mrs. Warner, you're not listening," she said. "You called this meeting. We didn't. There's a hurricane coming and the city's closing down. You want this ranger and the others looking for Joey to go out and risk their lives to find him. That's what you expect?"

"Yeah," Crystal said. "I tell them where to look, and they need to go out and find my kid. That's what cops are supposed to do."

"Yeah, well, you, as Joey's mother, you were supposed to protect him, not sell him to the highest bidder," Sylvia challenged. "And how did that turn out?"

She might have been young, but it was apparent that Crystal had been around. She didn't back down. "Five years," she said. "Or no deal."

"Seven," Sylvia countered, scratching out "ten" on the form, initialing the change, and pushing the paperwork back across the table at Crystal. "If you don't break your probation, you'll never serve a day for selling the kid. All you have to do is keep your nose clean. My final offer."

Smiling, Crystal picked up the agreement and read it. "I knew I could get a better deal than that Barnett idiot," she said, placing it on the table to sign it. "I knew I didn't need a lawyer. I told my parents that, but, like always, they didn't believe me."

"Good job, you've got what you want," I said. "Now tell us about the guy who has Joey."

For the next half hour, Crystal talked about someone she knew as Larry Montgomery, a good-looking, middle-aged man who approached her in the park and told her that he and his wife wanted a child and couldn't have one. "This Larry guy, he said that his wife wanted to raise Joey. He's got lots of money, and he can do all kinds of things for him that I can't do. He drove me past his house, a few blocks from the park. It's big with a big yard, and he said he'd put up a swing set and a sandbox. This Larry said he's going to give Joey everything he asks for."

"Did you ever meet his wife?" Sylvia asked.

"No," Crystal said with a shrug. "I asked to meet her, but Larry said he wanted to surprise her, to bring Joey home to her like a present."

"You weren't even curious about the woman who'd be raising your son?" I asked. "Not at all?"

"Larry said she was a wonderful person," Crystal said, visibly defensive. "He told me she loves kids, and that she always wanted a kid like Joey. They had a girl once, a little girl Joey's age, who looked like Joey, with kind of brown hair, not dark but a blondish brown like Joey. I guess the little girl, well, she had kind of big blue eyes like Joey's, too."

The description of the child Benoit had attempted to murder in New Orleans came to mind. "What happened to her?" I asked.

"A terrible accident. She drowned when they were living in Louisiana, in a bayou," Crystal said. "When Larry talked about it, he cried."

It was all lies, of course, twisted half-truths, memories out of the past contorted and manipulated. Like everything else Benoit had done, it was all a game, symbols and clues left behind to heighten the excitement. David was right: Benoit wanted us on his trail, just a step behind him. If we hadn't found his father to guide us, Benoit had made sure that he'd told Crystal just enough to suggest what he planned to do with the boy.

"What else do you know about him?" I asked.

"I can give you his address," she offered. "I know where he lives. He even said I could visit Joey once all the publicity about the kidnapping is over and you cops stop investigating."

"Write it down," Sylvia said, scooting her legal pad and a pen across the table. Crystal complied, writing out an address. Once she did, I tore off the page, copied the address in my notebook, and then walked over to a D.A.'s investigator Sylvia had brought with her, a carefully dressed man with a graying pompadour who'd been standing off to the side, listening. "Call major crimes. Tell them this is a lead on the Warner case and ask them to have the house checked out. See if the boy's there."

"Yes, Lieutenant," he said, nodding, and walked away. I returned my attention to Crystal, who sat across from Sylvia, literally twiddling thumbs, fingers interlocked, thumbs circling each other, as if she were bored. I wanted to shake her, but instead I hung back and bit my tongue. It wasn't time to unload yet.

"Did this Larry ever talk about

Galveston?" I asked, my voice calm.

"How did you know he'd talk about Galveston?" Crystal asked. She'd stopped playing around with her hands and looked at me, curious.

"This is your turn to answer questions, not mine," I said, determined not to give her any reason to stop talking. "Tell us what we need to know."

Crystal thought for a moment. "He told me that he has a place there, a place he likes to go, with a fishing pier and a beach, near a park. He said he was going to take Joey one day. He said it's a beautiful place."

That seemed to confirm what David had deduced, that Benoit would head to Galveston. I thought of the beaches with piers I knew, extending out into the water, and how the storm surge was already rising on the island. I wondered if David and the captain would make it across before the causeway became impassable. But before I called David, I needed more from Crystal Warner.

"Tell me about his car. Describe it," I said. "License plate number, anything you remember."

"It was some kind of an SUV, one of those Japanese ones, but not a Toyota. I don't remember what brand. Navy blue with big wheels," she said with a shrug. "I don't remember the license plate, but it had a sticker on the back bumper with kind of a weird drawing on it."

"What kind of a drawing?" I asked.

"Well, kind of . . . ," Crystal said, grabbing the pen and pad again. She drew a symbol, like two capital Es, with an I in between, the second E turned backward to face the first. "Maybe not exactly, but something like that. I said it reminded me of a butterfly, and I asked him what it meant, but he said he didn't know, that he just thought it was pretty."

"Is there anything else?" Sylvia asked. "Do you know anything, anything at all, that could help the lieutenant and the others find Joey?"

"No, that's it." Crystal thought for a minute and then shrugged. "I'm not a bad mom. I'm not. I love Joey. I just couldn't take care of him, is all. I was at the park one afternoon while Joey played with a bunch of kids, and Larry and me started talking. Well, I couldn't support Joey, and my parents wouldn't let us live with them, there wasn't room. And Evan had that blond bimbo he was shacking up with, and suddenly his parents took him back. They took him back as if Joey and me, well, we weren't ever part of his life. It was like they were saying if he dumped us, they wanted him and they'd help him. If he was with us, no deal."

"That must have been infuriating," I said, trying to sound sympathetic. "I can appreciate why you were so upset and desperate."

"I was desperate," she said, looking relieved that I understood. "I couldn't find a good job. I applied for a few, but nobody hired me, and I had the kid to take care of. Plus, I couldn't go out. Couldn't do anything. I mean, my friends, they weren't willing to have a kid come along, and Joey was there all the time."

Before the interview ended, I had some housekeeping to do, a few final questions I wanted answered, things that had been nagging at me. "When you went out last Saturday night, I heard your parents couldn't babysit. That must have been disappointing," I said. "What did you do?"

"Oh, it wasn't so hard," she said with a shrug. "I'd done it before. I just gave Joey cough medicine, the adult stuff. It put him to sleep."

"I see," I said, wondering how any woman, any mother, could be so callous, so fixated only on her own needs. Crystal didn't even look upset admitting that she'd drugged her child so she could have a night in a bar. Something else still puzzled me. "If you really sold the boy, if you knew he wasn't coming home, why didn't you put his toys away?" I asked. "Why leave them scattered around the house?"

She sat back in her chair. "I wanted to," she said with an exaggerated frown. "My mom wouldn't let me. I started to and she made me put them all back, right where they were, like it was some kind of a shrine or something. I told her Joey wasn't coming home, but she didn't believe me. She got really upset. It was sick."

"Yeah, it sounds pretty sick," I said, not meaning Crystal's mother. "So tell me about the thirty grand. You know, you almost had me believing you didn't know about it."

At the mention of the money, Crystal looked even more pleased with herself. "I figured you'd find out about it pretty quick, so I'd thought about it a lot, about how to react. And the more I thought about it, I didn't see how you could prove it wasn't a gift from some donor, especially if I went on TV and asked for donations, like I did," she said with a slight chuckle. "I wanted fifty, but I couldn't get Larry to go up past thirty. Thirty wasn't bad, though."

"Yeah," I said, fighting to keep my face from reflecting my utter disgust. "Good negotiating. You're a real pro." Crystal didn't catch the sarcasm, and she continued to grin, smug about her skillful bargaining. "Weren't you afraid he wouldn't pay you?"

"Nah," she said. "I made it clear to Larry that if that money didn't hit my account first thing the next morning, I'd be screaming about how I suddenly remembered a guy I saw in the park, the one who kept looking at Joey. I'd say I saw him drive home once and knew where he lived. With a good description, y'all would have found him in no time."

Moments passed, and none of us talked. I was absorbing all we'd learned, and I suspected Sylvia was as well.

As if to wrap up the conversation, Crystal asked, "You'll tell Evan how I helped, won't you? Make sure he knows I told you everything I could to help find Joey. We're getting back together, and once you find Joey, we're going to be a family again."

"If we find Joey. If he's still alive," I said,

deciding it was time to jerk her out of never-never land and reveal what was really going on. She frowned at me as if she didn't understand. "The thing is, Crystal, that this man who has Joey, he doesn't plan to raise him like he told you."

With that, I took out the photograph of Peter Benoit from the nursing home, the one his father had at the front desk out of fear his son would murder him. "Is this the Larry guy you sold Joey to?"

Crystal looked at the picture and frowned. "Yeah. How did you get a picture of him? Did you already find him?"

"His name's not Larry. It's Peter Benoit, and he's not planning to raise Joey, he's going to kill him," I said.

She eyed me, unsure. "I don't believe it. He was older, but pretty good-looking. A really nice guy. Smart, too. He said he had the money to give Joey a good life."

"Peter Benoit has tried to murder before, his father and at least one other child we know of. And he has Joey. You sold your son to a killer, a sick, sick man," I said. Crystal shook her head, disbelieving. "Crystal, Benoit is playing some kind of game, sending us messages that tell us that's precisely what he's going to do. Whether you believe it or not, this man is going to murder your son."

Despite everything, Crystal still looked unimpressed. "You're right. I don't believe it."

"You know, I don't have time to try to convince you, but it's the truth," I said. "I'm leaving now, and so is Sylvia."

"Do you know how to pray?" Sylvia asked the girl as we all stood and one of the guards moved forward. He had the handcuffs out, and he grabbed Crystal's arms and clicked them into place behind her back.

"Why?" she asked.

"I thought that perhaps you'd want to pray for your son. Barring that, you may want to pray for yourself. Because the agreement you signed was only for one offense, offering a child for sale," Sylvia said, giving her a look of absolute distaste. "What's not covered is what happens if Joey dies. Then the charge is different. Then we indict you for being a party to a murder."

For the first time, the young woman looked more than vaguely concerned. "What's being a party to a murder?" she asked. "You mean, like I helped?"

"Yeah," I said. "Like you did when you agreed to turn your back in the park so this creep could take your son."

Crystal thought about that, and her eyes opened wider. "But he never said he'd murder Joey," she said, her voice small. "I didn't know."

"You can tell that to the judge and jury. I'm sure they'll be impressed," I said. "In the meantime, like Ms. Vogel suggested, assuming you know how, this is a good time to pray."

FORTY

"She did sell the kid," I told David when I got him on the phone. "She met Benoit in the park. It sounds like he was watching, looking for an unhappy mom to target, one who wasn't paying attention to her kid, a mom who looked like she'd rather be *anywhere* else. These guys have antennae for that type of thing. Benoit told Crystal he wanted a child to raise, that he was rich and he'd give the boy everything he wanted, to give her an easy out. It gave her an excuse, like she was doing it for Joey, not the thirty grand."

"Yeah," David said, his voice overflowing with a deep loathing. "What did you find out about where he might take the kid? Anything that will help?"

"I'm not sure about this. It seems too easy. Maybe it's a false lead, to throw us off, but Crystal says Benoit did talk about taking Joey to Galveston, to the beach, someplace with a fishing pier near a park."

A thoughtful pause, time to consider, and then David agreed. "You're right. He could be trying to mislead us. But on the other hand, this guy breeds drama, and a pier in a hurricane is a perfect setting for his big moment." Again silence, and then: "Plus, Benoit has consistently given us clues to help us trail him but not catch him. Like we discussed, he wants us one step behind, like when you got close to catching him last night, the fourth bull in the field. Having us hot on his trail increases the thrill of this sick game he's playing. So his wanting us in Galveston, searching the island, could mean that's precisely where he's going. He hasn't given us any other clues leading anywhere else."

"All true," I said, still doubtful, wondering if Benoit would give us any guidance that was so precise. Still, I couldn't dispute David's logic. "So do you go with that?"

"Yeah, we have to. We haven't anything else," he said. "I'll run it by the captain, see if he has other ideas, but I think we'll concentrate on the piers, especially anything near a park. Try to find a safe vantage point and set up surveillance. Anything else?"

"A description of Benoit's car. Crystal says that he was driving a large Japanese

SUV, dark blue. She doesn't remember a license plate number, but it has a bumper sticker on the back. It's another symbol, two capital Es turned inward, facing each other, with an I in the center. Looks a little like a butterfly."

"Great. That could help. What does it mean?"

"It's another *Adinkra,* this one called *Pempamsie,*" I explained. "I found a reference to it on the Internet. It symbolizes strength that cannot be crushed."

"More gloating," David said. "More taunting."

"Yeah," I answered. "But maybe it'll backfire. Maybe it'll help you spot the SUV. I've already e-mailed the information on the vehicle to the sheriff's department and Houston and Galveston PD, so they can all start looking. I've also alerted Galveston to the description of the possible site, and they're pulling together information on the piers for you, both on the Gulf and on the bay side of the island, especially anything near a park."

"Yeah," he said. "Great."

In the background, I heard what sounded like a loud gust of wind. "David, where are you?"

"We just crossed the causeway onto the

island," he said. The connection was bad, cutting in and out. "It's getting pretty rough. We're hearing on the radio that the Gulf side of the island is beginning to flood, and the storm's not scheduled to hit here for another six hours."

"Be careful," I said. "Please, David, be careful."

At that, the phone went dead.

Forty-One

It felt as if they'd been driving for hours, circulating through nearly deserted streets. Joey wondered where the man was taking him, why he couldn't go home, go someplace where he could eat. He was so hungry, his stomach hurt. When he thought of food, Joey thought again about the nice lady at the store, the one who smiled at him and asked his name. The bad man said that Joey made him kill the woman, because he told her his name. Joey felt sad that the nice lady died. He wondered again about his momma, thinking how worried she must be, and about his poppa. He wasn't on the television looking for Joey like his momma was, but the boy knew that his poppa was upset and worried about him. His poppa worried a lot, and he tried to take care of Joey. *Maybe Poppa wasn't on the television because he was too busy looking for me?* Joey thought that had to be true, that his poppa was too busy to be on television because he was looking everywhere he could think of, trying to find Joey.

"My momma and poppa want me to go home," Joey whispered.

Behind the wheel, the man didn't respond, simply continued to drive. The boy was tied down to the backseat, ropes around his arms and legs making sure he couldn't raise his body, even an arm to wave at a passing car.

Joey thought maybe the man hadn't heard him, so he said it again, this time louder: "My momma and poppa want me to go home!"

In the driver's seat, Peter Benoit laughed, his voice echoing through the SUV. "No one knows where you are, Joey," he said, his voice filled with pride. "No one. Not your mother or father, your grandmother or grandfather. Not the police. And even if they are looking, they won't find you. Not until it's all over."

Joey thought about that. "When will that be?"

"When will what be?" Benoit mocked.

"When will it be over?" Joey asked again.

A dour smile on his lips, Benoit at first hesitated, but then answered, "When I'm done with you. When I'm satisfied."

Joey thought about that and felt better. "After that, can I go home?"

At that, Benoit turned and looked over his shoulder at the boy in the backseat, shaking his head with disgust at the child's naïveté. He turned back, fixed his eyes on the road, and mumbled, "Very soon, this will be over. This will end."

At first, Joey thought about the tone of the man's voice, the anger seething just below the surface. Still, when he thought about what the man had said, it sounded like good news. Soon, this would end. Relieved, Joey wondered if maybe he didn't need to be as frightened of the man. Since that first night, sometimes, when Benoit looked at him, it made the boy's heart beat fast in his chest. Sometimes it beat so fast, it hurt. And sometimes, when Joey felt very frightened, he felt his pants grow warm and wet. When that happened, Benoit seethed. It happened so often that Benoit had the boy in diapers from a store, the pull-up kind.

"I don't want you smelling up my car," he'd said when he tied the boy down. "And we're not stopping, not for anything, not until after dark."

"But the hurricane," Joey had said, his eyes wide. On the radio, they said the storm was coming and that people needed to hide.

"We have to be safe from the hurricane so it won't hurt us."

"You don't need to worry about the storm," Benoit had told him with a short laugh. "I'll take care of you."

Forty-Two

Maggie ran to me as soon as I stopped the Tahoe in the driveway. It appeared that she'd been waiting on the front porch, and she cried as she wrapped her arms around my waist. "Oh, Magpie," I whispered, rubbing her back. "I'm so sorry. It's okay. It's all okay."

"I heard about Sergeant Buckshot," she said, pulling her head back to look up at me with my late husband's eyes, a soft shade of the palest brown with flecks of green. "I heard about it on the news, how he was shot and his body burned up. They said he was dead, that somebody murdered him."

"I know," I said, feeling guiltier with each second ticking off the clock. Despite everything, I should have carved out a few minutes to call her, to try to smooth it over, instead of letting her find out from the television. It was understandable that Maggie was upset. She'd grown up knowing

Buckshot, and now he was gone. She must have been wondering if the same thing could happen to me.

"I got worried about where you were, if you were okay," she said, burying her head in my chest. "Gram said she talked to you, that you were all right, but I wanted to see you for myself."

"Maggie, Maggie, my beautiful daughter," I said, holding her in my arms and kissing the top of her head. "Magpie, I'm here, and everything is fine."

She attempted a small, brave smile. "I know," she said, the tears rolling down her cheeks. "But I got so scared."

We stood holding each other in the driveway as the moments slid by. Finally, she released me and stepped back, smiling at me, showing off her new braces, relieved that I was home. Bill had been a Texas Ranger, too, and ever since she'd been a small girl, we'd been honest with Maggie, never trying to deny that our jobs were dangerous. She saw us strapping on our rigs and putting our guns in our holsters before we walked out the door to work. We told her we were well trained and that we weren't foolhardy. We did our best to minimize the dangers. And maybe most important, that the reason we took chances was to help others. Working the job wasn't a quest to find excitement. We simply were trying our best to arrest the guilty and save those who could be saved. Then Bill died, but it had nothing to do with the job. Still, I knew Maggie worried. And now with Buckshot's death, I understood how frightened she was. She'd loved her father and lost him, and any reminder that I could die was too painful to bear.

Looking at my daughter on the threshold of growing into a teenager, I had no doubt that the tie between us was eternal and true. I put my hands on her shoulders. Every year, Maggie grew taller. Every year that passed, every inch she gained, brought us closer to the day she'd separate from me. In two years, she'd enter high school, then, four years later, college. Someday I'd be old, and she'd be the powerful one. But it wouldn't change what we were to each other. My daughter was one of the great loves of my life.

"Maggie, I'm okay," I said, leaning down and kissing her forehead. I looked her intently in the eyes. The captain and David were right: I belonged home with Maggie and Mom in the storm. I couldn't have made that decision, not with Joey Warner in danger, and I was grateful that it had been made for me. But there were things Maggie had to remember. "Please don't worry about me. I'm careful. I do my best. And I try hard not to take unnecessary chances. I can't guarantee what'll happen, but I can guarantee that I will always do my best to come home to you."

"I know, Mom," she said, again slipping her arms around me. "I'm sorry I got so scared."

"Don't be sorry," I said, holding her tight. "I get scared, too, sometimes. I love you, too."

At that, I turned, keeping one arm around her, and we walked toward the house. Mom stood on the porch, watching. "We're glad you're home, Sarah," she said, ruffling Maggie's hair and kissing me on the cheek as I passed her. "We've been looking forward to seeing you."

The rest of the afternoon dissolved in work. After a much needed hot shower and a change of clothes, I pored over the Warner case files, looking for something, anything that could help, anything we'd overlooked, while Mom, Maggie, and Frieda finished securing the stable and putting fly halters on the horses, covering their eyes. The theory was that limiting their vision would keep them calmer and that if the doors flew open, if somehow — because nearly anything was possible in a hurricane — they ran off, the halters would protect their eyes from flying debris. The most recent reports said that at the rate the hurricane traveled, Juanita would take twelve hours or more to pass through.

Inside the house, Mom had everything in place, from the battery-operated radio on the kitchen counter to a cot with bedding in the living room for Bobby. Before long, Mom, Frieda, and Maggie came in and showered, settling in to ride out the storm.

In the kitchen, Mom worked on dinner, while Frieda, who'd moved into the spare bed in Maggie's room for the duration, set up an altar in the dining room, on a battered yellow vinyl tablecloth on top of Mom's old table, decorating it with candles, skull masks shaped from sugar, silk daisies, and small wooden statues of skeletons painted black and white with maniacal grins, some wearing big hats and riding bicycles. Along with Halloween, this night was the beginning of the Mexican festival known as Día de los Muertos, the Day of the Dead, when the dead are thought to roam the earth, visiting family and friends.

When I went to check on them, Maggie

and Frieda sat in chairs, watching the candle flames flicker, Frieda's lips moving silently in prayer. In the center of the memorial, she'd placed a silver-framed photograph of an austere-looking woman with a gray bun and intense dark eyes — her mother, whose body was buried back in her native village in Mexico.

"Maggie, time to help Gram with dinner. She's making chicken and dumplings, and I bet she could use some help chopping veggies," I whispered. Yet neither Maggie nor I moved quickly. In the darkened dining room, the altar had a comforting sense of ritual, a reminder of ancient ways, and looking at it gave me a sense of peace.

"Isn't it beautiful?" Maggie asked.

"Yes, Magpie," I said, gazing at Frieda's memorial to the dead and thinking about all those I'd lost, my father, my husband. In the flames, I pictured Buckshot the last time I'd seen him, more than a day earlier at the office, in the meeting with the captain. I'd never see him again, and I already missed him. I pushed away thoughts that I was at least partly to blame for his death. "The altar is beautiful."

Frieda smiled at me but kept praying.

Bobby arrived just as the sun began to set. The winds had picked up, but we had yet to feel any real effects from the storm. Before long, Maggie sauntered off to the living room, where she turned on an old sitcom, while Bobby took her place helping Mom in the kitchen. He stirred the pot of simmering chicken and vegetables, the rich aroma enveloping the room, while they talked softly, trying not to disturb me as I worked at the kitchen table.

"What's Sarah doing?" Bobby asked, watching me with maps and pictures spread out on the table.

"She's trying to find that boy, that little one who went missing from the park earlier in the week," Mom whispered.

"Oh, they haven't found him yet?" he asked, and Mom shook her head. "Poor kid," he said. With that, Bobby went back to stirring, and Mom started cutting up the greens for the salad.

Wondering what was going on in Galveston, I picked up my cell and held down the key for David's number. I'd been trying to reach him for hours, but all I got was a fast busy. I understood it was probably a function of the storm. Reports said Hurricane Juanita had moved into Galveston with torrential rains, a twenty-foot storm surge, and gusts measuring more than 150 miles per hour. We were already hearing on the radio that power lines were down on the island, and one cell phone tower had collapsed under the strain. I wasn't so much worried about David and the captain as I was eager to talk to them. The problem was that the longer I looked at the map I'd drawn, one with the location of all four dead bulls and the Warner house, where the fifth symbol had been delivered, the more uneasy I felt about locking in on Galveston as the location.

Searching for answers while telling myself that I had to be wrong, that David and the captain were right and that they'd find the boy, I laid out the photographs and sketches of the symbols, this time lining them up with the locations on the map where they were found, marking each point with a dot. Everything had occurred in and around Houston, the killings of the four bulls on the outskirts of the city and the symbol left on the Warners' doorstep, inside Houston proper. The more I thought about it, the bigger the knot in my chest grew.

We'd called it wrong. I felt certain of it.

"Sarah, it's time to clear off the kitchen table," Mom said. "Dinner's ready."

Supper was a quiet occasion, all of us with much on our minds. Bobby raved over Mom's dumplings, while I let them slide down my throat in silence. They were hot and comforting, and again I was glad to be home.

A worried expression crowding her face, Frieda, who'd remained silent throughout the meal, mentioned the hurricane's falling on both Halloween and Día de los Muertos. "Do you think that's a bad omen?" she asked.

"No, it's not," Mom replied, putting her palm over Frieda's hand, resting on the table. "In your festival, isn't it deceased family and friends who come to visit? Those you've lost?"

"Yes," Frieda said, nodding.

"Then perhaps it's a good omen," Mom said with a kind smile. "If those we love are close, they'll watch over us. They'll help keep us safe."

"That's true," Frieda said, her face heavy with sadness. "I'll pray at the altar that my mother comes to protect us."

Maggie searched my face, and I said, "That would be appreciated, Frieda. We can always use prayers. But we'll be fine. You'll see. We'll be fine."

Afterward, I reclaimed the cleared kitchen table, again laying out my map and drawings. For hours I pored over them, and time slipped away, until I heard Bobby announce,

"Nora, Strings and the reverend just drove up. Looks like they're taking you up on your offer."

"Maggie, Strings is here!" I shouted.

I left the papers as they were and went with the others to greet our guests. In the past year, twelve-year-old Strings had shot up, and Maggie's best friend had to be nearing five feet four inches tall. He'd also let his curly black hair grow longer and traded in his round wire rims for oval glasses that darkened in the sunlight. His dad, the Reverend Fred Jacobs, pastored the Mount Zion African Church down the road from the ranch, an old, clapboard building in the center of Libertyville, a small settlement originally founded by freed slaves during Reconstruction. The spiritual leader of the oldest black church in the area, Strings' dad was a spindly man with rough-carved features and an angular jaw, who had a perpetual twinkle in his dark eyes.

The reverend and Strings struggled to unload three coolers from the back of their pickup truck as Bobby rushed down and offered, "Let me help you with that." Mom had already explained at dinner that since we had Bobby's generator, she'd called Strings's mom, Alba, and offered to store their frozen food in our extra freezer. Pretty soon we were all pitching in, lugging the coolers into the house.

"Would you like a bowl of chicken and dumplings?" Mom asked. It was rare that anyone dropped in at any hour, even one like this, nearly nine at night, that Mom didn't offer a plate of food, coffee, or a cool drink.

"Alba's already fed us, and fed us well," the reverend explained, patting his midsection. "We'll be eating a lot in the next couple of days. We've got a bunch of refrigerator food to consume before it spoils, if we're going to lose power."

"We won't have a lot, but if the generator works out okay, we'll bring you what ice we can make," Mom offered.

"That's kind of you, Nora," the reverend said, allowing his eyes to stray over to my paperwork on the kitchen table. "It's good of you to help us out like this. Can't tell you how much we appreciate your storing our frozen goods through the storm."

With that, he fingered a photograph of one of the symbols, the one found on the second bull, *Ako-ben,* a call to arms. "Maggie, are you doing a school project on *Adinkra?*" he asked. "You should have asked. I could have helped you. What's this symbol written on? Some kind of parchment?"

"It's not Maggie's. It's mine, for a case. That's drawn on the hide of a dead bull," I explained. "Are you familiar with *Adinkra?*"

"Of course," he said, picking up the other photos and paging through them. "On the hide of a dead bull, huh? That seems odd."

"Yeah," I said, wondering if there was something about cattle that made the location strike him as strange. "Any particular reason it seems odd?"

"No, no," he said. "Just seems like an unusual thing to do, is all."

"Sarah's working on that kidnapping case," Mom explained. "The little boy from the park."

"Saw something about that on the news," the reverend said.

Maggie and Strings took off for the dining room, where she wanted to show him Frieda's altar. Before long, I could hear Frieda explaining the symbolism of the sugar skull masks and the small figures.

"That poor little boy," said Reverend Fred, shaking his head. "What's his name? Joey, isn't it? I didn't know that you still hadn't found him. Breaks your heart, doesn't it? A little one like that out there, don't know where, in this storm. Something like this makes me wonder why there's so much evil in the world."

"Yes, it does," I agreed, sick at the image of the child at the mercy of a madman.

Reverend Fred peered down at the table. "What's the map for?"

"I used it to plot where the *Adinkra* symbols were left," I explained. Technically I should have hidden the photos, since it was all evidence in an ongoing investigation, but something about the way Strings's dad surveyed the map and the symbols piqued my interest. "Each of those dots on the map represents where a symbol was found. Any ideas?"

He chewed on that for a few minutes, picking up the photos of the scenes where the bulls were killed, then finally placing them back down. "I thought maybe, but no," he said. "I guess not. It seemed like maybe you had a crossroads going, but it doesn't look that way. Not with that one off center, not really in the middle."

"A crossroads?" I asked. "What're we talking about?"

Pointing down at the map, he indicated the dot marking the Warner house, where the note had been left on the doorstep. "Well, if that one wasn't there, you could connect the other four points on the map, north to south and east to west, where the bulls were found, and form a cross. Then all you'd have to do is draw circles on the ends of the lines, representing the circles in your pictures there," he said, holding up one of the photographs of Habanero, tracing the circle the killer had drawn around the bull's carcass in the dirt. Each of the scene photos had a similar circle, drawn around each of the four shotgunned bulls. "He the drew a circle at the intersection of the lines. This symbol is called a crossroads."

The reverend eyed me to see if I was getting it. I wasn't, not completely. "You see, there's a lot of symbolism in both Christian and African cultures regarding crossroads."

"So tracing the circles found where the bulls were killed onto the map, and then connecting them with two equal lines, I could have a crossroads?" I asked.

"Yeah," he said. "You sure could, at least the way I'm looking at it. The only problem is that you've got that other one."

I thought about that. The "other one," the dot marking the Warner house, was different from all the others. No circle had been drawn in the earth. Nothing had been killed or, perhaps, sacrificed, like the longhorns. All the Warners discovered on their doorstep was an envelope holding Joey's bloody underpants and the sheet of paper with the symbol. That dot on the map, the one the reverend called the "problem," well, maybe it wasn't part of the pattern.

"Can you tell me about it?" I asked. "This crossroads symbol."

The reverend glanced at his watch. The storm was approaching, and we could hear the first winds howling outside. He looked out at the trees, their leaves rustling. The hurricane was making everyone jumpy. "I guess there's time," he said. Then he called out to his son in the living room, "Strings, y'all come out here and put this food away in the freezer while I talk to Maggie's mom, please. We need to be leaving for home real soon."

"We'll do that," Mom offered, but the reverend objected.

"It's good for children to do their share, Nora," he said. Then, again, he called out to his son, "Strings, come on out."

Moments later, Mom, Bobby, Strings, and Maggie were hauling the coolers into the back room, where we had a freezer, clearing a section and unloading the contents, including Alba Jacobs's frozen homemade pies, for safekeeping. Meanwhile Reverend Fred, whose fiery Sunday sermons brought folks from far and wide to his little church in the country, placed a sheet of unlined paper over the top of the map and plotted the four outer markings, drawing circles around each. He then used a marker and a ruler to connect the northern point with the southern and an equally long second line to join the eastern and western kill sites. Finally, in the center, he drew a fifth and larger circle.

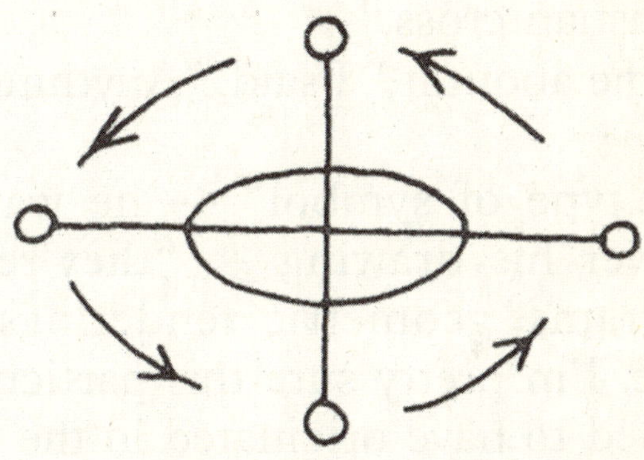

"It seems like crossroads have always interested folks," he said as he drew. "For Christians, the symbol resembles a cross. You know, long past, folks who committed suicide were banned from burial in the consecrated grounds of Christian cemeteries. So families sometimes took the bodies out to the countryside and buried them where roads intersected, believing the roads formed a cross, and it was as close to a Christian burial as their loved one could get."

"You said there are African connotations,

too," I reminded him. "Like the *Adinkra?*"

"Sure," he said. I motioned, and he looked at the chair I offered but shook his head. I could tell he was worried about time passing and the storm building. "Better not. Gotta be on our way soon, before the weather gets too treacherous. Anyway, the African symbolism has nothing to do with the Christian cross."

"Tell me about it," I said. "Anything might help."

"This type of symbol" — he waved his hand over his drawing — "they're called cosmograms, geometric renderings of the universe. I'm pretty sure this particular one is believed to have originated in the Kongo, an ancient civilization in Central Africa. The slaves brought it with them to the Americas, and over the decades, it became known as a crossroads symbol. There are different interpretations of what it symbolizes. Some saw the point at the top," he said, placing the tip of the pen at the upper circle on the map, "as God, or maybe dawn or the sun."

Tracing the line down to the lowest circle, he went on. "The opposite point, the one beneath, was midnight, darkness, or death, and the line that intersects them, in the case of this map connecting east and west, may have symbolized the earth or water."

Again I considered the dead bulls, how Benoit had taken the time to draw circles in the dirt around each, circles that resembled those on the map that the reverend had drawn.

"What about the center?" I asked, pointing to the circle Reverend Fred had drawn at the intersection of the two lines, at the axis of the crossroads.

"There are different theories on the importance of the center, but they all allude to a special significance, that it's a sacred location. These diagrams were sometimes drawn on the earth, traced onto the ground and such, and folks were known to stand on the center circle to take oaths," he said, excitement creeping into his voice. It was apparent that the symbolism held special meaning for the reverend, as sacred ancient symbols and rituals. "In this interpretation, as in most, it was believed that the center of the crossroads was the point where a man could go to be close to God. It was where God was able to see him."

"Go on," I urged.

"Well, there are other interpretations, especially after the slaves were transported to the New World. They began drawing the cosmogram in different places, inside the bricks they made to build the plantations, on the ground out in the fields, sometimes they made them out of stones, even drew them with white chalk on the bottoms of old black kettles they used to melt down the sugarcane to make syrup."

"A place to take oaths," I repeated, thinking back to what he'd said. "That's what the center was for, to be near God."

"Sometimes, yes. But like I said, there were other explanations. Some say the four circles on the tips of the crossroads symbol represent the stages in a man's life, from birth to adulthood, to old age, to death," he said, following along with his pen turned pointer as he mentioned each stage. "When a man stands in the center, it's also thought that he's suspended somewhere between life and death."

Reverend Fred paused, and I sat back in my chair and thought about what he was telling me. It seemed certain that Peter Benoit had grown up hearing his father, an expert on African symbolism, talk about just such things. The old man told us that he'd taught Peter about his work, explained ancient imagery and rituals. Was this diagram a map indicating where he had Joey?

"Like I said, I've studied a little on this because it interests me, and what I understand is that many of the African slaves had a slight twist on the cosmogram. They believed that God could see them at the center of the crossroads," the reverend continued, again pointing at that center circle. "That when they drew this mark and stood at the center, they were as close to God as they could be on this good earth."

"That's fascinating," I said. I thought about all he'd said, how it all made sense in the context of the symbolism Benoit had left behind. But I felt wary, worried about jumping to any conclusion. "Are there other meanings?"

"Seems to me that there are," he said, closing one eye and thinking on it a bit more. Then he smiled, as if he'd just recalled what had been on the tip of his tongue. "If I remember right, I'm pretty sure some folks back then believed that any man who stood at the center of the cosmogram was of elevated value, that he was to be respected, a man capable of governing others. If my memory is right, some figured that anyone who stood at the center of the crossroads had evolved to such a lofty point that he understood the unknowable, the great mysteries of our world, the meanings of both life and death."

As Reverend Fred talked, my mind raced. I thought of the string of dead longhorns and the meaning of the third symbol, *Aya:* "I am not afraid of you." Benoit had sounded so confident when he'd told me that over the telephone, so superior. Then, suddenly, what should have occurred to me early on took form, as my mind traced back to the heart-stopping moment I first saw Buckshot's burning body. Benoit set Buckshot's corpse on fire at the center of a country intersection, in the middle of a crossroads.

"You know, there's something else," Reverend Fred said, smiling at me. "I've always kind of liked one particular interpretation of the crossroads symbolism. Sometimes, I figure that if I ever need it, and I hope I won't, it might come in handy."

"What's that?" I asked.

"Well, I've heard it said by some folks, scholars and the like who study these things, that there's something else about this right here," he said, pointing again at the circle at the center of his diagram, the point where the lines intersected.

"What is it?" I asked, sounding perhaps more urgent than he expected. The reverend glanced over at me, and I saw a spark of interest and a slight questioning in his eyes. There wasn't time to tell him everything, but I needed to know all he could tell me, quickly. A little boy's life could be ending as we stood talking at the kitchen table. "Please, Reverend Fred. It's important. It could help with the case. It could help find that little boy. Please go on."

"Well, I've heard that some believe if you're in trouble, that's where you go," he explained, watching me. "I've heard it said that anyone who needs help can go to the center of the crossroads and wait. It's there that God will find you."

Forty-Three

"I'm sorry, Maggie," I said. "I understand this is a bad time to leave, with the hurricane coming, and I understand why you're upset, especially after Buckshot's death. I don't want to go. Please believe me when I say that I *don't* want to go. But there's a little four-year-old boy in grave danger, and I need to help him."

We stood in the garage, where I searched through the Tahoe's equipment locker, making sure I had everything I needed. When I pulled out a Kevlar vest and strapped it on over my white T-shirt, Maggie gasped.

"This is to be careful," I said, sorry I hadn't driven down the road and found someplace else to get dressed, someplace where she wouldn't have seen me. How could I be so thoughtless when I knew she was already frightened? "Maggie, listen, I've called the office, and two troopers have volunteered to back me up. They're already on their way downtown. I won't be alone. And I'll be careful."

"Mom, let the others go," my daughter said, tears cascading down her cheeks. "You don't have to go! You don't have to!"

"Please believe me, I don't have any other choice," I said. Looking at her, tears welling in her eyes, I felt an ache in my chest, as if my heart couldn't bear to do this to her. But I was still thinking through all the evidence, trying to interpret the clues. What I suspected was that to play out his game, his fantasy, Benoit had the boy somewhere in downtown Houston. My best guess was near the I-45 and I-10 underpass, where the two lines intersected on my map, the ones Reverend Fred had drawn connecting the locations where the bulls were found, north to south and east with west. It seemed logical that Benoit, playing out his awful game, had plotted out that area, since the overlapping of those two highways had to be considered Houston's major crossroads. On the reverend's map, that intersection fell directly in the center of the inner circle.

Outside, the hurricane blew in all around us, powered by what felt like an unquenchable fury. With every passing minute, the winds grew stronger. Although at the ranch we were still at the northern fringe of the storm, the limbs of heavy oaks danced like puppets controlled by a commanding hand, and the tall, thin-trunked pines bent nearly in half, bowing to the storm's great power. I had no illusions about escaping the full brunt of the hurricane. Where I was going, I'd be driving directly into the gale.

Yet I couldn't stay home. The troopers didn't know the case and could underestimate Benoit's capabilities. I couldn't put them in that danger, risk that they'd end up like Buckshot, whose death already hung heavy on my conscience. Besides, time to reconsider was something I didn't have. Each second I hesitated, the storm grew more potent, its driving rains fueling floods, the destruction of its treacherous winds. I had to leave quickly. Otherwise Joey Warner would die, and Peter Benoit would escape. All would be lost.

In a rush, I grabbed a black slicker from the locker, unrolled it with a snap of the wrist, then made sure the flaps identifying me as law enforcement, the badge painted on the front and "Texas Rangers" written across the back, were rolled up and secured, not visible. In this particular scenario, I didn't need to advertise my approach, not in the darkness, where the reflective yellow lettering could glow in streetlights or flash in bursts of lightning. I hadn't forgotten how Benoit had sidled up behind me at the plantation, unheard even in the stillness of a calm afternoon. This time, I wanted the element of surprise on *my* side, not his.

Searching through the locker, I chose a waterproof flashlight, which I hung on my belt, and a pair of night vision goggles, then I double-checked my Colt .45 in its holster, making sure I had backup ammunition. Instead of a shotgun, I chose a Bushmaster semiautomatic, a .223-caliber, and made sure it was loaded. I wrapped the black, assault-type rifle along with more ammo in a plastic bag, then slipped it all into a waterproof sack with a shoulder strap. Judging I was fully equipped, I took my sobbing daughter by the arm and walked out into the rain toward the house, telling myself I had no other choice. I couldn't reach David or the captain, but even if I could, now that the storm was under way and the causeway flooded, they were trapped on Galveston Island.

In the driveway, the rain saturated us in sheets and the wind slapped so hard that it left a burning sensation on my skin, but halfway to the house, Maggie planted her feet and pushed against me. I wore the rain jacket, but my daughter had on only an orange T-shirt, old black jeans, and a pair of white tennis shoes. I remembered that I'd been meaning to buy her new ones. In a growing spurt, Maggie had worn the shoes barely a few months before her feet pushed against the round toes. But I'd been so busy, so distracted, I'd forgotten. I wasn't a bad mother, I reminded myself. Being busy didn't make one a bad mother. And it wasn't entirely my fault. It wasn't fair that life slipped past so quickly. I wished I could hold time by the reins and pull it back, forcing it to slow.

"No, Mom. No. Please, don't go!" Maggie begged, her voice a hoarse scream. Her arms tightened around my waist, and I felt all the determination a twelve-year-old could muster.

As I had that afternoon, when she'd cried over Buckshot, I held Maggie in my arms. "I have to," I said as the rain beat down on us. "Maggie, I will do everything in my power to stay out of harm's way. You have my promise that I will do my best to come home to you," I shouted, my voice trailing off in the wind. "There's no one more important to me than you. I love you dearly. But there's a little four-year-old boy out there, frightened and in grave danger. I have to try to save him."

It wasn't fair to put such a burden on my daughter. She shouldn't be made to feel guilty for not wanting me to risk my life. It was understandable that she felt fearful, realizing I'd be tracking a killer during a dangerous storm. But Maggie had to understand it was important, that I wasn't leaving her on a whim.

"Oh, Mom . . ." She began to cry ever harder. "Why do you always have to be the one? Why? Mom, please don't —"

"I love you and I don't want to leave you, but I know you're safe here with Gram, Bobby, and Frieda," I interrupted. "I know they'll watch over you. That little boy, Maggie, he has no one to save him but me."

I looked down at my daughter's beautiful young face, traced her cheek with my hand, and she tracked my eyes with hers. Her tears mixed with the rain. Before long, she nodded. "Okay, Mom," she said, sucking in hard, as if marshaling the last of her nerve. "I understand. I'll be all right."

"I know you will, Maggie," I said, proud of her but sad that she was being forced to grow up so quickly. We'd been through so much in the past few years, including the death of her father. But we'd gotten through it together. I had to believe we would again. "And you know, even though I have to go, that I love you."

"I know," she agreed, again holding me tight. "I love you, too."

I kissed her one more time on the forehead and then motioned to the porch, where Mom and Bobby stood watching. Without hesitating, Mom walked out into the pounding rain and the sweeping gusts of wind and wrapped her arms around Maggie. My daughter searched my face, her eyes dark with fear, as my mother led her back to the porch. "I love you, Mom. I'll see you tomorrow," I shouted.

"Of course you will, Sarah," Mom answered, resolute, her expression willing it all to be true. "Sarah, I love you dearly. And we'll see you tomorrow, after the storm."

Forty-Four

Rain banged on the hood and strong winds buffeted the Tahoe's exterior, but it handled well for the first leg of the trip downtown. Holding tight to the steering wheel, fighting the powerful winds, I tried calling the captain and David again and got another round of fast busy signals. When I repeated the exercise a few minutes later, I got a crackly connection to his voice mail. "David, it's me, Sarah," I shouted so he would be able to hear me over the bellowing weather. "I don't think Benoit's in Galveston. I think he has the boy in downtown Houston, near the meeting point of I-45 and I-10, maybe on this one underpass I know where 10 goes under 45. It floods down there," I said, and then, thinking I needed to explain: "I got help with the symbols, more information. Anyway, I think I've got it figured out now, what all the clues mean, and my best guess is that's where he'll take the boy. I've called for backup. I know you can't help, that even if you get this message, you're stuck on the island. David, please find a safe place to ride out the storm. Please stay safe. I love you."

As soon as I closed the phone, I wondered if I should have finished the message with those three words. I'd never told David I loved him before, and he'd never said it to me. I wasn't sure until that moment that I did love him. I'd thought about the possibility but never really embraced it. I guess it scared me a little. And now, with our relationship hanging in the balance, it seemed a particularly unfortunate time to profess my feelings. Still, I couldn't take it back, and in case something did happen to me, if I didn't get to tell him in person, I wanted him to know what he meant to me.

The freeways were deserted. The mayor and police department had warned folks not to venture out into so powerful a storm, and they'd obeyed. At least I had no other drivers to contend with. Before long, I took the exit to the right off FM 249, the freeway that links Tomball with Houston, and got on the access ramp that leads to the Sam Houston Tollway. As the SUV accelerated upward, I felt Hurricane Juanita's brute strength. One lane with cement barriers on either side, the incline soared seventy feet into the air and offered no protection. Gusts hit the side of the Tahoe like blows from an invisible fist, and I fought the steering wheel, pulling the car to the left to keep from falling right, tipping over, and plummeting onto the concrete below.

"Hold on," I urged as I wrestled with the wheel, forcing the Tahoe into a gradual left. The rain intensified, hailing upon the car with such force that I wondered if water could dent the SUV's metal shell. The windshield wipers had no hope of keeping up, and I strained to see ahead. At the top of the ramp, the force of the wind coupled with a thin layer of water collecting on the cement, and the Tahoe took flight, rising off the road and hydroplaning to the right. The rear fishtailed to the left, and I drifted, suspended, until the back bumper slammed the concrete barrier. The impact shook the SUV, and I strained, forcing the wheel to the left, righting the wheels, and swinging back straight, as the ramp descended and the rain gushed in waterfalls from the rectangular openings in the base of the ramp's concrete barriers.

Once I'd made it onto the tollway heading east, I wove from lane to lane, searching for higher ground as the curve of the massive four-lane road undulated from side to side. Water pooled in the low-lying lanes, and I had no way to gauge its depth. Rainwater rapids on the feeder road rushed over the curbs, collected, and twisted down sewers in dangerous whirlpools. Above me, the freeway lights, beacons perched on hundred-foot-high poles, appeared to sway in the fierce winds. Driving in the right-hand lane, I heard a loud crack and thought, *Thunder.* Instead a thick, twisted limb of an ancient oak tumbled down, its fingerlike appendages reaching onto the tollway. I swung to the left and barely missed smashing head-on into a wide, bulky branch, but I couldn't escape running over its spindly fringes submerged beneath the water.

Overcompensating, I steered too hard left and hit a deep pool. Water splashed high over the SUV's hood, blocking my already sparse view. Unable to see where I was headed, I felt the front end rise, the tires float. Out of control, the Tahoe swerved to the left, then the right. Panic wrenched my chest into a tight knot as the SUV's wide tires with their deep grooves suddenly hit the road and slammed down hard. I jerked the wheel to the right, and the Tahoe jolted mercifully forward.

Overhead, freeway signs announced the

approach of I-45, my route downtown to the underpass where I believed Benoit intended to murder Joey Warner. On the right, the feeder roads overflowed, spilling off rainwater that gushed from the highway and neighboring roads, forming a swift current filled with broken branches and shingles blown from nearby roofs. The only other route was the overpass onto I-45. Like the one I'd taken onto the tollway, it surged up high over the flat landscape, and the Tahoe would again be exposed to the full force of the treacherous winds. As I approached I-45, I debated what to do, whether to risk the fierce gusts on the overpass or the swelling, debris-ridden floodwaters on the feeder road. In the end, I had no options. At the last exit before I-45, a massive pine lay on its side, its battle-scarred trunk blocking the exit ramp onto the feeder. With no alternative, I steered up onto the overpass.

Off the tollway, I swung to the right, the Tahoe climbing the ramp yet again prey to the hurricane's full force. The SUV was built solid and strong but boxy, not designed to encounter such strong winds, and I heard creaking steel as I fought to steer to the top of the ramp. Once there, I gunned the engine, eager to start the path down. The

SUV swayed, and I felt the driver's-side tires lift from the road, but as I took the curve at the top, the Tahoe righted itself and dropped to the pavement, again forging ahead.

Once on I-45, I considered what waited downtown. Would Joey already be dead? It was still early in the storm, and I thought the boy would be alive. As a twelve-year-old, Benoit had taken his time trying to kill the girl, drawing it out. As an adult, he'd chosen to poison his father, a slow death, not a quick one. This was a man who savored the killing.

"He'll take his time, and he'll want to be there," I whispered. "He'll want to see it happen."

The only vehicle on the freeway, I continued to weave between lanes as the water rose beneath the truck. I neared a section of highway thick with wreckage, broken glass, and bent steel. Flying debris had shattered windows across one side of an office building that loomed beside the freeway. The building remained standing, a damaged skeleton, while glass, furniture and paper, a copy machine, and computers rained out from wall-less offices. A glimmer caught my eye, and instinctively I sped up and turned the steering wheel to the left, but not in time to prevent a flying sheet of metal from hitting the windshield. Instantly, a crack webbed its way diagonally, etching jagged fingers into the glass.

"Damn," I whispered, wondering if the break would weaken the windshield enough for the strong winds to crash it in on me.

Then, a mile north of the 610 Loop, the inner circle around the city, Houston plunged into darkness.

No lights shone on the one-hundred-foot poles above the freeway or in the bordering neighborhoods and businesses. No streetlights or city lights lit my way for as far as I could see. The storm had taken control, and the power was out. I slowed, worried about the road ahead, unable to see what waited. The wet pavement glistened dark in my headlights. I no longer had any frame of reference, no way to estimate the depth of the water pooling on the road, if the pavement lay inches, a foot, or feet below the black, shimmering surface of the floodwaters.

Approaching a low spot in the freeway, I slowed to keep from splashing up into the undercarriage of the car, where water could stall the engine. Taking my time, I kept my foot steady on the gas pedal. A third of the way through what looked like a small pond, I felt the road dip, and I feared all was lost.

Instead, only a few feet ahead, the front tires hit a bump and the front of the Tahoe rose. I kept the gas steady, and the SUV crawled forward, out of the water. Somewhere ahead of me waited Houston's skyline. On any other night it sparkled, lit by tens of thousands of streetlights and office lights, car head- and taillights, neon signs, brightly lit restaurants and theaters, and the Ferris wheel along I-45, turning with riders who stared in wonder out at the city and up at the moon and stars. This night, nothing was visible, only the driving rain and the scrap of road ahead revealed in my headlights.

All remained shrouded in darkness until lightning hit, blinding white explosions of light. For just a moment, downtown Houston's ridge of skyscrapers lit, silhouetted in the glow. The lightning revealed the undersides of heavy black clouds tenting the night sky, and the overhead signs, too, became visible. I was only three miles from the I-10 exit, my destination. Perhaps less. Distracted, I didn't notice at first that out of the darkness something flew toward the car, something green and white, something that crashed into the passenger-side door and then ricocheted off, like a door popping open after it's been slammed. My heart pounding from the scare, I stared at the road ahead of me as a section of freeway sign, torn off by the wind, raced away, twirling and spinning until it smashed into a light pole and split in half.

Finally, I neared the I-10 exit and slowed, looking for the troopers who'd volunteered to be my backup. I saw no one. I pulled over to a high spot on the shoulder and put the Tahoe in park, and then I picked up my cell and called the office. No one answered. I tried again and got a fast busy. On the third attempt, my call went through.

"It's Lieutenant Armstrong," I said, the static-filled connection fading in and out. "I said it's Lieutenant Armstrong. Can you hear me? I'm at the rendezvous location."

"Is that you, Lieutenant?" someone replied.

"Yes, yes, it's me," I said. "Where are the troopers? I'm at the exit, waiting, but I don't see them."

"We lost contact with Hays and Branson about fifteen minutes ago," he said. "We keep trying, but no luck reaching them."

Then, only grating noise. "Where were they?" I asked. "When the phone cut out, where were they?"

"I can't hear you," he said. "But if you can hear me, listen. We don't think —" Then his voice disappeared behind a sheet of crackling static.

"Come on, come on," I said. "Where were they when you last heard from them?"

If the troopers were anywhere close, I could pick them up and take them with me. Again the connection broke up, but then, just as suddenly, it cleared. "Okay, if you can hear me, listen. The last we heard, their vehicle was flooded out on a feeder road, trying to get off the 610 Loop north and onto 45. We're not sure where. Like I said, we're trying to reach them but can't get through."

Bad news. I would have had to backtrack and still most likely would never find them. My last possibility for help had evaporated. I would have to face Benoit alone. "If you hear from them, tell them I'm at the meeting point," I said, my voice strong, fighting not to reveal my rising fear. "Tell them I'll wait for five minutes. Then I'm going in."

With that, I realized the phone was dead. I tried to call again, hungry for any connection to a human voice, but got no signal. Somewhere, I assumed, the hurricane had claimed yet another victim, the cell phone tower that was my only link to my office, my last hope for help. The storm raged, and I waited. One minute passed, three, five. I did nothing, just sat as six minutes clicked past, then seven. I felt unable to move. I was afraid.

Outside, the rain and wind ravaged the city, tearing at the darkened landscape. The clamor of the wind buffeting the SUV neared deafening, sounding and feeling as if it came from all directions. The Tahoe rocked, swayed by the force of the wind, and I held on to the steering wheel, put my head down on it, prayed, and considered what to do. I thought about Maggie, waiting for me at home. I thought about my promise, to do my best to stay safe. And I thought about Joey Warner, in the hands of a monster.

Ten minutes after my call to headquarters, I tried 911, my last-ditch effort. Again, I had no signal. Perhaps it wouldn't have mattered. The mayor had announced there would be no emergency services during the storm. There was no one to rush to my aid.

Not sure what to do, not wanting to go in alone, I thought about Buckshot, dead, his body smoldering in the street. Then, again, I thought about Joey, remembered his shy smile in the photograph David first showed me and the happy little boy tumbling through the grass in a photo his grandmother had displayed on the *Today* show. As frightened as I was, I didn't have a choice. I put the Tahoe in gear and pulled back onto the road, heading toward downtown.

Where I-10 wraps under I-45, I took the left-lane exit leading to I-10 east. At the end of a ramp, I threw the Tahoe into a lower gear and made a sharp U-turn, heading west on the deserted eastbound freeway. A distance ahead, I saw the underpass I was thinking of, the one that can become a lake in a bad storm, and I slowed. In the darkness, I searched, but in the slice exposed by my headlights, I saw nothing alive, only unceasing rain and debris flying in the violence of a gale-force wind. My headlights shimmered on the building body of water where the I-10 freeway should have been. I couldn't tell how deep it was in the center, but I thought maybe not too deep, maybe not impassable. Still, that wasn't my intention.

Watching the shadows but able to see little in the darkness, I pulled onto the right shoulder near the underpass and jerked the car to the left. The engine in park, I slipped on my night vision goggles and cinched the jacket's hood over my head, shut down the headlights, and took my .45 out of the holster. Holding my breath, I tried to open the driver's-side door. It didn't budge. From that angle, the wind hit the door head-on. Instead I clambered over the center console, lowered myself into the seat, and unlocked the passenger-side door. It swung open.

Although warm, the rain whipped down with a force that hurt like icicles hitting my face, and the wind howled so loud, I heard nothing else. Shielded by the Tahoe, I picked my way around its frame, but as soon as I passed the front fender, the wind hit, propelling me backward, pushing me down flat into a puddle on the rain-soaked cement.

"Damn," I chastised myself. "Get up!"

Fighting the wind, I crawled onto my feet. Rather than stand, I stopped at a crouch, reasoning that it made me smaller, less of a target. Carefully, I edged forward, watching, waiting, straining to see, and holding my .45 as if it were a buoy in a violent sea, my only hope for survival. Although it was just a short distance, it seemed to take forever before I stood in the darkened underpass, ankle-deep, scanning the surface, my vision limited by the confines of the goggles. Through the eyepieces, the concrete glowed yellow in a sea of green, and the water glistened dark, nearly black.

Taking my time, I inspected the concrete

forms, the massive pillars holding up the freeway over my head. At any moment, I feared, Benoit could lunge out of the darkness or shoot at me from behind cover. If he was watching, he had the advantage, waiting, already in place and undoubtedly prepared for my arrival. In the wind I lost ground, until I stood pinned against a concrete wall. Anxious to find the boy, sure he had to be there, I watched the water but saw nothing. My eyes searched first the flooded roadway and then the cement structure, even the underpinnings of the freeway over my head. When I saw no sign of either Benoit or the boy, I pushed myself off the wall, bending at the waist, and waded through the water, as though my upper body were a battering ram, toward the divider between the opposite lanes of the freeway. Once in the center, I held desperately to a railing and repeated my hunt, searching for someone, something, anything to indicate Benoit was or had been there, that this was the place his clues were intended to lead me, the site where he would murder the boy.

But I saw nothing, no one. My heart drilled as if it would break through my chest, and I knew I'd been wrong.

Slowly, I willed my feet to hold me upright through the cascading floodwaters running off the freeway into the underpass, and I picked my way back to the truck. Fighting great gusts of wind that threatened to topple me, I retraced my steps to the Tahoe, again to the passenger-side door. I thought about Joey, knowing I'd failed him. Somewhere, at that very moment, Benoit might be murdering the boy, and despite all my work, all my hopes, I'd been unable to find the child. In that moment, I knew that the four-year-old's face, like those of others I'd failed to save, would haunt me every day of the rest of my life.

Wondering if I should fight the storm home or try to find somewhere safe to hunker down for the next nine hours, until the hurricane had passed through, I opened the Tahoe's door and slid in. I climbed back over the console, took off the night goggles, and turned on the headlights, then put the SUV into drive. I stepped on the gas, eased into a slow U-turn, and made my way to the entrance ramp, where I retraced my path onto I-45. Once there, I drove north in the empty southbound lanes, toward Tomball and the ranch, all the time wondering where Benoit and little Joey were and thinking: *I had to be right. It had to have something to do with the crossroads. It fit so well. It had to be right.*

A sick ache in my stomach, I swallowed back bile that welled up from somewhere deep inside. All I could think of was what might be happening at that very moment, where the boy was, and what Benoit had planned for him. I had to be missing something. I had to have misjudged. In my mind, I reconstructed the diagram on the map and where Reverend Fred had drawn the intersection of the two lines, based on the kill sites of the longhorns. How could I have misinterpreted the clues? But there was no arguing with the obvious. I was wrong. I'd failed.

Despondent, I drove a short distance on the abandoned freeway, dodging rubble in the road, fighting the push of the wind against the side of the SUV. I felt as if all were lost. I looked for shelter, but nothing was open, no safe places. Every store and shop was closed for the duration of the storm. Their owners were undoubtedly holed up in their homes, wondering if they'd have businesses to return to. It turned out that was what I should have done, stayed home and ridden out the storm with my family. My rush downtown in the middle of a hurricane was well-intentioned but misguided. I'd accomplished nothing.

I decided I had no option but to brave the

storm and head home.

At least Maggie would be relieved. I'd take my time, be careful, and be there when she woke up in the morning. That made me smile, and I relaxed behind the wheel a bit, resigned. Buoyed by the prospect of returning to my family, I momentarily dropped my guard, despite the hurricane and my worries about the boy. That was when something occurred to me. I thought about how the map hadn't been big enough to precisely plot the ranches, much less the pastures where the bulls had died. That meant that the locations on the map were far from exact. After Reverend Fred connected the dots, I'd chosen the I-10 and I-45 intersection because it was near the center and it fit the description as Houston's main crossroads. *What if it's someplace else, someplace close but not precisely that underpass?* I thought. Ideas attacked my mind with all the force of the rain that pelted the Tahoe. While mentally flipping through the possibilities, I made another U-turn and once again drove toward downtown's skyline, still hidden in the powerless landscape of a violent night. Fighting the wind and watching the water rise and rush around me, I rethought all I knew about Benoit.

Where would he take the boy? I wondered.

This was a man who lived to play games, who relished leaving clues. Somehow, at some point, I felt certain he'd told me where he'd take the boy, where he planned to murder him. I just had to be smart enough to figure it out.

As I retraced my route, I replayed my final conversation with Benoit on the telephone. Although I analyzed every word, nothing that came to mind pointed at a location. It was only when I reconstructed my encounter with him at the Westover Plantation that I suddenly remembered something he'd mentioned in passing.

At the time, the way he'd stared at me, cold and distant, had kicked my instincts into high gear, but once I'd left the plantation, I'd thought little of what he'd said about his carefully constructed plans for the slaves quarters. Now it took on a whole new meaning: "The site is perfect, picturesque, on a slope near the pond. We've built the piers because, in any tropical storm or hurricane, that part of the park, the section closest to the pond, floods."

Forty-Five

The longer the tempest raged, the more dangerous the roads became. Sections of freeway I'd taken just minutes earlier were now submerged, newly formed lakes and rivers reflecting back at me through the high beams of my headlights. This time I drove past the I-10 underpass, only a few minutes farther south, still within the center circle on the reverend's map, directly toward Houston's shadow downtown. Another round of lightning and the black cloak lifted, revealing hidden skyscrapers towered by thunderclouds. In front of the skyscrapers, bordering I-45, waited Sam Houston Park, a brief green space tucked against the concrete-and-glass city. So many lazy afternoons I'd spent there with Maggie and Mom, munching picnic lunches of Mom's fried chicken and mayonnaise-and-mustard potato salad and enjoying the scenery.

As I drove, I fought to recall old memories,

trying to reconstruct what I knew about how the park was laid out, to decide where Benoit would have had the piers for the slaves quarters constructed. He'd said near the pond. As I remembered, that was on the edge of the park, near the winged statue, *The Spirit of the Confederacy.*

The McKinney exit loomed ahead, and I veered left to take it, down the ramp toward the center of the city, while still mulling over the design of the park and attempting to make sense of Benoit's plans. Perhaps if I'd been paying more attention, I would have seen the river of floodwater in time, before the Tahoe's tires disappeared and the water rushed in all around me, from the sides of the car, from underneath. Another mistake: I slammed on the brakes, a gut reaction but the wrong one, since it splashed even more water back into the car. I eased off, but it was too late. In the darkness I felt the SUV lift and float, then rock back and forth, as helpless as a toy bobbing in the fast-moving current. Panicking, I felt powerless as water surrounded the SUV on the outside and poured in all around me. Grabbing the handle, I fought to open the door, to get out before the SUV submerged, but the pressure of the outside water kept the door from budging. Reining in my terror, I counted out loud to compose myself: "One Mississippi. Two Mississippi. Three Mississippi . . ."

In the glow from the Tahoe's interior lights, the water swelled around my feet, climbing higher on my legs. Before long, the warm floodwaters inside the Tahoe rose to midshin, and, still fighting to remain calm, I unlatched my seat belt, tore off my jacket, and ripped off the Velcro straps that held my Kevlar vest. I threw the bulletproof vest into the backseat, pulled on the jacket, and then grabbed the bag containing the Bushmaster, slipping the strap over my head and across my chest. At the same time, I considered the irony of drowning while a dangerous killer waited for me just blocks away in the darkness. I thought about people trapped in mines and wells who find a rock or a pen to write on a wall, to leave sad farewells to friends and family, expressing their love. And I wondered if my death would leave anyone searching for that reassurance, if I'd told everyone who had a place in my heart how important they were to me.

The water rose, filling the Tahoe's interior up to my knees, and still I waited. I put on the goggles, and I was ready. I thought about Maggie and wondered if she'd someday be a university professor, as she planned. I had life insurance, enough to pay for a good education, and even with the panic that clutched my throat, I knew that if I died in a watery grave, Mom would take over for me. Maggie wouldn't be alone. She'd be cared for and loved, and someday, maybe, she'd forgive me for leaving her in a hurricane to try to save a four-year-old named Joey Warner.

Outside, the floodwater reached the base of the windows. The final moments would be less than minutes, but it felt like hours as inside the Tahoe the water climbed until it covered my waist, up onto my chest, higher and higher, until it reached the same level inside as outside, an equilibrium of air and water. If everything I'd been told about escaping a submerging vehicle worked, this was my opportunity.

With the pressure balanced between the interior and the exterior of the car, I reached down beneath the warm floodwaters and pulled the latch. The door opened as easily as if on dry land. I took a deep breath, held on to the top of the door frame, and stepped out, the ball of panic in my chest tightened when I tested with my left foot and felt no ground beneath me. I'd thought about the weight of the Kevlar vest but nothing else.

Instantly water filled my rubber boots, puddling around my tennis shoes, and I felt as if I had lead weights tied to my feet. The night vision goggles, heavy on my face, felt suffocating. Balancing on the door and the car frame, fighting the weight of the water-filled boots, I bobbed up and tried to grab on to the luggage rack, to use it to heave myself onto the Tahoe's roof, but the wind slammed the door against me and an angry flash of lightning pulsed overhead as I slipped from my perch. My arms gave way and I fell, plunging down. The floodwater covered my neck, my face, and I held my breath, reaching about me, hoping to once again grab the open door frame, praying, *Not this way, God. Not this way. Not now.*

Finally, my feet hit ground. Pushing off with my legs, I propelled myself upward, then grabbed the car and pulled myself up, breaking through the surface, and gasping hungrily for air. In an instant, I tore off the constricting goggles and threw them away, begging to breathe. Stilling my terror.

Holding on to the sinking car, I again pulled hard, forcing my chest out of the water, then my waist. Another flash of lightning, and I saw a wide pond at the end of the ramp, where it joined the city street. There was so much water and such a strong current. Once there, I'd be helpless, unable to escape. I had to get out of the water and onto land, and I had to do it quickly. Again, I used the door frame as leverage, thrusting myself upward, pushing with all my strength. This time I grabbed the luggage rack, groaning as I yanked myself onto the roof.

The SUV drifted, all the while sinking ever deeper into the water, as I yanked off my boots. With each burst of lightning, the current carried the Tahoe closer to the underside of a concrete bridge. Protruding from a cement pillar at the edge of the bridge were several rebar rungs stacked like steps on a ladder. I had only one hope: to reach out and grab one and hold tight. Once on the ladder, I could pull myself up and jump from the pillar to land.

The Tahoe swayed in the current, and I held on, waiting. A burst of lightning, and I whispered a prayer and jumped, reaching out for the rebar steps where I thought I would find them. My hands closed on air, and I was pulled into the fast-moving current, disappearing beneath it, the Bushmaster weighing on my back. The water swirled, and I swam as hard as I could. When I broke through the surface, I reached out, hoping to grab something, anything, but I found nothing.

Caught in the current, I was buffeted back and forth within the swells as the water toyed with me, pushing my head under and then above the surface. Swallowing gulps of water, choking on the foul-tasting mix of rain, debris, and pollution, I wondered about a life that could end without a whisper beneath a pool of floodwater. I thought of my late husband and what he must have thought at the final moments of his life as the flames of the fire engulfing his car consumed him.

Another burst of lightning lit the water, and I spotted the concrete pillar I'd aimed for not behind but just ahead, on my left. Somehow the rushing water had spun me backward. With all my might I swam, willing myself forward, the water fighting against me, pushing me an inch back, it seemed, for nearly every inch I gained. Finally, one hand hit the concrete and the other grabbed for the rebar. It felt sharp in my hand, and I held tight, pulling myself toward it, and then hoisted my body up, climbing the sharp metal rungs out of the water. After another burst of lightning, I saw my goal and jumped onto a cement-covered slope along the side of the ramp, above the waterline. My feet on wet but solid land, I collapsed, gasping, heaving in and panting out, the rain battering my skin, my sopping clothes hanging like threadbare dishrags, water rushing all around me on its way to the deadly pool of floodwaters below.

Gasping for breath for I don't know how long, I sat on that cement incline convincing myself that I was still alive, watching as the gathering pond swallowed the Tahoe's headlights, snuffing out their beams. The water churned around the SUV's roof as it sank below the water. Then nothing remained visible above the surface of the floodwaters but the rain and the wind. Finally, I pushed back my exhaustion. I stood and thought about Peter Benoit, and my anger grew.

FORTY-SIX

Without the night vision goggles, all I had to light my way were sporadic bursts of lightning and the waterproof flashlight from my belt. As I walked toward the park, I pulled the Bushmaster from the canvas bag and tore off the plastic, then slipped the rifle's strap back over my shoulder and stowed the extra ammo in my jacket pocket. Carefully, I stepped between the shards left from broken panes of glass, climbed over downed tree limbs, and skirted unidentifiable wreckage. All around me, I heard the shrill sounds of flying debris hitting the skyscrapers' windows, thick glass shattering and falling to the concrete below.

From my holster I retrieved my Colt .45, double-checking to make sure it was loaded even though I knew it was, all the while concentrating on mentally reconstructing the layout of Sam Houston Park. I thought again of what Benoit had said, of where he'd built the pilings for the slaves quarters. I remembered the steep grade of the green space that culminated in the small pond and the landscape of the park bordered by the old restored homes. Above it towered the city's massive skyscrapers. I considered what Benoit had planned. If his fantasy was to re-create his attempt at murdering the girl, he'd stake Joey out and then sit back and wait, watching as the water rose, minute by minute, the boy slowly drowning.

Where would he be? I thought about the pond and considered the structures closest to it, the places that offered shelter to hide from the brunt of the hurricane. Only one building came to mind, St. John Church, a white clapboard structure set on the hill above the pond. That had to be Benoit's choice, the structure closest to the pond with the best view.

Picking my way with the narrow beam from the flashlight, walking as fast as my exhausted legs could carry me, I pulled together what I remembered of the simple, one-room church. I knew it well. Mom loved the building; it was her favorite in the park. While Maggie and I inhaled lunch, Mom reminisced about the many churches she remembered like it when she was a girl, small German Lutheran churches founded by Houston's early settlers. I could picture the old black, white, and gold altar at the back of the church. We'd toured it so often, I remembered the translation of the stenciled German passage above the altar: "Blessed are they that hear the word of God and keep it."

On the opposite end, facing the pond, a steeple soared from the roof, high above the doors. An ear-to-ear grin on her face, Maggie had often stood in that very spot, under the steeple, pulling the thick rope that extended through the ceiling into the tower, over and over again ringing a centuries-old bell that once called a long-dead congregation to services. Over the front door, a second German passage read: "The Lord preserve your going out and your coming in. Amen."

Another burst of lightning, and I noticed a dark SUV parked on the street and then the park and the church ahead. I crossed the street, aimed my flashlight's beam, and saw the bumper sticker with the symbol, just as Crystal had described it — the two capital Es turned inward with an I in the center, resembling a butterfly. What did it mean? So much cluttered my mind, but I tried to remember. Then it came to me, *Pempamsie,* which translated to "strength that cannot be crushed."

We'll see, I thought.

Worried Benoit would notice its beam, I turned off my flashlight and headed to the park. From that point forward, as much as it was my enemy, the darkness was my friend. In a burst of lightning, I saw fallen trees, their strong limbs and trunks broken, lying like the skeletons of the dead along my path. I took a right, off the street, and walked toward the church, through an opening in the spear-topped black wrought-iron fence surrounding the park. It was then that I glimpsed a shaft of light glowing from the front of the church, a bright funnel that cut through the rain into darkness, illuminating a patch of grass near the pond. Only one person could be holding that flashlight, Peter Benoit. And he'd want to watch only one thing, the culmination of his plan, Joey Warner's death.

"That he hasn't left means the boy is still alive," I whispered. From the direction of Benoit's flashlight beam, he had to have the boy staked out as I'd suspected, on the bank of the pond directly below the church. All the while, the heavy rains pummeled me, and I thought of the floodwaters rising.

Fighting the urge to rush to free the child, since that would put both of us in the line of fire, I knew that before anything else, I had to rid the world of Peter Benoit.

The next revelation presented itself in yet another burst of light from the heavens, a mammoth oak tree uprooted, its trunk crushing the back corner of the small church's south wall and part of the roof above it. I walked forward warily, holding my Colt .45, and once I reached it, I stood outside the church, looking in. I waited for the next burst of lightning, then peered inside but saw nothing but a brief flash of the church's interior. Where was Benoit?

Quickly, I scrambled a few feet up on the fallen tree trunk and again waited. Another bolt of lightning, and this time I had a better vantage point and enough light to fully search the inside of the church, through the opening the fallen tree had torn in the wall. I saw lines of pews, the altar, and a silent organ. What I didn't see was Peter Benoit. Suddenly, I realized something else was missing. There was no sound coming from the steeple. The bell inside the tower should have been ringing, banging in the violent winds.

"That's where Benoit is," I whispered. "The bell isn't ringing because he's tied it up."

In the glow of yet another bolt of lightning, I saw a ladder below the steeple, and I knew I was right. There were no other possibilities. I climbed higher on the trunk, toward the roof, but then stopped. I thought about the nearly two-hundred-year-old church, its wood siding and frame all but petrified by age. I thought about what that aged wood could do to the path of a bullet, how it would twist it and send it reeling off course. Needing to make sure every shot counted, I holstered my .45 and grabbed the Bushmaster from over my shoulder. Clutching it in my right hand, I used my left to hold on as I picked my way up the trunk of the fallen oak. In the darkness, with the deafening sound of the storm, I had a chance, one chance, to surprise Benoit.

As I felt for branches ahead of me, I fought to keep my tennis shoes from slipping on the wet bark, and my mind filled with images of arriving at the country crossroads and seeing Buckshot's body in flames. Benoit owed David, and he owed me. He owed his father. He owed the little girl he'd tried to murder when he was still a child. But most of all, he owed Buckshot and Joey Warner.

Peter Benoit had an open account that needed to be paid.

My hands reached the pitched roof, and I

used a tree limb to pull myself up, then held on to a higher limb, supporting myself while standing on the shingles as all around me bursts of pulsating lightning lit the skyline and the church's tall, straight, silent bell tower. Benoit had knocked out the shutters, and I clearly saw his silhouette through a window, his back turned toward me. I climbed higher, still bracing myself against a thick, twisted branch, fighting the wind, and I thought about the excitement that must have been flooding through Benoit as he watched the culmination of his intricate plan, his fantasy played out in the form of the rising water creeping ever closer to his young victim.

Finally, I straightened up and stood, and I took aim at Benoit's back.

Surrounded by the clamor of the storm, he couldn't have heard me, but as if he sensed my presence, Benoit turned, and the beam from his flashlight found my face. Instantly, I let loose, pulling the Bushmaster's trigger over and over, the rifle slicing easily through the old wood, splintering it into gaping holes, exploding out sections of the aged church steeple.

All I could think of was obliterating the monster inside.

■ ■ ■ ■

When I stopped firing, the tower bell began to sound. Rocked by the howling wind and the relentless rain, it rang and rang as I crouched down, watching. I couldn't see Benoit, and I wondered if he'd fallen or jumped into the church below. Hurrying down the tree, I slipped from one branch to the next, barely keeping my footing. Halfway down, I stopped and turned on my flashlight, peering into the church. Benoit lay crumpled on the floor beneath the bell tower, blood pooling near his chest. I started to go inside, then thought of Joey, and the sheets of rain falling, the water from the pond rising with each passing moment. I looked again at Benoit and made a decision. I turned and ran to the pond.

Rushing forward on the saturated earth, I scanned the ground with my flashlight, searching. I hadn't gone far when I saw a series of brick-and-mortar pillars, the pilings for the slaves quarters. I followed those to where the earth sloped and saw a rope leading to a small figure, flush on the ground.

The boy's arms and legs were tied to two of the pilings, and the water had already risen to his shoulders, covering his feet and legs, past his waist, collecting around his neck. With little time to spare, I ran to him, but my tennis shoes slipped out from under me and I fell, hitting my right hip hard. Instead of trying to stand in the rushing rainwater, I rolled over and slithered the rest of the way on my stomach. As I reached him, I grabbed one of the pilings to brace myself. The rain stung my skin as I pulled closer to the boy. His eyes shut tight to keep out the pounding storm, he didn't see me and couldn't hear me in the hurricane's clamor.

Until I wrapped my arm around him, Joey didn't realize I was even there. I braced myself by wrapping my legs around the higher of the two pillars and pulled out my pocketknife to cut him free, the ropes on his feet first. The boy's eyes opened, terrified, for just a moment, then snapped shut in the driving rain. Frightened, he squirmed in my grasp. I strained to cut through the final rope, releasing his hands, and the child responded by wrenching his small body away from me. I held tight, reminding myself that he had no way of knowing who I was or why I was there.

My arms tight around him, I carefully eased up onto my knees. As exhausted as my body was, I dragged the boy with me as I crawled up the hill. When I had solid footing on level land, I stood and leaned over to pick him up. The boy felt bone thin but continued to fight with surprising strength to break my hold.

As I made my way back toward the church, I reminded myself to check Benoit, to be sure he was dead. I climbed the steps to the church's front door and put down the boy. Before I could even try to explain, he turned and ran down the stairs. When I grabbed his arm, I shouted, "I'm a police officer." If he heard me in the deafening noise of the storm, he didn't believe me. Again he turned to run, and I clutched his hand tight. I couldn't hold the boy and the gun and open the door at the same time, and I decided my best option was to return to the hole in the south wall. My shoulders aching, I picked up the boy and carried him.

Fighting the driving wind, I walked along the front of the church, head bowed to keep the rain from my eyes. Just as I neared the corner of the church, there was another burst of lightning so close that for a moment the park glowed as if in daylight, followed by an earsplitting clap of thunder. Frightened, Joey kicked and flailed his arms, at the same time burying his head against my chest. Confused, he didn't appear to know if he wanted to break free or hide in my arms. As I rounded the corner, I saw what the lightning had hit, a large branch off a second oak tree that lay crossways on top of the tree trunk I'd climbed to the roof.

Still carrying Joey, I hurried to the side of the church. At the foot of the fallen tree, I put the boy down but held him by the hand. Again I shouted, "Joey, I'm a police officer. Can you hear me? I'm a police officer."

Again, he tried to wrench away, either not hearing me or not understanding. Realizing what I had to do, I pulled the Velcro that held up the flap on the front of my jacket, and the badge painted in yellow dropped. I shone the flashlight on it, pointed at it, and again shouted, "I'm a police officer!" At first, the child looked confused, but then I saw a glimmer of understanding as he realized the badge identified me as someone who could help. Sobbing, he threw his arms around my leg, holding on tight.

Gently, I pushed the boy back until he was beside the church wall, unwrapped his arms from my left shin, and motioned for him to wait. With my Colt .45 in hand, I carefully made my way up the fallen tree trunk, looking for a way into the church. The climb was treacherous as the branch slipped and rocked atop the tree trunk. The higher I climbed, the more obvious it became that the first tree and the newly fallen branch combined to form a tight web, one that blocked my way. I couldn't squeeze through to get inside the church. Again I focused my flashlight on the floor, directly under the steeple. To my relief, Benoit lay there, still as death.

All around us the storm raged, torrential rain and fierce wind. Another round of ear-shattering thunder and ragged branches of lightning sliced through the black sky. Beneath me, Joey wrapped his arms around his head and screamed, in a state of near panic. Fearing he'd turn and run, I decided I had no choice but to quickly get the boy to safety.

"It's okay, Joey," I shouted above the storm as I slid down the tree and grabbed him. "We'll be okay."

Once again in my arms, his small body tensed against mine. He hugged my neck tight, and his head tucked into my shoulder. In another blast of lightning, the boy shuddered, and I surveyed Houston's skyline, wondering where to take him to hide from the storm. We needed to be on higher ground, somewhere protected from the rain and the wind.

Ahead of us stood Heritage Plaza, a monolithic skyscraper with the relief of a Mayan temple at the crest. It was one of Houston's tallest buildings and would certainly be locked, but I carried the boy, fighting the wind, across the street toward the building. All the while, trash blew past us, and broken window glass crunched under my tennis shoes. Running as fast as I could, I worried that a windowpane would drop from above us, showering us with shards of glass.

"Keep your eyes closed," I shouted as I covered the boy's head with one hand, holding him in the crook of the elbow of the other arm. My eyes barely open, I felt my way around the building. Once I saw an entrance to the garage ahead, I hurried, pushing myself forward. I skirted the wooden arm blocking the entry and climbed the ramp. When I got far enough inside, where the rain wasn't boring down on us, exhaustion took over and my knees began to buckle. Perhaps feeling my weakness, Joey pulled away from my shoulder and looked at me, his face a blotchy mass of red bruises from the beating it had taken in the storm.

"Can you walk?" I asked.

The boy nodded. He appeared stunned

and still riding on the edge of fear, but he understood.

I put him down carefully on the parking structure's concrete floor, then took his hand, and we slowly walked up the ramps and farther up into the garage, looking for a way into the building with the beam from my flashlight. At each deserted floor, we stopped at the entrances to the building, but all were locked. On the garage's third floor, I tried to break the thick industrial glass insert in the door with the Bushmaster's barrel, but the rifle merely bounced off.

On level four, I found three vehicles parked against the interior wall, two pickups and an old black Jeep Cherokee. I left Joey standing in an alcove at a door into the building, protected from the wind. I searched the bed of the first pickup, found nothing to help, then the second, and again came away empty-handed. It took two attempts with my rifle barrel to break the Jeep's window. Once I did, I flipped the locks and opened the back. The alarm went off, and I waited a few moments, but no one came. I pulled up the mat in the back of the Jeep, found the tool kit, and took out the jack. Back at the door, I moved Joey away from the panel of glass in the small window. With the jack's handle, I struck the window over and over again.

Nothing. Not even a crack in the glass.

After so many tries, my entire body throbbed with pain and exhaustion. I returned to the pickup trucks, broke the glass with the jack handle, and rifled through both. In the second, I discovered a glass-break, a metal tool with a point on the end designed to allow those inside to break a car window to escape if caught in water. "Now this would have come in handy a little earlier," I said, looking at Joey, who stared up at me questioningly, undoubtedly wondering about the strange woman who'd emerged out of the storm to save him.

It took four hits to shatter the door's glass insert. I reached in and was flooded with disappointment when I realized it had a keyed lock, not one with a lever I could flip to get inside. I'd nearly given up when a security guard came around a corner into the hallway leading to the door, his gun drawn. He looked as frightened as I was.

"I'm a Texas Ranger," I shouted, aiming the flashlight on the badge on my jacket and my face, hoping to put him at ease. "I've got a little boy here who was kidnapped. We need help."

■ ■ ■ ■

The cell phones weren't working, but the building had a generator running, fueling limited lights and the telephones and cameras in the security office, which was how the guard spotted me. I considered calling Evan Warner, to tell him I had his son, but I didn't know his parents' phone number, and directory assistance led to a fast busy. Instead, I put in a call to the Rocking Horse.

"Are you all right?" I screamed into the headset. "Is everybody okay?"

"Yeah, Mom," Maggie said. "Are you all right?"

"Maggie, I've got Joey," I reassured my daughter. "We're safe. It's all right. Everything's all right."

All I could hear was my daughter sobbing. Mom took the telephone and said, "We're fine, Sarah. Everything is fine."

An hour later, the security guards shared their stash with us, and Joey and I each consumed a peanut-butter-and-jelly sandwich and drank a can of orange pop. Our clothes were soaked, and afterward, one guard found a maintenance uniform for me to wear. Another took off his white cotton undershirt for Joey. Then they opened an office for us, a law firm's posh reception area with two big, soft leather couches. I laid Joey on one couch and then claimed the other, my battered body sore. Moments passed and I'd started to drift into sleep when I felt the boy slip onto the couch with me, nesting his small body against mine, looking for comfort. I said nothing, only held him. We'd both been through so much, but he was alive. He'd have the opportunity to grow up, to one day be a man.

As I felt myself finally give in to my overwhelming fatigue, Joey said his first words to me, and I thought my heart might break.

"Did my momma send you?" he asked. "When the storm's over, can we call her to come get me?"

Forty-Seven

One of the guards roused Joey and me about two the following afternoon, after the hurricane had passed. The boy looked confused at first, as if he couldn't remember where he'd fallen asleep, but when he saw me, he smiled.

The first words he spoke were, "Did you call my momma?"

"She'll find out you're safe," I tried to reassure him. "And guess what?"

"What?" he asked, very serious.

"As soon as we get to the police station, we'll call your dad!"

For the moment, all seemed right with the world as the four-year-old jumped up and down, screaming, "Call my poppa! Call my poppa!"

We both laughed, and I promised, "As soon as we get to the police station, Joey. As soon as we can, we'll call him."

The power remained out throughout

much of Houston, including downtown, and none of the elevators worked in the skyscrapers, so we used flashlights to make our way through the windowless corridors and as we walked down the stairway to the first floor. The security guards gave us each a doughnut, a day old but tasty. Even though mine didn't have my customary chocolate frosting and jimmies, it couldn't have tasted better. Our clothes were still damp, so Joey wore the undershirt and I had on the same gray coveralls I'd slept in. A few minutes later, a squad car and a sheriff's department unmarked car pulled up outside, and Jim Ruskin, one of the major crimes detectives who'd been working the abduction case with David, walked into the lobby to claim us.

"Where's the bad guy?" he asked.

"Across the street, in Sam Houston Park, inside St. John Church," I said. It gave me great pleasure to add, "Dead."

A gruff man with buzz-cut hair and black-rimmed glasses, Ruskin called it in, asking for one of the police integrity prosecutors to respond to the scene along with detectives and an assistant medical examiner. "Do I need to bring the lieutenant in for questioning?" he asked his superiors. The normal course of events when a cop shoots a civilian is for an investigation to swing into full force. I'd be expected at the scene to do a walk-through, answering questions. But when Ruskin hung up, he waved it off. "Under the circumstances, they said you should write up a report and file it later. No hurry."

Outside, the sidewalk was strewn with rubbish and broken glass, and holes gaped in the glass façades of the skyscrapers, where windows had shattered and fallen. The city and county cleaning crews weren't out yet, and the city's bustling business district remained deserted. Like a rainstorm that clears the air, the hurricane had washed away the oppressive heat. The summer that had refused to end was finally over, replaced by a cool fall breeze. Above, the sky was a perfect blue with hardly a cloud. And across the street, in the park, the bell in St. John's tower, with no wind or bullets to strike it, was silent.

At Lockwood, in a cubicle in major crimes, Joey propelled a black vinyl office chair in circles as he inhaled a Hershey's bar. "Doesn't that make you feel sick?" I asked, laughing.

"No, it's fun," the boy said, wrinkling up his nose. "The world spins fast and it makes my heart get excited!"

"One thing you'll learn when you get older, Joey, is that the world spins pretty fast on its own," I said. He looked at me, smiled, and then pushed on the chair to spin again.

Ruskin, who sat across the squad room, laughed. We were both still looking at Joey Warner as if he'd risen from the dead. Remarkably, the doc who'd examined the boy at the ER said at least physically his ordeal had done little damage, only left him with scratches, bruises, and bug bites. Psychologically? That was something the future would answer. Every time I thought of the park and the watery grave Benoit had planned for the boy, I shuddered.

I truly didn't expect what happened next. It had never crossed my mind that it was even a possible turn of events, but Ruskin's office phone rang, and I saw his expression change from relief to dread.

"It's for you," he said, handing over the headset. "Your office."

The captain's voice came on the line. "Sarah, you're okay?"

"Yeah," I said. "Fine."

"And you found the Warner boy. He's safe?"

"Right here beside me, playing spin-around in Ruskin's office chair," I said, smiling at Joey. "Laughing like a four-year-old."

At that, I turned my back on the boy, not wanting him to hear. "What's wrong?" I asked. "Is David all right? Are you?"

"Oh, nothing like that," he said. "We're both safe and sound, back at the office. We got a chopper to fly in and pick us up about an hour ago. Bring us here. David got your voice mail, that you were tracking Benoit. We were worried. The cells are down, but we called the sheriff's office and they told us what happened."

"What is it, then?" I asked. "What's wrong?"

The captain paused. "Well," he said, his voice somber. My imagination took over. I wondered if he had bad news about Mom or Maggie. Had something happened at the ranch after I'd talked to them the night before? But then the captain said, "Tell me again about where you left Benoit."

"I didn't leave him," I said, relieved that he hadn't called with bad news about my family. There'd just been some miscommunication, I reassured myself. They didn't understand what I'd said about where they could find Benoit. "I left *his body* on the floor at St. John Church, the little church in Sam Houston Park. Didn't they look there?"

"Well, yeah," the captain said. "Sarah, they did look there."

At that, I felt my head drift back and my eyes close, almost an involuntary reaction. I took two long breaths to calm myself. Then I uttered the words I would have paid dearly never to say: "He wasn't there."

"No," the captain said. "They found blood on the wooden floorboards, but Benoit's not there. No body. No Benoit."

I flashed back to the scene in the church the night before, the motionless figure on the floor, my first impulse to check him, to make sure Benoit was dead. Fatigue and worry about the boy got the better of me. I hadn't finished him off. Benoit was a monster, and he didn't deserve to live, and my mistake had given him more time and the opportunity to kill again. He'd murdered my friend, and he hadn't paid.

I hung around Lockwood long enough to greet Evan and his parents when they came to claim Joey. The boy ran to his father, screaming, throwing his hands up in the air as if Joey were a teenage fan and Evan a rock star. Jackson and Alicia Warner tried to talk to the child, but Joey appeared shy at first, hiding his handsome young face in his father's shirt, looking up at them with his curious blue eyes. Finally, when Evan explained that these were his parents, Joey's grandparents, the boy lit up like a kid at a carnival first in line to get on the spinning teacups. "Another oma and opa?" Joey asked, sounding as if it were too astonishing to believe. As I walked out the door, I heard everyone laughing.

The Tahoe was being towed, but I figured it was headed to the scrap heap. Two hours later, the squad that chauffeured me home pulled under the arch over the driveway at the ranch, the one with the Rocking Horse emblem at the top, wrapped in more of Maggie's Christmas lights. We'd barely parked when Maggie ran out, so excited to see me that she took the time to slip on only one flip-flop. She hit the gravel, realized one foot was bare, and pulled back, screaming and laughing.

"Magpie, I love you dearly and forever!" I said, scooping her into my arms.

"Forever and ever!" Maggie echoed.

Mom and Bobby came out, and pretty soon everyone was hugging and laughing and telling hurricane stories. They already knew the outline of mine, that I'd swamped the Tahoe and that Joey was safe, that we'd spent the night in a skyscraper; so I listened to them. I was practically on the porch when

I realized what Maggie was saying, that the corral elm tree had come down in the storm. I swiveled back and looked at it, the great tree on its side, its massive roots yanked from the earth, a tangled ball encased in dirt. We walked over to the fence, and I stared at the tree.

"It must have been a tornado," Bobby said with a shrug. "About five this morning, we heard this loud noise, like a train. We all huddled together in the closet to get away from the windows, and then we heard a big crack."

"After it was over, we looked out, and the tree was down," Mom said, picking up the story. "Such a shame. That tree's got to be sixty years old, maybe more. It was here before your pop and I built the place. And to lose it like this doesn't seem right."

"Maggie, I'm so sorry," I said, my arm around her thin shoulders, staring out at the elm, its leaves still wrapped in the thousands of white Christmas lights my daughter relied on to help her feel closer to her dead father. "I know that tree was special to you."

"It's okay," she said, smiling up at me.

"We'll plant another," I volunteered, wishing I could salvage the tree, sorry that no one could. "It'll take a while to grow, but in the meantime we'll string lights on the other trees around the house. And someday the one we plant will be big enough. You'll see."

Maggie didn't answer, she just looked up at me and grinned. Then she hugged me again and whispered, "It doesn't matter, Mom. It really doesn't. All that matters is that we're all okay, and that you're home."

Epilogue

Every member of law enforcement in Harris County had a photograph and a description of Peter Benoit. For three days, as Houston slowly awoke after the hurricane, we searched. We followed leads as far away as Louisiana and Arkansas and sent out bulletins to every state in the Union and down into Mexico and up into Canada. We would never give up on looking for Benoit, but his trail was cold. His dark blue SUV was found abandoned on a country road, in the middle of an intersection, a crossroads, with no explanation as to how he'd disappeared.

It did, however, seem that he made a stop before leaving the area. On the second day after the hurricane, my cell phone rang; it was the administrator at Alex Benoit's nursing home. "One of the nurses found the professor dead this morning," she said. "We're having his body autopsied. His nose is bruised, and we're thinking that it may be broken."

"Sounds like suffocation," I agreed. "Was his son seen near the home?"

At that moment, I remembered the photo he'd given us that night, the one of Peter Benoit that we'd taken from the main desk, the photo that was supposed to keep Alex Benoit safe so that his son would be recognized and barred from his room. So much had already happened, and now I worried that taking the photo had cost the old man his life.

"No, we didn't see him, and we were watching for him. The local police were still supposed to be keeping an eye on the nursing home, but the old man's son may have found a way to get past them. The professor's window was broken from the inside," she said. "We'll keep you posted, but we're pretty sure this isn't natural causes."

Everything had been slowed down by the hurricane, so it was nearly a week before we buried Sergeant George "Buckshot" Fields. So many attended the service that loudspeakers had to be set up outside the church to ensure all could hear the eulogy. His ex-wife left her new husband, Buckshot's old friend, in California and came alone. At the service, Peggy held her daughter's hand, comforting her at the loss of her father.

"Today we bury a fallen hero," the preacher said. "Sergeant Fields was a great man, a righter of wrongs, a man loyal and true, one who could be trusted to always do what was right, even if it wasn't easy. He was the father of a daughter he loved, one he will always love."

From the church, we drove to a quiet cemetery north of Houston, where a grave yawned open below the bronze-colored casket. It was there that Buckshot would find eternal rest, under a crepe myrtle that flowered pure white. The tent the family sat under was the head of a triangular span of mourners so deep and so dense that if Buckshot looked down and saw how many cared about him, he would have been proud. When the preacher finished his final prayer, we walked away from the casket, still propped up on scaffolding over the open grave. I tried not to think of Buckshot's body the last time I saw it, of the awful destruction of the fire.

Depressed from the lack of success at finding Benoit but having to admit we had no leads to follow, David and I took off the weekend after the funeral and left for the Hill Country. The power was still out at his house and at the ranch, along with a big chunk of Houston. I hadn't wanted to go, but Mom insisted. She and Bobby were enjoying the quiet of no television and video games, watching Maggie play cards with Strings on the porch and working with the horses, while they ate all the baked goods Mom's nerves had stockpiled before the hurricane hit. The generator, they insisted, made the house livable, especially since the newly arrived fall breezes kept the place cool. I wasn't convinced, figuring what was really going on was that my entire family was conspiring to make sure David and I finally had time alone together.

We found a little B&B in the rolling hills west of Austin, on a horse ranch. Our second day there, we rode two of the owners' Arabians. The place bordered a forest, and trails took us along a creek and down into ravines. When we arrived back at the small cottage we'd rented, we sat on the swing and held hands. Afterward, David, who'd brought three coolers full of supplies, started constructing dinner.

"Lord bless a man who can cook!" I exclaimed, chuckling, while I watched from the couch. My job had been to bring the wine for the trip, and my cheeks were flushed from a glass of red Zinfandel. I sized him up, forming my hands into a square to make a frame, and peered at him. "You know, you'd look cute in an apron."

"Don't get any ideas," David said with a smirk. He put down a knife and the zucchini he'd been chopping and came over and nestled against my neck, whispering, "Although I'd be happy to dress up like a French maid if I thought you'd find the game playing inspiring."

I ran my hands over his arms, felt the tightness of his muscles under the thin cotton shirt, and sighed. "You know, I'm tempted," I admitted. I raised my face toward him, and he met me halfway with a warm, long, ravenous kiss. At that precise moment, my stomach rumbled, and I laughed. I put my hand on his cheek and looked into his eyes. "You know, I think you'd better feed me first."

Bending at the waist, he bowed. "Whatever my lady wishes."

Dinner disappeared quickly, a feast of sautéed veggies and chicken breast, along with a salad I splashed with a light vinaigrette. Afterward, we sat together on the porch swing, breathing in the crisp air, a blanket warming our legs. I thought back to the hurricane. It had been a full week since I'd left David that voice mail, the one that I'd concluded by confiding that I loved him.

He hadn't mentioned it once. He'd also said nothing about the decision hanging over both of us, whether or not he'd move to Denver and try one more time to reconcile with his ex-wife.

I winnowed a place for my head on his shoulder and wondered if he'd heard my confession or if the cell phone tower, in the middle of the storm, had chosen that moment to send out static instead of my profession of love. I wondered where life would take us and if we had a future together. It was then that he stood up and took me by the hands. "It's time to go inside, where it's warm."

"It's pretty nice out here," I said, acting as if I didn't understand.

"Inside, woman," he ordered with a laugh. "Your chef commands."

A roguish look in his eyes, he led me inside, locked the door, then escorted me to the bedroom and the four-poster bed. There, he peeled off my T-shirt and unhooked my bra, a white lace one I'd purchased in my continuing effort to be more of a girl. I let it fall from my shoulders, then drop to the old wood floor. The cool air made me shiver, and David leaned in to kiss me, cupping my breasts in his strong, warm palms while I slowly unbuttoned his shirt.

When I finished, I pushed his shirt to the side and unlatched his belt, the buckle a silver one with a star I'd given him months earlier, calling it his rodeo belt and saying that wearing it would make him a real Texan.

Our bodies naked, we rolled onto the bed, clutching each other. Not satiated by mere food, our mouths were desperate for each other. He stroked my body, and I felt every nerve take notice, an excitement that left me longing for more. Soon, he was on top of me, and I kneaded his muscular shoulders as he rose and fell, my legs wrapped around his strong thighs. I pushed against him, and he writhed, rocking and bringing me along with him, heightening the enjoyment and the thrill of each passing moment. Finally, a warm release, a throwing back of the head in what could have been mistaken for agony, and we both cried out.

Afterward, we spooned together, him behind me, smelling of sex and food. His left arm lay beneath me, wrapped around my chest, and his right hand played with the flesh between my thighs. I groaned.

"This isn't fair, David," I whispered. "It's really not."

"What?" he asked, mischievousness lacing his voice. "What's not fair?"

"This isn't fair," I said. "Making me want you like this."

At that he released his hold on me, and I regretted my words. He moved away, and I rolled onto my back and looked up at him. Before I could speak, he ran his hands lightly over my sides and down my thighs and then lifted me up until my hips were off the bed. Again on top of me, he made love to me, transporting me to a place I couldn't go alone.

When it was over, we again lay together. In the morning we'd go home, and I needed to know.

"David," I said as he held me tight, "I don't want to ruin this, but I deserve an answer."

At first he said and did nothing, only lay still and held me. Then he slowly unfolded, releasing me. He sat on the side of the bed, his eyes deeply troubled, immensely sad. He never said a word, but I knew.

"You're moving to Denver," I said. "You brought me here to say good-bye."

"I do love you, Sarah," he said with a melancholy half smile. "When I heard you say that on my voice mail, that you love me, I understood that I feel the same way. I want you to believe that I do love you."

Shaking my head as if it were too strange

a turn of events, I asked, "Then, why?"

"Because I have to," he said, moving closer and wiping a tear off my cheek. "Because I love Jan, too. She wanted the divorce, I didn't. I never completely stopped loving her. Because we were married for a decade, and we have a fifteen-year-old son I want to be a father to."

"I can understand that," I said, thinking I needed to step back, to not protest. It was his life. His family. I wasn't proud of it, but I had to ask. "But what'll be different now? Your ex-wife couldn't live with you on the job before, the long hours, the time on the road. Your situation hasn't changed."

From the look on his face, his lips knotted in a crooked frown, I knew he'd thought long and hard about just that. "You're right," he admitted. "Absolutely right. And maybe it won't work. But I have to try."

When I said nothing, he wrapped his arms around me. "Don't hate me for this, Sarah. Please, try to understand."

"I'd never hate you," I said, meaning it, yet feeling a coldness in the room. I grabbed the green comforter and pulled it up around me. "But you said you love me, and I don't understand."

A tense pause, and then David whispered, "If Bill came back, if somehow something happened and your dead husband walked into this room, think about it. You said you love me, but wouldn't you still love him? Wouldn't you want to put your family back together, to restore what you had? Wouldn't you leave me to be with him and give Maggie her mother and her father?"

My head bowed. He was right. We spent the rest of that night lying together, holding each other, and in the morning, we drove home in silence.

Maybe in another world it could have all ended there, David dropping me off at the ranch the next morning and Mom eyeing me and seeing my sadness. She slipped her arms around me and walked me inside our home, where Strings played the guitar in the kitchen while Maggie sang along. That night, I sat on the porch rocking chair and wondered if there was any place safe for love. If somewhere love always won. My mind drifted back to my last night with David, then from David to Bill, and I questioned what it would be like never to leave the confines of a lover's arms, never to have to confront the hard realities that wait with a rising sun and a new day. If such a place exists, I haven't found it.

Yet I'm no stranger to life's contrasts, the

good and the bad.

Sometimes I believe I live in two worlds: one with those I love, my family and my friends, and the other, the day-to-day horrors of my work, where I regularly confront the certainty that evil exists. In this second world, joy is too often replaced by sadness, celebration by grief, and exhilaration by tragedy. Love is the most vulnerable of all. It falls victim to fear, anger, jealousy, and even greed.

In one week; I'd suffered the pain of losing a good friend, the joy of saving a little lost boy, and the resigned sadness of watching the man I love drive away, perhaps never to return. It seemed that just when I convinced myself that good would triumph and that someday all might be right with the world, someone, God, the devil, someone, felt compelled to slap me on the side of the head and shout, "Pay attention, Sarah. Take heed. Never let down your guard. Never take for granted what waits around the next corner."

At my office the following week, the phone rang. Sylvia Vogel, the prosecutor on the Warner case, had news. "We're going to arrest Crystal Warner," she said. "We got an indictment from the grand jury."

"What about the immunity agreement?" I

asked, surprised.

"Crystal shouldn't have been so cocksure. She should have had her attorney involved. I wrote it so narrowly, we didn't have any problem finding exceptions," Sylvia said, sounding as pleased as I was at the turn of events. "All Crystal has immunity for is selling the kid. We're going to hit her with a restaurant menu of other charges, including child endangerment and lying to law enforcement personnel."

"Ah," I said, smiling. "Maybe there is justice, at least now, this one time. Maybe the bad will be punished."

"Yeah," Vogel said, her voice a hoarse cough. "Maybe. At least we can hope."

Afterward, I walked into Buckshot's office. His daughter had already come and taken all she'd wanted, mementos to remember her father by. I knew what I was looking for, something that summed up the friend I'd lost, something to keep him near. What I chose was a small glass vial filled with lead buckshot, taken from the hide of a rustler, the very buckshot that christened George Fields with his nickname.

Back in my office, I placed the remembrance on my desk, proud to have it center stage. I fingered it, wondering if we'd ever find Peter Benoit, if he'd ever pay for his crimes, especially murdering my friend. Then, before heading home to the ranch, I decided to tackle the stack of mail in my inbox. I was halfway through when I found a handwritten envelope with no return address. I cut it open with the pewter letter opener Mom had given me for Christmas a few years earlier, the one with a horse-head handle, and then slipped out a single sheet of unlined white paper. My hands trembled, and images of the small skulls waiting in my workroom flashed into my mind. How many times had I thought about those two unidentified children while looking for Joey? How many times had I wondered if the cases could be connected?

When I read the short note tucked inside the envelope, I no longer had to wonder. I knew.

Lieutenant Armstrong,

Thank you for the lesson. What I learned: it's easier when their mothers simply agree to disappear and not report them missing. Current tally:

Benoit. 2

Armstrong. 1

The game will be continued.

ACKNOWLEDGMENTS

For their assistance, I'd like to thank:

My friend, former teacher, and much appreciated reader, Ken Hammond

Senior crime scene analyst David Rossi

Prosecutors Edward Porter and Kelly Siegler

Forensic expert Andrea Campbell

Criminal profiler Pat Brown

Christopher Boutros, D.V.M.

Doug Dickey at Apex Helicopters

Forensic pathologist Elizabeth Peacock, M.D.

Sergeant Tracy Shipley

Florida Department of Law Enforcement criminal profiler Leslie D'Ambrosia

Jerry and Sherry Dunn

Donna Weaver, who explored Houston with me

Retired Texas Ranger Marrie Aldridge

My agent, Jane Dystel, and her partner, Miriam Goderich, at Dystel & Goderich

At St. Martin's Minotaur: my editor, Daniela Rapp; my publicist, Bridget Hartzler; and my copy editor, Sona Vogel.

A special thank-you to Sue Vandegrift for her powers of organization. Sarah and I both appreciate her efforts. And, as always, I'd like to express my heartfelt gratitude to my family and friends. I could never find a way sufficient to thank all of you for your generous support.

ABOUT THE AUTHOR

Kathryn Casey is a former magazine reporter and the author of five highly acclaimed true-crime books. This is Kathryn's third work of fiction, following *Singularity* and *Blood Lines.* She lives in Houston with her husband.

Visit her Web site at www.kathryncasey.com.

The employees of Thorndike Press hope you have enjoyed this Large Print book. All our Thorndike, Wheeler, and Kennebec Large Print titles are designed for easy reading, and all our books are made to last. Other Thorndike Press Large Print books are available at your library, through selected bookstores, or directly from us.

For information about titles, please call:

(800) 223-1244

or visit our Web site at:

http://gale.cengage.com/thorndike

To share your comments, please write:

Publisher
Thorndike Press
295 Kennedy Memorial Drive
Waterville, ME 04901